I

I first met Césarine Vivian in the stalls at the Ambiguities Theatre.

I had promised to take Mrs. Latham and Irene to see the French plays which were then being acted by Marie Leroux's celebrated Palais Royal company. I wasn't at the time exactly engaged to poor Irene: it has always been a comfort to me that I wasn't engaged to her, though I knew Irene herself considered it practically equivalent to an understood engagement. We had known one another intimately from childhood upward, for the Lathams were a sort of second cousins of ours, three times removed: and we had always called one another by our Christian names, and been very fond of one another in a simple girlish and boyish fashion as long as we could either of us remember. Still, I maintain, there was no definite understanding between us; and if Mrs. Latham thought I had been paying Irene attentions, she must have known that a young man of two and twenty, with a decent fortune and a nice estate down in Devonshire, was likely to look about him for a while before he thought of settling down and marrying quietly.

I had brought the yacht up to London Bridge, and was living on board in picnic style, and running about town casually, when I took Irene and her mother to see "Faustine," at the Ambiguities. As soon as we had got in and taken our places, Irene whispered to me, touching my hand lightly with her fan, "Just look at the very dark girl on the other side of you, Harry! Did you ever in your life see anybody so perfectly beautiful?"

It has always been a great comfort to me, too, that Irene herself was the first person to call my attention to Césarine Vivian's extraordinary beauty.

I turned round, as if by accident, and gave a passing glance, where Irene waved her fan, at the girl beside me. She was beautiful, certainly, in a terrible, grand, statuesque style of beauty; and I saw at a glimpse that she had Southern blood in her veins, perhaps Negro, perhaps Moorish, perhaps only Spanish, or Italian, or Provençal. Her features were proud and somewhat Jewish-looking; her eyes large, dark, and haughty; her black hair waved slightly in sinuous undulations as it passed across her high, broad forehead; her complexion, though a dusky olive in tone, was clear and rich, and daintily transparent; and her lips were thin and very slightly curled at the delicate corners, with a peculiarly imperious and almost scornful expression of fixed disdain. I had never before beheld anywhere such a magnificently repellent specimen of womanhood. For a second or so, as I looked, her eyes met mine with a defiant inquiry, and I was conscious that moment of some strange and weird fascination in her glance that seemed to draw me irresistibly towards her, at the same time that I hardly dared to fix my gaze steadily upon the piercing eyes that looked through and through me with their keen penetration.

"She's very beautiful, no doubt," I whispered back to Irene in a low undertone, "though I must confess I don't exactly like the look of her. She's a trifle too much of a tragedy queen for my taste: a Lady Macbeth, or a Beatrice Cenci, or a Clytemnestra. I prefer our simple little English prettiness to this southern splendour. It's more to our English liking than these tall and stately Italian enchantresses. Besides, I fancy the girl looks as if she had a drop or two of black blood somewhere about her."

"Oh, no," Irene cried warmly. "Impossible, Harry. She's exquisite: exquisite. Italian, you know, or something of that sort. Italian girls have always got that peculiar gipsy-like type of beauty."

Low as we spoke, the girl seemed to know by instinct we were talking about her; for she drew away the ends of her light wrap coldly, in a significant fashion, and turned with her opera-glass in the opposite direction, as if on purpose to avoid looking towards us.

A minute later the curtain rose, and the first act of Halévy's "Faustine" distracted my attention for the moment from the beautiful stranger.

Marie Leroux took the part of the great empress. She was grand, stately, imposing, no doubt, but somehow it seemed to me she didn't come up quite so well as usual that evening to one's ideal picture of the terrible, audacious, superb Roman woman. I leant over and murmured so to Irene. "Don't you know why?" Irene whispered back to me with a faint movement of the play-bill toward the beautiful stranger.

"No," I answered; "I haven't really the slightest conception."

"Why," she whispered, smiling; "just look beside you. Could anybody bear comparison for a moment as a Faustine with that splendid creature in the stall next to you?"

I stole a glance sideways as she spoke. It was quite true. The girl by my side was the real Faustine, the exact embodiment of the dramatist's creation; and Marie Leroux, with her stagey effects and her actress's pretences, could not in any way stand the contrast with the genuine empress who sat there eagerly watching her.

The girl saw me glance quickly from her towards the actress and from the actress back to her, and shrank aside, not with coquettish timidity, but half angrily and half as if flattered and pleased at the implied compliment. "Papa," she said to the very English-looking gentleman who sat beyond her, "ce monsieur-ci...." I couldn't catch the end of the sentence.

She was French, then, not Italian or Spanish; yet a more perfect Englishman than the man she called "papa" it would be difficult to discover on a long summer's day in all London.

"My dear," her father whispered back in English, "if I were you...." and the rest of that sentence also was quite inaudible to me.

My interest was now fully roused in the beautiful stranger, who sat evidently with her father and sister, and drank in every word of the play as it proceeded with the intensest interest. As for me, I hardly cared to look at the actors, so absorbed was I in my queenly neighbour. I made a bare pretence of watching the stage every five minutes, and saying a few words now and again to Irene or her mother; but my real attention was all the time furtively directed to the girl beside me. Not that I was taken with her; quite the contrary; she distinctly repelled me; but she seemed to exercise over me for all that the same strange and indescribable fascination which is often possessed by some horrible sight that you would give worlds to avoid, and yet cannot for your life help intently gazing upon.

Between the third and fourth acts Irene whispered to me again, "I can't keep my eyes off her, Harry. She's wonderfully beautiful. Confess now: aren't you over head and ears in love with her?"

The Beckoning Hand & Other Stories by Grant Allen

Charles Grant Blairfindie Allen was born on February 24th, 1848 at Alwington, near Kingston, Canada West (now part of Ontario).

Home schooled until 13 when his family moved to England, Grant was to become a highly regarded science writer who branched out to a fiction career and became enormously popular.

His work helped propel several genres of fiction and whilst his career was short it was enormously productive.

Grant's scientific background enabled him to root much of his work in a plausibility that was denied to others. He had little fear in challenging a society that treated women as second class citizens and creating best sellers from such works.

On October 25th 1899 Grant Allen died at his home in Hindhead, Haslemere, Surrey, England. He died just before finishing Hilda Wade. The novel's final episode, which he dictated to his friend, doctor and neighbour Sir Arthur Conan Doyle from his bed appeared under the appropriate title, The Episode of the Dead Man Who Spoke in 1900.

Index of Contents

THE BECKONING HAND.
I
II
III
IV
V
VI
VII
VIII
IX
LUCRETIA
THE THIRD TIME
I
II
III
IV
V
VI
THE GOLD WULFRIC
PART I
I
II
III
IV
PART II
I
II

III

IV

V

VI

MY UNCLE'S WILL

I

II

III

IV

THE TWO CARNEGIES

I

II

III

IV

V

VI

OLGA DAVIDOFF'S HUSBAND

I

II

III

IV

V

VI

JOHN CANN'S TREASURE

II

III

IV

V

VI

VII

VIII

ISALINE AND I

I

II

III

PROFESSOR MILLITER'S DILEMMA

IN STRICT CONFIDENCE

I

II

III

IV

V

THE SEARCH PARTY'S FIND

HARRY'S INHERITANCE

I

II

III

IV

V

I looked at Irene's sweet little peaceful English face, and I answered truthfully, "No, Irene. If I wanted to fall in love, I should find somebody—"

"Nonsense, Harry," Irene cried, blushing a little, and holding up her fan before her nervously. "She's a thousand times prettier and handsomer in every way—"

"Prettier?"

"Than I am."

At that moment the curtain rose, and Marie Leroux came forward once more with her imperial diadem, in the very act of defying and bearding the enraged emperor.

It was a great scene. The whole theatre hung upon her words for twenty minutes. The effect was sublime. Even I myself felt my interest aroused at last in the consummate spectacle. I glanced round to observe my neighbour. She sat there, straining her gaze upon the stage, and heaving her bosom with suppressed emotion. In a second, the spell was broken again. Beside that tall, dark southern girl, in her queenly beauty, with her flashing eyes and quivering nostrils, intensely moved by the passion of the play, the mere actress who mouthed and gesticulated before us by the footlights was as sounding brass and a tinkling cymbal. My companion in the stalls was the genuine Faustine: the player on the stage was but a false pretender.

As I looked a cry arose from the wings: a hushed cry at first, a buzz or hum; rising louder and ever louder still, as a red glare burst upon the scene from the background. Then a voice from the side boxes rang out suddenly above the confused murmur and the ranting of the actors "Fire! Fire!"

Almost before I knew what had happened, the mob in the stalls, like the mob in the gallery, was surging and swaying wildly towards the exits, in a general struggle for life of the fierce old selfish barbaric pattern. Dense clouds of smoke rolled from the stage and filled the length and breadth of the auditorium; tongues of flame licked up the pasteboard scenes and hangings, like so much paper; women screamed, and fought, and fainted; men pushed one another aside and hustled and elbowed, in one wild effort to make for the doors at all hazards to the lives of their neighbours. Never before had I so vividly realized how near the savage lies to the surface in our best and highest civilized society. I had to realize it still more vividly and more terribly afterwards.

One person alone I observed calm and erect, resisting quietly all pushes and thrusts, and moving with slow deliberateness to the door, as if wholly unconcerned at the universal noise and hubbub and tumult around her. It was the dark girl from the stalls beside me.

For myself, my one thought of course was for poor Irene and Mrs. Latham. Fortunately, I am a strong and well-built man, and by keeping the two women in front of me, and thrusting hard with my elbows on either side to keep off the crush, I managed to make a tolerably clear road for them down the central row of stalls and out on to the big external staircase. The dark girl, now separated from her father and sister by the rush, was close in front of me. By a careful side movement, I managed to include her also in our party. She looked up to me gratefully with her big eyes, and her mouth broke into a charming smile as she turned and said in perfect English, "I am much obliged to you for your kind assistance." Irene's cheek was pale as death; but through the strange young lady's olive skin the bright blood still burned and glowed amid that frantic panic as calmly as ever.

We had reached the bottom of the steps, and were out into the front, when suddenly the strange lady turned around and gave a little cry of disappointment. "Mes lorgnettes! Mes lorgnettes!" she said. Then glancing round carelessly to me she went on in English: "I have left my opera-glasses inside on the vacant seat. I think, if you will excuse me, I'll go back and fetch them."

"It's impossible," I cried, "my dear madam. Utterly impossible. They'll crush you underfoot. They'll tear you to pieces."

She smiled a strange haughty smile, as if amused at the idea, but merely answered, "I think not," and tried to pass lightly by me.

I held her arm. I didn't know then she was as strong as I was. "Don't go," I said imploringly. "They will certainly kill you. It would be impossible to stem a mob like this one."

She smiled again, and darted back in silence before I could stop her.

Irene and Mrs. Latham were now fairly out of all danger. "Go on, Irene," I said loosing her arm. "Policeman, get these ladies safely out. I must go back and take care of that mad woman."

"Go, go quick," Irene cried. "If you don't go, she'll be killed, Harry."

I rushed back wildly after her, battling as well as I was able against the frantic rush of panic-stricken fugitives, and found my companion struggling still upon the main staircase. I helped her to make her way back into the burning theatre, and she ran lightly through the dense smoke to the stall she had occupied, and took the opera-glasses from the vacant place. Then she turned to me once more with a smile of triumph. "People lose their heads so," she said, "in all these crushes. I came back on purpose to show papa I wasn't going to be frightened into leaving my opera-glasses. I should have been eternally ashamed of myself if I had come away and left them in the theatre."

"Quick," I answered, gasping for breath. "If you don't make haste, we shall be choked to death, or the roof itself will fall in upon us and crush us!"

She looked up where I pointed with a hasty glance, and then made her way back again quickly to the staircase. As we hurried out, the timbers of the stage were beginning to fall in, and the engines were already playing fiercely upon the raging flames. I took her hand and almost dragged her out into the open. When we reached the Strand, we were both wet through, and terribly blackened with smoke and ashes. Pushing our way through the dense crowd, I called a hansom. She jumped in lightly. "Thank you so much," she said, quite carelessly. "Will you kindly tell him where to drive? Twenty-seven, Seymour Crescent."

"I'll see you home, if you'll allow me," I answered. "Under these circumstances, I trust I may be permitted."

"As you like," she said, smiling enchantingly. "You are very good. My name is Césarine Vivian. Papa will be very much obliged to you for your kind assistance."

I drove round to the Lathams' after dropping Miss Vivian at her father's door, to assure myself of Irene's safety, and to let them know of my own return unhurt from my perilous adventure. Irene met me on the doorstep, pale as death still. "Thank heaven," she cried, "Harry, you're safe back again! And that poor girl? What has become of her?"

"I left her," I said, "at Seymour Crescent."

Irene burst into a flood of tears. "Oh, Harry," she cried, "I thought she would have been killed there. It was brave of you, indeed, to help her through with it."

II

Next day, Mr. Vivian called on me at the Oxford and Cambridge, the address on the card I had given his daughter. I was in the club when he called, and I found him a pleasant, good-natured Cornishman, with very little that was strange or romantic in any way about him. He thanked me heartily, but not too effusively, for the care I had taken of Miss Vivian overnight; and he was not so overcome with parental emotion as not to smoke a very good Havana, or to refuse my offer of a brandy and seltzer. We got on very well together, and I soon gathered from what my new acquaintance said that, though he belonged to one of the best families in Cornwall, he had been an English merchant in Haiti, and had made his money chiefly in the coffee trade. He was a widower, I learned incidentally, and his daughters had been brought up for some years in England, though at their mother's request they had also passed part of their lives in convent schools in Paris and Rouen. "Mrs. Vivian was a Haitian, you know," he said casually: "Catholic of course. The girls are Catholics. They're good girls, though they're my own daughters; and Césarine, your friend of last night, is supposed to be clever. I'm no judge myself: I don't know about it. Oh, by the way, Césarine said she hadn't thanked you half enough herself yesterday, and I was to be sure and bring you round this afternoon to a cup of tea with us at Seymour Crescent."

In spite of the impression Mdlle. Césarine had made upon me the night before, I somehow didn't feel at all desirous of meeting her again. I was impressed, it is true, but not favourably. There seemed to me something uncanny and weird about her which made me shrink from seeing anything more of her if I could possibly avoid it. And as it happened, I was luckily engaged that very afternoon to tea at Irene's. I made the excuse, and added somewhat pointedly—on purpose that it might be repeated to Mdlle. Césarine—"Miss Latham is a very old and particular friend of mine, a friend whom I couldn't for worlds think of disappointing."

Mr. Vivian laughed the matter off. "I shall catch it from Césarine," he said good-humouredly, "for not bringing her cavalier to receive her formal thanks in person. Our West-Indian born girls, you know, are very imperious. But if you can't, you can't, of course, so there's an end of it, and it's no use talking any more about it."

I can't say why, but at that moment, in spite of my intense desire not to meet Césarine again, I felt I would have given whole worlds if he would have pressed me to come in spite of myself. But, as it happened, he didn't.

At five o'clock, I drove round in a hansom as arranged, to Irene's, having almost made up my mind, if I found her alone, to come to a definite understanding with her and call it an engagement. She wasn't alone, however. As I entered the drawing-room, I saw a tall and graceful lady sitting opposite her, holding a cup of tea, and with her back towards me. The lady rose, moved round, and bowed. To my immense surprise, I found it was Césarine.

I noted to myself at the moment, too, that in my heart, though I had seen her but once before, I thought of her already simply as Césarine. And I was pleased to see her: fascinated: spell-bound.

Césarine smiled at my evident surprise. "Papa and I met Miss Latham this afternoon in Bond Street," she said gaily, in answer to my mute inquiry, "and we stopped and spoke to one another, of course, about last night; and papa said you couldn't come round to tea with us in the Crescent, because you were engaged already to Miss Latham. And Miss Latham very kindly asked me to drive over and take tea with her, as I was so anxious to thank you once more for your great kindness to me yesterday."

"And Miss Vivian was good enough to waive all ceremony," Irene put in, "and come round to us as you see, without further introduction."

I stopped and talked all the time I was there to Irene; but, somehow, whatever I said, Césarine managed to intercept it, and I caught myself quite guiltily looking at her from time to time, with an inexpressible attraction that I could not account for.

By-and-by, Mr. Vivian's carriage called for Césarine, and I was left a few minutes alone with Irene.

"Well, what do you think of her?" Irene asked me simply.

I turned my eyes away: I dare not meet hers. "I think she's very handsome," I replied evasively.

"Handsome! I should think so. She's wonderful. She's splendid. And doesn't she talk magnificently, too, Harry?"

"She's clever, certainly," I answered shuffling. "But I don't know why, I mistrust her, Irene."

I rose and stood by the door with my hat in my hand, hesitating and trembling. I felt as if I had something to say to Irene, and yet I was half afraid to venture upon saying it. My fingers quivered, a thing very unusual with me. At last I came closer to her, after a long pause, and said, "Irene."

Irene started, and the colour flushed suddenly into her cheeks. "Yes, Harry," she answered tremulously.

I don't know why, but I couldn't utter it. It was but to say "I love you," yet I hadn't the courage. I stood there like a fool, looking at her irresolutely, and then—

The door opened suddenly, and Mrs. Latham entered and interrupted us.

III

I didn't speak again to Irene. The reason was that three days later I received a little note of invitation to lunch at Seymour Crescent from Césarine Vivian.

I didn't want to accept it, and yet I didn't know how to help myself. I went, determined beforehand as soon as ever lunch was over to take away the yacht to the Scotch islands, and leave Césarine and all her enchantments for ever behind me. I was afraid of her, that's the fact, positively afraid of her. I couldn't look her in the face without feeling at once that she exerted a terrible influence over me.

The lunch went off quietly enough, however. We talked about Haiti and the West Indies; about the beautiful foliage and the lovely flowers; about the moonlight nights and the tropical sunsets; and Césarine grew quite enthusiastic over them all. "You should take your yacht out there some day, Mr. Tristram," she said softly. "There is no place on earth so wild and glorious as our own beautiful neglected Haiti."

She lifted her eyes full upon me as she spoke. I stammered out, like one spell-bound, "I must certainly go, on your recommendation, Mdlle. Césarine."

"Why Mademoiselle?" she asked quickly. Then, perceiving I misunderstood her by the start I gave, she added with a blush, "I mean, why not 'Miss Vivian' in plain English?"

"Because you aren't English," I said confusedly. "You're Haitian, in reality. Nobody could ever for a moment take you for a mere Englishwoman."

I meant it for a compliment, but Césarine frowned. I saw I had hurt her, and why; but I did not apologize. Yet I was conscious of having done something very wrong, and I knew I must try my best at once to regain my lost favour with her.

"You will take some coffee after lunch?" Césarine said, as the dishes were removed.

"Oh, certainly, my dear," her father put in. "You must show Mr. Tristram how we make coffee in the West Indian fashion."

Césarine smiled, and poured it out, black coffee, very strong, and into each cup she poured a little glass of excellent pale neat cognac. It seemed to me that she poured the cognac like a conjuror's trick; but everything about her was so strange and lurid that I took very little notice of the matter at that particular moment. It certainly was delicious coffee: I never tasted anything like it.

After lunch, we went into the drawing-room, and thence Césarine took me alone into the pretty conservatory. She wanted to show me some of her beautiful Haitian orchids, she said; she had brought the orchids herself years ago from Haiti. How long we stood there I could never tell. I seemed as if intoxicated with her presence. I had forgotten now all about my distrust of her: I had forgotten all about Irene and what I wished to say to her: I was conscious only of Césarine's great dark eyes, looking through and through me with their piercing glance, and Césarine's figure, tall and stately, but very voluptuous, standing close beside me, and heaving regularly as we looked at the orchids. She talked to me in a low and dreamy voice; and whether the Château Larose at lunch had got into my head, or whatever it might be, I felt only dimly and faintly aware of what was passing around me. I was unmanned with love, I suppose: but, however it may have been, I certainly moved and spoke that afternoon like a man in a trance from which he cannot by any effort of his own possibly awake himself.

"Yes, yes," I overheard Césarine saying at last, as through a mist of emotion, "you must go some day and see our beautiful mountainous Haiti. I must go myself. I long to go again. I don't care for this gloomy, dull, sunless England. A hand seems always to be beckoning me there. I shall obey it someday, for Haiti, our lovely Haiti, is too beautiful."

Her voice was low and marvellously musical. "Mademoiselle Césarine," I began timidly.

She pouted and looked at me. "Mademoiselle again," she said in a pettish way. "I told you not to call me so, didn't I?"

"Well, then, Césarine," I went on boldly. She laughed low, a little laugh of triumph, but did not correct or check me in any way.

"Césarine," I continued, lingering I know not why over the syllables of the name, "I will go, as you say. I shall see Haiti. Why should we not both go together?"

She looked up at me eagerly with a sudden look of hushed inquiry. "You mean it?" she asked, trembling visibly. "You mean it, Mr. Tristram? You know what you are saying?"

"Césarine," I answered, "I mean it. I know it. I cannot go away from you and leave you. Something seems to tie me. I am not my own master.... Césarine, I love you."

My head whirled as I said the words, but I meant them at the time, and heaven knows I tried ever after to live up to them.

She clutched my arm convulsively for a moment. Her face was aglow with a wonderful light, and her eyes burned like a pair of diamonds. "But the other girl!" she cried. "Her! Miss Latham! The one you call Irene! You are ... in love with her! Are you not? Tell me!"

"I have never proposed to Irene," I replied slowly. "I have never asked any other woman but you to marry me, Césarine."

She answered me nothing, but my face was very near hers, and I bent forward and kissed her suddenly. To my immense surprise, instead of struggling or drawing away, she kissed me back a fervent kiss, with lips hard pressed to mine, and the tears trickled slowly down her cheeks in a strange fashion. "You are mine," she cried. "Mine for ever. I have won you. She shall not have you. I knew you were mine the moment I looked upon you. The hand beckoned me. I knew I should get you."

"Come up into my den, Mr. Tristram, and have a smoke," my host interrupted in his bluff voice, putting his head in unexpectedly at the conservatory door. "I think I can offer you a capital Manilla."

The sound woke me as if from some terrible dream, and I followed him still in a sort of stupor up to the smoking room.

IV

That very evening I went to see Irene. My brain was whirling even yet, and I hardly knew what I was doing; but the cool air revived me a little, and by the time I reached the Lathams' I almost felt myself again.

Irene came down to the drawing-room to see me alone. I saw what she expected, and the shame of my duplicity overcame me utterly.

I took both her hands in mine and stood opposite her, ashamed to look her in the face, and with the terrible confession weighing me down like a burden of guilt. "Irene," I blurted out, without preface or comment, "I have just proposed to Césarine Vivian."

Irene drew back a moment and took a long breath. Then she said, with a tremor in her voice, but without a tear or a cry, "I expected it, Harry. I thought you meant it. I saw you were terribly, horribly in love with her."

"Irene," I cried, passionately and remorsefully flinging myself upon the sofa in an agony of repentance, "I do not love her. I have never cared for her. I'm afraid of her, fascinated by her. I love you, Irene, you and you only. The moment I'm away from her, I hate her, I hate her. For heaven's sake, tell me what am I to do! I do not love her. I hate her, Irene."

Irene came up to me and soothed my hair tenderly with her hand. "Don't, Harry," she said, with sisterly kindliness. "Don't speak so. Don't give way to it. I know what you feel. I know what you think. But I am not angry with you. You mustn't talk like that. If she has accepted you, you must go and marry her. I have nothing to reproach you with: nothing, nothing. Never say such words to me again. Let us be as we have always been, friends only."

"Irene," I cried, lifting up my head and looking at her wildly, "it is the truth: I do not love her, except when I am with her: and then, some strange enchantment seems to come over me. I don't know what it is, but I can't escape it. In my heart, Irene, in my heart of hearts, I love you, and you only. I can never love her as I love you, Irene. My darling, my darling, tell me how to get myself away from her."

"Hush," Irene said, laying her hand on mine persuasively. "You're excited to-night, Harry. You are flushed and feverish. You don't know what you're saying. You mustn't talk so. If you do, you'll make me hate you and despise you. You must keep your word now, and marry Miss Vivian."

V

The next six weeks seem to me still like a vague dream: everything happened so hastily and strangely. I got a note next day from Irene. It was very short. "Dearest Harry, Mamma and I think, under the circumstances, it would be best for us to leave London for a few weeks. I am not angry with you. With best love, ever yours affectionately, Irene."

I was wild when I received it. I couldn't bear to part so with Irene. I would find out where they were going and follow them immediately. I would write a note and break off my mad engagement with Césarine. I must have been drunk or insane when I made it. I couldn't imagine what I could have been doing.

On my way round to inquire at the Latham's, a carriage came suddenly upon me at a sharp corner. A lady bowed to me from it. It was Césarine with her father. They pulled up and spoke to me. From that moment my doom was sealed. The old fascination came back at once, and I followed Césarine blindly home to her house to luncheon, her accepted lover.

In six weeks more we were really married.

The first seven or eight months of our married life passed away happily enough. As soon as I was actually married to Césarine, that strange feeling I had at first experienced about her slowly wore off in the closer, commonplace, daily intercourse of married life. I almost smiled at myself for ever having felt it. Césarine was so beautiful and so queenly a person, that when I took her down home to Devonshire, and introduced her to the old manor, I really found myself immensely proud of her. Everybody at Teignbury was delighted and struck with her; and, what was a great deal more to the point, I began to discover that I was positively in love with her myself, into the bargain. She softened and melted immensely on nearer acquaintance; the Faustina air faded slowly away, when one saw her in her own home among her own occupations; and I came to look on her as a beautiful, simple, innocent girl, delighted with all our country pleasures, fond of a breezy canter on the slopes of Dartmoor, and taking an affectionate interest in the ducks and chickens, which I could hardly ever have conceived even as possible when I first saw her in Seymour Crescent. The imperious, mysterious, terrible Césarine disappeared entirely, and I found in her place, to my immense relief, that I had married a graceful, gentle, tender-hearted English girl, with just a pleasant occasional touch of southern fire and impetuosity.

As winter came round again, however, Césarine's cheeks began to look a little thinner than usual, and she had such a constant, troublesome cough, that I began to be a trifle alarmed at her strange symptoms. Césarine herself laughed off my fears. "It's nothing, Harry," she would say; "nothing at all, I assure you, dear. A few good rides on the moor will set me right again. It's all the result of that horrid London. I'm a country-born girl, and I hate big towns. I never want to live in town again, Harry."

I called in our best Exeter doctor, and he largely confirmed Césarine's own simple view of the situation. "There's nothing organically wrong with Mrs. Tristram's constitution," he said confidently. "No weakness of the lungs or heart in any way. She has merely run down, outlived her strength a little. A winter in some warm, genial climate would set her up again, I haven't the least hesitation in saying."

"Let us go to Algeria with the yacht, Reeney," I suggested, much reassured.

"Why Algeria?" Césarine replied, with brightening eyes. "Oh, Harry, why not dear old Haiti? You said once you would go there with me, you remember when, darling; why not keep your promise now, and go there? I want to go there, Harry: I'm longing to go there." And she held out her delicately moulded hand in front of her, as if beckoning me, and drawing me on to Haiti after her.

"Ah, yes; why not the West Indies?" the Exeter doctor answered meditatively. "I think I understood you that Mrs. Tristram is West Indian born. Quite so. Quite so. Her native air. Depend upon it, that's the best place for her. By all means, I should say, try Haiti."

I don't know why, but the notion for some reason displeased me immensely. There was something about Césarine's eyes, somehow, when she beckoned with her hand in that strange fashion, which reminded me exactly of the weird, uncanny, indescribable impression she had made upon me when I first knew her. Still I was very fond of Césarine, and if she and the doctor were both agreed that Haiti would be the very best place for her, it would be foolish and wrong for me to interfere with their joint wisdom. Depend upon it, a woman often knows what is the matter with her better than any man, even her husband, can possibly tell her.

The end of it all was, that in less than a month from that day, we were out in the yacht on the broad Atlantic, with the cliffs of Falmouth and the Lizard Point fading slowly behind us in the distance, and the white spray dashing in front of us, like fingers beckoning us on to Haiti.

VI

The bay of Port-au-Prince is hot and simmering, a deep basin enclosed in a ringing semicircle of mountains, with scarce a breath blowing on the harbour, and with tall cocoa-nut palms rising unmoved into the still air above on the low sand-spits that close it in to seaward. The town itself is wretched, squalid, and hopelessly ramshackled, a despondent collection of tumbledown wooden houses, interspersed with indescribable negro huts, mere human rabbit-hutches, where parents and children herd together, in one higgledy-piggledy, tropical confusion. I had never in my days seen anything more painfully desolate and dreary, and I feared that Césarine, who had not been here since she was a girl of fourteen, would be somewhat depressed at the horrid actuality, after her exalted fanciful ideals of the remembered Haiti. But, to my immense surprise, as it turned out, Césarine did not appear at all shocked or taken aback at the squalor and wretchedness all around her. On the contrary, the very air of the place seemed to inspire her from the first with fresh vigour; her cough disappeared at once as if by magic; and the colour returned forthwith to her cheeks, almost as soon as we had fairly cast anchor in Haitian waters.

The very first day we arrived at Port-au-Prince, Césarine said to me, with more shyness than I had ever yet seen her exhibit, "If you wouldn't mind it, Harry, I should like to go at once, this morning, and see my grandmother."

I started with astonishment. "Your grandmother, Césarine!" I cried incredulously. "My darling! I didn't know you had a grandmother living."

"Yes, I have," she answered, with some slight hesitation, "and I think if you wouldn't object to it, Harry, I'd rather go and see her alone, the first time at least, please dearest."

In a moment, the obvious truth, which I had always known in a vague sort of fashion, but never thoroughly realized, flashed across my mind in its full vividness, and I merely bowed my head in silence. It was natural she should not wish me to see her meeting with her Haitian grandmother.

She went alone through the streets of Port-au-Prince, without inquiry, like one who knew them familiarly of old, and I dogged her footsteps at a distance unperceived, impelled by the same strange fascination which had so often driven me to follow Césarine wherever she led me. After a few hundred yards, she turned out of the chief business place, and down a tumbledown alley of scattered negro cottages, till she came at last to a rather better house that stood by itself in a little dusty garden of guava-trees and cocoa-nuts. A rude paling, built negro-wise of broken barrel-staves, nailed rudely together, separated the garden from the compound next to it. I slipped into the compound before Césarine observed me, beckoned the lazy negro from the door of the hut, with one finger placed as a token of silence upon my lips, dropped a dollar into his open palm, and stood behind the paling, looking out into the garden beside me through a hole made by a knot in one of the barrel staves.

Césarine knocked with her hand at the door, and in a moment was answered by an old negress, tall and bony, dressed in a loose sack-like gown of coarse cotton print, with a big red bandanna tied around her short grey hair, and a huge silver cross dangling carelessly upon her bare and wrinkled black neck. She wore no sleeves, and bracelets of strange beads hung loosely around her shrunken and skinny wrists. A more hideous old hag I had never in my life beheld before; and yet I saw, without waiting to observe it, that she had Césarine's great dark eyes and even white teeth, and something of Césarine's figure lingered still in her lithe and sinuous yet erect carriage.

"Grand'mère!" Césarine said convulsively, flinging her arms with wild delight around that grim and withered gaunt black woman. It seemed to me she had never since our marriage embraced me with half the fervour she bestowed upon this hideous old African witch creature.

"Hé, Césarine, it is thee, then, my little one," the old negress cried out suddenly, in her thin high voice and her muffled Haitian patois. "I did not expect thee so soon, my cabbage. Thou hast come early. Be the welcome one, my granddaughter."

I reeled with horror as I saw the wrinkled and haggard African kissing once more my beautiful Césarine. It seemed to me a horrible desecration. I had always known, of course, since Césarine was a quadroon, that her grandmother on one side must necessarily have been a full-blooded negress, but I had never yet suspected the reality could be so hideous, so terrible as this.

I crouched down speechless against the paling in my disgust and astonishment, and motioned with my hand to the negro in the hut to remain perfectly quiet. The door of the house closed, and Césarine disappeared: but I waited there, as if chained to the spot, under a hot and burning tropical sun, for fully an hour, unconscious of anything in heaven or earth, save the shock and surprise of that unexpected disclosure.

At last the door opened again, and Césarine apparently came out once more into the neighbouring garden. The gaunt negress followed her close, with one arm thrown caressingly about her beautiful neck and shoulders. In London, Césarine would not have permitted anybody but a great lady to take such a liberty with her; but here in Haiti, she submitted to the old negress's horrid embraces with perfect calmness. Why should she not, indeed! It was her own grandmother.

They came close up to the spot where I was crouching in the thick drifted dust behind the low fence, and then I heard rather than saw that Césarine had flung herself passionately down upon her knees on the ground, and was pouring forth a muttered prayer, in a tongue unknown to me, and full of harsh and uncouth gutturals. It was not Latin; it was not even the coarse Creole French, the negro patois in which I heard the people jabbering to one another loudly in the streets around me: it was some still more hideous and barbaric language, a mass of clicks and inarticulate noises, such as I could never have believed might possibly proceed from Césarine's thin and scornful lips.

At last she finished, and I heard her speaking again to her grandmother in the Creole dialect. "Grandmother, you will pray and get me one. You will not forget me. A boy. A pretty one; an heir to my husband!" It was said wistfully, with an infinite longing. I knew then why she had grown so pale and thin and haggard before we sailed away from England.

The old hag answered in the same tongue, but in her shrill withered note, "You will bring him up to the religion, my little one, will you?"

Césarine seemed to bow her head. "I will," she said. "He shall follow the religion. Mr. Tristram shall never know anything about it."

They went back once more into the house, and I crept away, afraid of being discovered, and returned to the yacht, sick at heart, not knowing how I should ever venture again to meet Césarine.

But when I got back, and had helped myself to a glass of sherry to steady my nerves, from the little flask on Césarine's dressing-table, I thought to myself, hideous as it all seemed, it was very natural Césarine should wish to see her grandmother. After all, was it not better, that proud and haughty as she was, she should not disown her own flesh and blood? And yet, the memory of my beautiful Césarine wrapped in that hideous old black woman's arms made the blood curdle in my very veins.

As soon as Césarine returned, however, gayer and brighter than I had ever seen her, the old fascination overcame me once more, and I determined in my heart to stifle the horror I could not possibly help feeling. And that evening, as I sat alone in the cabin with my wife, I said to her, "Césarine, we have never spoken about the religious question before: but if it should be ordained we are ever to have any little ones of our own, I should wish them to be brought up in their mother's creed. You could make them better Catholics, I take it, than I could ever make them Christians of any sort."

Césarine answered never a word, but to my intense surprise she burst suddenly into a flood of tears, and flung herself sobbing on the cabin floor at my feet in an agony of tempestuous cries and writhings.

VII

A few days later, when we had settled down for a three months' stay at a little bungalow on the green hills behind Port-au-Prince, Césarine said to me early in the day, "I want to go away to-day, Harry, up into the mountains, to the chapel of Notre Dame de Bon Secours."

I bowed my head in acquiescence. "I can guess why you want to go, Reeney," I answered gently. "You want to pray there about something that's troubling you. And if I'm not mistaken, it's the same thing that made you cry the other evening when I spoke to you down yonder in the cabin."

The tears rose hastily once more into Césarine's eyes, and she cried in a low distressed voice, "Harry, Harry, don't talk to me so. You are too good to me. You will kill me. You will kill me."

I lifted her head from the table, where she had buried it in her arms, and kissed her tenderly. "Reeney," I said, "I know how you feel, and I hope Notre Dame will listen to your prayers, and send you what you ask of her. But if not, you need never be afraid that I shall love you any the less than I do at present."

Césarine burst into a fresh flood of tears. "No, Harry," she said, "you don't know about it. You can't imagine it. To us, you know, who have the blood of Africa running in our veins, it is not a mere matter of fancy. It is an eternal disgrace for any woman of our race and descent not to be a mother. I cannot help it. It is the instinct of my people. We are all born so: we cannot feel otherwise."

It was the only time either of us ever alluded in speaking with one another to the sinister half of Césarine's pedigree.

"You will let me go with you to the mountains, Reeney?" I asked, ignoring her remark. "You mustn't go so far by yourself, darling."

"No, Harry, you can't come with me. It would make my prayers ineffectual, dearest. You are a heretic, you know, Harry. You are not Catholic. Notre Dame won't listen to my prayer if I take you with me on my pilgrimage, my darling."

I saw her mind was set upon it, and I didn't interfere. She would be away all night, she said. There was a rest-house for pilgrims attached to the chapel, and she would be back again at Maisonette (our bungalow) the morning after.

That afternoon she started on her way on a mountain pony I had just bought for her, accompanied only by a negro maid. I couldn't let her go quite unattended through those lawless paths, beset by cottages of half savage Africans; so I followed at a distance, aided by a black groom, and tracked her road along the endless hill-sides up to a fork in the way where the narrow bridle-path divided into two, one of which bore away to leftward, leading, my guide told me, to the chapel of Notre Dame de Bon Secours.

At that point the guide halted. He peered with hand across his eyebrows among the tangled brake of tree-ferns with a terrified look; then he shook his woolly black head ominously. "I can't go on,

Monsieur," he said, turning to me with an unfeigned shudder. "Madame has not taken the path of Our Lady. She has gone to the left along the other road, which leads at last to the Vaudoux temple."

I looked at him incredulously. I had heard before of Vaudoux. It is the hideous African canibalistic witchcraft of the relapsing half-heathen Haitian negroes. But Césarine a Vaudoux worshipper! It was too ridiculous. The man must be mistaken: or else Césarine had taken the wrong road by some slight accident.

Next moment, a horrible unspeakable doubt seized upon me irresistibly. What was the unknown shrine in her grandmother's garden at which Césarine had prayed in those awful gutturals? Whatever it was, I would probe this mystery to the very bottom. I would know the truth, come what might of it.

"Go, you coward!" I said to the negro. "I have no further need of you. I will make my way alone to the Vaudoux temple."

"Monsieur," the man cried, trembling visibly in every limb, "they will tear you to pieces. If they ever discover you near the temple, they will offer you up as a victim to the Vaudoux."

"Pooh," I answered, contemptuous of the fellow's slavish terror. "Where Madame, a woman, dares to go, I, her husband, am certainly not afraid to follow her."

"Monsieur," he replied, throwing himself submissively in the dust on the path before me, "Madame is Creole; she has the blood of the Vaudoux worshippers flowing in her veins. Nobody will hurt her. She is free of the craft. But Monsieur is a pure white and uninitiated.... If the Vaudoux people catch him at their rites, they will rend him in pieces, and offer his blood as an expiation to the Unspeakable One."

"Go," I said, with a smile, turning my horse's head up the right-hand path toward the Vaudoux temple. "I am not afraid. I will come back again to Maisonette to-morrow."

I followed the path through a tortuous maze, beset with prickly cactus, agave, and fern-brake, till I came at last to a spur of the hill, where a white wooden building gleamed in front of me, in the full slanting rays of tropical sunset. A skull was fastened to the lintel of the door. I knew at once it was the Vaudoux temple.

I dismounted at once, and led my horse aside into the brake, though I tore his legs and my own as I went with the spines of the cactus plants; and tying him by the bridle to a mountain cabbage palm, in a spot where the thick underbrush completely hid us from view, I lay down and waited patiently for the shades of evening.

It was a moonless night, according to the Vaudoux fashion; and I knew from what I had already read in West Indian books that the orgies would not commence till midnight.

From time to time, I rubbed a fusee against my hand without lighting it, and by the faint glimmer of the phosphorus on my palm, I was able to read the figures of my watch dial without exciting the attention of the neighbouring Vaudoux worshippers.

Hour after hour went slowly by, and I crouched there still unseen among the agave thicket. At last, as the hands of the watch reached together the point of twelve, I heard a low but deep rumbling noise coming ominously from the Vaudoux temple. I recognized at once the familiar sound. It was the note of the bull-roarer, that mystic instrument of pointed wood, whirled by a string round the head of the hierophant, by whose aid savages in their secret rites summon to their shrines their gods and spirits. I had often made one myself for a toy when I was a boy in England.

I crept out through the tangled brake, and cautiously approached the back of the building. A sentinel was standing by the door in front, a powerful negro, armed with revolver and cutlas. I skulked round noiselessly to the rear, and lifting myself by my hands to the level of the one tiny window, I peered in through a slight scratch on the white paint, with which the glass was covered internally.

I only saw the sight within for a second. Then my brain reeled, and my fingers refused any longer to hold me. But in that second, I had read the whole terrible, incredible truth: I knew what sort of a woman she really was whom I had blindly taken as the wife of my bosom.

Before a rude stone altar covered with stuffed alligator skins, human bones, live snakes, and hideous sorts of African superstition, a tall and withered black woman stood erect, naked as she came from her mother's womb, one skinny arm raised aloft, and the other holding below some dark object, that writhed and struggled awfully in her hand on the slab of the altar, even as she held it. I saw in a flash of the torches behind it was the black hag I had watched before at the Port-au-Prince cottage.

Beside her, whiter of skin, and faultless of figure, stood a younger woman, beautiful to behold, imperious and haughty still, like a Greek statue, unmoved before that surging horrid background of naked black and cringing savages. Her head was bent, and her hand pressed convulsively against the swollen veins in her throbbing brow; and I saw at once it was my own wife, a Vaudoux worshipper, Césarine Tristram.

In another flash, I knew the black woman had a sharp flint knife in her uplifted hand; and the dark object in the other hand I recognized with a thrill of unspeakable horror as a negro girl of four years old or thereabouts, gagged and bound, and lying on the altar.

Before I could see the sharp flint descend upon the naked breast of the writhing victim, my fingers in mercy refused to bear me, and I fell half fainting on the ground below, too shocked and unmanned even to crawl away at once out of reach of the awful unrealizable horror.

But by the sounds within, I knew they had completed their hideous sacrifice, and that they were smearing over Césarine, my own wife, the woman of my choice, with the warm blood of the human victim.

Sick and faint, I crept away slowly through the tangled underbrush, tearing my skin as I went with the piercing cactus spines; untied my horse from the spot where I had fastened him; and rode him down without drawing rein, cantering round sharp angles and down horrible ledges, till he stood at last, white with foam, by the grey dawn, in front of the little piazza at Maisonette.

VIII

That night, the thunder roared and the lightning played with tropical fierceness round the tall hilltops away in the direction of the Vaudoux temple. The rain came down in fearful sheets, and the torrents roared and foamed in cataracts, and tore away great gaps in the rough paths on the steep hill-sides. But at eight o'clock in the morning Césarine returned, drenched with wet, and with a strange frown upon her haughty forehead.

I did not know how to look at her or how to meet her.

"My prayers are useless," she muttered angrily as she entered. "Some heretic must have followed me unseen to the chapel of Notre Dame de Bon Secours. The pilgrimage is a failure."

"You are wet," I said, trembling. "Change your things, Césarine." I could not pretend to speak gently to her.

She turned upon me with a fierce look in her big black eyes. Her instinct showed her at once I had discovered her secret. "Tell them, and hang me," she cried fiercely.

It was what the law required me to do. I was otherwise the accomplice of murder and cannibalism. But I could not do it. Profoundly as I loathed her and hated her presence, now, I couldn't find it in my heart to give her up to justice, as I knew I ought to do.

I turned away and answered nothing.

Presently, she came out again from her bedroom, with her wet things still dripping around her. "Smoke that," she said, handing me a tiny cigarette rolled round in a leaf of fresh tobacco.

"I will not," I answered with a vague surmise, taking it from her fingers. "I know the smell. It is manchineal. You cannot any longer deceive me."

She went back to her bedroom once more. I sat, dazed and stupefied, in the bamboo chair on the front piazza. What to do, I knew not, and cared not. I was tied to her for life, and there was no help for it, save by denouncing her to the rude Haitian justice.

In an hour or more, our English maid came out to speak to me. "I'm afraid, sir," she said, "Mrs. Tristram is getting delirious. She seems to be in a high fever. Shall I ask one of these poor black bodies to go out and get the English doctor?"

I went into my wife's bedroom. Césarine lay moaning piteously on the bed, in her wet clothes still; her cheeks were hot, and her pulse was high and thin and feverish. I knew without asking what was the matter with her. It was yellow fever.

The night's exposure in that terrible climate, and the ghastly scene she had gone through so intrepidly, had broken down even Césarine's iron constitution.

I sent for the doctor and had her put to bed immediately. The black nurse and I undressed her between us. We found next her bosom, tied by a small red silken thread, a tiny bone, fresh and ruddy-looking. I knew what it was, and so did the negress. It was a human finger-bone, the last joint of a small child's fourth finger. The negress shuddered and hid her head. "It is Vaudoux, Monsieur!" she said. "I have seen it on others. Madame has been paying a visit, I suppose, to her grandmother."

For six long endless days and nights I watched and nursed that doomed criminal, doing everything for her that skill could direct or care could suggest to me: yet all the time fearing and dreading that she might yet recover, and not knowing in my heart what either of our lives could ever be like if she did live through it.

A merciful Providence willed it otherwise.

On the sixth day, the fatal vomito negro set in, the symptom of the last incurable stage of yellow fever, and I knew for certain that Césarine would die. She had brought her own punishment upon her. At midnight that evening she died delirious.

Thank God, she had left no child of mine behind her to inherit the curse her mother's blood had handed down to her!

IX

On my return to London, whither I went by mail direct, leaving the yacht to follow after me, I drove straight to the Lathams' from Waterloo Station. Mrs. Latham was out, the servant said, but Miss Irene was in the drawing-room.

Irene was sitting at the window by herself, working quietly at a piece of crewel work. She rose to meet me with her sweet simple little English smile. I took her hand and pressed it like a brother.

"I got your telegram," she said simply. "Harry, I know she is dead; but I know something terrible besides has happened. Tell me all. Don't be afraid to speak of it before me. I am not afraid, for my part, to listen."

I sat down on the sofa beside her, and told her all, without one word of excuse or concealment, from our last parting to the day of Césarine's death in Haiti: and she held my hand and listened all the while with breathless wonderment to my strange story.

At the end I said, "Irene, it has all come and gone between us like a hideous nightmare. I cannot imagine even now how that terrible woman, with all her power, could ever for one moment have bewitched me away from you, my beloved, my queen, my own heart's darling."

Irene did not try to hush me or to stop me in any way. She merely sat and looked at me steadily, and said nothing.

"It was fascination," I cried. "Infatuation, madness, delirium, enchantment."

"It was worse than that, Harry," Irene answered, rising quietly. "It was poison; it was witchcraft; it was sheer African devilry."

In a flash of thought, I remembered the cup of coffee at Seymour Crescent, the curious sherry at Port-au-Prince, the cigarette with the manchineal she had given me on the mountains, and I saw forthwith that Irene with her woman's quickness had divined rightly. It was more than infatuation; it was intoxication with African charms and West Indian poisons.

"What a man does in such a woman's hands is not his own doing," Irene said slowly. "He has no more control of himself in such circumstances than if she had drugged him with chloroform or opium."

"Then you forgive me, Irene?"

"I have nothing to forgive, Harry. I am grieved for you. I am frightened." Then bursting into tears, "My darling, my darling; I love you, I love you!"

I will acknowledge that I was certainly a very young man in the year '67; indeed, I was only just turned of twenty, and was inordinately proud of a slight downy fringe on my upper lip, which I was pleased to speak of as my moustache. Still, I was a sturdy young fellow enough, in spite of my consumptive tendencies, and not given to groundless fears in a general way; but I must allow that I was decidedly frightened by my adventure in the Richmond Hotel on the Christmas Eve of that aforesaid year of grace. It may be a foolish reminiscence, yet I dare say you won't mind listening to it.

When I say the Richmond Hotel, you must not understand me to speak of the Star and Garter in the town of that ilk situated in the county of Surrey, England. The Richmond where I passed my uncomfortable Christmas Eve stands on the banks of the pretty St. Francis River in Lower Canada. I had gone out to the colony in the autumn of that year, to look after a small property of my mother's near Kamouraska; and I originally intended to spend the winter in Quebec. But as November and December wore away, and the snow grew deeper and deeper upon the plains of Abraham, I became gradually aware that a Canadian winter was not the best adapted tonic in the world for a hearty young man with a slight hereditary predisposition to consumption. I had seen enough of Arctic life in Quebec during those two initial months to give me a good idea of its pleasures and its drawbacks. I had steered by toboggan down the ice-cone at the Falls of Montmorenci; I had driven a sleigh, tête-à-tête with a French Canadian belle, to a surprise picnic in a house at Sainte Anne; I had skated, snow-shoed, and curled to my heart's content; and I had caught my death of cold on the frozen St. Lawrence, not to mention such minor misfortunes as getting my nose, ears, and feet frostbitten during a driving party up the banks of the Chaudière. So a few days before Christmas, I determined to strike south. I would go for a tour through Virginia and the Carolinas, to escape the cold weather, waiting for the return of the summer sun to catch a glimpse of Niagara and the great lakes.

For this purpose I must first go to Montreal; and, that being the case, what could be more convenient than to spend Christmas Day itself with the rector at Richmond, to whom I had letters of introduction, his wife being in fact a first cousin of my mother's? Richmond lies half-way on the Grand Trunk line between Quebec and Montreal, and it would be more pleasant, by breaking my journey there, to eat my turkey and plum-pudding in a friend's family than in that somewhat cheerless hotel, the Dominion Hall. So off I started from the Point Levy station, at four o'clock on the twenty-fourth of December, hoping to arrive at my journey's end about one o'clock on Christmas morning.

Now, those were the days, just after the great American civil war, when gold was almost unknown either in the States or Canada, and everybody used greasy dollar notes of uncertain and purely local value. Hence I was compelled to take the money for expenses on my projected tour in the only form of specie which was available, that of solid silver. A hundred and fifty pounds in silver dollars amounts to a larger bulk and a heavier weight than you would suppose; and I thought it safer to carry the sum in my own hands, loosely bundled into a large leather reticule. Hinc illoe lacrimoe:— that was the real cause of my night's adventure and of the present story.

When I got into the long open American railway-carriage, with its comfortable stove and warm foot-bricks, I found only one seat vacant, and that was a red velvet sofa, opposite to another occupied by a girl of singular beauty. I can remember to this day exactly how she was dressed. I dare say my lady readers will think it horribly old-fashioned at the present time, but it was the very latest and most enchanting style in the year '67. On her head was a coquettish little cheese-plate bonnet, bound round with one of those warm, soft, fleecy woollen veils or head-wraps which Canadian girls know as Nubias. Her dress was a short winter walking costume of the period, trimmed with fur, and vandyked at the bottom so as to show a glimpse of the quilted down petticoat underneath. Her little high-heeled boots, displayed by the short costume, were buttoned far above the ankle, and bound with fur to match the dress; while a tiny tassel at the side added just a suspicion of Parisian coquetry. Her cloak was lined with sable, or what seemed so to my undiscriminating eyes; and her rug was a splendid piece of wolverine skins. As to her eyes, her lips, her figure, I had rather not attempt them. I can manage clothes, but not goddesses. Altogether, quite a dream of Canadian beauty, not devoid of that indefinable grace which goes only with the French blood.

I was not bold in '67, and I would have preferred to take any other seat rather than face this divine apparition; but there was no help for it, since all the others were filled: so I sat down a little sheepishly, I dare say. Almost before we were well out of the station we had got into a conversation, and it was she who began it.

"You are an Englishman, I think?" she said, looking at me with a frank and pleasant smile.

"Yes," I answered, colouring, though why I should have been ashamed of my nationality for that solitary moment of my life I cannot imagine, unless, perhaps, because she was a Canadian; "but how on earth did you discover it?"

"You would have been more warmly wrapped up if you had lived long in Canada," she replied. "In spite of our stoves and hot bricks, you'll find yourself very cold before you get to your journey's end."

"Yes," I said; "I suppose it's rather chilly late at night in these big cars."

"Dreadfully; oh, quite terribly. You ought to have a rug, you really ought. Won't you let me lend you one? I have another under the seat here."

"But you brought that for yourself," I interposed. "You will want it by-and-by, when it gets a little colder."

"Oh no, I shan't. This is warm enough for me; it's wolverine. You have a mother?"

What an extraordinary question, I thought, and what an unusually friendly girl! Was she really quite as simple-minded as she seemed, or could she be the "designing woman" of the novels? Yes, I admitted to her cautiously that I possessed a maternal parent, who was at that moment safely drinking her tea in a terrace at South Kensington.

"I have none," she said, with an emphasis on the personal pronoun, and a sort of appealing look in her big eyes. "But you should take care of yourself, for her sake. You really must take my rug. Hundreds, oh, thousands of young Englishmen come out here, and kill themselves their first winter by imprudence."

Thus adjured, I accepted the rug with many thanks and apologies, and wrapped myself warmly up in the corner, with a splendid view of my vis-à-vis.

Exactly at that moment, the ticket collector came round upon his official tour. Now, on American and Canadian railways, you do not take your ticket beforehand, but pay your fare to the collector, who walks up and down through the open cars from end to end, between every station. I lifted up my bag of silver, which lay on the seat beside me, and imprudently opened it to take out a few dollars full in sight of my enchanting neighbour. I saw her look with unaffected curiosity at the heap of coin within, and I was proud at being able to give such an unequivocal proof of my high respectability, for what better guarantee of all the noblest moral qualities can any man produce all the world over than a bag of dollars?

"What a lot of money!" she said, as the collector passed on. "What can you want with it all in coin?"

"I'm going on a tour in the Southern States," I confided in reply, "and I thought it better to take specie." (I was very proud ten or twelve years ago of that word specie.)

"And I suppose those are your initials on the reticule? What a pretty monogram! Your mother gave you that for a birthday present."

"You must be a conjurer or a clairvoyant," I said, smiling. "So she did;" and I added that the initials represented my humble patronymic and baptismal designations.

"My name's Lucretia," said my neighbour artlessly, as a child might have said it, without a word as to surname or qualifying circumstances; and from that moment she became to me simply Lucretia. I think of her as Lucretia to the present day. As she spoke, she pointed to the word engraved in tiny letters on her pretty silver locket.

I suppose she thought my confidence required a little more confidence in return, for after a slight pause she repeated once more, "My name's Lucretia, and I live at Richmond."

"Richmond!" I cried. "Why, that's just where I'm going. Do you know the rector?"

"Mr. Pritchard? Oh yes, intimately. He's our greatest friend. Are you going to stop with him?"

"For a day or two at least, on my way to Montreal. Mrs. Pritchard is my mother's cousin."

"How delightful! Then we may consider ourselves acquaintances. But you don't mean to knock them up to-night? They'll all be in bed long before one o'clock."

"No, I haven't even written to tell them I was coming," I answered. "They gave me a general invitation, and said I might drop in whenever I pleased."

"Then you must stop at the hotel to-night. I'm going there myself. My people keep the hotel."

Was it possible! I was thunderstruck. I had pictured Lucretia to myself as at least a countess of the ancien régime, a few of whom still linger on in Montreal and elsewhere. Her locket, her rugs, her eyes, her chiselled features, all of them seemed to me redolent of the old French noblesse. And here it turned out that this living angel was only the daughter of an inn-keeper! But in that primitive and pleasant Canadian society such things, I thought, can easily be. No doubt she is the petted child of the house, the one heiress of the old man's savings; and after spending a winter holiday among the gaieties of Quebec, she is now returning to pass the Christmas season with her own family. I will not conceal the fact that I had already fallen over head and ears in love with Lucretia at first sight, and that frank avowal made me love her all the more. Besides, these Canadian hotel-keepers are often very rich; and was not her manner perfect, and was she not an intimate friend of the rector and his wife? All these things showed at least that she was accustomed to refined society. I caught myself already speculating as to what my mother would think of such a match.

In five minutes it was all arranged about the hotel, and I had got into the midst of a swimming conversation with Lucretia. She told me about herself and her past; how she had been educated at a convent in Montreal, and loved the nuns, oh so dearly, though she was a Protestant herself, and only French on her mother's side. (This, I thought, was well, as a safeguard against parental prejudice.) She told me all the gossip of Richmond, and whom I should meet at the rector's, and what a dull little town it was. But Quebec was delightful, and Montreal, oh, if she could only live in Montreal, it would be perfect bliss. And so I thought myself, if only Lucretia would live there with me; but I prudently refrained from saying so, as I thought it rather premature. Or perhaps I blushed and stammered too much to get the words out. "Had she ever been in Europe?" No, never, but she would so like it. "Ah, it would be delightful to spend a month or two in Paris," I suggested, with internal pictures of a honeymoon floating through my brain. "Yes, that would be most enjoyable," she answered. Altogether, Lucretia and I kept chatting uninterruptedly the whole way to Richmond, and the other passengers must have voted us most unconscionable bores; for they evidently could not sleep by reason of our incessant talking. We did not sleep, nor wish to sleep. And I am bound to say that a more frankly enchanting or seemingly guileless girl than Lucretia I have never met from that day to this.

At last we reached Richmond Depôt (as the Canadians call the stations), very cold and tired externally, but lively enough as regards the internal fires. We got out, and looked after our luggage. A sleepy porter promised to bring it next morning to the hotel. There were no sleighs in waiting, Richmond is too much of a country station for that, so I took my reticule in my hand, threw Lucretia's rug across her shoulders, and proceeded to walk with her to the hotel.

Now, the "Depôt" is in a suburb known as Melbourne, while Richmond itself lies on the other side of the river St. Francis, here crossed by a long covered bridge, a sort of rough wooden counterpart of the famous one at Lucerne. As we passed out into the cold night, it was snowing heavily, and the frost was very bitter. Lucretia took my arm without a word of prelude, as naturally as if she were my sister, and guided me through the snow-covered path to the bridge. When we got under the shelter of the wooden covering, we had to pass through the long dark gallery, as black as night, heading only for the dim square of moonlight at the other end. But Lucretia walked and chatted on as unconcernedly as if she had always been in the habit of traversing that lonely tunnel-like bridge with a total stranger every evening of her life. I confess I was surprised. I fancied a prim English girl in a similar situation, and I began to wonder whether all this artlessness was really as genuine as it looked.

At the opposite end of the bridge we emerged upon a street of wooden frame houses. In one of them only was there a light. "That's the hotel!" said Lucretia, nodding towards it, and again I suffered a thrill of disappointment. I had pictured to myself a great solid building like the St. Lawrence Hall at Montreal, forgetting that Richmond was a mere country village; and here I found a bit of a frame cottage as the whole domain of Lucretia's supposed father. It was too awful!

We reached the door and entered. Fresh surprises were in store for me. The passage led into a bar, where half-a-dozen French Canadians were sitting with bottles and glasses, playing some game of cards. One rather rough-looking young man jumped up in astonishment as we entered, and exclaimed, "Why, Lucretia, we didn't expect you for another hour. I meant to take the sleigh for you." I could have knocked him down for calling her by her Christian name, but the conviction flashed upon me that this was Lucretia's brother. He glanced up at the big Yankee clock on the mantelpiece, which pointed to a quarter past twelve, then pulled out his watch and whistled. "Stopped three quarters of an hour ago, by Jingo," was his comment. "Why, I forgot to wind it up. Upon my word, Lucretia, I'm awfully sorry. But who is the gentleman?"

"A friend of the Pritchards, Tom dear, who wants a bed here to-night. I couldn't imagine why the sleigh didn't come for me. It's so unlike you not to remember it." And she gave him a look to melt adamant.

Tom was profuse in his apologies, and made it quite clear that his intentions at least had been most excellent; besides, he kissed Lucretia with so much brotherly tenderness that I relented of my desire to knock him down. Then brother and sister retired for a while, apparently to see after my bedroom, and I was left alone in the bar.

I cannot say I liked the look of it. The men were drinking whiskey and playing écarté, two bad things, I thought in my twenty-year-old propriety. My dear mother hated gambling, which hatred she had instilled into my youthful mind, and this was evidently a backwoods gambling-house. Moreover, I carried a bag of silver coin, quite large enough to make it well worth while, to rob me. The appearances were clearly against Lucretia's home; but surely Lucretia herself was a guarantee for anything.

Presently Tom returned, and told me my room was ready. I followed him up the stairs with a beating heart and a heavy reticule. At the top of the landing Lucretia stood smiling, my candle in her hand, and showed me into the room. Tom and she looked around to see that all was comfortable, and then they both shook hands with me, which certainly seemed a curious thing for an inn-keeper and his sister. As soon as they were gone, I began to look about me and consider the situation. The room had two doors, but the key was gone from both. I opened one towards the passage, but found no key outside; the other, which probably communicated with a neighbouring bedroom, was locked from the opposite side. Moreover, there had once been a common bolt on this second door, but it had been removed. I looked close at the screw-holes, and was sure they were quite fresh. Could the bolt have been taken off while I was waiting in the bar? All at once it flashed upon my mind that I had been imprudently confiding in my disclosures to Lucretia. I had told her that I carried a hundred and fifty pounds in coin, an easy thing to rob and a difficult thing to identify. She had heard that nobody was aware of my presence in Richmond, except herself and her brother. I had not written to tell the Pritchards I was coming, and she knew that I had not told any one of my whereabouts, because I did not decide where I should go until I talked with her about the matter. No one in Canada would miss me. If these people chose to murder me for my money (and inn-keepers often murder their guests, I thought), nobody would think of inquiring or know where to inquire for me. Weeks would elapse before my mother wrote from England to ask my whereabouts, and by that time all traces might well be lost. I left Quebec only telling the people at my hotel that I was going to Montreal. Then I thought of Lucretia's eagerness to get into conversation, her observation about my money, her suggestion that I should come to the Richmond Hotel. And how could she, a small inn-keeper's daughter, afford to get all those fine furs and lockets by fair means? Did she really know the Pritchards, or was it likely, considering her position? All these things came across me in a moment. What a fool I had been ever to think of trusting such a girl!

I got up and walked about the room. It was evidently Lucretia's own bedroom; "part of the decoy," said I to myself sapiently. But could so beautiful a girl really hurt one? A piece of music was lying on the dressing-table. I took it up and looked at it casually. Gracious heavens! it was a song from "Lucrezia Borgia!" Her very name betrayed her! She too was a Lucretia. I walked over to the mantelpiece. A little ivory miniature hung above the centre: I gave it a glance as I passed. Incredible! It was the Beatrice Cenci! Talk of beautiful women! Why, they poison one, they stab one, they burn one alive, with a smile on their lips. Lucretia must have a taste for murderesses. Evidently she is a connoisseur.

At least, thought I, I shall sell my life dearly. I could not go to bed; but I pulled the bedstead over against one of the doors, the locked one, and I laid the mattress down in front of the other. Then I lay down on the mattress, my money-bag under my head, and put the poker conveniently by my side. If they came to rob and murder me, they should at least have a broken head to account for next day. But I soon got tired of this defensive attitude, and reflected that, if I must lie awake all night, I might as well have something to read. So I went over to the little book-case and took down the first book which came to hand. It bore on the outside the title "OEuvres de Victor Hugo. Tome I'er. Théâtre." "This, at any rate," said I to myself, "will be light and interesting." I returned to my mattress, opened the volume, and began to read Le Roi s'amuse.

I had never before dipped into that terrible drama, and I devoured it with a horrid avidity. I read how Triboulet bribed the gipsy to murder the king; how the gipsy's sister beguiled him into the hut; how the plot was matured; and how the sack containing the corpse was delivered over to Triboulet. It was an awful play to read on such a night and in such a place, with the wind howling round the corners and the snow gathering deeply upon the window-panes. I was in a considerable state of fright when I began it: I was in an agony of terror before I had got half-way through. Now and then I heard footsteps on the stairs: again I could distinguish two voices, one a woman's, whispering outside the door; a little later, the other door was very slightly opened and then pushed back again stealthily by a man's hand. Still I read on. At last, just as I reached the point where Triboulet is about to throw the corpse into the river, my candle, a mere end, began to sputter in its socket, and after a few ineffectual flickers suddenly went out, leaving me in the dark till morning.

I lay down once more, trembling but wearied out. A few minutes later the voices came again. The further door was opened a second time, and I saw dimly a pair of eyes (not, I felt sure, Lucretia's) peering in the gloom, and reflecting the light from the snow on the window. A man's voice said huskily in an undertone, "It's all right now;" and then there was a silence. I knew they were coming to murder me. I clutched the poker firmly, stood on guard over the dollars, and waited the assault. The moment that intervened seemed like a lifetime.

A minute. Five minutes. A quarter of an hour. They are evidently trying to take me off my guard. Perhaps they saw the poker; in any case, they must have felt the bedstead against the door. That would show them that I expected them. I held my watch to my ear and counted the seconds, then the minutes, then the hours. When the candle went out it was three o'clock. I counted up till about half-past five.

After that I must have fallen asleep from very weariness. My head glided back upon the reticule, and I dozed uneasily until morning. Every now and then I started in my sleep, but the murderers hung back. When I awoke it was eight o'clock, and the dollars were still safe under my head. I rose wearily, washed myself, and arranged the tumbled clothes in which I had slept, for my portmanteau had not yet arrived from the Depôt. Next, I put back the bed and mattress, and then I took the dollars and went downstairs to the bar, hardly knowing whether to laugh at my last night's terror, or to congratulate myself on my lucky escape from a den of robbers. At the foot of the stairs, whom should I come across but Lucretia herself!

In a moment the doubt was gone. She was enchanting. Quite a different style of dress, but equally lovely and suitable. A long figured gown of some fine woollen material, giving very nearly the effect of a plain neat print, and made quite simply to fit her perfect little figure. A plain linen collar, and a quiet silver brooch. Hair tied in a single broad knot above the head, instead of yesterday's chignon and cheese-plate. Altogether, a model winter morning costume for a cold climate. And as she advanced frankly, holding out her hand with a smile, I could have cut my own throat with a pocket-knife as a merited punishment for daring to distrust her. Such is human nature at the ripe age of twenty!

"We were so afraid you didn't sleep, Tom and I," she said with a little tone of anxiety; "we saw a light in your room till so very late, and Tom opened the door a wee bit once or twice to see if you were sleeping; but he said you seemed to have pulled the mattress on the floor. I do hope you weren't ill."

What on earth could I answer? Dare I tell this angel how I had suspected her? Impossible! "Well," I stammered out, colouring up to my eyes, "I was rather over-tired, and couldn't get to rest, so I put the candle on a chair, took a book, and lay on the floor so as to have a light to read by. But I slept very well after the candle went out, thank you."

"There were none but French books in the room, though," she said quickly: "perhaps you read French?"

"I read Le Roi s'amuse, or part of it," said I.

"Oh, what a dreadful play to read on Christmas Eve!" cried Lucretia, with a little deprecating gesture. "But you must come and have your breakfast."

I followed her into the dining-room, a pretty little bright-looking room behind the bar. Frightened as I was during the night, I could not fail to notice how tastefully the bedroom was furnished; but this little salle-à-manger was far prettier. The paper, the carpet, the furniture, were all models of what cheap and simple cottage decorations ought to be. They breathed of Lucretia. The Montreal nuns had evidently taught her what "art at home" meant. The table was laid, and the white table-cloth, with its bright silver and sprays of evergreen in the vase, looked delightfully appetising. I began to think I might manage a breakfast after all.

"How pretty all your things are!" I said to Lucretia.

"Do you think so?" she answered. "I chose them, and I laid the table."

I looked surprised; but in a moment more I was fairly overwhelmed when Lucretia left the room for a minute, and then returned carrying a tray covered with dishes. These she rapidly and dexterously placed upon the table, and then asked me to take my seat.

"But," said I, hesitating, "am I to understand.... You don't mean to say.... Are you ... going ... to wait upon me?"

Lucretia's face was one smile of innocent amusement from her white little forehead to her chiselled little chin. "Why, yes," she answered, laughing, "of course I am. I always wait upon our guests when I'm at home. And I cooked these salmon cutlets, which I'm sure you'll find nice if you only try them while they're hot." With which recommendation she uncovered all the dishes, and displayed a breakfast that might have tempted St. Anthony. Not being St. Anthony, I can do Lucretia's breakfast the justice to say that I ate it with unfeigned heartiness.

So my princess was, after all, the domestic manager and assistant cook of a small country inn! Not a countess, not even a murderess (which is at least romantic), but only a prosaic housekeeper! Yet she was a princess for all that. Did she not read Victor Hugo, and play "Lucrezia Borgia," and spread her own refinement over the village tavern? In no other country could you find such a strange mixture of culture and simplicity; but it was new, it was interesting, and it was piquant. Lucretia in her morning dress officiously insisting upon offering me the buckwheat pancakes with her own white hands was Lucretia still, and I fell deeper in love than ever.

After breakfast came a serious difficulty. I must go to the Pritchards, but before I went, I must pay. Yet, how was I to ask for my bill? I couldn't demand it of Lucretia. So I sat a while ruminating, and at last I said, "I wonder how people do when they want to leave this house."

"Why," said Lucretia, promptly, "they order the sleigh."

"Yes," I answered sheepishly, "no doubt. But how do they manage about paying?"

Lucretia smiled. She was so absolutely transparent, and so accustomed to her simple way of doing business, that I suppose she did not comprehend my difficulty. "They ask me, of course, and I tell them what they owe. You owe us half-a-dollar."

Half-a-dollar, two shillings sterling, for a night of romance and terror, a bed and bedroom, a regal breakfast, and—Lucretia to wait upon one! It was too ridiculous. And these were the good simple Canadian villagers whom I had suspected of wishing to rob and murder me! I never felt so ashamed of my own stupidity in the whole course of my life.

I must pay it somehow, I supposed, but I could not bear to hand over two shilling pieces into Lucretia's outstretched palm. It was desecration, it was sheer sacrilege. But Lucretia took the half-dollar with the utmost calmness, and went out to order the sleigh.

I drove to the rector's, after saying good-bye to Lucretia, with a clear determination that before I left Richmond she should have consented to become my wife. Of course there were social differences, but those would be forgotten in South Kensington, and nobody need ever know what Lucretia had been in Canada. Besides, she was fit to shine in the society of duchesses, a society into which I cannot honestly pretend that I habitually penetrate.

The rector and his wife gave me a hearty welcome, and I found Mrs. Pritchard a good motherly sort of body, just the right woman for helping on a romantic love-match. So, in the course of the morning, as we walked back from church, I managed to mention to her casually that a very nice young woman had come down in the train with me from Quebec.

"You don't mean Lucretia?" cried good Mrs. Pritchard.

"Lucretia," I answered in a cold sort of way, "I think that was her name. In fact, I remember she told me so."

"Oh yes, everybody calls her Lucretia, indeed, she's hardly got any other name. She's the dearest creature in the world, as simple as a child, yet the most engaging and kind-hearted girl you ever met. She was brought up by some nuns at Montreal, and being a very clever girl, with a great deal of taste, she was their favourite pupil, and has turned out a most cultivated person."

"Does she paint?" I asked, thinking of the Beatrice.

"Oh, beautifully. Her ivory miniatures always take prizes at the Toronto Exhibition. And she plays and sings charmingly."

"Are they well off?"

"Very, for Canadians. Lucretia has money of her own, and they have a good farm besides the hotel."

"She said she knew you very well," I ventured to suggest.

"Oh yes; in fact, she's coming here this evening. We have an early dinner, you know our simple Canadian habits, and a few friends will drop in to high tea after evening service. She and Tom will be among them, you met Tom, of course?"

"I had the pleasure of making Tom's acquaintance at one o'clock this morning," I answered. "But, excuse my asking it, isn't it a little odd for you to mix with people in their position?"

The rector smiled and put in his word. "This is a democratic country," he said; "a mere farmer community, after all. We have little society in Richmond, and are very glad to know such pleasant intelligent people as Tom and Lucretia."

"But then, the convenances," I urged, secretly desiring to have my own position strengthened. "When I got to the hotel last night, or rather this morning, there were a lot of rough-looking hulking fellows drinking whiskey and playing cards."

"Ah, I dare say. Old Picard, and young Le Patourel from Melbourne, and the Post Office people sitting over a quiet game of écarté while they waited for the last train. The English mail was in last night. As for the whiskey, that's the custom of the country. We Canadians do nothing without whiskey. A single glass of Morton's proof does nobody any harm."

And these were my robbers and gamblers? A party of peaceable farmers and sleepy Post officials, sitting up with a sober glass of toddy and beguiling the time with écarté for love, in expectation of Her Majesty's mails. I shall never again go to bed with a poker by my side as long as I live.

About seven o'clock our friends came in. Lucretia was once more charming; this time in a long evening dress, a peach-coloured silk with square-cut boddice, and a little lace cap on her black hair. I dare say I saw almost the full extent of her wardrobe in those three changes; but the impression she produced upon me was still that of boundless wealth. However, as she had money of her own, I no longer wondered at the richness of her toilette, and I reflected that a comfortable little settlement might help to outweigh any possible prejudice on my mother's part.

Lucretia was the soul of the evening. She talked, she flirted innocently with every man in the room (myself included), she played divinely, and she sang that very song from "Lucrezia Borgia" in a rich contralto voice. As she rose at last from the piano, I could contain myself no longer. I must find some opportunity of proposing to her there and then. I edged my way to the little group where she was standing, flushed with the compliments on her song, talking to our hostess near the piano. As I approached from behind, I could hear that they were speaking about me, and I caught a few words distinctly. I paused to listen. It was very wrong, but twenty is an impulsive age.

"Oh, a very nice young man indeed," Lucretia was saying; "and we had a most enjoyable journey down. He talked so simply, and seemed such an innocent boy, so I took quite a fancy to him." (My heart beat about two hundred pulsations to the minute.) "Such a clever, intelligent talker too, full of wide English views and interests, so different from our narrow provincial Canadian lads." (Oh, Lucretia, I feel sure of you now. Love at first sight on both sides, evidently!) "And then he spoke to me so nicely about his mother. I was quite grieved to think he should be travelling alone on

Christmas Eve, and so pleased when I heard he was to spend his Christmas with you, dear. I thought what I should have felt if—"

I listened with all my ears. What could Lucretia be going to say?

"If one of my own dear boys was grown up, and passing his Christmas alone in a strange land."

I reeled. The room swam before me. It was too awful. So all that Lucretia had ever felt was a mere motherly interest in me as a solitary English boy away from his domestic turkey on the twenty-fifth of December! Terrible, hideous, blighting fact! Lucretia was married!

The rector's refreshments in the adjoining dining-room only went to the length of sponge-cake and weak claret-cup. I managed to get away from the piano without fainting, and swallowed about a quart of the intoxicating beverage by tumblerfuls. When I had recovered sufficiently from the shock to trust my tongue, I ventured back into the drawing-room. It struck me then that I had never yet heard Lucretia's surname. When she and her brother arrived in the early part of the evening, Mrs. Pritchard had simply introduced them to me by saying, "I think you know Tom and Lucretia already." Colonial manners are so unceremonious.

I joined the fatal group once more. "Do you know," I said, addressing Lucretia with as little tremor in my voice as I could easily manage, "it's very curious, but I have never heard your surname yet."

"Dear me," cried Lucretia, "I quite forgot. Our name is Arundel."

"And which is Mr. Arundel?" I continued. "I should like to make his acquaintance."

"Why," answered Lucretia with a puzzled expression of face, "you've met him already. Here he is!" And she took a neighbouring young man in unimpeachable evening dress gently by the arm. He turned round. It required a moment's consideration to recognize in that tall and gentlemanly young fellow with the plain gold studs and turndown collar my rough acquaintance of last night, Tom himself!

I saw it in a flash. What a fool I had been! I might have known they were husband and wife. Nothing but a pure piece of infatuated preconception could ever have made me take them for brother and sister. But I had so fully determined in my own mind to win Lucretia for myself that the notion of any other fellow having already secured the prize had never struck me.

It was all the fault of that incomprehensible Canadian society, with its foolish removal of the natural barriers between classes. My mother was quite right. I should henceforth be a high-and-dry conservative in all matters matrimonial, return home in the spring with heart completely healed, and after passing correctly through a London season, marry the daughter of a general or a Warwickshire squire, with the full consent of all the high contracting parties, at St. George's, Hanover Square. With this noble and moral resolution firmly planted in my bosom, I made my excuses to the rector and his good little wife, and left Richmond for ever the very next morning, without even seeing Lucretia once again.

But, somehow, I have never quite forgotten that journey from Quebec on Christmas Eve; and though I have passed through several London seasons since that date, and undergone increasingly active sieges from mammas and daughters, as my briefs on the Oxford Circuit grow more and more numerous, I still remain a bachelor, with solitary chambers in St. James's. I sometimes fancy it might have been otherwise if I could only once have met a second paragon exactly like Lucretia.

I

If Harry Lewin had never come to Stoke Peveril, Edie Meredith would certainly have married her cousin Evan.

For Evan Meredith was the sort of man that any girl of Edie's temperament might very easily fall in love with. Tall, handsome, with delicate, clear-cut Celtic face, piercing yet pensive black Welsh eyes, and the true Cymric gifts of music and poetry, Evan Meredith had long been his pretty cousin's prime favourite among all the young men of all Herefordshire. She had danced with him over and over again at every county ball; she had talked with him incessantly at every lawn-tennis match and garden-party; she had whispered to him quietly on the sofa in the far corner while distinguished amateurs were hammering away conscientiously at the grand piano; and all the world of Herefordshire took it for granted that young Mr. Meredith and his second cousin were, in the delightfully vague slang of society, "almost engaged."

Suddenly, like a flaming meteor across the quiet evening skies, Harry Lewin burst in all his dashing splendour upon the peaceful and limited Herefordshire horizon. He came from that land of golden possibilities, Australia; but he was Irish by descent, and his father had sent him young to Eton and Oxford, where he picked up the acquaintance of everybody worth knowing, and a sufficient knowledge of things in general to pass with brilliant success in English society. In his vacations, having no home of his own to go to, he had loitered about half the capitals and spas of Europe, so that Vichy and Carlsbad, Monte Carlo and Spezzia, Berlin and St. Petersburg, were almost as familiar to him as London and Scarborough. Nobody knew exactly what his father had been: some said a convict, some a gold-miner, some a bush-ranger; but whatever he was, he was at least exceedingly rich, and money covers a multitude of sins quite as well and as effectually as charity. When Harry Lewin came into his splendid property at his father's death, and purchased the insolvent Lord Tintern's old estate at Stoke Peveril, half the girls and all the mothers in the whole of Herefordshire rose at once to a fever of anxiety in their desire to know upon which of the marriageable young women of the county the wealthy new-comer would finally bestow himself in holy matrimony.

There was only one girl in the Stoke district who never appeared in the slightest degree flattered or fluttered by Harry Lewin's polite attentions, and that girl was Edie Meredith. Though she was only the country doctor's daughter—"hardly in our set at all, you know," the county people said depreciatingly—she had no desire to be the mistress of Peveril Court, and she let Harry Lewin see pretty clearly that she didn't care the least in the world for that distinguished honour.

It was at a garden party at Stoke Peveril Rectory that Edie Meredith met one afternoon her cousin Evan and the rich young Irish-Australian. Harry Lewin had stood talking to her with his easy jaunty manner, so perfectly self-possessed, so full of Irish courtesy and Etonian readiness, when Evan Meredith, watching them half angrily out of his dark Welsh eyes from the corner by the laburnum tree, walked slowly over to interrupt their tête-à-tête of set purpose. He chose certainly an awkward moment: for his earnest serious face and figure showed to ill advantage just then and there beside the light-hearted cheery young Oxonian's. Edie fancied as he strolled up to her that she had never seen her cousin Evan look so awkward, so countrified, and so awfully Welsh. (On the border counties, to look like a Welshman is of course almost criminal.) She wondered she had overlooked till now the fact that his was distinctly a local and rustic sort of handsomeness. He looked like a

Herefordshire squireen gentleman, while Harry Lewin, with his Irish chivalry and his Oxford confidence, looked like a cosmopolitan and a man of society.

As Evan came up, glancing blackly at him from under his dark eyebrows, Harry Lewin moved away carelessly, raising his hat and strolling off as if quite unconcerned, to make way for the new-comer. Evan nodded to him a distant nod, and then turned to his cousin Edie.

"You've been talking a great deal with that fellow Lewin," he said sharply, almost angrily, glancing straight at her with his big black eyes.

Edie was annoyed at the apparent assumption of a right to criticise her. "Mr. Lewin's a very agreeable man," she answered quietly, without taking the least notice of his angry tone. "I always like to have a chat with him, Evan. He's been everywhere and knows all about everything, Paris and Vienna, and I don't know where. So very different, of course, from our Stoke young men, who've never been anywhere in their whole lives beyond Bristol or Hereford."

"Bristol and Hereford are much better places, I've no doubt, for a man to be brought up in than Paris or Vienna," Evan Meredith retorted hastily, the hot blood flushing up at once into his dusky cheek. "But as you seem to be so very much taken up with your new admirer, Edie, I'm sure I'm very sorry I happened at such an unpropitious moment to break in upon your conversation."

"So am I," Edie answered, quietly and with emphasis.

She hardly meant it, though she was vexed with Evan; but Evan took her immediately at her word. Without another syllable he raised his hat, turned upon his heel, and left her standing there alone, at some little distance from her mother, by the edge of the oval grass-plot. It was an awkward position for a girl to be left in, for everybody would have seen that Evan had retired in high dudgeon, had not Harry Lewin promptly perceived it, and with quiet tact managed to return quite casually to her side, and walk back with her to her mother's protection, so as to hide at once her confusion and her blushes. As for Evan, he wandered off moodily by himself among the lilacs and arbutus bushes of the lower shrubbery.

He had been pacing up and down there alone for half an hour or more, nursing his wrath and jealousy in his angry heart, when he saw between the lilac branches on the upper walk the flash of Edie's pretty white dress, followed behind at a discreet distance by the rustle of Mrs. Meredith's black satin. Edie was walking in front with Harry Lewin, and Mrs. Meredith, attempting vainly to affect a becoming interest in the rector's conversation, was doing the proprieties at twenty paces.

As they passed, Evan Meredith heard Harry Lewin's voice murmuring something in a soft, gentle, persuasive flow, not a word of which he could catch individually, though the general accent and intonation showed him at once that Harry was pleading earnestly with his cousin Edie. Evan could have written her verses, pretty enough verses, too, by the foolscap ream; but though he had the Welsh gift of rhyme, he hadn't the Irish gift of fluency and eloquence; and he knew in his own heart that he could never have poured forth to any woman such a steady, long, impassioned flood of earnest solicitation as Harry Lewin was that moment evidently pouring forth to his cousin Edie. He held his breath in silent expectation, and waited ten whole endless seconds, a long eternity, to catch the tone of Edie's answer.

Instead of the mere tone, he caught distinctly the very words of that low soft musical reply. Edie murmured after a slight pause: "No, no, Mr. Lewin, I must not—I cannot. I do not love you."

Evan Meredith waited for no more. He knew partly from that short but ominous pause, and still more from the half-hearted, hesitating way in which the nominal refusal was faintly spoken, that his cousin Edie would sooner or later accept his rival. He walked away, fiercely indignant, and going home, sat down to his desk, and wrote at white-heat an angry letter, beginning simply "Edith Meredith," in which he released her formally and unconditionally from the engagement which both of them declared had never existed.

Whether his letter expedited Harry Lewin's wooing or not, it is at least certain that in the end Evan Meredith's judgment was approved by the result; and before the next Christmas came round again, Edie was married to Harry Lewin, and duly installed as mistress of Peveril Court.

II

The first three months of Edie Lewin's married life passed away happily and pleasantly. Harry was always kindness itself to her; and as she saw more of him, she found in him what she had not anticipated, an unsuspected depth and earnestness of purpose. She had thought him at first a brilliant, dashing, clever Irishman; she discovered upon nearer view that he had something more within him than mere showy external qualities. He was deeply in love with her: he respected and admired her: and in the midst of all his manly chivalry of demeanour towards his wife there was a certain indefinable air of self-restraint and constant watchfulness over his own actions which Edie noticed with some little wifely pride and pleasure. She had not married a mere handsome rich young fellow; she had married a man of character and determination.

About three months after their marriage, Harry Lewin was called away for the first time to leave his bride. An unexpected letter from his lawyer in London, immediate business, those bothering Australian shares and companies! Would Edie forgive him? He would run up for the day only, starting early and getting back late the same night. It's a long run from Stoke to London, but you can just manage it if you fit your trains with dexterous ingenuity. So Harry went, and Edie was left alone, for the first time in her life, in the big rooms of Peveril Court for a whole day.

That very afternoon Evan Meredith and his father happened to call. It was Evan's first visit to the bride, for he couldn't somehow make up his mind to see her earlier. He was subdued, silent, constrained, regretful, but he said nothing in allusion to the past, nothing but praise of the Peveril Court grounds, the beauty of the house, the charm of the surroundings, the magnificence of the old Romneys and Sir Joshuas.

"You have a lovely place, Edie," he said, hesitating a second before he spoke the old familiar name, but bringing it out quite naturally at last. "And your husband? I hope I may have the, the pleasure of seeing him again."

Edie coloured. "He has gone up to town to-day," she answered simply.

"By himself?"

"By himself, Evan."

Evan Meredith coughed uneasily, and looked at her with a silent look which said more plainly than words could have said it, "Already!"

"He will be back this evening," Edie went on apologetically, answering aloud his unspoken thought. "I—I'm sorry he isn't here to see you, Evan."

"I'm sorry too, very sorry," Evan answered with a half-stifled sigh. He didn't mean to let her see the ideas that were passing through his mind; but his quick, irrepressible Celtic nature allowed the internal emotions to peep out at once through the thin cloak of that conventionally polite expression of regret. Edie knew he meant he was very sorry that Harry should have gone away so soon and left her.

That evening, about ten o'clock, as Edie, sitting alone in the blue drawing-room, was beginning to wonder when Harry's dogcart would be heard rolling briskly up the front avenue, there came a sudden double rap at the front door, and the servant brought in a sealed telegram. Edie tore it open with some misgiving. It was not from Harry. She read it hastily: "From Proprietor, Norton's Hotel, Jermyn Street, London, to Mrs. Lewin, Peveril Court, Stoke Peveril, Herefordshire. Mr. Lewin unfortunately detained in town by urgent business. He will not be able to return before to-morrow."

Edie laid down the telegram with a sinking heart. In itself there was nothing so very strange in Harry's being detained by business; men are always being detained by business; she knew it was a way they had, a masculine peculiarity. But why had not Harry telegraphed himself? Why had he left the proprietor of Norton's Hotel to telegraph for him? Why was he at Norton's Hotel at all? And if he really was there, why could he not have written the telegram himself? It was very mysterious, perplexing, and inexplicable. Tears came into Edie's eyes, and she sat long looking at the flimsy pink Government paper, as if the mere inspection of the hateful message would help her to make out the meaning of the enclosed mystery.

Soon the question began to occur to her, what should she do for the night's arrangements? Peveril Court was so big and lonely; she hated the idea of stopping there alone. Should she have out the carriage and drive round to spend the night as of old at her mother's? But no; it was late, and the servants would think it so very odd of her. People would talk about it; they would say Harry had stopped away from her unexpectedly, and that she had gone back in a pique to her own home. Young wives, she knew, are always doing those foolish things, and always regretting them afterwards when they find the whole county magnifying the molehill into a veritable mountain. Much as she dreaded it, she must spend the night alone in that big bedroom, the haunted bedroom where the last of the Peverils died. Poor little Edie! with her simple, small, village ways, she hated that great rambling house, and all its halls and staircases and corridors! But there was no help for it. She went tearfully up to her own room, and flung herself without undressing on the great bed with the heavy crimson tapestry hangings.

There she lay all night, tossing and turning, crying and wondering, dozing off at times and starting up again fitfully, but never putting out the candles on the dressing-table, which had burned away deep in the sockets by the time morning began to peep through the grey Venetians of the east window.

III

Next morning Evan Meredith heard accidentally that Harry Lewin had stopped for the night in London, and had telegraphed unexpectedly to Edie that he had been detained in town on business.

Evan shook his head with an ominous look. "Poor child," he said to himself pityingly; "she would marry a man who had been brought up in Paris and Vienna!"

And when Harry came back that evening by the late train, Evan Meredith was loitering casually by the big iron gates of Peveril Court to see whether Edie's husband was really returning.

There was a very grave and serious look on Harry's face that surprised and somewhat disconcerted Evan. He somehow felt that Harry's expression was not that of a careless, dissipated fellow, and he said to himself, this time a little less confidently: "Perhaps after all I may have been misjudging him."

Edie was standing to welcome her husband on the big stone steps of the old manor house. He stepped from the dogcart, not lightly with a spring as was his usual wont, but slowly and almost remorsefully, like a man who has some evil tidings to break to those he loves dearest. But he kissed Edie as tenderly as ever, even more tenderly, she somehow imagined; and he looked at her with such a genuine look of love that Edie thought it was well worth while for him to go away for the sake of such a delightful meeting.

"Well, darling," she asked, as she went with him into the great dining-room, "why didn't you come back to the little wifie, as you promised yesterday?"

Harry looked her full in the face, not evasively or furtively, but with a frank, open glance, and answered in a very quiet voice, "I was detained on business, Edie."

"What business?" Edie asked, a little piqued at the indefiniteness of the answer.

"Business that absolutely prevented me from returning," Harry replied, with a short air of perfect determination.

Edie tried in vain to get any further detail out of him. To all her questions Harry only answered with the one set and unaltered formula, "I was detained on important business."

But when she had asked him for the fiftieth time in the drawing-room that evening, he said at last, not at all angrily, but very seriously, "It was business, Edie, closely connected with your own happiness. If I had returned last night, you would have been sorry for it, sooner or later. I stayed away for your own sake, darling. Please ask me no more about it."

Edie couldn't imagine what he meant; but he spoke so seriously, and smoothed her hand with such a tender, loving gesture, that she kissed him fervently, and brushed away the tears from her swimming eyes without letting him see them. As for Harry, he sat long looking at the embers in the smouldering fire, and holding his pretty little wife's hand tight in his without uttering a single syllable. At last, just as they were rising to go upstairs, he laid his hand upon the mantelpiece as if to steady himself, and said very earnestly, "Edie, with God's help, I hope it shall never occur again."

"What, Harry darling? What do you mean? What will never occur again?"

He paused a moment. "That I should be compelled to stop a night away from you unexpectedly," he answered then very slowly.

And when he had said it he took up the candle from the little side table and walked away, with two tears standing in his eyes, to his own dressing-room.

From that day forth Edie Lewin noticed two things. First, that her husband seemed to love her even more tenderly and deeply than ever. And second, that his strange gravity and self-restraint seemed to increase daily upon him.

And Evan Meredith, watching closely his cousin and her husband, thought to himself with a glow of satisfaction, for he was too generous and too true in his heart to wish ill to his rival—"After all, he loves her truly; he is really in love with her. Edie will be rich now, and will have a good husband. What could I ever have given her compared to what Harry Lewin can give her? It is better so. I must not regret it."

IV

For five or six months more, life passed as usual at Peveril Court, or at Harry Lewin's new town house in Curzon Street, Mayfair. The season came and went pleasantly enough, with its round of dances, theatres, and dinners; and in the autumn Edie Lewin found herself once more back for the shooting in dear old Herefordshire. Harry was always by her side, the most attentive and inseparable of husbands; he seemed somehow to cling to her passionately, as if he could not bear to be out of her sight for a single moment. Edie noticed it, and felt grateful for his love. Evan Meredith noticed it too, and reproached himself bitterly more than once that he should ever so unworthily have distrusted the man who had been brought up in Paris and Vienna.

One day, however, Harry had ridden from Stoke to Hereford, for the exercise alone, and Edie expected him back to dinner. But at half-past seven, just as the gong in the hall was burrr-ing loudly, a telegram arrived once more for Mrs. Lewin, which Edie tore open with trembling fingers. It was almost exactly the same mystifying message over again, only this time it was sent by Harry himself, not by an unknown hotel-keeping deputy. "I have been suddenly detained here by unexpected business. Do not expect me home before to-morrow. Shall return as early as possible. God bless you!"

Those last words, so singular in a telegram, roused and accentuated all Edie's womanly terrors. "God bless you!"—what on earth could Harry mean by that solemn adjuration under such strange and mysterious circumstances? There was something very serious the matter, Edie felt sure; but what it could be she could not even picture to herself. Her instinctive fears did not take that vulgarly mistrustful form that they might have taken with many a woman of lower and more suspicious nature; she knew and trusted Harry far too well for that; she was too absolutely certain of his whole unshaken love and tenderness; but the very vagueness and indefiniteness of the fears she felt made them all the harder and more terrible to bear. When you don't know what it is you dread, your fancy can dress up its terrors afresh every moment in some still more painful and distressing disguise.

If Harry had let her know where he was stopping, she would have ordered the carriage then and there, and driven over to Hereford, not to spy him out, but to be with him in his trouble or difficulty. That, however, was clearly impossible, for Harry had merely sent his telegram as from "H. Lewin, Hereford;" and to go about from hotel to hotel through the county town, inquiring whether her husband was staying there, would of course have been open to the most ridiculous misinterpretation. Everybody would have said she was indeed keeping a tight hand upon him! So with many bitter tears brushed hastily away, Edie went down in solemn and solitary state to dinner, hating herself for crying so foolishly, and burning hot with the unpleasant consciousness that the butler and footman were closely observing her face and demeanour. If she could have dined quite alone in her own boudoir very furtively it wouldn't have been quite so dreadful; but to keep up appearances with a sinking heart before those two eminently respectable and officious men-servants, it was really enough to choke one.

That night again Edie Lewin never slept for more than a few troubled minutes together; and whenever she awoke, it was with a start and a scream, and a vague consciousness of some impending evil.

When Harry came again next day he didn't laugh it off carelessly and lightly; he didn't soothe her fears and uneasiness with ready kisses and prompt excuses; he didn't get angry with her and tell her not to ask him too many questions about his own business: he met her as gravely and earnestly as before, with the same tender, loving, half self-reproachful tone, and yet with the same evident desire and intention to love and cherish her more fondly than ever. Edie was relieved, but she was by no means satisfied. She knew Harry loved her tenderly, devotedly; but she knew also there was some sort of shadow or secret looming ominously between them.

Another wife, supposed dead? He would have trusted her and told her. Another love? Oh, no: she could trust him; it was impossible.

And so the weeks wore away, and Edie wondered all to no purpose. At last, by dint of constant wondering, she almost wore out the faculty of wonder, and half ceased to think about it any longer.

But she noticed that from day to day the old bright, brilliant Irish character was slowly fading out of Harry's nature, and that in its place there was growing up a settled, noble, not unbecoming earnestness. He seemed perhaps a trifle less striking and attractive than formerly, but a great deal worthier of any true woman's enduring love and admiration.

Evan Meredith noticed the change as well. He and Harry had grown now into real friends. Harry saw and recognized the genuine depth of Evan's nature. Evan had made amends and apologies to Harry for a single passing rudeness or two. Both liked the other better for the momentary rivalry and for the way he had soon forgotten it. "He's a good fellow," Evan said to his father often, "and Edie, with her quiet, simple English nature, has made quite another man of him, given him the ballast and the even steadiness he once wanted."

V

Spring came, and then summer; and with summer, the annual visitation of garden parties. The Trenches at Malbury Manor were going to give a garden party, and Harry and Edie drove across to it. Edie took her husband over in the pony-carriage with the two little greys she loved so well to drive herself: the very prettiest and best-matched ponies, everybody said, in the whole county of Hereford.

As they walked about on the lawn together, they met Edie's father and mother. Somehow, Edie happened to fasten herself accidentally upon her mother, while Harry strolled away alone, and stood talking with something of his old brilliancy to one group or another of loungers independently. For awhile, Edie missed him; he had gone off to look at the conservatories or something. Then, she saw him chatting with Canon Wilmington and his daughters over by one of the refreshment tables, and handing them champagne cup and ices, while he talked with unusual volubility and laughter. Presently he came up to her again, and to her great surprise said, with a yawn, "Edie, this is getting dreadfully slow. I can't stand it any longer. I think I shall just slip away quietly and walk home; you can come after me whenever you like with the ponies! Good-bye till dinner. God bless you, darling!"

It wasn't a usual form of address with him, and Edie vaguely noted it in passing, but thought nothing more about the matter after the first moment. "Good-bye, Harry," she said laughingly. "Perhaps Evan will see me home. Good-bye."

Harry smiled rather sadly. "Evan has ridden over on one of my cobs," he answered quietly, "and so I suppose he'll have to ride back again."

"He's the best fellow that ever lived," Evan said, as Harry turned away with a friendly nod. "Upon my word, I'm quite ashamed of the use I make of your husband's stables, Edie."

"Nonsense, Evan; we're always both delighted when you will use anything of ours as if it were your own."

At six o'clock the ponies were stopping the way, and Edie prepared to drive home alone. She took the bye-road at the back of the grounds in preference to the turnpike, because it wouldn't be so crowded or so dusty for her to drive upon.

They had gone about a mile from the house, and had passed the Beehive, where a group of half-tipsy fellows was loitering upon the road outside the tavern, when a few hundred yards further Edie suddenly checked the greys for no immediately apparent reason.

"Got a stone in his hoof, ma'am?" the groom asked, looking down curiously at the off horse, and preparing to alight for the expected emergency.

"No," Edie answered with a sudden shake of her head. "Look there, William! On the road in front of us! What a disgusting brute. I nearly ran over him."

The groom looked in the direction where Edie pointed with her whip, and saw lying on the ground, straight before the horses' heads, a drunken man, asleep and helpless, with a small pocket flask clasped in his hand, quite empty.

"Pick him up!" Edie said in a tone of disgust. "Carry him over and lay him on the side of the road there, will you, William?"

The man went off to do as he was directed. At that moment, Evan Meredith, coming up from behind on Harry's cob, called out lightly, "Can I help you, Edie? What's the matter? Ho! One of those beastly fellows from the Beehive yonder. Hold a minute, William, you've got a regular job there, more than an armful. Drunken men are heavy to carry. Wait a bit, and I'll come and help you."

Ho rode forward, to the groom's side just as the groom raised in his arms the drunkard's head and exposed to view his down-turned face. Then, with a sudden cry of horror and pity, Evan Meredith, not faltering for a moment, drove his heel into his horse's flank, and rode off, speechless with conflicting emotions, leaving Edie there alone, face to face with her fallen husband.

It was Harry Lewin.

Apoplexy? Epilepsy? An accident? A sunstroke? No, no. Edie could comfort herself with none of those instantaneous flashes of conjecture, for his face and his breath would alone have told the whole story, even if the empty flask in his drunken hand had not at once confirmed the truth of her first apprehension. She sat down beside him on the green roadside, buried her poor face in her trembling hands, and cried silently, silently, silently, for twenty minutes.

The groom, standing motionless officially beside her, let her tears have free vent, and knew not what to say or do under such extraordinary and unprecedented circumstances.

One thing only Edie thought once or twice in the midst of that awful blinding discovery. Thank God that Evan Meredith had not stopped there to see her misery and degradation. An Englishman might have remained like a fool, with the clumsy notion of assisting her in her trouble, and getting him safely home to Peveril Court for her. Evan, with his quick Welsh perception, had seen in a second that the only possible thing for her own equals to do on such an occasion was to leave her alone with her unspeakable wretchedness.

After a while, she came to a little, by dint of crying and pure exhaustion, and began to think that something must at least be done to hide this terrible disgrace from the prying eyes of all Herefordshire.

She rose mechanically, without a word, and motioning the groom to take the feet, she lifted Harry's head, her own husband's head, that drunken wretch's head, great heavens, which was it? and helped to lay him silently on the floor of the pony carriage. He was helpless and motionless as a baby. Her eyes were dry now, and she hardly even shuddered. She got into the carriage again, covered over the breathing mass of insensible humanity at the bottom with her light woollen wrapper, and drove on in perfect silence till she reached Peveril Court. As she drew up in front of the door, the evening was beginning to close in rapidly. The groom, still silent, jumped from the carriage, and ran up the steps with his usual drilled accuracy to ring the bell. Edie beckoned to him imperiously with her hand to stop and come back to her. He paused, and turned down the steps again to hear what she wished. Edie's lips were dry; she couldn't utter a word: but she pointed mutely to her husband's prostrate form, and the groom understood at once that she wished him to lift Harry out of the carriage. Hastily and furtively they carried him in at the library door, the first room inside the house, and there they laid him out upon the sofa, Edie putting one white finger passionately on her lip to enjoin silence. As soon as that was done, she sat down to the table with marvellous resolution, and wrote out a cheque for twenty pounds from her own cheque-book. Then at last she found speech with difficulty. "William," she said, her dry husky throat almost choking with the effort, "take that, instead of notice. Go away at once, I'll drive you to the station, go to London, and never say a single word of this to anyone."

William touched his hat in silence, and walked back slowly to the carriage. Edie, now flushed and feverish, but dry of lips and erect of mien, turned the key haughtily in the door, and stalked out to the greys once more. Silently still she drove to the station, and saw William take the London train. "You shall have a character," she said, very quietly; "write to me for it. But never say a word of this for your life to anybody."

William touched his hat once more, and went away, meaning conscientiously in his own soul to keep this strange and unexpected compact.

Then Edie drove herself back to Peveril Court, feeling that only Evan Meredith knew besides; and she could surely count at least on Evan's honour.

But to-morrow! to-morrow! what could she ever do to-morrow?

Hot and tearless still, she rang the drawing-room bell. "Mr. Lewin will not be home to-night," she said, with no further word of explanation. "I shall not dine. Tell Watkins to bring me a cup of tea in my own bedroom."

The maid brought it, and Edie drank it. It moistened her lips and broke the fever. Then she flung herself passionately upon the bed, and cried, and cried, and cried, wildly, till late in the evening.

Eleven o'clock came. Twelve o'clock. One. She heard them tolling out from the old clock-tower, clanging loudly from the church steeple, clinking and tinkling from all the timepieces in all the rooms of Peveril Court. But still she lay there, and wept, and sobbed, and thought of nothing. She didn't even figure it or picture it to herself; her grief and shame and utter abasement were too profound for mind to fathom. She only felt in a dim, vague, half-unconscious fashion that Harry, the Harry she had loved and worshipped, was gone from her forever and ever.

In his place, there had come that irrational, speechless, helpless Thing that lay below, breathing heavily in its drunken sleep, down on the library sofa.

VI

By half-past one the lights had long been out in all the rooms, and perfect silence reigned throughout the household. Impelled by a wild desire to see him once more, even though she loathed him, Edie took a bedroom candle in her hand, and stole slowly down the big staircase.

Loathed him? Loved him, ay, loved him even so. Loved him, and the more she loved him, the more utterly loathed him.

If it had been any lesser or lower man, she might have forgiven him. But him, Harry, it was too unspeakable.

Creeping along the passage to the library door, she paused and listened. Inside, there was a noise of footsteps, pacing up and down the room hurriedly. He had come to himself, then! He had slept off his drunken helplessness! She paused and listened again to hear further.

Harry was stalking to and fro across the floor with fiery eagerness, sobbing bitterly to himself, and pausing every now and then with a sort of sudden spasmodic hesitation. From time to time she heard him mutter aloud, "She must have seen me! She must have seen me! They will tell her, they will tell her! Oh, God! they will tell her!"

Should she unlock the door, and fling herself wildly into his arms? Her instinct told her to do it, but she faltered and hesitated. A drunkard! a drunkard! Oh no! she could not. The evil genius conquered the good, and she checked the impulse that alone could have saved her.

She crept up again, with heart standing still and failing within her, and flung herself once more upon her own bed.

Two o'clock. Three. Half-past three. A quarter to four.

How long the night seems when you are watching and weeping!

Suddenly, at the quarter-hour just gone, a sharp ring at a bell disturbed her lethargy, a ring two or three times repeated, which waked the butler from his sound slumber.

Edie walked out cautiously to the top of the stairs and listened. The butler stood at the library door and knocked in vain. Edie heard a letter pushed under the door, and in a muffled voice heard Harry saying, "Give that letter to your mistress, Hardy—to-morrow morning."

A vague foreboding of evil overcame her. She stole down the stairs in the blank dark and took the letter without a word from the half-dressed and wondering butler. Then she glided back to her own room, sat down eagerly by the dressing-table, and began to read it.

"EDIE,

"This is the third time, and I determined with myself that the third time should be the last one. Once in London; once at Hereford; once now. I can stand it no longer. My father died a drunkard. My mother died a drunkard. I cannot resist the temptation. It is better I should not stop here. I have tried hard, but I am beaten in the struggle. I loved you dearly: I love you still far too much to burden your life by my miserable presence. I have left you everything. Evan will make you happier than I could. Forgive me.

"HARRY."

She dropped the letter with a scream, and almost would have fainted.

But even before the faintness could wholly overcome her, another sound rang out sharper and clearer far from the room below her. It brought her back to herself immediately. It was the report of a pistol.

Edie and the butler hurried back in breathless suspense to the library door. It was locked still. Edie took the key from her pocket and turned it quickly. When they entered, the candles on the mantelpiece were burning brightly, and Harry Lewin's body, shot through the heart, lay in a pool of gurgling blood right across the spattered hearthrug.

THE GOLD WULFRIC

PART I

I

There are only two gold coins of Wulfric of Mercia in existence anywhere. One of them is in the British Museum, and the other one is in my possession.

The most terrible incident in the whole course of my career is intimately connected with my first discovery of that gold Wulfric. It is not too much to say that my entire life has been deeply coloured by it, and I shall make no apology therefore for narrating the story in some little detail. I was stopping down at Lichfield for my summer holiday in July, 1879, when I happened one day accidentally to meet an old ploughman who told me he had got a lot of coins at home that he had ploughed up on what he called the "field of battle," a place I had already recognized as the site of the Mercian kings' wooden palace.

I went home with him at once in high glee, for I have been a collector of old English gold and silver coinage for several years, and I was in hopes that my friendly ploughman's find might contain something good in the way of Anglo-Saxon pennies or shillings, considering the very promising place in which he had unearthed it.

As it turned out, I was not mistaken. The little hoard, concealed within a rude piece of Anglo-Saxon pottery (now No. 127 in case LIX. at the South Kensington Museum), comprised a large number of common Frankish Merovingian coins (I beg Mr. Freeman's pardon for not calling them Merwings), together with two or three Kentish pennies of some rarity from the mints of Ethelbert at Canterbury and Dover. Amongst these minor treasures, however, my eye at once fell upon a single gold piece, obviously imitated from the imperial Roman aureus of the pretender Carausius, which I saw immediately must be an almost unique bit of money of the very greatest numismatic interest. I took it up and examined it carefully. A minute's inspection fully satisfied me that it was indeed a genuine mintage of Wulfric of Mercia, the like of which I had never before to my knowledge set eyes upon.

I immediately offered the old man five pounds down for the whole collection. He closed with the offer forthwith in the most contented fashion, and I bought them and paid for them all upon the spot without further parley.

When I got back to my lodgings that evening I could do nothing but look at my gold Wulfric. I was charmed and delighted at the actual possession of so great a treasure, and was burning to take it up at once to the British Museum to see whether even in the national collection they had got another like it. So being by nature of an enthusiastic and impulsive disposition, I determined to go up to town the very next day, and try to track down the history of my Wulfric. "It'll be a good opportunity," I said to myself, "to kill two birds with one stone. Emily's people haven't gone out of town yet. I can call there in the morning, arrange to go to the theatre with them at night, and then drive at once to the Museum and see how much my find is worth."

Next morning I was off to town by an early train, and before one o'clock I had got to Emily's.

"Why, Harold," she cried, running down to meet me and kiss me in the passage (for she had seen me get out of my hansom from the drawing-room window), "how on earth is it that you're up in town to-day? I thought you were down at Lichfield still with your Oxford reading party."

"So I am," I answered, "officially at Lichfield; but I've come up to-day partly to see you, and partly on a piece of business about a new coin I've just got hold of."

"A coin!" Emily answered, pretending to pout. "Me and a coin! That's how you link us together mentally, is it? I declare, Harold, I shall be getting jealous of those coins of yours some day, I'm certain. You can't even come up to see me for a day, it seems, unless you've got some matter of a coin as well to bring you to London. Moral: never get engaged to a man with a fancy for collecting coins and medals."

"Oh, but this is really such a beauty, Emily," I cried enthusiastically. "Just look at it, now. Isn't it lovely? Do you notice the inscription—'Wulfric Rex!' I've never yet seen one anywhere else at all like it."

Emily took it in her hands carelessly. "I don't see any points about that coin in particular," she answered in her bantering fashion, "more than about any other old coin that you'd pick up anywhere."

That was all we said then about the matter. Subsequent events engrained the very words of that short conversation into the inmost substance of my brain with indelible fidelity. I shall never forget them to my dying moment.

I stopped about an hour altogether at Emily's, had lunch, and arranged that she and her mother should accompany me that evening to the Lyceum. Then I drove off to the British Museum, and asked for leave to examine the Anglo-Saxon coins of the Mercian period.

The superintendent, who knew me well enough by sight and repute as a responsible amateur collector, readily gave me permission to look at a drawerful of the earliest Mercian gold and silver coinage. I had brought one or two numismatic books with me, and I sat down to have a good look at those delightful cases.

After thoroughly examining the entire series and the documentary evidence, I came to the conclusion that there was just one other gold Wulfric in existence besides the one I kept in my pocket, and that was the beautiful and well-preserved example in the case before me. It was described in the last edition of Sir Theophilus Wraxton's "Northumbrian and Mercian Numismatist" as an absolutely unique gold coin of Wulfric of Mercia, in imitation of the well-known aureus of the false emperor Carausius. I turned to the catalogue to see the price at which it had been purchased by the nation. To my intense surprise I saw it entered at a hundred and fifty pounds.

I was perfectly delighted at my magnificent acquisition.

On comparing the two examples, however, I observed that, though both struck from the same die and apparently at the same mint (to judge by the letter), they differed slightly from one another in two minute accidental particulars. My coin, being of course merely stamped with a hammer and then cut to shape, after the fashion of the time, was rather more closely clipped round the edge than the Museum specimen; and it had also a slight dent on the obverse side, just below the W of Wulfric. In all other respects the two examples were of necessity absolutely identical.

I stood for a long time gazing at the case and examining the two duplicates with the deepest interest, while the Museum keeper (a man of the name of Mactavish, whom I had often seen before on previous visits) walked about within sight, as is the rule on all such occasions, and kept a sharp look-out that I did not attempt to meddle with any of the remaining coins or cases.

Unfortunately, as it turned out, I had not mentioned to the superintendent my own possession of a duplicate Wulfric; nor had I called Mactavish's attention to the fact that I had pulled a coin of my own for purposes of comparison out of my waistcoat pocket. To say the truth, I was inclined to be a little secretive as yet about my gold Wulfric, because until I had found out all that was known about it I did not want anybody else to be told of my discovery.

At last I had fully satisfied all my curiosity, and was just about to return the Museum Wulfric to its little round compartment in the neat case (having already replaced my own duplicate in my waistcoat pocket), when all at once, I can't say how, I gave a sudden start, and dropped the coin with a jerk unexpectedly upon the floor of the museum.

It rolled away out of sight in a second, and I stood appalled in an agony of distress and terror in the midst of the gallery.

Next moment I had hastily called Mactavish to my side, and got him to lock up the open drawer while we two went down on hands and knees and hunted through the length and breadth of the gallery for the lost Wulfric.

It was absolutely hopeless. Plain sailing as the thing seemed, we could see no trace of the missing coin from one end of the room to the other.

At last I leaned in a cold perspiration against the edge of one of the glass cabinets, and gave it up in despair with a sinking heart. "It's no use, Mactavish," I murmured desperately; "the thing's lost, and we shall never find it."

Mactavish looked me quietly in the face. "In that case, sir," he answered firmly, "by the rules of the Museum I must call the superintendent." He put his hand, with no undue violence, but in a strictly official manner, upon my right shoulder. Then he blew a whistle. "I'm sorry to be rude to you, sir," he went on, apologetically, "but by the rules of the Museum I can't take my hand off you till the superintendent gives me leave to release you."

Another keeper answered the whistle. "Send the superintendent," Mactavish said quietly. "A coin missing."

In a minute the superintendent was upon the spot. When Mactavish told him I had dropped the gold Wulfric of Mercia he shook his head very ominously. "This is a bad business, Mr. Tait," he said gloomily. "A unique coin, as you know, and one of the most valuable in the whole of our large Anglo-Saxon collection."

"Is there a mouse-hole anywhere," I cried in agony; "any place where it might have rolled down and got mislaid or concealed for the moment?"

The superintendent went down instantly on his own hands and knees, pulled up every piece of the cocoa-nut matting with minute deliberation, searched the whole place thoroughly from end to end, but found nothing. He spent nearly an hour on that thorough search; meanwhile Mactavish never for a moment relaxed his hold upon me.

At last the superintendent desisted from the search as quite hopeless, and approached me very politely.

"I'm extremely sorry, Mr. Tait," he said in the most courteous possible manner, "but by the rules of the Museum I am absolutely compelled either to search you for the coin or to give you into custody. It may, you know, have got caught somewhere about your person. No doubt you would prefer, of the two, that I should look in all your pockets and the folds of your clothing."

The position was terrible. I could stand it no longer.

"Mr. Harbourne," I said, breaking out once more from head to foot into a cold sweat, "I must tell you the truth. I have brought a duplicate gold Wulfric here to-day to compare with the Museum specimen, and I have got it this very moment in my waistcoat pocket."

The superintendent gazed back at me with a mingled look of incredulity and pity.

"My dear sir," he answered very gently, "this is altogether a most unfortunate business, but I'm afraid I must ask you to let me look at the duplicate you speak of."

I took it, trembling, out of my waistcoat pocket and handed it across to him without a word. The superintendent gazed at it for a moment in silence; then, in a tone of the profoundest commiseration, he said slowly, "Mr. Tait, I grieve to be obliged to contradict you. This is our own specimen of the gold Wulfric!"

The whole Museum whirled round me violently, and before I knew anything more I fainted.

II

When I came to I found myself seated in the superintendent's room, with a policeman standing quietly in the background.

As soon as I had fully recovered consciousness, the superintendent motioned the policeman out of the room for a while, and then gently forced me to swallow a brandy and soda.

"Mr. Tait," he said compassionately, after an awkward pause, "you are a very young man indeed, and, I believe, hitherto of blameless character. Now, I should be very sorry to have to proceed to extremities against you. I know to what lengths, in a moment of weakness, the desire to possess a rare coin will often lead a connoisseur, under stress of exceptional temptation. I have not the slightest doubt in my own mind that you did really accidentally drop this coin; that you went down on your knees honestly intending to find it; that the accident suggested to you the ease with which you might pick it up and proceed to pocket it; that you yielded temporarily to that unfortunate impulse; and that by the time I arrived upon the scene you were already overcome with remorse and horror. I saw as much immediately in your very countenance. Nevertheless, I determined to give you the benefit of the doubt, and I searched over the whole place in the most thorough and conscientious manner.... As you know, I found nothing.... Mr. Tait, I cannot bear to have to deal harshly with you. I recognize the temptation and the agony of repentance that instantly followed it. Sir, I give you one chance. If you will retract the obviously false story that you just now told me, and confess that the coin I found in your pocket was in fact, as I know it to be, the Museum specimen, I will forthwith dismiss the constable, and will never say another word to any one about the whole matter. I don't want to ruin you, but I can't, of course, be put off with a falsehood. Think the matter carefully over with yourself. Do you or do you not still adhere to that very improbable and incredible story?"

Horrified and terror-stricken as I was, I couldn't avoid feeling grateful to the superintendent for the evident kindness with which he was treating me. The tears rose at once into my eyes.

"Mr. Harbourne," I cried passionately, "you are very good, very generous. But you quite mistake the whole position. The story I told you was true, every word of it. I bought that gold Wulfric from a ploughman at Lichfield, and it is not absolutely identical with the Museum specimen which I dropped upon the floor. It is closer clipped round the edges, and it has a distinct dent upon the obverse side, just below the W of Wulfric."

The superintendent paused a second, and scanned my face very closely.

"Have you a knife or a file in your pocket?" he asked in a much sterner and more official tone.

"No," I replied, "neither, neither."

"You are sure?"

"Certain."

"Shall I search you myself, or shall I give you in custody?"

"Search me yourself," I answered confidently.

He put his hand quietly into my left-hand breast pocket, and to my utter horror and dismay drew forth, what I had up to that moment utterly forgotten, a pair of folding pocket nail-scissors, in a leather case, of course with a little file on either side.

My heart stood still within me.

"That is quite sufficient, Mr. Tait," the superintendent went on, severely. "Had you alleged that the Museum coin was smaller than your own imaginary one you might have been able to put in the facts as good evidence. But I see the exact contrary is the case. You have stooped to a disgraceful and unworthy subterfuge. This base deception aggravates your guilt. You have deliberately defaced a valuable specimen in order if possible to destroy its identity."

What could I say in return? I stammered and hesitated.

"Mr. Harbourne," I cried piteously, "the circumstances seem to look terribly against me. But, nevertheless, you are quite mistaken. Tho missing Wulfric will come to light sooner or later and prove me innocent."

He walked up and down the room once or twice irresolutely, and then he turned round to me with a very fixed and determined aspect which fairly terrified me.

"Mr. Tait," he said, "I am straining every point possible to save you, but you make it very difficult for me by your continued falsehood. I am doing quite wrong in being so lenient to you; I am proposing, in short, to compound a felony. But I cannot bear, without letting you have just one more chance, to give you in charge for a common robbery. I will let you have ten minutes to consider the matter; and I beseech you, I beg of you, I implore you to retract this absurd and despicable lie before it is too late for ever. Just consider that if you refuse I shall have to hand you over to the constable out there, and that the whole truth must come out in court, and must be blazoned forth to the entire world in every newspaper. The policeman is standing here by the door. I will leave you alone with your own thoughts for ten minutes."

As he spoke he walked out gravely, and shut the door solemnly behind him. The clock on the chimney-piece pointed with its hands to twenty minutes past three.

It was an awful dilemma. I hardly knew how to act under it. On the one hand, if I admitted for the moment that I had tried to steal the coin, I could avoid all immediate unpleasant circumstances; and as it would be sure to turn up again in cleaning the Museum, I should be able at last to prove my innocence to Mr. Harbourne's complete satisfaction. But, on the other hand, the lie, for it was a lie, stuck in my throat; I could not humble myself to say I had committed a mean and dirty action which I loathed with all the force and energy of my nature. No, no! come what would of it, I must stick by the truth, and trust to that to clear up everything.

But if the superintendent really insisted on giving me in charge, how very awkward to have to telegraph about it to Emily! Fancy saying to the girl you are in love with, "I can't go with you to the theatre this evening, because I have been taken off to gaol on a charge of stealing a valuable coin from the British Museum." It was too terrible!

Yet, after all, I thought to myself, if the worst comes to the worst, Emily will have faith enough in me to know it is ridiculous; and, indeed, the imputation could in any case only be temporary. As soon as the thing gets into court I could bring up the Lichfield ploughman to prove my possession of a gold Wulfric; and I could bring up Emily to prove that I had shown it to her that very morning. How lucky that I had happened to take it out and let her look at it! My case was, happily, as plain as a pikestaff. It was only momentarily that the weight of the evidence seemed so perversely to go against me.

Turning over all these various considerations in my mind with anxious hesitancy, the ten minutes managed to pass away almost before I had thoroughly realized the deep gravity of the situation.

As the clock on the chimney-piece pointed to the half-hour, the door opened once more, and the superintendent entered solemnly. "Well, Mr. Tait," he said in an anxious voice, "have you made up your mind to make a clean breast of it? Do you now admit, after full deliberation, that you have endeavoured to steal and clip the gold Wulfric?"

"No," I answered firmly, "I do not admit it; and I will willingly go before a jury of my countrymen to prove my innocence."

"Then God help you, poor boy," the superintendent cried despondently. "I have done my best to save you, and you will not let me. Policeman, this is your prisoner. I give him in custody on a charge of stealing a gold coin, the property of the trustees of this Museum, valued at a hundred and seventy-five pounds sterling."

The policeman laid his hand upon my wrist. "You will have to go along with me to the station, sir," he said quietly.

Terrified and stunned as I was by the awfulness of the accusation, I could not forget or overlook the superintendent's evident reluctance and kindness. "Mr. Harbourne," I cried, "you have tried to do your best for me. I am grateful to you for it, in spite of your terrible mistake, and I shall yet be able to show you that I am innocent."

He shook his head gloomily. "I have done my duty," he said with a shudder. "I have never before had a more painful one. Policeman, I must ask you now to do yours."

III

The police are always considerate to respectable-looking prisoners, and I had no difficulty in getting the sergeant in charge of the lock-up to telegraph for me to Emily, to say that I was detained by important business, which would prevent me taking her and her mother to the theatre that evening. But when I explained to him that my detention was merely temporary, and that I should be able to disprove the whole story as soon as I went before the magistrates, he winked most unpleasantly at the constable who had brought me in, and observed in a tone of vulgar sarcasm, "We have a good many gentlemen here who says the same, sir, don't we, Jim? but they don't always find it so easy as they expected when they stands up afore the beak to prove their statements."

I began to reflect that even a temporary prison is far from being a pleasant place for a man to stop in.

Next morning they took me up before the magistrate; and as the Museum authorities of course proved a primâ facie case against me, and as my solicitor advised me to reserve my defence, owing to the difficulty of getting up my witness from Lichfield in reasonable time, I was duly committed for trial at the next sessions of the Central Criminal Court.

I had often read before that people had been committed for trial, but till that moment I had no idea what a very unpleasant sensation it really is.

However, as I was a person of hitherto unblemished character, and wore a good coat made by a fashionable tailor, the magistrate decided to admit me to bail, if two sureties in five hundred pounds each were promptly forthcoming for the purpose. Luckily, I had no difficulty in finding friends who believed in my story; and as I felt sure the lost Wulfric would soon be found in cleaning the museum, I suffered perhaps a little less acutely than I might otherwise have done, owing to my profound confidence in the final triumph of the truth.

Nevertheless, as the case would be fully reported next morning in all the papers, I saw at once that I must go straight off and explain the matter without delay to Emily.

I will not dwell upon that painful interview. I will only say that Emily behaved as I of course knew she would behave. She was horrified and indignant at the dreadful accusation; and, woman like, she was very angry with the superintendent. "He ought to have taken your word for it, naturally, Harold," she cried through her tears. "But what a good thing, anyhow, that you happened to show the coin to me. I should recognize it anywhere among ten thousand."

"That's well, darling," I said, trying to kiss away her tears and cheer her up a little. "I haven't the slightest doubt that when the trial comes we shall be able triumphantly to vindicate me from this terrible, groundless accusation."

IV

When the trial did actually come on, the Museum authorities began by proving their case against me in what seemed the most horribly damning fashion. The superintendent proved that on such and such a day, in such and such a case, he had seen a gold coin of Wulfric of Mercia, the property of the Museum. He and Mactavish detailed the circumstances under which the coin was lost. The superintendent explained how he had asked me to submit to a search, and how, to avoid that indignity, I had myself produced from my waistcoat-pocket a gold coin of Wulfric of Mercia, which I asserted to be a duplicate specimen, and my own property. The counsel for the Crown proceeded thus with the examination:—

"Do you recognize the coin I now hand you?"

"I do."

"What is it?"

"The unique gold coin of Wulfric of Mercia, belonging to the Museum."

"You have absolutely no doubt as to its identity?"

"Absolutely none whatsoever."

"Does it differ in any respect from the same coin as you previously saw it?"

"Yes. It has been clipped round the edge with a sharp instrument, and a slight dent has been made by pressure on the obverse side, just below the W of Wulfric."

"Did you suspect the prisoner at the bar of having mutilated it?"

"I did, and I asked him whether he had a knife in his possession. He answered no. I then asked him whether he would submit to be searched for a knife. He consented, and on my looking in his pocket I found the pair of nail-scissors I now produce, with a small file on either side."

"Do you believe the coin might have been clipped with those scissors?"

"I do. The gold is very soft, having little alloy in its composition; and it could easily be cut by a strong-wristed man with a knife or scissors."

As I listened, I didn't wonder that the jury looked as if they already considered me guilty: but I smiled to myself when I thought how utterly Emily's and the ploughman's evidence would rebut this unworthy suspicion.

The next witness was the Museum cleaner. His evidence at first produced nothing fresh, but just at last, counsel set before him a paper, containing a few scraps of yellow metal, and asked him triumphantly whether he recognized them. He answered yes.

There was a profound silence. The court was interested and curious. I couldn't quite understand it all, but I felt a terrible sinking.

"What are they?" asked the hostile barrister.

"They are some fragments of gold which I found in shaking the cocoa-nut matting on the floor of gallery 27 the Saturday after the attempted theft."

I felt as if a mine had unexpectedly been sprung beneath me. How on earth those fragments of soft gold could ever have got there I couldn't imagine; but I saw the damaging nature of this extraordinary and inexplicable coincidence in half a second.

My counsel cross-examined all the witnesses for the prosecution, but failed to elicit anything of any value from any one of them. On the contrary, his questions put to the metallurgist of the Mint, who was called to prove the quality of the gold, only brought out a very strong opinion to the effect that the clippings were essentially similar in character to the metal composing the clipped Wulfric.

No wonder the jury seemed to think the case was going decidedly against me.

Then my counsel called his witnesses. I listened in the profoundest suspense and expectation.

The first witness was the ploughman from Lichfield. He was a well-meaning but very puzzle-headed old man, and he was evidently frightened at being confronted by so many clever wig-wearing barristers.

Nevertheless, my counsel managed to get the true story out of him at last with infinite patience, dexterity, and skill. The old man told us finally how he had found the coins and sold them to me for five pounds; and how one of them was of gold, with a queer head and goggle eyes pointed full face upon its surface.

When he had finished, the counsel for the Crown began his cross-examination. He handed the ploughman a gold coin. "Did you ever see that before?" he asked quietly.

"To be sure I did," the man answered, looking at it open-mouthed.

"What is it?"

"It's the bit I sold Mr. Tait there, the bit as I got out o' the old basin."

Counsel turned triumphantly to the judge. "My lord," he said, "this thing to which the witness swears is a gold piece of Ethelwulf of Wessex, by far the commonest and cheapest gold coin of the whole Anglo-Saxon period."

It was handed to the jury side by side with the Wulfric of Mercia; and the difference, as I knew myself, was in fact extremely noticeable. All that the old man could have observed in common between them must have been merely the archaic Anglo-Saxon character of the coinage.

As I heard that, I began to feel that it was really all over.

My counsel tried on the re-examination to shake the old man's faith in his identification, and to make him transfer his story to the Wulfric which he had actually sold me. But it was all in vain. The ploughman had clearly the dread of perjury for ever before his eyes, and wouldn't go back for any consideration upon his first sworn statement. "No, no, mister," he said over and over again in reply to my counsel's bland suggestion, "you ain't going to make me forswear myself for all your cleverness."

The next witness was Emily. She went into the box pale and red-eyed, but very confident. My counsel examined her admirably; and she stuck to her point with womanly persistence, that she had herself seen the clipped Wulfric, and no other coin, on the morning of the supposed theft. She knew it was so, because she distinctly remembered the inscription, "Wulfric Rex," and the peculiar way the staring open eyes were represented with barbaric puerility.

Counsel for the Crown would only trouble the young lady with two questions. The first was a painful one, but it must be asked in the interests of justice. Were she and the prisoner at the bar engaged to be married to one another?

The answer came, slowly and timidly, "Yes."

Counsel drew a long breath, and looked her hard in the face. Could she read the inscription on that coin now produced?—handing her the Ethelwulf.

Great heavens! I saw at once the plot to disconcert her, but was utterly powerless to warn her against it.

Emily looked at it long and steadily. "No," she said at last, growing deadly pale and grasping the woodwork of the witness-box convulsively; "I don't know the character in which it is written."

Of course not: for the inscription was in the peculiar semi-runic Anglo-Saxon letters! She had never read the words "Wulfric Rex" either. I had read them to her, and she had carried them away vaguely in her mind, imagining no doubt that she herself had actually deciphered them.

There was a slight pause, and I felt my blood growing cold within me. Then the counsel for the Crown handed her again the genuine Wulfric, and asked her whether the letters upon it which she professed to have read were or were not similar to those of the Ethelwulf.

Instead of answering, Emily bent down her head between her hands, and burst suddenly into tears.

I was so much distressed at her terrible agitation that I forgot altogether for the moment my own perilous position, and I cried aloud, "My lord, my lord, will you not interpose to spare her any further questions?"

"I think," the judge said to the counsel for the Crown, "you might now permit the witness to stand down."

"I wish to re-examine, my lord," my counsel put in hastily.

"No," I said in his ear, "no. Whatever comes of it, not another question. I had far rather go to prison than let her suffer this inexpressible torture for a single minute longer."

Emily was led down, still crying bitterly, into the body of the court, and the rest of the proceedings went on uninterrupted.

The theory of the prosecution was a simple and plausible one. I had bought a common Anglo-Saxon coin, probably an Ethelwulf, valued at about twenty-two shillings, from the old Lichfield ploughman. I had thereupon conceived the fraudulent idea of pretending that I had a duplicate of the rare Wulfric. I had shown the Ethelwulf, clipped in a particular fashion, to the lady whom I was engaged to marry. I had then defaced and altered the genuine Wulfric at the Museum into the same shape with the aid of my pocket nail-scissors. And I had finally made believe to drop the coin accidentally upon the floor, while I had really secreted it in my waistcoat pocket. The theory for the defence had broken down utterly. And then there was the damning fact of the gold scrapings found in the cocoa-nut matting of the British Museum, which was to me the one great inexplicable mystery in the whole otherwise comprehensible mystification.

I felt myself that the case did indeed look very black against me. But would a jury venture to convict me on such very doubtful evidence?

The jury retired to consider their verdict. I stood in suspense in the dock, with my heart loudly beating. Emily remained in the body of the court below, looking up at me tearfully and penitently.

After twenty minutes the jury retired.

"Guilty or not guilty?"

The foreman answered aloud, "Guilty."

There was a piercing cry in the body of the court, and in a moment Emily was carried out half fainting and half hysterical.

The judge then calmly proceeded to pass sentence. He dwelt upon the enormity of my crime in one so well connected and so far removed from the dangers of mere vulgar temptations. He dwelt also upon the vandalism of which I had been guilty, myself a collector, in clipping and defacing a valuable and unique memorial of antiquity, the property of the nation. He did not wish to be severe upon a young man of hitherto blameless character; but the national collection must be secured against such a peculiarly insidious and cunning form of depredation. The sentence of the court was that I should be kept in—

Five years' penal servitude.

Crushed and annihilated as I was, I had still strength to utter a single final word. "My lord," I cried, "the missing Wulfric will yet be found, and will hereafter prove my perfect innocence."

"Remove the prisoner," said the judge, coldly.

They took me down to the courtyard unresisting, where the prison van was standing in waiting.

On the steps I saw Emily and her mother, both crying bitterly. They had been told the sentence already, and were waiting to take a last farewell of me.

"Oh, Harold!" Emily cried, flinging her arms around me wildly, "it's all my fault! It's my fault only! By my foolish stupidity I've lost your case. I've sent you to prison. Oh, Harold, I can never forgive myself. I've sent you to prison. I've sent you to prison."

"Dearest," I said, "it won't be for long. I shall soon be free again. They'll find the Wulfric sooner or later, and then of course they'll let me out again."

"Harold," she cried, "oh, Harold, Harold, don't you see? Don't you understand? This is a plot against you. It isn't lost. It isn't lost. That would be nothing. It's stolen; it's stolen!"

A light burst in upon me suddenly, and I saw in a moment the full depth of the peril that surrounded me.

PART II

I

It was some time before I could sufficiently accustom myself to my new life in the Isle of Portland to be able to think clearly and distinctly about the terrible blow that had fallen upon me. In the midst of all the petty troubles and discomforts of prison existence, I had no leisure at first fully to realize the fact that I was a convicted felon with scarcely a hope, not of release; for that I cared little, but of rehabilitation.

Slowly, however, I began to grow habituated to the new hard life imposed upon me, and to think in my cell of the web of circumstance which had woven itself so irresistibly around me.

I had only one hope. Emily knew I was innocent. Emily suspected, like me, that the Wulfric had been stolen. Emily would do her best, I felt certain, to heap together fresh evidence, and unravel this mystery to its very bottom.

Meanwhile, I thanked Heaven for the hard mechanical daily toil of cutting stone in Portland prison. I was a strong athletic young fellow enough. I was glad now that I had always loved the river at Oxford; my arms were stout and muscular. I was able to take my part in the regular work of the gang to which I belonged. Had it been otherwise, had I been set down to some quiet sedentary occupation, as first-class misdemeanants often are, I should have worn my heart out soon with thinking perpetually of poor Emily's terrible trouble.

When I first came, the Deputy-Governor, knowing my case well (had there not been leaders about me in all the papers?), very kindly asked me whether I would wish to be given work in the book-keeping department, where many educated convicts were employed as clerks and assistants. But I begged particularly to be put into an outdoor gang, where I might have to use my limbs constantly, and so keep my mind from eating itself up with perpetual thinking. The Deputy-Governor immediately consented, and gave me work in a quarrying gang, at the west end of the island, near Deadman's Bay on the edge of the Chesil.

For three months I worked hard at learning the trade of a quarryman, and succeeded far better than any of the other new hands who were set to learn at the same time with me. Their heart was not in it; mine was. Anything to escape that gnawing agony.

The other men in the gang were not agreeable or congenial companions. They taught me their established modes of intercommunication, and told me several facts about themselves, which did not tend to endear them to me. One of them, 1247, was put in for the manslaughter of his wife by kicking; he was a low-browed, brutal London drayman, and he occupied the next cell to mine, where he disturbed me much in my sleepless nights by his loud snoring. Another, a much slighter and more intelligent-looking man, was a skilled burglar, sentenced to fourteen years for "cracking a crib" in the neighbourhood of Hampstead. A third was a sailor, convicted of gross cruelty to a defenceless Lascar. They all told me the nature of their crimes with a brutal frankness which fairly surprised me; but when I explained to them in return that I had been put in upon a false accusation, they treated my remarks with a galling contempt that was absolutely unsupportable. After a short time I ceased to communicate with my fellow-prisoners in any way, and remained shut up with my own thoughts in utter isolation.

By-and-by I found that the other men in the same gang were beginning to dislike me strongly, and that some among them actually whispered to one another, what they seemed to consider a very strong point indeed against me, that I must really have been convicted by mistake, and that I was a regular stuck-up sneaking Methodist. They complained that I worked a great deal too hard, and so made the other felons seem lazy by comparison; and they also objected to my prompt obedience to our warder's commands, as tending to set up an exaggerated and impossible standard of discipline.

Between this warder and myself, on the other hand, there soon sprang up a feeling which I might almost describe as one of friendship. Though by the rules of the establishment we could not communicate with one another except upon matters of business, I liked him for his uniform courtesy, kindliness, and forbearance; while I could easily see that he liked me in return, by contrast with the other men who were under his charge. He was one of those persons whom some experience of prisons then and since has led me to believe less rare than most people would imagine, men in whom the dreary life of a prison warder, instead of engendering hardness of heart and cold unsympathetic sternness, has engendered a certain profound tenderness and melancholy of spirit. I grew quite fond of that one honest warder, among so many coarse and criminal faces; and I found, on the other hand, that my fellow-prisoners hated me all the more because, as they expressed it in their own disgusting jargon, I was sucking up to that confounded dog of a barker. It happened once, when I was left for a few minutes alone with the warder, that he made an attempt for a moment, contrary to regulations, to hold a little private conversation with me.

"1430," he said in a low voice, hardly moving his lips, for fear of being overlooked, "what is your outside name?"

I answered quietly, without turning to look at him, "Harold Tait."

He gave a little involuntary start. "What!" he cried. "Not him that took a coin from the British Museum?"

I bridled up angrily. "I did not take it," I cried with all my soul. "I am innocent, and have been put in here by some terrible error."

He was silent for half a second. Then he said musingly, "Sir, I believe you. You are speaking the truth. I will do all I can to make things easy for you."

That was all he said then. But from that day forth he always spoke to me in private as "Sir," and never again as "1430."

An incident arose at last out of this condition of things which had a very important effect upon my future position.

One day, about three months after I was committed to prison, we were all told off as usual to work in a small quarry on the cliff-side overhanging the long expanse of pebbly beach known as the Chesil. I had reason to believe afterwards that a large open fishing boat lying upon the beach below at the moment had been placed there as part of a concerted scheme by the friends of the Hampstead burglar; and that it contained ordinary clothing for all the men in our gang, except myself only. The idea was evidently that the gang should overpower the warder, seize the boat, change their clothes instantly, taking turns about meanwhile with the navigation, and make straight off for the shore at Lulworth, where they could easily disperse without much chance of being recaptured. But of all this I was of course quite ignorant at the time, for they had not thought well to intrust their secret to the ears of the sneaking virtuous Methodist.

A few minutes after we arrived at the quarry, I was working with two other men at putting a blast in, when I happened to look round quite accidentally, and to my great horror, saw 1247, the brutal wife-kicker, standing behind with a huge block of stone in his hands, poised just above the warder's head, in a threatening attitude. The other men stood around waiting and watching. I had only just time to cry out in a tone of alarm, "Take care, warder, he'll murder you!" when the stone descended upon the warder's head, and he fell at once, bleeding and half senseless, upon the ground beside me. In a second, while he shrieked and struggled, the whole gang was pressing savagely and angrily around him.

There was no time to think or hesitate. Before I knew almost what I was doing, I had seized his gun and ammunition, and, standing over his prostrate body, I held the men at bay for a single moment. Then 1247 advanced threateningly, and tried to put his foot upon the fallen warder.

I didn't wait or reflect one solitary second. I drew the trigger, and fired full upon him. The bang sounded fiercely in my ears, and for a moment I could see nothing through the smoke of the rifle.

With a terrible shriek he fell in front of me, not dead, but seriously wounded.

"The boat, the boat," the others cried loudly. "Knock him down! Kill him! Take the boat, all of you."

At that moment the report of my shot had brought another warder hastily to the top of the quarry.

"Help, help!" I cried. "Come quick, and save us. These brutes are trying to murder our warder!"

The man rushed back to call for aid; but the way down the zigzag path was steep and tortuous, and it was some time before they could manage to get down and succour us.

Meanwhile the other convicts pressed savagely around us, trying to jump upon the warder's body and force their way past to the beach beneath us. I fired again, for the rifle was double-barrelled; but it was impossible to reload in such a tumult, so, after the next shot, which hit no one, I laid about me fiercely with the butt end of the gun, and succeeded in knocking down four of the savages, one after another. By that time the warders from above had safely reached us, and formed a circle of fixed bayonets around the rebellious prisoners.

"Thank God!" I cried, flinging down the rifle, and rushing up to the prostrate warder. "He is still alive. He is breathing! He is breathing!"

"Yes," he murmured in a faint voice, "I am alive, and I thank you for it. But for you, sir, these fellows here would certainly have murdered me."

"You are badly wounded yourself, 1430," one of the other warders said to me, as the rebels were rapidly secured and marched off sullenly back to prison. "Look, your own arm is bleeding fiercely."

Then for the first time I was aware that I was one mass of wounds from head to foot, and that I was growing faint from loss of blood. In defending the fallen warder I had got punched and pummelled on every side, just the same as one used to get long ago in a bully at football when I was a boy at Rugby, only much more seriously.

The warders brought down seven stretchers: one for me; one for the wounded warder; one for 1247, whom I had shot; and four for the convicts whom I had knocked over with the butt end of the rifle. They carried us up on them, strongly guarded, in a long procession.

At the door of the infirmary the Governor met us. "1430," he said to me, in a very kind voice, "you have behaved most admirably. I saw you myself quite distinctly from my drawing-room windows. Your bravery and intrepidity are well deserving of the highest recognition."

"Sir," I answered, "I have only tried to do my duty. I couldn't stand by and see an innocent man murdered by such a pack of bloodthirsty ruffians."

The Governor turned aside a little surprised. "Who is 1430?" he asked quietly.

A subordinate, consulting a book, whispered my name and supposed crime to him confidentially. The Governor nodded twice, and seemed to be satisfied.

"Sir," the wounded warder said faintly from his stretcher, "1430 is an innocent man unjustly condemned, if ever there was one."

II

On the Thursday week following, when my wounds were all getting well, the whole body of convicts was duly paraded at half-past eleven in front of the Governor's house.

The Governor came out, holding an official-looking paper in his right hand. "No. 1430," he said in a loud voice, "stand forward." And I stood forward.

"No. 1430, I have the pleasant duty of informing you, in face of all your fellow-prisoners, that your heroism and self-devotion in saving the life of Warder James Woollacott, when he was attacked and almost overpowered on the twentieth of this month by a gang of rebellious convicts, has been reported to Her Majesty's Secretary of State for the Home Department; and that on his recommendation Her Majesty has been graciously pleased to grant you a Free Pardon for the remainder of the time during which you were sentenced to penal servitude."

For a moment I felt quite stunned and speechless. I reeled on my feet so much that two of the warders jumped forward to support me. It was a great thing to have at least one's freedom. But in another minute the real meaning of the thing came clearer upon me, and I recoiled from the bare sound of those horrid words, a free pardon. I didn't want to be pardoned like a convicted felon: I wanted to have my innocence proved before the eyes of all England. For my own sake, and still more for Emily's sake, rehabilitation was all I cared for.

"Sir," I said, touching my cap respectfully, and saluting the Governor according to our wonted prison discipline, "I am very greatly obliged to you for your kindness in having made this representation to the Home Secretary; but I feel compelled to say I cannot accept a free pardon. I am wholly guiltless of the crime of which I have been convicted; and I wish that instead of pardoning me the Home Secretary would give instructions to the detective police to make a thorough investigation of the case, with the object of proving my complete innocence. Till that is done, I prefer to remain an inmate of Portland Prison. What I wish is not pardon, but to be restored as an honest man to the society of my equals."

The Governor paused for a moment, and consulted quietly in an undertone with one or two of his subordinates. Then he turned to me with great kindness, and said in a loud voice, "No. 1430, I have no power any longer to detain you in this prison, even if I wished to do so, after you have once obtained Her Majesty's free pardon. My duty is to dismiss you at once, in accordance with the terms of this document. However, I will communicate the substance of your request to the Home Secretary, with whom such a petition, so made, will doubtless have the full weight that may rightly attach to it. You must now go with these warders, who will restore you your own clothes, and then formally set you at liberty. But if there is anything further you would wish to speak to me about, you can do so afterward in your private capacity as a free man at two o'clock in my own office."

I thanked him quietly and then withdrew. At two o'clock I duly presented myself in ordinary clothes at the Governor's office.

We had a long and confidential interview, in the course of which I was able to narrate to the Governor at full length all the facts of my strange story exactly as I have here detailed them. He listened to me with the greatest interest, checking and confirming my statements at length by reference to the file of papers brought to him by a clerk. When I had finished my whole story, he said to me quite simply, "Mr. Tait, it may be imprudent of me in my position and under such peculiar circumstances to say so, but I fully and unreservedly believe your statement. If anything that I can say or do can be of any assistance to you in proving your innocence, I shall be very happy indeed to exert all my influence in your favour."

I thanked him warmly with tears in my eyes.

"And there is one point in your story," he went on, "to which I, who have seen a good deal of such doubtful cases, attach the very highest importance. You say that gold clippings, pronounced to be similar in character to the gold Wulfric, were found shortly after by a cleaner at the Museum on the cocoa-nut matting of the floor where the coin was examined by you?"

I nodded, blushing crimson. "That," I said, "seems to me the strangest and most damning circumstance against me in the whole story."

"Precisely," the Governor answered quietly. "And if what you say is the truth (as I believe it to be), it is also the circumstance which best gives us a clue to use against the real culprit. The person who stole the coin was too clever by half, or else not quite clever enough for his own protection. In manufacturing that last fatal piece of evidence against you he was also giving you a certain clue to his own identity."

"How so?" I asked, breathless.

"Why, don't you see? The thief must in all probability have been somebody connected with the Museum. He must have seen you comparing the Wulfric with your own coin. He must have picked it up and carried it off secretly at the moment you dropped it. He must have clipped the coin to manufacture further hostile evidence. And he must have dropped the clippings afterwards on the cocoa-nut matting in the same gallery on purpose in order to heighten the suspicion against you."

"You are right," I cried, brightening up at the luminous suggestion—"you are right, obviously. And there is only one man who could have seen and heard enough to carry out this abominable plot—Mactavish!"

"Well, find him out and prove the case against him, Mr. Tait," the Governor said warmly, "and if you send him here to us I can promise you that he will be well taken care of."

I bowed and thanked him, and was about to withdraw, but he held out his hand to me with perfect frankness.

"Mr. Tait," he said, "I can't let you go away so. Let me have your hand in token that you bear us no grudge for the way we have treated you during your unfortunate imprisonment, and that I, for my part, am absolutely satisfied of the truth of your statement."

III

The moment I arrived in London I drove straight off without delay to Emily's. I had telegraphed beforehand that I had been granted a free pardon, but had not stopped to tell her why or under what conditions.

Emily met me in tears in the passage. "Harold! Harold!" she cried, flinging her arms wildly around me. "Oh, my darling! my darling! how can I ever say it to you? Mamma says she won't allow me to see you here any longer."

It was a terrible blow, but I was not unprepared for it. How could I expect that poor, conventional, commonplace old lady to have any faith in me after all she had read about me in the newspapers?

"Emily," I said, kissing her over and over again tenderly, "you must come out with me, then, this very minute, for I want to talk with you over matters of importance. Whether your mother wishes it or not, you must come out with me this very minute."

Emily put on her bonnet hastily and walked out with me into the streets of London. It was growing dark, and the neighbourhood was a very quiet one; or else perhaps even my own Emily would have felt a little ashamed of walking about the streets of London with a man whose hair was still cropped short around his head like a common felon's.

I told her all the story of my release, and Emily listened to it in profound silence.

"Harold!" she cried, "my darling Harold!" (when I told her the tale of my desperate battle over the fallen warder), "you are the bravest and best of men. I knew you would vindicate yourself sooner or later. What we have to do now is to show that Mactavish stole the Wulfric. I know he stole it; I read it at the trial in his clean-shaven villain's face. I shall prove it still, and then you will be justified in the eyes of everybody."

"But how can we manage to communicate meanwhile, darling?" I cried eagerly. "If your mother won't allow you to see me, how are we ever to meet and consult about it?"

"There's only one way, Harold, only one way; and as things now stand you mustn't think it strange of me to propose it. Harold, you must marry me immediately, whether mamma will let us or not!"

"Emily!" I cried, "my own darling! your confidence and trust in me makes me I can't tell you how proud and happy. That you should be willing to marry me even while I am under such a cloud as this gives me a greater proof of your love than anything else you could possibly do for me. But, darling, I am too proud to take you at your word. For your sake, Emily, I will never marry you until all the world has been compelled unreservedly to admit my innocence."

Emily blushed and cried a little. "As you will, Harold, dearest," she answered, trembling, "I can afford to wait for you. I know that in the end the truth will be established."

IV

A week or two later I was astonished one morning at receiving a visit in my London lodgings from the warder Woollacott, whose life I had been happily instrumental in saving at Portland Prison.

"Well, sir," he said, grasping my hand warmly and gratefully, "you see I haven't yet entirely recovered from that terrible morning. I shall bear the marks of it about me for the remainder of my lifetime. The Governor says I shall never again be fit for duty, so they've pensioned me off very honourable."

I told him how pleased I was that he should have been liberally treated, and then we fell into conversation about myself and the means of re-establishing my perfect innocence.

"Sir," said he, "I shall have plenty of leisure, and shall be comfortably off now. If there's anything that I can do to be of service to you in the matter, I shall gladly do it. My time is entirely at your disposal."

I thanked him warmly, but told him that the affair was already in the hands of the regular detectives, who had been set to work upon it by the Governor's influence with the Home Secretary.

By-and-by I happened to mention confidentially to him my suspicions of the man Mactavish. An idea seemed to occur to the warder suddenly; but he said not a word to me about it at the time. A few days later, however, he came back to me quietly and said, in a confidential tone of voice, "Well, sir, I think we may still manage to square him."

"Square who, Mr. Woollacott? I don't understand you."

"Why, Mactavish, sir. I found out he had a small house near the Museum, and his wife lets a lodging there for a single man. I've gone and taken the lodging, and I shall see whether in the course of time something or other doesn't come out of it."

I smiled and thanked him for his enthusiasm in my cause; but I confess I didn't see how anything on earth of any use to me was likely to arise from this strange proceeding on his part.

V

It was that same week, I believe, that I received two other unexpected visitors. They came together. One of them was the Superintendent of Coins at the British Museum; the other was the well-known antiquary and great authority upon the Anglo-Saxon coinage, Sir Theophilus Wraxton.

"Mr. Tait," the superintendent began, not without some touch of natural shamefacedness in his voice and manner, "I have reason to believe that I may possibly have been mistaken in my positive identification of the coin you showed me that day at the Museum as our own specimen of the gold Wulfric. If I was mistaken, then I have unintentionally done you a most grievous wrong; and for that wrong, should my suspicions turn out ill-founded, I shall owe you the deepest and most heartfelt apologies. But the only reparation I can possibly make you is the one I am doing to-day by bringing here my friend Sir Theophilus Wraxton. He has a communication of some importance to make to you; and if he is right, I can only beg your pardon most humbly for the error I have committed in what I believed to be the discharge of my duties."

"Sir," I answered, "I saw at the time you were the victim of a mistake, as I was the victim of a most unfortunate concurrence of circumstances; and I bear you no grudge whatsoever for the part you bore in subjecting me to what is really in itself a most unjust and unfounded suspicion. You only did what you believed to be your plain duty; and you did it with marked reluctance, and with every desire to leave me every possible loophole of escape from what you conceived as a momentary yielding to a vile temptation. But what is it that Sir Theophilus Wraxton wishes to tell me?"

"Well, my dear sir," the old gentleman began, warmly, "I haven't the slightest doubt in the world myself that you have been quite unwarrantably disbelieved about a plain matter of fact that ought at once to have been immediately apparent to anybody who knew anything in the world about the gold Anglo-Saxon coinage. No reflection in the world upon you, Harbourne, my dear friend, no reflection in the world upon you in the matter; but you must admit that you've been pig-headedly hasty in jumping to a conclusion, and ignorantly determined in sticking to it against better evidence. My dear sir, I haven't the very slightest doubt in the world that the coin now in the British Museum is not the one which I have seen there previously, and which I have figured in the third volume of my 'Early Northumbrian and Mercian Numismatist!' Quite otherwise; quite otherwise, I assure you."

"How do you recognize that it is different, sir?" I cried excitedly. "The two coins were struck at just the same mint from the same die, and I examined them closely together, and saw absolutely no difference between them, except the dent and the amount of the clipping."

"Quite true, quite true," the old gentleman replied with great deliberation. "But look here, sir. Here is the drawing I took of the Museum Wulfric fourteen years ago, for the third volume of my 'Northumbrian Numismatist.' That drawing was made with the aid of careful measurements, which you will find detailed in the text at page 230. Now, here again is the duplicate Wulfric, permit me to call it your Wulfric; and if you will compare the two you'll find, I think, that though your Wulfric is a great deal smaller than the original one, taken as a whole, yet on one diameter, the diameter from the letter U in Wulfric to the letter R in Rex, it is nearly an eighth of an inch broader than the specimen I have there figured. Well, sir, you may cut as much as you like off a coin, and make it smaller; but hang me if by cutting away at it for all your lifetime you can make it an eighth of an inch broader anyhow, in any direction."

I looked immediately at the coin, the drawing, and the measurements in the book, and saw at a glance that Sir Theophilus was right.

"How on earth did you find it out?" I asked the bland old gentleman, breathlessly.

"Why, my dear sir, I remembered the old coin perfectly, having been so very particular in my drawing and measurement; and the moment I clapped eyes on the other one yesterday, I said to my good friend Harbourne, here: 'Harbourne,' said I, 'somebody's been changing your Wulfric in the case over yonder for another specimen.' 'Changing it!' said Harbourne: 'not a bit of it; clipping it, you mean.' 'No, no, my good fellow,' said I: 'do you suppose I don't know the same coin again when I see it, and at my time of life too? This is another coin, not the same one clipped. It's bigger across than the old one from there to there.' 'No, it isn't,' says he. 'But it is,' I answer. 'Just you look in my "Northumbrian and Mercian" and see if it isn't so.' 'You must be mistaken,' says Harbourne. 'If I am, I'll eat my head,' says I. Well, we get down the 'Numismatist' from the bookshelf then and there; and sure enough, it turns out just as I told him. Harbourne turned as white as a ghost, I can tell you, as soon as he discovered it. 'Why,' says he, 'I've sent a poor young fellow off to Portland Prison, only three or four months ago, for stealing that very Wulfric.' And then he told me all the story. 'Very well,' said I, 'then the only thing you've got to do is just to go and call on him to-morrow, and let him know that you've had it proved to you, fairly proved to you, that this is not the original Wulfric.'"

"Sir Theophilus," I said, "I'm much obliged to you. What you point out is by far the most important piece of evidence I've yet had to offer. Mr. Harbourne, have you kept the gold clippings that were found that morning on the cocoa-nut matting?"

"I have, Mr. Tait," the superintendent answered anxiously. "And Sir Theophilus and I have been trying to fit them upon the coin in the Museum shelves; and I am bound to admit I quite agree with him that they must have been cut off a specimen decidedly larger in one diameter and smaller in another than the existing one, in short, that they do not fit the clipped Wulfric now in the Museum."

VI

It was just a fortnight later that I received quite unexpectedly a telegram from Rome directed to me at my London lodgings. I tore it open hastily; it was signed by Emily, and contained only these few words: "We have found the Museum Wulfric. The superintendent is coming over to identify and reclaim it. Can you manage to run across immediately with him?"

For a moment I was lost in astonishment, delight, and fear. How and why had Emily gone over to Rome? Who could she have with her to take care of her and assist her? How on earth had she tracked the missing coin to its distant hiding-place? It was all a profound mystery to me; and after my first outburst of joy and gratitude, I began to be afraid that Emily might have been misled by her eagerness and anxiety into following up the traces of the wrong coin.

However, I had no choice but to go to Rome and see the matter ended; and I went alone, wearing out my soul through that long journey with suspense and fear; for I had not managed to hit upon the superintendent, who, through his telegram being delivered a little the sooner, had caught a train six hours earlier than the one I went by.

As I arrived at the Central Station at Rome, I was met, to my surprise, by a perfect crowd of familiar faces. First, Emily herself rushed to me, kissed me, and assured me a hundred times over that it was all right, and that the missing coin was undoubtedly recovered. Then, the superintendent, more shamefaced than ever, and very grave, but with a certain moisture in his eyes, confirmed her statement by saying that he had got the real Museum Wulfric undoubtedly in his pocket. Then Sir Theophilus, who had actually come across with Lady Wraxton on purpose to take care of Emily, added his assurances and congratulations. Last of all, Woollacott, the warder, stepped up to me and said simply, "I'm glad, sir, that it was through me as it all came out so right and even."

"Tell me how it all happened," I cried, almost faint with joy, and still wondering whether my innocence had really been proved beyond all fear of cavil.

Then Woollacott began, and told me briefly the whole story. He had consulted with the superintendent and Sir Theophilus, without saying a word to me about it, and had kept a close watch upon all the letters that came for Mactavish. A rare Anglo-Saxon coin is not a chattel that one can easily get rid of every day; and Woollacott shrewdly gathered from what Sir Theophilus had told him that Mactavish (or whoever else had stolen the coin) would be likely to try to dispose of it as far away from England as possible, especially after all the comments that had been made on this particular Wulfric in the English newspapers. So he took every opportunity of intercepting the postman at the front door, and looking out for envelopes with foreign postage stamps. At last one day a letter arrived for Mactavish with an Italian stamp and a cardinal's red hat stamped like a crest on the flap of the envelope. Woollacott was certain that things of that sort didn't come to Mactavish every day about his ordinary business. Braving the penalties for appropriating a letter, he took the liberty to open this suspicious communication, and found it was a note from Cardinal Trevelyan, the Pope's Chamberlain, and a well-known collector of antiquities referring to early Church history in England, and that it was in reply to an offer of Mactavish's to send the Cardinal for inspection a rare gold coin not otherwise specified. The Cardinal expressed his readiness to see the coin, and to pay a hundred and fifty pounds for it, if it proved to be rare and genuine as described. Woollacott felt certain that this communication must refer to the gold Wulfric. He therefore handed the letter to

Mrs. Mactavish when the postman next came his rounds, and waited to see whether Mactavish any day afterwards went to the post to register a small box or packet. Meanwhile he communicated with Emily and the superintendent, being unwilling to buoy me up with a doubtful hope until he was quite sure that their plan had succeeded. The superintendent wrote immediately to the Cardinal, mentioning his suspicions, and received a reply to the effect that he expected a coin of Wulfric to be sent him shortly. Sir Theophilus, who had been greatly interested in the question of the coin, kindly offered to take Emily over to Rome, in order to get the criminating piece, as soon as it arrived, from Cardinal Trevelyan. That was, in turn, the story that they all told me, piece by piece, in the Central Station at Rome that eventful morning.

"And Mactavish?" I asked of the superintendent eagerly.

"Is in custody in London already," he answered somewhat sternly. "I had a warrant out against him before I left town on this journey."

At the trial the whole case was very clearly proved against him, and my innocence was fully established before the face of all my fellow-countrymen. A fortnight later my wife and I were among the rocks and woods at Ambleside; and when I returned to London, it was to take a place in the department of coins at the British Museum, which the superintendent begged of me to accept as some further proof in the eyes of everybody that the suspicion he had formed in the matter of the Wulfric was a most unfounded and wholly erroneous one. The coin itself I kept as a memento of a terrible experience; but I have given up collecting on my own account entirely, and am quite content nowadays to bear my share in guarding the national collection from other depredators of the class of Mactavish.

MY UNCLE'S WILL

I

"My dear Mr. Payne," said my deceased uncle's lawyer with an emphatic wag of his forefinger, "I assure you there's no help for it. The language of the will is perfectly simple and explicit. Either you must do as your late uncle desired, or you must let the property go to the representative of his deceased wife's family."

"But surely, Blenkinsopp," I said deprecatingly, "we might get the Court of Chancery to set it aside, as being contrary to public policy, or something of that sort. I know you can get the Court of Chancery to affirm almost anything you ask them, especially if it's something a little abstruse and out of the common; it gratifies the Court's opinion of its own acumen. Now, clearly, it's contrary to public policy that a man should go and make his own nephew ridiculous by his last will and testament, isn't it?"

Mr. Blenkinsopp shook his head vigorously. "Bless my soul, Mr. Payne," he answered, helping himself to a comprehensive pinch from his snuff-box (an odious habit, confined, I believe, at the present day to family solicitors), "bless my soul, my dear sir, the thing's simply impossible. Here's your uncle, the late Anthony Aikin, Esquire, deceased, a person of sound mind and an adult male above the age of twenty-one years, to be quite accurate, oetatis suoe, seventy-eight, makes his will, and duly attests the same in the presence of two witnesses; everything quite in order: not a single point open to exception in any way. Well, he gives and bequeaths to his nephew, Theodore Payne, gentleman, that's you, after a few unimportant legacies, the bulk of his real and personal estate, provided only that you adopt the surname of Aikin, prefixed before and in addition to your own surname of Payne. But, and this is very important, if you don't choose to adopt and use the said surname of Aikin, in the manner hereinbefore recited, then and in that case, my dear sir, why, then and in that case, as clear as currant jelly, the whole said residue of his real and personal estate is to go to the heir or heirs-at-law of the late Amelia Maria Susannah Aikin, wife of the said Anthony Aikin, Esquire, deceased. Nothing could be simpler or plainer in any way, and there's really nothing on earth for you to do except to choose between the two alternatives so clearly set before you by your deceased uncle."

"But look here, you know, Blenkinsopp," I said appealingly, "no fellow can really be expected to go and call himself Aikin-Payne, now can he? It's positively too ridiculous. Mightn't I stick the Payne before the Aikin, and call myself Payne-Aikin, eh? That wouldn't be quite so absurdly suggestive of a perpetual toothache. But Aikin-Payne! Why, the comic papers would take it up immediately. Every footman in London would grin audibly when he announced me. I fancy I hear the fellows this very moment: flinging open the door with a violent attempt at seriousness, and shouting out, 'Mr. Haching-Pain, ha, ha, ha!' with a loud guffaw behind the lintel. It would be simply unendurable!"

"My dear sir," answered the unsympathetic Blenkinsopp (most unsympathetic profession, an attorney's, really), "the law doesn't take into consideration the question of the probable conduct of footmen. It must be Aikin-Payne or nothing. I admit the collocation does sound a little ridiculous, to be sure; but your uncle's will is perfectly unequivocal upon the subject, in fact, ahem! I drew it up myself, to say the truth; and unless you call yourself Aikin-Payne, 'in the manner hereinbefore recited,' then and in that case, observe (there's no deception), then and in that case the heir or heirs-at-law of the late Amelia Maria Susannah aforesaid will be entitled to benefit under the will as fully in every respect as if the property was bequeathed directly to him, her, or them, by name, and to no other person."

"And who the dickens are these heirs-at-law, Blenkinsopp?" I ventured to ask after a moment's pause, during which the lawyer had refreshed himself with another prodigious sniff from his snuff-box.

"Who the dickens are they, Mr. Payne? I should say Mr. Aikin-Payne, ahem, why, how the dickens should I know, sir? You don't suppose I keep a genealogical table and full pedigree of all the second cousins of all my clients hung up conspicuously in some spare corner of my brain, do you, eh? Upon my soul I really haven't the slightest notion. All I know about them is that the late Mrs. Amelia Maria Susannah Aikin, deceased, had one sister, who married somebody or other somewhere, against Mr. Anthony Aikin's wishes, and that he never had anything further to say to her at any time. 'But where she's gone and how she fares, nobody knows and nobody cares,' sir, as the poet justly remarks."

I was not previously acquainted with the poet's striking observation on this matter, but I didn't stop to ask Mr. Blenkinsopp in what author's work these stirring lines had originally appeared. I was too much occupied with other thoughts at that moment to pursue my investigations into their authorship and authenticity. "Upon my word, Blenkinsopp," I said, "I've really half a mind to shy the thing up and go on with my schoolmastering."

Mr. Blenkinsopp shrugged his shoulders. "Believe me, my dear young friend," he said sententiously, "twelve hundred a year is not to be sneezed at. Without inquiring too precisely into the exact state of your existing finances, I should be inclined to say your present engagement can't be worth to you more than three hundred a year."

I nodded acquiescence. "The exact figure," I murmured.

"And your private means are?"

"Non-existent," I answered frankly.

"Then, my dear sir, excuse such plainness of speech in a man of my profession; but if you throw it up you will be a perfect fool, sir; a perfect fool, I assure you."

"But perhaps, Blenkinsopp, the next-of-kin won't step in to claim it!"

"Doesn't matter a bit, my dear fellow. Executors are bound to satisfy themselves before paying you over your legacy that you have assumed and will use the name of Aikin before and in addition to your own name of Payne, in the manner hereinbefore recited. There's no getting over that in any way."

I sighed aloud. "Twelve hundred a year is certainly very comfortable," I said. "But it's a confounded bore that one should have a condition tacked on to it which will make one a laughing-stock for life to all the buffoons and idiots of one's acquaintance."

Blenkinsopp nodded in modified assent. "After all," he answered, "I wouldn't mind taking it on the same terms myself."

"Well," said I, "che sara sara. If it must be, it must be; and you may put an advertisement into the Times accordingly. Tell the executors that I accept the condition."

II

"I won't stop in town," said I to myself, "to be chaffed by all the fellows at the club and in the master's room at St. Martin's. I'll run over on the Continent until the wags (confound them) have forgotten all about it. I'm a sensitive man, and if there's anything on earth I hate it's cheap and easy joking and punning on a name or a personal peculiarity which lays itself open obviously to stupid buffoonery. Of course I shall chuck up the schoolmastering now;—it's an odious trade at any time, and I may as well take a pleasant holiday while I'm about it. Let me see, Nice or Cannes or Florence would be the best thing at this time of year. Escape the November fogs and January frosts. Let's make it Cannes, then, and try the first effect of my new name upon the corpus vile of the Cannois."

So I packed up my portmanteau hurriedly, took the 7.45 to Paris, and that same evening found myself comfortably ensconced in a wagon lit, making my way as fast as the Lyons line would carry me en route for the blue Mediterranean.

The Hôtel du Paradis at Cannes is a very pleasant and well managed place, where I succeeded in making myself perfectly at home. I gave my full name to the concierge boldly. "Thank Heaven," I thought, "Aikin-Payne will sound to her just as good a label to one's back as Howard or Cholmondely. She won't see the absurdity of the combination." She was a fat Vaudoise Swiss by origin, and she took it without moving a muscle. But she answered me in very tolerable English, me, who thought my Parisian accent unimpeachable! "Vary well, sirr, your lettares shall be sent to your apartments." I saw there was the faintest twinkle of a smile about the corner of her mouth, and I felt that even she, a mere foreigner, a Swiss concierge, perceived at once the incongruity of the two surnames. Incongruity! that's the worst of it! Would that they were incongruous! But it's their fatal and obvious congruity with one another that makes their juxtaposition so ridiculous. Call a man Payne, and I venture to say, though I was to the manner born, and it's me that says it as oughtn't to say it, you couldn't find a neater or more respectable surname in all England: call him plain Aikin, and though that perhaps is less aristocratic, it's redeemed by all the associations of childhood with the earliest literature we imbibed through the innocuous pages of "Evenings at Home:" but join the two together, in the order of alphabetical precedence, and you get an Aikin-Payne, which is a thing to make a sensitive man, compelled to bear it for a lifetime, turn permanently red like a boiled lobster. My uncle must have done it on purpose, in order to inflict a deadly blow on what he would doubtless have called my confounded self-conceit!

However, I changed my tourist suit for a black cutaway, and made my way down to the salle-à-manger. The dinner was good in itself, and was enlivened for me by the presence of an extremely pretty girl of, say nineteen, who sat just opposite, and whose natural protector I soon managed to draw casually into a general conversation. I say her natural protector, because, though I took him at the time for her father, I discovered afterwards that he was really her uncle. Experience has taught me that when you sit opposite a pretty girl at an hotel, you ought not to open fire by directing your observations to herself in person; you should begin diplomatically by gaining the confidence of her male relations through the wisdom or the orthodoxy of your political and social opinions. Mr. Shackleford, that, I found afterwards, was the uncle's name, happened to be a fiery Tory, while I have the personal misfortune to be an equally rabid Radical: but on this occasion I successfully dissembled, acquiescing with vague generality in his denunciation of my dearest private convictions; and by the end of dinner we had struck up quite an acquaintance with one another.

"Ruby," said the aunt to the pretty girl, as soon as dinner was over, "shall we take a stroll out in the gardens?"

Ruby! what a charming name really. I wonder, now, what is her surname? And what a beautiful graceful figure, as she rises from the table, and throws her little pale blue Indian silk scarf around her pretty shoulders! Clearly, Ruby is a person whose acquaintance I ought to cultivate.

"Uncle won't come, of course," said Ruby, with a pleasant smile (what teeth!). "The evening air would be too much for him. You know," she added, looking across to me, "almost everybody at Cannes is in the invalid line, and mustn't stir out after sunset. Aunt and I are unfashionable enough to be quite strong, and to go in for a stroll by moonlight."

"I happen to be equally out of the Cannes fashion," I said, directing my observation, with great strategic skill, rather to the aunt than to Miss Ruby in person; "and if you will allow me I should be very glad to accompany you."

So we turned out on the terrace of the Paradis, and walked among the date-palms and prickly pears that fill the pretty tropical garden. It was a lovely moonlight evening in October; and October is still almost a summer month in the Riviera. The feathery branches of the palms stood out in clear-cut outline against the pale moonlit sky; the white houses of Cannes gleamed with that peculiarly soft greenish Mediterranean tint in the middle distance; and the sea reflected the tremulous shimmer in the background, between the jagged sierra of the craggy Esterel and the long low outline of the Ile Ste. Marguerite. Altogether, it was an ideal poet's evening, the very evening to stroll for the first time with a beautiful girl through the charmed alleys of a Provençal garden!

Ruby Estcourt, she gave me her name before long, was quite as pleasant to talk to as she was beautiful and graceful to behold. Fortunately, her aunt was not one of the race of talkative old ladies, and she left the mass of the conversation entirely to Ruby and myself. In the course of half an hour or so spent in pacing up and down that lovely terrace, I had picked out, bit by bit, all that I most wanted to know about Ruby Estcourt. She was an orphan, without brothers or sisters, and evidently without any large share of this world's goods; and she lived with her aunt and uncle, who were childless people, and who usually spent the summer in Switzerland, retiring to the Riviera every winter for the benefit of Mr. Shackleford's remaining lung. Quite simple and unaffected Ruby seemed, though she had passed most of her lifetime in the too-knowing atmosphere of Continental hotels, among that cosmopolitan public which is so sharp-sighted that it fancies it can see entirely through such arrant humbug as honour in men and maidenly reserve in women. Still, from that world Ruby Estcourt had somehow managed to keep herself quite unspotted; and a simpler, prettier, more natural little fairy you wouldn't find anywhere in the English villages of half a dozen counties.

It was all so fresh and delightful to me, the palms, the Mediterranean, the balmy evening air, the gleaming white town, and pretty Ruby Estcourt, that I walked up and down on the terrace as long as they would let me; and I was really sorry when good Mrs. Shackleford at last suggested that it was surely getting time for uncle's game of cribbage. As they turned to go, Ruby said good evening, and then, hesitating for a moment as to my name, said quite simply and naturally, "Why, you haven't yet told us who you are, have you?"

I coloured a little, happily invisible by moonlight, as I answered, "That was an omission on my part, certainly. When you told me you were Miss Estcourt, I ought to have mentioned in return that my own name was Aikin-Payne, Theodore Aikin-Payne, if you please: may I give you a card?"

"Aching Pain!" Ruby said, with a smile. "Did I hear you right? Aching Pain, is it? Oh, what a very funny name!"

I drew myself up as stiffly as I was able. "Not Aching Pain," I said, with a doleful misgiving in my heart, it was clear everybody would put that odd misinterpretation upon it for the rest of my days. "Not Aching Pain, but Aikin-Payne, Miss Estcourt. A-i-k-i-n, Aikin, the Aikins of Staffordshire; P-a-y-n-e, Payne, the Paynes of Surrey. My original surname was Payne, a surname that I venture to say I'm a little proud of; but my uncle, Mr. Aikin, from whom I inherit property," I thought that was rather a good way of putting it, "wished me to adopt his family name in addition to my own, in fact, made it a condition, sine quâ non, of my receiving the property."

"Payne—Aikin," Ruby said, turning the names over to herself slowly. "Ah, yes, I see. Excuse my misapprehension, Mr.—Mr. Aikin-Payne. It was very foolish of me; but really, you know, it does sound so very ludicrous, doesn't it now?"

I bit my lip, and tried to smile back again. Absurd that a man should be made miserable about such a trifle; and yet I will freely confess that at that moment, in spite of my uncle's twelve hundred a year, I felt utterly wretched. I bowed to pretty little Ruby as well as I was able, and took a couple more turns by myself hurriedly around the terrace.

Was it only fancy, or did I really detect, as Ruby Estcourt said the two names over to herself just now, that she seemed to find the combination a familiar one? I really didn't feel sure about it; but it certainly did sound as if she had once known something about the Paynes or the Aikins. Ah, well! there are lots of Paynes and Aikins in the world, no doubt; but alas! there is only one of them doomed to go through life with the absurd label of an Aikin-Payne fastened upon his unwilling shoulders.

III

"Good morning, Mr.—Mr. Aikin-Payne," said Ruby Estcourt, stumbling timidly over the name, as we met in the salle-à-manger at breakfast next day. "I hope you don't feel any the worse for the chilly air last evening."

I bowed slightly. "You seem to have some difficulty in remembering my full name, Miss Estcourt," I said suggestively. "Suppose you call me simply Mr. Payne. I've been accustomed to it till quite lately, and to tell you the truth, I don't altogether relish the new addition."

"I should think not, indeed," Ruby answered frankly. "I never heard such a ridiculous combination in all my life before. I'm sure your uncle must have been a perfect old bear to impose it upon you."

"It was certainly rather cruel of him," I replied, as carelessly as I could, "or at least rather thoughtless. I dare say, though, the absurdity of the two names put together never struck him. What are you going to do with yourselves to-day, Mr. Shackleford? Everybody at Cannes has nothing to do but to amuse themselves, I suppose?"

Mr. Shackleford answered that they were going to drive over in the morning to Vallauris, and that if I cared to share a carriage with them, he would be happy to let me accompany his party. Nothing could have suited my book better. I was alone, I wanted society and amusement, and I had never seen a prettier girl than Ruby Estcourt. Here was the very thing I needed, ready cut out to my hand by propitious fortune. I found out as time went on that Mr. Shackleford, being a person of limited income, and a bad walker, had only one desire in life, which was to get somebody else to pay half his carriage fares for him by arrangement. We went to a great many places together, and he always divided the expenses equally between us, although I ought only to have paid a quarter, as his party consisted of three people, while I was one solitary bachelor. This apparent anomaly he got over on the ingenious ground that if I had taken a carriage by myself it would have cost me just twice as much. However, as I was already decidedly anxious for pretty little Ruby Estcourt's society, this question of financial detail did not weigh heavily upon me. Besides, a man who has just come into twelve hundred a year can afford to be generous in the matter of hackney carriages.

We had a delightful drive along the shore of that beautiful blue gulf to Vallauris, and another delightful drive back again over the hills to the Paradis. True, old Mr. Shackleford proved rather a bore through his anxiety to instruct me in the history and technical nature of keramic ware in general, and of the Vallauris pottery in particular, when I wanted rather to be admiring the glimpses of Bordighera and the Cap St. Martin and the snow-clad summits of the Maritime Alps with Ruby Estcourt. But in spite of all drawbacks—and old Mr. Shackleford with his universal information really was a serious drawback—I thoroughly enjoyed that first morning by the lovely Mediterranean. Ruby herself was absolutely charming. Such a light, bright, fairy-like little person, moving among the priceless vases and tazzas at Clément Massier's as if she were an embodied zephyr, too gentle even to knock them over with a whiff of her little Rampoor shawl, but there, I can't describe her, and I won't attempt it. Ruby, looking over my shoulder at this moment, says I always was an old stupid: so that, you see, closes the question.

An old stupid I certainly was for the next fortnight. Old Mr. Shackleford, only too glad to have got hold of a willing victim in the carriage-sharing fraud, dragged me about the country to every available point of view or object of curiosity within ten miles of the Square Brougham. Ruby usually accompanied us; and as the two old people naturally occupied the seat of honour at the back of the carriage, why, of course Ruby and I had to sit together with our backs to the horses, a mode of progression which I had never before known to be so agreeable. Every evening, Ruby and I walked out on the terrace in the moonlight; and I need hardly say that the moon, in spite of her pretended coldness, is really the most romantic and sentimental satellite in the whole solar system. To cut a long story short, by the end of the fortnight I was very distinctly in love with Ruby; and if you won't think the avowal a conceited one, I venture to judge by the sequel that Ruby was almost equally in love with me.

One afternoon, towards the close of my second week at Cannes, Ruby and I were sitting together on the retired seat in the grounds beside the pond with the goldfish. It was a delicious sunny afternoon, with the last touch of southern summer in the air, and Ruby was looking even prettier than usual, in her brocade pattern print dress, and her little straw hat with the scarlet poppies. (Ruby always dressed, I may say dresses, in the very simplest yet most charming fashion). There was something in the time and place that moved me to make a confession I had for some time been meditating; so I looked straight in her face, and not being given to long speeches, I said to her just this, "Ruby, you are the sweetest girl I ever saw in my life. Will you marry me?"

Ruby only looked at me with a face full of merriment, and burst out laughing. "Why, Mr. Payne," she said (she had dropped that hideous prefix long ago), "you've hardly known me yet a fortnight, and here you come to me with a regular declaration. How can I have had time to think about my answer to such a point-blank question?"

"If you like, Ruby," I answered, "we can leave it open for a little; but it occurs to me you might as well say 'yes' at once: for if we leave it open, common sense teaches me that you probably mean to say yes in the long-run." And to clench the matter outright, I thought it best to stoop across and kiss Ruby just once, by way of earnest. Ruby took the kiss calmly and sedately; so then I knew the matter was practically settled.

"But there's one thing, Mr. Payne, I must really insist upon," Ruby said very quietly; "and that is that I mustn't be called Mrs. Aikin-Payne. If I marry you at all, I must marry you as plain Mr. Payne without any Aikin. So that's clearly understood between us."

Here was a terrible condition indeed! I reasoned with Ruby, I explained to Ruby, I told Ruby that if she positively insisted upon it I must go back to my three hundred a year and my paltry schoolmastership, and must give up my uncle Aikin's money. Ruby would hear of no refusal.

"You have always the alternative of marrying somebody else, you know, Mr. Payne," she said with her most provoking and bewitching smile; "but if you really do want to marry me, you know the conditions."

"But, Ruby, you would never care to live upon a miserable pittance of three hundred a year! I hate the name as much as you do, but I think I should try to bear it for the sake of twelve hundred a year and perfect comfort."

No, Ruby was inexorable. "Take me or leave me," she said with provoking calmness, "but if you take me, give up your uncle's ridiculous suggestion. You can have three days to make your mind up. Till then, let us hear no more about the subject."

IV

During those three days I kept up a brisk fire of telegrams with old Blenkinsopp in Chancery Lane; and at the end of them I came mournfully to the conclusion that I must either give up Ruby or give up the twelve hundred a year. If I had been a hero of romance I should have had no difficulty at all in deciding the matter: I would have nobly refused the money off-hand, counting it as mere dross compared with the loving heart of a beautiful maiden. But unfortunately I am not a hero of romance; I am only an ordinary graduate of an English university. Under these circumstances, it did seem to me very hard that I must throw away twelve hundred a year for a mere sentimental fancy. And yet, on the other hand, not only did I hate the name myself, but I couldn't bear to impose it on Ruby; and as to telling Ruby that I wouldn't have her, because I preferred the money, that was clearly quite impossible. The more I looked the thing in the face, the more certain it appeared that I must relinquish my dream of wealth and go back (with Ruby) to my schoolmastering and my paltry three hundred. After all, lots of other fellows marry on that sum; and to say the truth, I positively shrank myself from going through life under the ridiculous guise of an Aikin-Payne.

The upshot of it all was that at the end of the three days, I took Ruby a little walk alone among the olive gardens behind the shrubbery. "Ruby," I said to her, falteringly, "you're the most fantastic, self-willed, imperious little person I ever met with, and I want to make just one more appeal to you. Won't you reconsider your decision, and take me in spite of the surname?"

Ruby grubbed up a little weed with the point of her parasol, and looked away from me steadfastly as she answered with her immovable and annoying calmness, "No, Mr. Payne, I really can't reconsider the matter in any way. It was you who took three days to make your mind up. Have you made it up yet or not, pray?"

"I have made it up, Ruby."

"And you mean—?" she said interrogatively, with a faint little tremor in her voice which I had never before noticed, and which thrilled through me with the ecstasy of a first discovery.

"And I mean," I answered, "to marry you, Ruby, if you will condescend to take me, and let my Uncle Aikin's money go to Halifax. Can you manage, Ruby, to be happy, as a poor schoolmaster's wife in a very tiny cottage?"

To my joy and surprise, Ruby suddenly seized both my hands in hers, kissed me twice of her own accord, and began to cry as if nothing could stop her. "Then you do really and truly love me," she said through her tears, holding fast to my hands all the time; "then you're really willing to make this great sacrifice for me!"

"Ruby," I said, "my darling, don't excite yourself so. And indeed it isn't a very great sacrifice either, for I hate the name so much I hardly know whether I could ever have endured to bear it."

"You shan't bear it," Ruby cried, eagerly, now laughing and clapping her hands above me. "You shan't bear it, and yet you shall have your Uncle Aikin's money all the same for all that."

"Why, what on earth do you mean, Ruby?" I asked in amazement. "Surely, my darling, you can't understand how strict the terms of the will actually are. I'm afraid you have been deluding yourself into a belief in some impossible compromise. But you must make your mind up to one thing at once, that unless I call myself Aikin-Payne, you'll have to live the rest of your life as a poor schoolmaster's wife. The next-of-kin will be sharp enough in coming down upon the money."

Ruby looked at me and laughed and clapped her hands again. "But what would you say, Mr. Payne," she said with a smile that dried up all her tears, "what would you say if you heard that the next-of-kin was, who do you think?—why me, sir, me, Ruby Estcourt?"

I could hardly believe my ears. "You, Ruby?" I cried in my astonishment. "You! How do you know? Are you really sure of it?"

Ruby put a lawyer's letter into my hand, signed by a famous firm in the city. "Read that," she said simply. I read it through, and saw in a moment that what Ruby said was the plain truth of it.

"So you want to do your future husband out of the twelve hundred a year!" I said, smiling and kissing her.

"No," Ruby answered, as she pressed my hand gently. "It shall be settled on you, since I know you were ready to give it up for my sake. And there shall be no more Aikin-Paynes henceforth and for ever."

There was never a prettier or more blushing bride than dear little Ruby that day six weeks.

THE TWO CARNEGIES

I

"Harold," said Ernest Carnegie to his twin-brother at breakfast one morning, "have you got a tooth aching slightly to-day?"

"Yes, by Jove, I have!" Harold answered, laying down the Times, and looking across the table with interest to his brother; "which one was yours?"

"The third from the canine on the upper left side," Ernest replied quickly. "And yours?"

"Let me see. This is the canine, isn't it? One, two, three; yes. The same, of course. It's really a very singular coincidence. How about the time? Was that as usual?"

"I'll tell you in a minute. Mine came on the day of the Guthries' hop. I was down at Brighton that morning. What date? Let me think; why, the 9th, I'm certain. To-day's what, mother?"

"The 23rd," said Harold, glancing for confirmation at the paper. "The law works itself out once more as regularly as if by machinery. I'm just a fortnight later than you, Ernest, as always."

Ernest drummed upon the table with his finger for a minute. "I'm afraid you'll have it rather badly to-day, Harold," he said, after a pause. "Mine got unbearable towards midday, and if I hadn't had it looked to in the afternoon, I couldn't have danced a single dance to save my life that evening. I advise you to go round to the dentist's immediately, and try to get it stopped before it goes any further."

Harold finished his cup of coffee, and looked out of the window blankly at the fog outside. "It's an awful thought," he said at last, "this living, as we two do, by clockwork! Everybody else lives exactly the same way, but they don't have their attention called to it, as we do. Just to think that from the day you and I were born, Ernest, it was written in the very fabric of our constitutions that when we were twenty-three years and five months old, the third molar in our upper left jaws should begin to fail us! It's really appalling in its unanswerable physical fatalism, when ones comes to think upon it."

"So I said to myself at the Guthries', the morning it began to give me a twinge," said Ernest, in the self-same tone. "It seemed to me such a terrible idea that in a fortnight's time, as certain as the sun, the very same tooth in your head would begin to go, as the one that was going in mine. It's too appalling, really."

"But do you actually mean to say," asked pretty little Nellie Holt, the visitor, newly come the day before from Cheshire, "that whenever one of you gets a toothache, the other one gets a toothache in the same tooth a fortnight later?"

"Not a toothache only," Ernest answered, he was studying for his degree as a physician, and took this department upon himself as by right—"but every other disease or ailment whatsoever. We're like two clocks wound up to strike at fixed moments; only, we're not wound up to strike exactly together. I'm fourteen days in advance of Harold, so to speak, and whatever happens to me to-day will happen to him, in all probability, exactly a fortnight later."

"How very extraordinary!" said Nellie, looking quickly, from one handsome clear-cut face to its exact counterpart in the other. "And yet not so extraordinary, after all, when one comes to think how very much alike you both are."

"Ah, that's not all," said Ernest, slowly; "it's something that goes a good deal deeper than that, Miss Holt. Consider that every one of us is born with a certain fixed and recognizable constitution, which we inherit from our fathers and mothers. In us, from our birth upward, are the seeds of certain diseases, the possibilities of certain actions and achievements. One man is born with hereditary consumption; another man with hereditary scrofula; a third with hereditary genius or hereditary drunkenness, each equally innate in the very threads and strands of his system. And it's all bound to come out, sooner or later, in its own due and appointed time. Here's a fellow whose father had gout at forty: he's born with such a constitution that, as the hands on his life-dial reach forty, out comes the gout in his feet, wherever he may be, as certain as fate. It's horrible to think of, but it's the truth, and there's no good in disguising it."

Nellie Holt shuddered slightly. "What a dreadful materialistic creed, Mr. Carnegie," she said, looking at him with a half-frightened air. "It's almost as bad as Mohammedan fatalism."

"No, not so bad as that," Ernest Carnegie answered; "not nearly so bad as that. The Oriental belief holds that powers above you compel your life against your will: we modern scientific thinkers only hold that your own inborn constitution determines your whole life for you, will included. But whether we like it or dislike it, Miss Holt, there are the facts, and nobody can deny them. If you'd lived with a twin-sister, as Harold and I have lived together for twenty-three years, you'd see that the clocks go as they are set, with fixed and predestined regularity. Twins, you know, are almost exactly alike in all things, and in the absolute coincidence of their constitutions you can see the inexorable march of disease, and the inexorable unfolding of the predetermined life-history far better than in any other conceivable case. I'm a scientific man myself, you see, and I have such an opportunity of watching it all as no other man ever yet had before me."

"My dear," said Mrs. Carnegie, the mother, from the head of the table, "you've no idea how curiously their two lives have always resembled one other. When they were babies, they were so much alike that we had to tie red and blue ribbons round their necks to distinguish them. Ernest was red and Harold blue, no, Ernest was blue and Harold red: at least, I'm not quite certain which way it was, but I know we have a note of it in the family Bible, for Mr. Carnegie made it at the time for fear we should get confused between them when we were bathing them. So we put the ribbons on the moment they were christened, and never took them both off together for a second, even to bathe them, so as to prevent accidents. Well, do you know, dear, from the time they were babies, they were always alike in everything; but Ernest was always a fortnight before Harold. He said "Mamma" one day, and just a fortnight later Harold said the very same word. Then Ernest said "sugar," and so did Harold in another fortnight. Ernest began to toddle a fortnight the earliest. They took the whooping cough and the measles in the same order; and they cut all their teeth so, too, the same teeth first on each side, and just at a fortnight's distance from one another. It's really quite an extraordinary coincidence."

"The real difficulty would be," said Harold, "to find anything in which we didn't exactly resemble one another. Well, now I must be off to this horrid office with the Pater. Are you ready, Pater? I'll call in at Estwood's in the course of the morning, Ernest, and tell him to look after my teeth. I don't want to miss the Balfours' party this evening. Curious that we should be going to a party this evening too. That isn't fated in our constitutions, anyhow, is it, Ernest? Good morning, Miss Holt; the first waltz, remember. Come along, Pater." And he went out, followed immediately by his father.

"I must be going too," said Ernest, looking at his watch; "I have an appointment with Dowson at Guy's at half-past ten, a very interesting case: hereditary cataract; three brothers, all of them get it, each as he reaches twelve years old, and Dowson has performed the operation on two, and is going to perform it on the other this very day. Good morning, Miss Holt; the second waltz for me; you won't forget, will you?"

"How awfully alike they really are, Mrs. Carnegie," said Nellie, as they were left alone. "I'm sure I shall never be able to tell them apart. I don't even know their names yet. The one that has just gone out, the one that's going to be a doctor, that's Mr. Harold, isn't it?"

"Oh no, dear," Mrs. Carnegie answered, putting her arm round Nellie's waist affectionately, "that's Ernest. Harold's the lawyer. You'll soon learn the difference between them. You can tell Ernest easily, because he usually wears a horrid thing for a scarf-pin, an ivory skull and cross-bones: he wears it, he says, just to distinguish him professionally from Harold. Indeed, that was partly why Mr. Carnegie was so anxious that Harold should go into his own office; so as to make a distinction of profession between them. If Harold had followed his own bent, he would have been a doctor too; they're both full of what they call physiological ideas, dreadful things, I think them. But Mr. Carnegie thought as they were so very much alike already we ought to do something to give them some individuality, as he says: for if they were both to be doctors or both solicitors, you know, there'd really be no knowing them apart, even for ourselves; and I assure you, my dear, as it is now even they're exactly like one person."

"Are they as alike in character, then, as they are in face?" asked Nellie.

"Alike in character! My dear, they're absolutely identical. Whatever the one thinks, or says, or does, the other thinks, says, and does at the same time, independently. Why, once Ernest went over to Paris for a week's holiday, while Harold went on some law business of his father's to Brussels. Would you believe it, when they came back they'd each got a present for the other. Ernest had seen a particular Indian silver cigar-case in a shop on the Boulevards, and he brought it home as a surprise for Harold. Well, Harold had bought an exactly similar one in the Montagne de la Cour, and brought it home as a surprise for Ernest. And what was odder still, each of them had had the other's initials engraved upon the back in some sort of heathenish Oriental characters."

"How very queer," said Nellie. "And yet they seem very fond of one another. As a rule, one's always told that people who are exactly alike in character somehow don't get on together."

"My dear child, they're absolutely inseparable. Their devotion to one another's quite unlimited. You see they've been brought up together, played together, sympathized with one another in all their troubles and ailments, and are sure of a response from each other about everything. It was the greatest trouble of their lives when Mr. Carnegie decided that Harold must become a solicitor for the sake of the practice. They couldn't bear at first to be separated all day; and when they got home in the evening, Ernest from the hospital and Harold from the office, they met almost like a pair of lovers. They've talked together about their work so much that Harold knows almost as much medicine now as Ernest, while Ernest's quite at home, his father declares, in 'Benjamin on Sales,' and 'Chitty on Contract.' It's quite delightful to see how fond they are of one another."

At five o'clock Ernest Carnegie returned from his hospital. He brought two little bunches of flowers with him, some lilies of the valley and a carnation, and he handed them with a smile, one to his sister and one to pretty little Nellie. "I thought you'd like them for this evening, Miss Holt," he said. "I chose a carnation on purpose, because I fancied it would suit your hair."

"Oh, Ernest," said his sister, "you ought to have got a red camelia. That's the proper thing for a brunette like Nellie."

"Nonsense, Edie," Ernest answered, "I hate camelias. Ugliest flowers out: so stiff and artificial. One might as well wear a starchy gauze thing from the milliner's."

"I'm so glad you brought Nellie Holt a flower. She's a sweet girl, Ernest, isn't she?" said Mrs. Carnegie a minute or two later, as Edie and Nelly ran upstairs. "I wish either of you two boys could take a fancy to a nice girl like her, now."

"My dear mother," Ernest answered, turning up his eyes appealingly. "A little empty-headed, pink-and-white thing like that! I don't know what Harold thinks, but she'd never do for me, at any rate. Very pretty to look at, very timid to talk to, very nice and shrinking, and all that kind of thing, I grant you; but nothing in her. Whenever I marry, I shall marry a real live woman, not a dainty piece of delicate empty drapery."

At six o'clock, Mr. Carnegie and Harold came in from the office. Harold carried in his hand two little button-hole bouquets, of a few white lilies and a carnation. "Miss Holt," he said, as he entered the drawing-room, "I've brought you and Edie a flower to wear at the Balfours' this evening. This is for you, Edie, with the pale pink; the dark will suit Miss Holt's hair best."

Edie looked at Ernest, and smiled significantly. "Why didn't you get us camelias, Harold?" she asked, with a faint touch of mischief in her tone.

"Camelias! My dear girl, what a question! I gave Miss Holt credit for better taste than liking camelias. Beastly things, as stiff and conventional as dahlias or sunflowers. You might just as well have a wax rose from an artificial flower-maker while you are about it."

Edie laughed and looked at Nellie. "See here," she said, taking up Ernest's bunches from the little specimen vases where she had put them to keep them fresh in water, "somebody else has thought of the flowers already."

Harold laughed, too, a little uneasily. "Aha," he said, "I see Ernest has been beforehand with me as usual. I'm always a day too late. It seems to me I'm the Esau of this duet, and Ernest's the Jacob. Well, Miss Holt, you must take the will for the deed; and after all, one will do for your dress and the other for your hair, won't they?"

"Harold," said his father, as they went upstairs together to dress for dinner, "Nellie Holt's a very nice girl, and I've reason to believe, you know I don't judge these matters without documentary evidence, I have reason to believe that she'll come into the greater part of old Stanley Holt's money. She's his favourite niece, and she benefits largely, as I happen to know, under his will. Verbum sap., my dear boy; she's a pretty girl, and has sweet manners. In my opinion, she'd make—"

"My dear Pater," Harold exclaimed, interrupting him, "for Heaven's sake don't say so. Pretty enough, I grant you; and no doubt old Stanley Holt's money would be a very nice thing in its way; but just seriously consider now, if you were a young man yourself, what on earth could you see in Nellie Holt to attract your love or admiration? Why, she shrinks and blushes every time she speaks to you. No, no, whenever I marry I should like to marry a girl of some presence and some character."

"Well, well," said his father, pausing a second at his bedroom door, "perhaps if she don't suit you, Harold, she'll suit Ernest."

"I should have thought, Pater, you knew us two better than that by this time."

"But, my dear Harold, you can't both marry the same woman!"

"No, we can't, Pater, but it's my opinion we shall both fall unanimously in love with her, at any rate, whenever we happen to see her."

II

The Balfours were very rich people, city people; "something in the stockbroking or bankruptcy line, I believe," Ernest Carnegie told Nelly Holt succinctly as they drove round in the brougham with his sister; and their dance was of the finest modern moneyed fashion. "Positively reeks with Peruvian bonds and Deferred Egyptians, doesn't it?" said Harold, as they went up the big open staircase and through the choice exotic flowers on the landing. "Old Balfour has so much money, they say, that if he tries his hardest he can't spend his day's income in the twenty-four hours. He had a good hard try at it once. Prince of Wales or somebody came to a concert for some sort of public purpose, hospital, or something, and old B. got the whole thing up on the tallest possible scale of expenditure. Spent a week in preparation. Had in dozens of powdered footmen; ordered palms and orange-trees in boxes from Nice; hung electric lights all over the drawing-room; offered Pattalini and Goldoni three times as much for their services as the total receipts for the charity were worth; and at the end of it all he called in a crack accountant to reckon up the cost of the entertainment. Well, he found, with all his efforts, he'd positively lived fifty pounds within his week's income. Extraordinary, isn't it?"

"Very extraordinary indeed," said Nellie, "if it's quite true, you know."

"You owe me the first waltz," Harold said, without noticing the reservation. "Don't forget it, please, Miss Holt."

"I say, Balfour," Ernest Carnegie observed to the son of the house, shortly after they had entered the ballroom, "who's that beautiful tall dark girl over there? No, not the pink one, that other girl behind her in the deep red satin."

"She? oh, she's nothing in particular," Harry Balfour answered carelessly (the girl in pink was worth eighty thousand, and her figure cast into the shade all her neighbours in Harry Balfour's arithmetical eyes). "Her name's Walters, Isabel Walters, daughter of a lawyer fellow, no offence meant to your profession, Carnegie. Let me see: you are the lawyer, aren't you? No knowing you two fellows apart, you know, especially when you've got white ties on."

"No, I'm not the lawyer fellow," Ernest answered quietly; "I'm the doctor fellow. But it doesn't at all matter; we're used to it. Would you mind introducing me to Miss Walters?"

"Certainly not. Come along. I believe she's a very nice girl in her way, you know, and dances capitally; but not exactly in our set, you see; not exactly in our set."

"I should have guessed as much to look at her," Ernest answered, with a faint undertone of sarcasm in his voice that was quite thrown away upon Harry Balfour. And he walked across the room after his host to ask Isabel Walters for the first waltz.

"Tall," he thought to himself as he looked at her: "dark, fine face, beautiful figure, large eyes; makes her own dresses; strange sort of person to meet at the Balfours' dances."

Isabel Walters danced admirably. Isabel Walters talked cleverly. Isabel Walters had a character and an individuality of her own. In five minutes she had told Ernest Carnegie that she was the Poor Relation, and in that quality she was asked once yearly to one of the Balfours' Less Distinguished dances. "This is a Less Distinguished," she said quickly; "but I suppose you go to the More Distinguished too?"

"On the contrary," Ernest answered, laughing; "though I didn't know the nature of the difference before, I've no doubt that I have to thank the fact of my being Less Distinguished myself for the pleasure of meeting you here this evening."

Isabel smiled quietly. "It's a family distinction only," she said. "Of course the Balfours wouldn't like the people they ask to know it. But we always notice the difference ourselves. My mother, you know, was the first Mrs. Balfour's half-sister. But in those days, I need hardly tell you, Mr. Balfour hadn't begun to do great things in Grand Trunk Preferences. Do you know anything about Grand Trunk Preferences?"

"Absolutely nothing," Ernest replied. "But, to come down to a more practical question: Are you engaged for the next Lancers?"

"A square dance. Oh, why a square dance? I hate square dances."

"I like them," said Ernest. "You can talk better."

"And yet you waltz capitally. As a rule, I notice the men who like square dances are the sticks who can't waltz without upsetting one. No, I'm not engaged for the next Lancers. Yes, with pleasure."

Ernest went off to claim little Nellie Holt from his brother.

"By Jove, Ernest," Harold said, as he met him again a little later in the evening, "that's a lovely girl you were dancing with just now. Who is she?"

"A Miss Walters," Ernest answered drily.

"I'll go and get introduced to her," Harold went on, looking at his brother with a searching glance. "She's the finest girl in the room, and I should like to dance with her."

"You think so?" said Ernest. And he turned away a little coldly to join a group of loungers by the doorway.

"This is not our Lancers yet, Mr. Carnegie," Isabel said, as Harold stalked up to her with her cousin by his side. "Ours is number seven."

"I'm not the same Mr. Carnegie," Harold said, smiling, "though I see I need no introduction now. I'm number seven's brother, and I've come to ask whether I may have the pleasure of dancing number six with you."

Isabel looked up at him in doubt. "You are joking, surely," she said. "You danced with me just now, the first waltz."

"You see my brother over by the door," Harold answered. "But we're quite accustomed to be taken for one another. Pray don't apologize; we're used to it."

Before the end of the evening Isabel Walters had danced three times with Ernest Carnegie, and twice with Harold. Before the end of the evening, too, Ernest and Harold were both at once deeply in love with her. She was not perhaps what most men would call a lovable girl; but she was handsome, clever, dashing, and decidedly original. Now, to both the Carnegies alike, there was no quality in a woman so admirable as individuality. Perhaps it was their own absolute identity of tastes and emotions that made them prize the possession of a distinct personality by others so highly; but in any case, there was no denying the fact that they were both head over ears in love with Isabel Walters.

"She's a splendid girl, Edie," said Harold, as he went down with his sister to the cab in which he was to take her home; "a splendid girl; just the sort of girl I should like to marry."

"Not so nice by half as Nellie Holt," said Edie simply. "But there, brothers never do marry the girls their sisters want them to."

"Very unreasonable of the brothers, no doubt," Harold replied, with a slight curl of his lip: "but possibly explicable upon the ground that a man prefers choosing a wife who'll suit himself to choosing one who'll suit his sisters."

"Mother," said Ernest, as he took her down to the brougham, with little Nellie Holt on his other arm, "that's a splendid girl, that Isabel Walters. I haven't met such a nice girl as that for a long time."

"I know a great many nicer," his mother answered, glancing half unconsciously towards Nellie, "but boys never do marry as their parents would wish them."

"They do not, mother dear," said Ernest quietly. "It's a strange fact, but I dare say it's partly dependent upon the general principle that a man is more anxious to live happily with his own wife than to provide a model daughter-in-law for his father and mother."

"Isabel," Mrs. Walters said to her daughter, as they took their seats in the cab that was waiting for them at the door, "what on earth did you mean by dancing five times in one evening with that young man with the light moustache? And who on earth is he, tell me?"

"He's two people, mamma," Isabel answered seriously; "and I danced three times with one of him, and twice with the other, I believe; at least so he told me. His name's Carnegie, and half of him's called Ernest and the other half Harold, though which I danced with which time I'm sure I can't tell you. He's a pair of twins, in fact, one a doctor and one a lawyer; and he talks just the same sort of talk in either case, and is an extremely nice young man altogether. I really like him immensely."

"Carnegie!" said Mrs. Walters, turning the name over carefully. "Two young Carnegies! How very remarkable! I remember somebody was speaking to me about them, and saying they were absolutely indistinguishable. Not sons of Mr. Carnegie, your uncle's solicitor, are they?"

"Yes; so Harry Balfour told me."

"Then, Isabel, they're very well off, I understand. I hope people won't think you danced five times in the evening with only one of them. They ought to wear some distinctive coat or something to prevent misapprehensions. Which do you like best, the lawyer or the doctor?"

"I like them both exactly the same, mamma. There isn't any difference at all between them, to like one of them better than the other for. They both seem very pleasant and very clever. And as I haven't yet discovered which is which, and didn't know from one time to another which I was dancing with, I can't possibly tell you which I prefer of two identicals. And as to coats, mamma, you know you couldn't expect one of them to wear a grey tweed suit in a ballroom, just to show he isn't the other one."

In the passage at the Carnegies', Ernest and Harold stopped one moment, candle in hand, to compare notes with one another before turning into their bedrooms. There was an odd constraint about their manner to each other that they had never felt before during their twenty-three years of life together.

"Well?" said Ernest, inquiringly, looking in a hesitating way at his brother.

"Well?" Harold echoed, in the same tone.

"What did you think of it all, Harold?"

"I think, Ernest, I shall propose to Miss Walters."

There was a moment's silence, and a black look gathered slowly on Ernest Carnegie's brow. Then he said very deliberately, "You are in a great hurry coming to conclusions, Harold. You've seen very little of her yet; and remember, it was I who first discovered her!"

Harold glanced at him angrily and half contemptuously.

"You discovered her first!" he said. "Yes, and you are always beforehand with me; but you shall not be beforehand with me this time. I shall propose to her at once, to prevent your anticipating me. So now you know my intentions plainly, and you can govern yourself accordingly."

Ernest looked back at him with a long look from head to foot.

"It is war then," he said, "Harold; war, you will have it? We are rivals?"

"Yes, rivals," Harold answered; "and war to the knife if so you wish it."

"War?"

"War!"

"Good night, Harold."

"Good night, Ernest."

And they turned in to their bedrooms, in anger with one another, for the first time since they had quarrelled in boyish fashion over tops and marbles years ago together.

III

That night the two Carnegies slept very little. They were both in love, very seriously in love; and anybody who has ever been in the same condition must have noticed that the symptoms, which may have been very moderate or undecided during the course of the evening, become rapidly more pronounced and violent as you lie awake in the solitude of your chamber through the night watches. But more than that, they had both begun to feel simultaneously the stab of jealousy. Each of them had been very much taken indeed by Isabel Walters; still, if they had seen no chance of a rival looming in the distance, they might have been content to wait a little, to see a little more of her, to make quite sure of their own affection before plunging headlong into a declaration. After all, it's very absurd to ask a girl to be your companion for life on the strength of an acquaintanceship which has extended over the time occupied by three dances in a single evening. But then, thought each, there was the chance of Ernest's proposing to her, or of Harold's proposing to her, before I do. That idea made precipitancy positively imperative; and by the next morning each of the young men had fully made up his mind to take the first opportunity of asking Isabella Walters to be his wife.

Breakfast passed off very silently, neither of the twins speaking much to one another; but nobody noticed their reticence much; for the morning after the occasional orgy or dance is apt to prove a very limp affair indeed in professional homes, where dances are not of nightly occurrence. After breakfast, Harold went off quickly to the office, and Ernest, having bespoken a holiday at the hospital, joined his sister and Nellie Holt in the library.

"Do you know, Ernest," Edie said to him, mindful of her last night's conversation with her other brother, "I really believe Harold has fallen desperately in love at first sight with that tall Miss Walters."

"I can easily believe it," Ernest answered testily; "she's very handsome and very clever."

Edie raised her eyebrows a little. "But it's awfully foolish, Ernest, to fall in love blindfold in that way, isn't it now?" she said, with a searching look at her brother. "He can't possibly know what sort of a girl she really is from half an hour's conversation in a ballroom."

"For my part, I don't at all agree with you, Edie," said Ernest, in his coldest manner. "I don't believe there's any right way of falling in love except at first sight. If a girl is going to please you, she ought to please you instantaneously and instinctively; at least, so I think. It isn't a thing to be thought about and reasoned about, but a thing to be felt and apprehended intuitively. I couldn't reason myself into marrying a girl, and what's more, I don't want to."

He sat down to the table, took out a sheet or two of initialed notepaper, and began writing a couple of letters. One of them, which he marked "Private" in the corner, ran as follows:—

"MY DEAR MISS WALTERS,

"Perhaps you will think it very odd of me to venture upon writing to you on the strength of such a very brief and casual acquaintance as that begun last night; but I have a particular reason for doing so, which I think I can justify to you when I see you. You mentioned to me that you were asked to the Montagus' steam-launch expedition up the river from Surbiton to-morrow; but I understood you to say you did not intend to accept the invitation. I write now to beg of you to be there, as I am going, and I am particularly anxious to meet you and have a little conversation with you on a subject of importance. I know you are not a very conventional person, and therefore I think you will excuse me for asking this favour of you. Please don't take the trouble to write in reply; but answer by going to the Montagus', and I shall then be able to explain this very queer letter. In haste,

"Yours very truly, "ERNEST CARNEGIE."

He read this note two or three times over to himself, looking not very well satisfied with its contents; and then at last, with the air of a man who determines to plunge and stake all upon a single venture, he folded it up and put it in its envelope. "It'll mystify her a little, no doubt," he thought to himself; "and being a woman, she'll be naturally anxious to unravel the mystery. But of course she'll know I mean to make her an offer, and perhaps she'll think me a perfect idiot for not doing it outright, instead of beating about the bush in this incomprehensible fashion. However, it's too cold-blooded, proposing to a girl on paper; I very much prefer the vivâ voce system. It's only till to-morrow; and I doubt if Harold will manage to be beforehand with me in that time. He'll be deep in business all morning, and have no leisure to think about her. Anyhow, all's fair in love and war; he said it should be war; and I'll try to steal a march upon him, for all his lawyer's quibbles and quiddits."

He took another sheet from his blotting-book, and wrote a second note, much more rapidly than the first one. It ran after this fashion—

"DEAR MRS. MONTAGU,

"Will you think it very rude of me if I ask you to let me be one of your party on your expedition up the river to-morrow? I heard of it from your son Algernon last night at the Balfours', and I happen to be very anxious to meet one of the ladies you have invited. Now, I know you're kindness itself to all your young friends in all these little matters, and I'm sure you won't be angry with me for so coolly inviting myself. If I hadn't felt perfect confidence in your invariable goodness, I wouldn't have ventured to do so. Please don't answer unless you've no room for me, but expect me to turn up at half-past two.

"Yours very sincerely, "ERNEST CARNEGIE.

"P.S.—We might call at Lady Portlebury's lawn, and look over the conservatories."

"Now, that's bold, but judicious," Ernest said to himself, admiringly, as he held the letter at arm's-length, after blotting it. "She might have been angry at my inviting myself, though I don't think she would be; but I'm sure she'll be only too delighted if I offer to take her guests over Aunt Portlebury's conservatories. The postscript's a stroke of genius. What a fuss these people will make, even over the widow of a stupid old cavalry officer, because her husband happens to have been knighted. It's all the better that she's a widow, indeed. The delicious vagueness of the title 'Lady' is certainly one of its chief recommendations. Sir Antony being out of the way, Mrs. Montagu's guests can't really tell but that poor dear old Aunt Portlebury may be a real live Countess." And he folded his second letter up with the full satisfaction of an approving conscience.

When Isabel Walters received Ernest Carnegie's mysterious note, she was certainly mystified by it as he had expected, and also not a little gratified. He meant to propose to her, that was certain; and there was never a woman in the whole world who was not flattered by a handsome young man's marked attentions. It was a very queer letter, no doubt; but it had been written skilfully enough to suit the particular personality of Isabel Walters: for Ernest Carnegie was a keen judge of character, and he flattered himself that he knew how to adapt his correspondence to the particular temperament of the persons he happened to be addressing. And though Isabel had no very distinct idea of what the two Carnegies were severally like (it could hardly have been much more distinct if she had known them both intimately), she felt they were two very good-looking, agreeable young men, and she was not particularly averse to the attentions of either. After all, upon what straws we all usually hang our love-making! We see one another once or twice under exceptionally deceptive circumstances; we are struck at first sight with something that attracts us on either side; we find the attraction is mutual; we flounder at once into a declaration of undying attachment; we get married, and on the whole we generally find we were right after all, in spite of our precipitancy, and we live happily ever afterwards. So it was not really very surprising that Isabel Walters, getting such a note from one of the two handsome young Mr. Carnegies, should have been in some doubt which of the two identicals it actually was, and yet should have felt indefinitely pleased and flattered at the implied attention. Which was Ernest and which Harold could only mean to her, when she came to think on it, which was the one she danced with first last night, and which the one she danced with second. She decided in her own mind that it would be better for her to go to the Montagus' picnic to-morrow, but to say nothing about it to her mother. "Mamma wouldn't understand the letter," she said to herself complacently; "she's so conventional; and when I come back to-morrow I can tell her one of the young Carnegies was there, and that he proposed to me. She need never know there was any appointment."

IV

At six o'clock, Harold Carnegie returned from the office. He, too, had been thinking all day of Isabel Walters, and the moment he got home he went into the library to write a short note to her, before Ernest had, as usual, forestalled him. As he did so he happened to see a few words dimly transferred to the paper in the blotting-book. They were in Ernest's handwriting, and he was quite sure the four first words read, "My dear Miss Walters." Then Ernest had already been beforehand with him, after all! But not by a fortnight: that was one good point; not this time by a fortnight! He would be even with him yet; he would catch up this anticipatory twin-brother of his, by force or fraud, rather than let him steal away Isabel Walters from him once and for ever. "All's fair in love and war," he muttered to himself, taking up the blotting-book carefully, and tearing out the tell-tale leaf in a furtive fashion. "Thank Heaven, Ernest writes a thick black hand, the same as I do; and I shall probably be able to read it by holding it up to the light." In his own soul Harold Carnegie loathed himself for such an act of petty meanness; but he did it; with love and jealousy goading him on, and the fear of his own twin-brother stinging him madly, he did it; remorsefully and shamefacedly, but still did it.

He took the page up to his own bedroom, and held it up to the window-pane. Blurred and indistinct, the words nevertheless came out legibly in patches here and there, so that with a little patient deciphering Harold could spell out the sense of both letters, though they crossed one another obliquely at a slight angle. "Very brief and casual acquaintance ... Montagus' steam-launch expedition up the river from Surbiton to-morrow ... am going and am particularly anxious to meet you ... this favour of you...." "So that's his plan, is it?" Harold said to himself. "Softly, softly, Mr. Ernest, I think I can checkmate you! What's this in the one to Mrs. Montagu? 'Expect me to turn up at half-past two.' Aha, I thought so! Checkmate, Mr. Ernest, checkmate: a scholar's mate for you! He'll be at the hospital till half-past one; then he'll take the train to Clapham Junction, expecting to catch the South-Western at 2.10. But to-morrow's the first of the month; the new time-tables come into force; I've got one and looked it out already. The South-Western now leaves at 2.4, three minutes before Mr. Ernest's train arrives at Clapham Junction. I have him now, I have him now, depend upon it. I'll go down instead of him. I'll get the party under way at once. I'll monopolize Isabel, pretty Isabel. I'll find my opportunity at Aunt Portlebury's, and Ernest won't get down to Surbiton till the 2.50 train. Then he'll find his bird flown already. Aha! that'll make him angry. Checkmate, my young friend, checkmate. You said it should be war, and war you shall have it. I thank thee, friend, for teaching me that word. Rivals now, you said; yes, rivals. 'Dolus an virtus, quis in hoste requirat?' Why, that comes out of the passage about Androgeos! An omen, a good omen. There's nothing like war for quickening the intelligence. I haven't looked at a Virgil since I was in the sixth form; and yet the line comes back to me now, after five years, as pat as the Catechism."

Chuckling to himself at the fraud to stifle conscience (for he had a conscience), Harold Carnegie dressed hastily for dinner, and went down quickly in a state of feverish excitement. Dinner passed off grimly enough. He knew Ernest had written to Isabel; and Ernest guessed from the other's excited, triumphant manner (though he tried hard to dissemble the note of triumph in it) that Harold must have written too—perhaps forestalling him by a direct proposal. In a dim way Mrs. Carnegie guessed vaguely that some coldness had arisen between her two boys, the first time for many years; and so she held her peace for the most part, or talked in asides to Nellie Holt and her daughter. The conversation was therefore chiefly delegated to Mr. Carnegie himself, who discoursed with much animation about the iniquitous nature of the new act for reducing costs in actions for the recovery of small debts, a subject calculated to arouse the keenest interest in the minds of Nellie and Edie.

Next morning, Harold Carnegie started for the office with prospective victory elate in his very step, and yet with the consciousness of his own mean action grinding him down to the pavement as he walked along it. What a dirty, petty, dishonourable subterfuge! and still he would go through with it. What a self-degrading bit of treachery! and yet he would carry it out. "Pater," he said, as he walked along, "I mean to take a holiday this afternoon. I'm going to the Montagus' water-party."

"Very inconvenient, Harold, my boy; 'Wilkins versus the Great Northern Railway Company' coming on for hearing; and, besides, Ernest's going there too. They won't want a pair of you, will they?"

"Can't help it, Pater," Harold answered. "I have particular business at Surbiton, much more important to me than 'Wilkins versus the Great Northern Railway Company.'"

His father looked at him keenly. "Ha!" he said, "a lady in the case, is there? Very well, my boy, if you must you must, and that's the end of it. A young man in love never does make an efficient lawyer. Get it over quickly, pray; get it over quickly, that's all I beg of you."

"I shall get it over, I promise you," Harold answered, "this very afternoon."

The father whistled. "Whew," he said, "that's sharp work, too, Harold, isn't it? You haven't even told me her name yet. This is really very sudden." But as Harold volunteered no further information, Mr. Carnegie, who was a shrewd man of the world, held it good policy to ask him nothing more about it for the present; and so they walked on the rest of the way to the father's office in unbroken silence.

At one o'clock, Harold shut up his desk at the office and ran down to Surbiton. At Clapham Junction he kept a sharp look-out for Ernest, but Ernest was not there. Clearly, as Harold anticipated, he hadn't learnt the alteration in the time-tables, and wouldn't reach Clapham Junction till the train for Surbiton had started.

At Surbiton, Harold pushed on arrangements as quickly as possible, and managed to get the party off before Ernest arrived upon the scene. Mrs. Montagu, seeing "one of the young Carnegies" duly to hand, and never having attempted to discriminate between them in any way, was perfectly happy at the prospect of getting landed at Lady Portlebury's without any minute investigation of the intricate question of Christian names. The Montagus were nouveaux riches in the very act of pushing themselves into fashionable society; and a chance of invading the Portlebury lawn was extremely welcome to them upon any terms whatsoever.

Isabel Walters was looking charming. A light morning dress became her even better than the dark red satin of the night before last; and she smiled at Harold with the smile of a mutual confidence when she took his hand, in a way that made his heart throb fast within him. From that moment forward, he forgot Ernest and the unworthy trick he was playing, and thought wholly and solely of Isabel Walters.

What a handsome young man he was, really, and how cleverly and brilliantly he talked all the way up to Portlebury Lodge! Everybody listened to him; he was the life and soul of the party. Isabel felt more flattered than ever at his marked attention. He was the doctor, wasn't he? No, the lawyer. Well, really, how impossible it was to distinguish and remember them. And so well connected, too. If he were to propose to her, now, she could afford to be so condescending to Amy Balfour.

At Lady Portlebury's lawn the steam-launch halted, and Harold managed to get Isabel alone among the walks, while his aunt escorted the main body of visitors thus thrust upon her hands over the conservatories. Eager and hasty, now, he lost no time in making the best of the situation.

"I guessed as much, of course, from your letter, Mr. Carnegie," Isabel said, playing with her fan with downcast eyes, as he pressed his offer upon her; "and I really didn't know whether it was right of me to come here without showing it to mamma and asking her advice about it. But I'm quite sure I oughtn't to give you an answer at once, because I've seen so very little of you. Let us leave the question open for a little. It's asking so much to ask one for a definite reply on such a very short acquaintance."

"No, no, Miss Walters," Harold said quickly. "For Heaven's sake, give me an answer now, I beg of you, I implore you. I must have an answer at once, immediately. If you can't love me at first sight, for my own sake, as I loved you the moment I saw you, you can never, never, never love me! Doubt and hesitation are impossible in true love. Now, or refuse me forever! Surely you must know in your own heart whether you can love me or not; if your heart tells you that you can, then trust it—trust it—don't argue and reason with it, but say at once you will make me happy forever."

"Mr. Carnegie," Isabel said, lifting her eyes for a moment, "I do think, perhaps, I don't know, but perhaps, after a little while, I could love you. I like you very much; won't that do for the present? Why are you in such a hurry for an answer? Why can't you give me a week or two to decide in?"

"Because," said Harold, desperately, "if I give you a week my brother will ask you, and perhaps you will marry him instead of me. He's always before me in everything, and I'm afraid he'll be before me in this. Say you'll have me, Miss Walters, oh, do say you'll have me, and save me from the misery of a week's suspense!"

"But, Mr. Carnegie, how can I say anything when I haven't yet made up my own mind about it? Why, I hardly know you yet from your brother."

"Ah, that's just it," Harold cried, in a voice of positive pain. "You won't find any difference at all between us, if you come to know us; and then perhaps you'll be induced to marry my brother. But you know this much already, that here am I, begging and pleading before you this very minute, and surely you won't send me away with my prayer unanswered!"

There was such a look of genuine anguish and passion in his face that Isabel Walters, already strongly prepossessed in his favour, could resist no longer. She bent her head a little, and whispered very softly, "I will promise, Mr. Carnegie; I will promise."

Harold seized her hand eagerly, and covered it with kisses. "Isabel," he cried in a fever of joy, "you have promised. You are mine, mine, mine. You are mine, now and forever!"

Isabel bowed her head, and felt a tear standing dimly in her eye, though she brushed it away hastily. "Yes," she said gently; "I will be yours. I think—I think—I feel sure I can love you."

Harold took her ungloved hand tenderly in his, and drew a ring off her finger. "Before I give you mine," he said, "you will let me take this one? I want it for a keepsake and a memorial."

Isabel whispered, "Yes."

Harold drew another ring from his pocket and slipped it softly on her third finger. Isabel saw by the glitter that there was a diamond in it. Harold had bought it the day before for that very purpose. Then he took from a small box a plain gold locket, with the letter H raised on it. "I want you to wear this," he said, "as a keepsake for me."

"But why H?" Isabel asked him, looking a little puzzled. "Your name's Ernest, isn't it?"

Harold smiled as well as he was able. "How absurd it is!" he said, with an effort at gaiety. "This ridiculous similarity pursues us everywhere. No, my name's Harold."

Isabel stood for a moment surprised and hesitating. She really hardly knew for the second which brother she ought to consider herself engaged to. "Then it wasn't you who wrote to me?" she said, with a tone of some surprise and a little start of astonishment.

"No, I certainly didn't write to you; but I came here to-day expecting to see you, and meaning to ask you to be my wife. I learned from my brother ("there can be no falsehood in putting it that way," he thought vainly to himself) that you were to be here; and I determined to seize the opportunity. Ernest meant to have come, too, but I believe he must have lost the train at Clapham Junction." That was all literally true, and yet it sounded simple and plausible enough.

Isabel looked at him with a puzzled look, and felt almost compelled to laugh, the situation was so supremely ridiculous. It took a moment to think it all out rationally. Yet, after all, though the letter came from the other brother, Ernest, it was this particular brother, Harold, she had been talking to and admiring all the day; it was this particular brother, Harold, who had gained her consent, and whom she had promised to love and to marry. And at that moment it would have been doing Isabel

Walters an injustice not to admit that in her own soul she did then and there really love Harold Carnegie.

"Harold," she said slowly, as she took the locket and hung it round her neck, "Harold. Yes, now I know. Then, Harold Carnegie, I shall take your locket and wear it always as a keepsake from you." And she looked up at him with a smile in which there was something more than mere passing coquettish fancy. You see, he was really terribly in earnest; and the very fact that he should have been so anxious to anticipate his brother, and should have anticipated him successfully, made her woman's heart go forth toward him instinctively. As Harold himself said, he was there bodily present before her; while Ernest, the writer of the mysterious letter, was nothing more to her in reality than a name and a shadow. Harold had asked her, and won her; and she was ready to love and cleave to Harold from that day forth for that very reason. What woman of them all has a better reason to give in the last resort for the faith that is in her?

V

Meanwhile, at Clapham Junction, Ernest Carnegie had arrived three minutes too late for the Surbiton train, and had been forced to wait for the 2.40. Of that he thought little: they would wait for him, he knew, if they waited an hour; for Mrs. Montagu would not for worlds have missed the chance of showing her guests round Lady Portlebury's gardens. So he settled himself down comfortably in the snug corner of his first-class carriage, and ran down by the later train in perfect confidence that he would find the steam launch waiting.

"No, sir, they've gone up the river in the launch, sir," said the man who opened the door for him; "and, I beg pardon, sir, but I thought you were one of the party."

In a moment Ernest's fancy, quickened by his jealousy, jumped instinctively at the true meaning of the man's mistake. "What," he said, "was there a gentleman very like me, in a grey coat and straw hat, same ribbon as this one?"

"Yes, sir. Exactly, sir. Well, indeed, I should have said it was yourself, sir; but I suppose it was the other Mr. Carnegie."

"It was!" Ernest answered between his clenched teeth, almost inarticulate with anger. "It was he. Not a doubt of it. Harold! I see it all. The treachery, the base treachery! How long have they been gone, I say? How long, eh?"

"About half an hour, sir; they went up towards Henley, sir."

Ernest Carnegie turned aside, reeling with wrath and indignation. That his brother, his own familiar twin-brother, should have played him this abominable, disgraceful trick! The meanness of it! The deceit of it! The petty spying and letter-opening of it! For somehow or other, inconceivable how, Harold must have opened his brother's letters. And then, quick as lightning, for those two brains jumped together, the thought of the blotting-book flashed across Ernest's mind. Why, he had noticed this morning that a page was gone out of it. He must have read the letters. And then the trains! Harold always got a time-table on the first of each month, with his cursed methodical lawyer ways. And he had never told him about the change of service. The dirty low trick! The mean trick! Even to think of it made Ernest Carnegie sick at heart and bitterly indignant.

In a minute he saw it all and thought it all out. Why did he, how did he? Why, he knew as clearly as if he could read Harold's thoughts, exactly how the whole vile plot had first risen upon him, and worked itself out within his traitorous brain. How? Ah, how? That was the bitterest, the most horrible, the deadliest part of it all. Ernest Carnegie knew, because he felt in his own inmost soul that, had he been put in the same circumstances, he would himself have done exactly as Harold had done.

Yes, exactly in every respect. Harold must have seen the words in the blotting-book, "My dear Miss Walters"—Ernest remembered how thickly and blackly he had written, must have seen those words; and in their present condition, either of the twins, jealous, angry, suspicious, half driven by envy of one another out of their moral senses, would have torn out the page then and there and read it all. He, too, would have kept silence about the train; he would have gone down to Surbiton; he would have proposed to Isabel Walters; he would have done in everything exactly as he knew Harold must have done it; but that did not make his anger and loathing for his brother any the weaker. On the contrary, it only made them all the more terrible. His consciousness of his own equal potential meanness roused his rage against Harold to a white heat. He would have done the same himself, no doubt; yes; but Harold, the mean, successful, actually accomplishing villain—Harold had really gone down and done it all in positive fact and reality.

Flushing scarlet and blanching white alternately with the fierceness of his anger, Ernest Carnegie turned down, all on fire, to the river's edge. Should he take a boat and row up after them to prevent the supplanter at least from proposing to Isabel unopposed? That would at any rate give him something to do, muscular work for his arms, if nothing else, to counteract the fire within him; but on second thoughts, no, it would be quite useless. The steam launch had had a good start of him, and no oarsman could catch up with it now by any possibility. So he walked about up and down near the river, chafing in soul and nursing his wrath against Harold for three long weary hours. And all that time Harold, false-hearted, fair-spoken, mean-spirited Harold, was enjoying himself and playing the gallant to Isabel Walters!

Minute by minute the hours wore away, and with every minute Ernest's indignation grew deeper and deeper. At last he heard the snort of the steam-launch ploughing its way lustily down the river, and he stood on the bank waiting for the guilty Harold to disembark.

As Harold stepped from the launch, and gave his hand to Isabel, he saw the white and bloodless face of his brother looking up at him contemptuously and coldly from beside the landing. Harold passed ashore and close by him, but Ernest never spoke a word. He only looked a moment at Isabel, and said to her with enforced calmness, "You got my letter, Miss Walters?"

Isabel, hardly comprehending the real solemnity of the occasion, answered with a light smile, "I did, Mr. Carnegie, but you didn't keep your appointment. Your brother came, and he has been beforehand with you." And she touched his hand lightly and went on to join her hostess.

Still Ernest Carnegie said nothing, but walked on, as black as night, beside his brother. Neither spoke a word; but after the shaking of hands and farewells were over, both turned together to the railway station. The carriage was crowded, and so Ernest still held his tongue.

At last, when they reached home and stood in the passage together, Ernest looked at his brother with a look of withering scorn, and, livid with anger, found his voice at last.

"Harold Carnegie," he said, in a low husky tone, "you are a mean intercepter of other men's letters; a sneaking supplanter of other men's appointments; a cur and a traitor whom I don't wish any longer to associate with. I know what you have done, and I know how you have done it. You have kept my engagement with Isabel Walters by reading the impression of my notes on the blotting-book. You are unfit for a gentleman to speak to, and I cast you off, now and for ever."

Harold looked at him defiantly, but said never a word.

"Harold Carnegie," Ernest said again, "I could hardly believe your treachery until it was forced upon me. This is the last time I shall ever speak to you."

Harold looked at him again, this time perhaps with a tinge of remorse in his expression, and said nothing but, "Oh, Ernest."

Ernest made a gesture with his hands as though he would repel him. "Don't come near me," he said; "Harold Carnegie, don't touch me! Don't call me by my name! I will have nothing more to say or do with you."

Harold turned away in dead silence, and went to his own room, trembling with conscious humiliation and self-reproach. But he did not attempt to make the only atonement in his power by giving up Isabel Walters. That would have been too much for human nature.

VI

When Harold Carnegie was finally married to Isabel Walters, Ernest stopped away from the wedding, and would have nothing whatever to say either to bride or bridegroom. He would leave his unnatural brother, he said, solely and entirely to the punishment of his own guilty conscience.

Still, he couldn't rest quiet in his father's house after Harold was gone, so he took himself small rooms near the hospital, and there he lived his lonely life entirely by himself, a solitary man, brooding miserably over his own wrongs and Harold's treachery. There was only one single woman in the world, he said, with whom he could ever have been really happy, Isabel Walters: and Harold had stolen Isabel Walters away from him by the basest treason. Once he could have loved Isabel, and her only; now, because she was Harold's wife, he bitterly hated her. Yes, hated her! With a deadly hatred he hated both of them.

Months went by slowly for Ernest Carnegie, in the dull drudgery of his hopeless professional life, for he cared nothing now for ambition or advancement; he lived wholly in the past, nursing his wrath, and devouring his own soul in angry regretfulness. Months went by, and at last Harold's wife gave birth to a baby, a boy, the exact image of his father and his uncle. Harold looked at the child in the nurse's arms, and said remorsefully, "We will call him Ernest. It is all we can do now, Isabel. We will call him Ernest, after my dear lost brother." So they called him Ernest, in the faint hope that his uncle's heart might relent a little; and Harold wrote a letter full of deep and bitter penitence to his brother, piteously begging his forgiveness for the grievous wrong he had wickedly and deliberately done him. But Ernest still nursed his righteous wrath silently in his own bosom, and tore up the letter into a thousand fragments, unanswered.

When the baby was five months old, Edie Carnegie came round hurriedly one morning to Ernest's lodgings near the hospital. "Ernest, Ernest," she cried, running up the stairs in great haste, "we want you to come round and see Harold. We're afraid he's very ill. Don't say you won't come and see him!"

Ernest Carnegie listened and smiled grimly. "Very ill," he muttered, with a dreadful gleam in his eyes. "Very ill, is he? and I have had nothing the matter with me! How curious! Very ill! I ought to have had the same illness a fortnight ago. Ha, ha! The cycle is broken! The clocks have ceased to strike together! His marriage has altered the run of his constitution, mine remains the same steady striker as ever. I thought it would! I thought it would! Perhaps he'll die, now, the mean, miserable traitor!"

Edie Carnegie looked at him in undisguised horror. "Oh, Ernest," she cried, with the utmost dismay; "your own brother! Your own brother! Surely you'll come and see him, and tell us what's the matter."

"Yes, I'll come and see him," Ernest answered, unmoved, taking up his hat. "I'll come and see him, and find out what's the matter." But there was an awful air of malicious triumph in his tone, which perfectly horrified his trembling sister.

When Ernest reached his brother's house, he went at once to Harold's bedside, and without a word of introduction or recognition he began inquiring into the nature of his symptoms, exactly as he would have done with any unknown and ordinary patient. Harold told him them all, simply and straightforwardly, without any more preface than he would have used with any other doctor. When Ernest had finished his diagnosis, he leaned back carelessly in his easy chair, folded his arms sternly, and said in a perfectly cold, clear, remorseless voice, "Ah, I thought so; yes, yes, I thought so. It's a serious functional disorder of the heart; and there's very little hope indeed that you'll ever recover from it. No hope at all, I may say; no hope at all, I'm certain. The thing has been creeping upon you, creeping upon you, evidently, for a year past, and it has gone too far now to leave the faintest hope of ultimate recovery."

Isabel burst into tears at the words, calmly spoken as though they were perfectly indifferent to both speaker and hearers; but Harold only rose up fiercely in the bed, and cried in a tone of the most imploring agony, "Oh, Ernest, Ernest, if I must die, for Heaven's sake, before I die, say you forgive me, do say, do say you forgive me. Oh, Ernest, dear Ernest, dear brother Ernest, for the sake of our long, happy friendship, for the sake of the days when we loved one another with a love passing the love of women, do, do say you will at last forgive me."

Ernest rose and fumbled nervously for a second with the edge of his hat. "Harold Carnegie," he said at last, in a voice trembling with excitement, "I can never forgive you. You acted a mean, dirty part, and I can never forgive you. Heaven may, perhaps it will; but as for me, I can never, never, never forgive you!"

Harold fell back feebly and wearily upon the pillows. "Ernest, Ernest," he cried, gasping, "you might forgive me! you ought to forgive me! you must forgive me! and I'll tell you why. I didn't want to say it, but now you force me. I know it as well as if I'd seen you do it. In my place, I know to a certainty, Ernest, you'd have done exactly as I did. Ernest Carnegie, you can't look me straight in the face and tell me that you wouldn't have acted exactly as I did."

That terrible unspoken truth, long known, but never confessed, even to himself, struck like a knife on Ernest's heart. He raised his hat blindly, and walked with unsteady steps out of the sick-room. At that moment, his own conscience smote him with awful vividness. Looking into the inmost recesses of his angry heart, he felt with a shudder that Harold had spoken the simple truth, and he dared not lie by contradicting him. In Harold's place he would have done exactly as Harold did! And that was just what made his deathless anger burn all the more fiercely and fervidly against his brother!

Groping his way down the stairs alone in a stunned and dazzled fashion, Ernest Carnegie went home in his agony to his lonely lodgings, and sat there solitary with his own tempestuous thoughts for the next eight-and-forty hours. He did not undress or lie down to sleep, though he dozed a little at times uneasily in his big arm-chair; he did not eat or drink much; he merely paced up and down his room feverishly, and sent his boy round at intervals of an hour or two to know how the doctor thought Mr. Harold Carnegie was getting on. The boy returned every time with uniformly worse and worse reports. Ernest rubbed his hands in horrid exultation: "Ah," he said to himself, eagerly, "he will die! he will die! he will pay the penalty of his dirty treachery! He has brought it all upon himself by marrying that wicked woman! He deserves it every bit for his mean conduct."

On the third morning, Edie came round again, this time with her mother. Both had tears in their eyes, and they implored Ernest with sobs and entreaties to come round and see Harold once more before he died. Harold was raving and crying for him in his weakness and delirium. But Ernest was like adamant. He would not go to see him, he said, not if they went down bodily on their knees before him.

At midday, the boy went again, and stayed a little longer than usual. When he returned, he brought back word that Mr. Harold Carnegie had died just as the clock was striking the hour. Ernest listened with a look of terror and dismay, and then broke down into a terrible fit of sobbing and weeping. When Edie came round a little later to tell him that all was over, she found him crying like a child in his own easy chair, and muttering to himself in a broken fashion how dearly he and Harold had loved one another years ago, when they were both happy children together.

Edie took him round to his brother's house, and there, over the deaf and blind face that lay cold upon the pillows, he cried the cry that he would not cry over his living, imploring brother. "Oh, Harold, Harold," he groaned in his broken agony, "I forgive you, I forgive you. I too sinned as you did. What you would do, I would do. It was bound up in both our natures. In your place I would have done as you did. But now the curse of Cain is upon me! A worse curse than Cain's is upon me! I have more than killed my brother!"

For a day or two Ernest went back, heart-broken, to his father's house, and slept once more in the old room where he used to sleep so long, next door to Harold's. At the end of three days, he woke once from one of his short snatches of sleep with a strange fluttering feeling in his left side. He knew in a moment what it was. It was the same disease that Harold had died of.

"Thank Heaven!" he said to himself eagerly, "thank Heaven, thank Heaven for that! Then I didn't wholly kill him! His blood isn't all upon my poor unhappy head. After all, his marriage didn't quite upset the harmony of the two clocks; it only made the slower one catch up for a while and pass the faster. I'm a fortnight later in striking than Harold this time; that's all. In three days more the clock will run down, and I shall die as he did."

And, true to time, in three days more, as the clock struck twelve, Ernest Carnegie died as his brother Harold had done before him, with the agonized cry for forgiveness trembling on his fevered lips, who knows whether answered or unanswered?

OLGA DAVIDOFF'S HUSBAND

I

Tobolsk, though a Siberian metropolis, is really a very pleasant place to pass a winter in. Like the western American cities, where everybody has made his money easily and spends it easily, it positively bubbles over with bad champagne, cheap culture, advanced thought, French romances, and all the other most recent products of human industry and ingenuity. Everybody eats pâté de foie gras, quotes Hartmann and Herbert Spencer, uses electric bells, believes in woman's rights, possesses profound views about the future of Asia, and had a grandfather who was a savage Samoyede or an ignorant Buriat. Society is extremely cultivated, and if you scratch it ever so little, you see the Tartar. Nevertheless, it considers itself the only really polite and enlightened community on the whole face of this evolving terrestrial planet.

The Davidoffs, however, who belonged to the most advanced section of mercantile society in all Tobolsk, were not originally Siberians, or even Russians, by birth or nationality. Old Mr. Davidoff, the grandfather, who founded the fortunes of the family in St. Petersburg, was a Welsh Davids; and he had altered his name by the timely addition of a Slavonic suffix in order to conciliate the national susceptibilities of Orthodox Russia. His son, Dimitri, whom for the same reason he had christened in honour of a Russian saint, removed the Russian branch of the house to Tobolsk (they were in the Siberian fur-trade), and there marrying a German lady of the name of Freytag, had one daughter and heiress, Olga Davidoff, the acknowledged belle of Tobolskan society. It was generally understood in Tobolsk that the Davidoffs were descended from Welsh princes (as may very likely have been the case, though one would really like to know what has become of all the descendants of Welsh subjects), if indeed they were not even remotely connected with the Prince of Wales himself in person.

The winter of 1873 (as everybody will remember) was a very cold one throughout Siberia. The rivers froze unusually early, and troikas had entirely superseded torosses on all the roads as early as the very beginning of October. Still, Tobolsk was exceedingly gay for all that; in the warm houses of the great merchants, with their tropical plants kept at summer heat by stoves and flues all the year round, nobody noticed the exceptional rigour of that severe season. Balls and dances followed one another in quick succession, and Olga Davidoff, just twenty, enjoyed herself as she had never before done in all her lifetime. It was such a change to come to the concentrated gaieties and delights of Tobolsk after six years of old Miss Waterlow's Establishment for Young Ladies, at The Laurels, Clapham.

That winter, for the first time, Baron Niaz, the Buriat, came to Tobolsk.

Exquisitely polished in manners, and very handsome in face and bearing, there was nothing of the Tartar anywhere visible about Baron Niaz. He had been brought up in Paris, at a fashionable Lycée, and he spoke French with perfect fluency, as well as with some native sparkle and genuine cleverness. His taste in music was unimpeachable: even Madame Davidoff, née Freytag, candidly admitted that his performances upon the violin were singularly brilliant, profound, and appreciative. Moreover, though a Buriat chief, he was a most undoubted nobleman: at the Governor's parties he took rank, by patent of the Emperor Nicholas, as a real Russian baron of the first water. To be sure, he was nominally a Tartar; but what of that? His mother and his grandmother, he declared, had both been Russian ladies; and you had only to look at him to see that there was scarcely a drop of Tartar blood still remaining anywhere in him. If the half-caste negro is a brown mulatto, the quarter-caste a light quadroon, and the next remove a practically white octoroon, surely Baron Niaz, in spite of his remote Buriat great-grandfathers, might well pass for an ordinary everyday civilized Russian.

Olga Davidoff was fairly fascinated by the accomplished young baron. She met him everywhere, and he paid her always the most marked and flattering attention. He was a Buriat, to be sure: but at

Tobolsk, you know—. Well, one mustn't be too particular about these little questions of origin in an Asiatic city.

It was at the Governor's dance, just before Christmas, that the Baron got his first good chance of talking with her for ten minutes alone among the fan palms and yuccas in the big conservatory. There was a seat in the far corner beside the flowering oleander, where the Baron led her after the fourth waltz, and leant over her respectfully as she played with her Chinese fan, half trembling at the declaration she knew he was on the point of making to her.

"Mademoiselle Davidoff," the Baron began in French, with a lingering cadence as he pronounced her name, and a faint tremor in his voice that thrilled responsively through her inmost being; "Mademoiselle Davidoff, I have been waiting long for this opportunity of speaking to you alone, because I have something of some importance, to me at least, mademoiselle, about which I wish to confer with you. Mademoiselle, will you do me the honour to listen to me patiently a minute or two? The matter about which I wish to speak to you is one that may concern yourself, too, more closely than you at first imagine."

What a funny way to begin proposing to one! Olga Davidoff's heart beat violently as she answered as unconcernedly as possible, "I shall be glad, M. le Baron, I'm sure, to listen to any communication that you may wish to make to me."

"Mademoiselle," the young man went on almost timidly, how handsome he looked as he stood there bending over her in his semi-barbaric Tartar uniform!—"mademoiselle, the village where I live in our own country is a lonely one among the high mountains. You do not know the Buriat country, it is wild, savage, rugged, pine-clad, snow-clad, solitary, inaccessible, but very beautiful. Even the Russians do not love it; but we love it, we others, who are to the manner born. We breathe there the air of liberty, and we prefer our own brawling streams and sheer precipices to all the artificial stifling civilization of Paris and St. Petersburg."

Olga looked at him and smiled quietly. She saw at once how he wished to break it to her, and held her peace like a wise maiden.

"Yes, mademoiselle," the young man went on, flooding her each moment with the flashing light from his great luminous eyes; "my village in the Buriat country lies high up beside the eternal snows. But though we live alone there, so far from civilization that we seldom see even a passing traveller, our life is not devoid of its own delights and its own interests. I have my own people all around me; I live in my village as a little prince among his own subjects. My people are few, but they are very faithful. Mademoiselle has been educated in England, I believe?"

"Yes," Olga answered. "In London, M. le Baron. I am of English parentage, and my father sent me there to keep up the connection with his old fatherland, where one branch of our House is still established."

"Then, mademoiselle, you will doubtless have read the tales of Walter Scott?"

Olga smiled curiously. "Yes," she said, amused at his naïveté, "I have certainly read them." She began to think that after all the handsome young Buriat couldn't mean really to propose to her.

"Well, you know, in that case, what was the life of a Highland chieftain in Scotland, when the Highland chieftains were still practically all but independent. That, mademoiselle, is exactly the life of a modern Buriat nobleman under the Russian empire. He has his own little territory and his own little people; he lives among them in his own little antiquated fortress; he acknowledges nominally the sovereignty of the most orthodox Czar, and even perhaps exchanges for a Russian title the Tartar chieftainship handed down to him in unbroken succession from his earliest forefathers. But in all the rest he still remains essentially independent. He rules over a little principality of his own, and cares not a fig in his own heart for czar, or governor, or general, or minister."

"This is rather treasonable talk for the Governor's palace," Olga put in, smiling quietly. "If we were not already in Tobolsk we might both, perhaps, imagine we should be sent to Siberia."

The Baron laughed, and showed his two rows of pearly white teeth to the best advantage. "They might send me to the mines," he said, "for aught I care, mademoiselle. I could get away easily enough from village to village to my own country; and once there, it would be easier for the Czar to take Constantinople and Bagdad and Calcutta than to track and dislodge Alexander Niaz in his mountain fortress."

Alexander Niaz! Olga noted the name to herself hurriedly. He was converted then! he was an orthodox Christian! That at least was a good thing, for so many of these Buriats are still nothing more than the most degraded Schamanists and heathens!

"But, mademoiselle," the young man went on again, playing more nervously now than ever with the jewelled hilt of his dress sword, "there is one thing still wanting to my happiness among our beautiful Siberian mountains. I have no lovely châtelaine to help me guard my little feudal castle. Mademoiselle, the Buriat women are not fit allies for a man who has been brought up among the civilization and the learning of the great Western cities. He needs a companion who can sympathize with his higher tastes: who can speak with him of books, of life, of art, of music. Our Buriat women are mere household drudges; to marry one of them would be utterly impossible. Mademoiselle, my father and my grandfather came away from their native wilds to seek a lady who would condescend to love them, in the polite society of Tobolsk. I have gone farther afield: I have sought in Paris, Berlin, Vienna, St. Petersburg. But I saw no lady to whose heart my heart responded, till I came back once more to old Tobolsk. There, mademoiselle, there I saw one whom I recognized at once as fashioned for me by heaven. Mademoiselle Davidoff, I tremble to ask you, but—I love you,—will you share my exile?"

Olga looked at the handsome young man with unconcealed joy and admiration. "Your exile!" she murmured softly, to gain time for a moment. "And why your exile, M. le Baron?"

"Mademoiselle," the young Buriat continued very earnestly, "I do not wish to woo or wed you under false pretences. Before you give me an answer, you must understand to what sort of life it is that I venture to invite you. Our mountains are very lonely: to live there would be indeed an exile to you, accustomed to the gaieties and the vortex of London." (Olga smiled quietly to herself, as she thought for a second of the little drawing-room at The Laurels, Clapham.) "But if you can consent to live in it with me, I will do my best to make it as easy for you as possible. You shall have music, books, papers, amusements, but not society, during the six months of summer which we must necessarily pass at my mountain village; you shall visit Tobolsk, Moscow, Petersburg, London, which you will, during the six months of holiday in winter; above all, you shall have the undying love and devotion of one who has never loved another woman, Alexander Niaz.... Mademoiselle, you see the conditions. Can you accept them? Can you condescend of your goodness to love me—to marry me?"

Olga Davidoff lifted her fan with an effort and answered faintly, "M. le Baron, you are very flattering. I—I will try my best to deserve your goodness."

Niaz took her pretty little hand in his with old-fashioned politeness, and raised it chivalrously to his trembling lips. "Mademoiselle," he said, "you have made me eternally happy. My life shall be passed in trying to prove my gratitude to you for this condescension."

"I think," Olga answered, shaking from head to foot, "I think, M. le Baron, you had better take me back into the next room to my mother."

II

Olga Davidoff's wedding was one of the most brilliant social successes of that Tobolsk season. Davidoff père surpassed himself in the costliness of his exotics, the magnificence of his presents, the reckless abundance of his Veuve Clicquot. Madame Davidoff successfully caught the Governor and the General, and the English traveller from India viâ the Himalayas. The Baron looked as gorgeous as he was handsome in his half Russian, half Tartar uniform and his Oriental display of pearls and diamonds. Olga herself was the prettiest and most blushing bride ever seen in Tobolsk, a simple English girl, fresh from the proprieties of The Laurels at Clapham, among all that curious mixed cosmopolitan society of semi-civilized Siberians, Catholic Poles, and orthodox Russians.

As soon as the wedding was fairly over, the bride and bridegroom started off by toross to make their way across the southern plateau to the Baron's village.

It was a long and dreary drive, that wedding tour, in a jolting carriage over Siberian roads, resting at wayside posting-houses, bad enough while they were still on the main line of the Imperial mails, but degenerating into true Central-Asian caravanserais when once they had got off the beaten track into the wild neighbourhood of the Baron's village. Nevertheless, Olga Davidoff bore up against the troubles and discomforts of the journey with a brave heart, for was not the Baron always by her side? and who could be kinder, or gentler, or more thoughtful than her Buriat husband? Yes, it was a long and hard journey, up among those border mountains of the Chinese and Tibetan frontier; but Olga felt at home at last when, after three weeks of incessant jolting, they arrived at the Buriat mountain stronghold, under cover of the night; and Niaz led her straightway to her own pretty little European boudoir, which he had prepared for her beforehand at immense expense and trouble in his upland village.

The moment they entered, Olga saw a pretty little room, papered and carpeted in English fashion, with a small piano over in the corner, a lamp burning brightly on the tiny side-table, and a roaring fire of logs blazing and crackling upon the simple stone hearth. A book or two lay upon the shelf at the side: she glanced casually at their titles as she passed, and saw that they were some of Tourgénieff's latest novels, a paper-covered Zola fresh from Paris, a volume each of Tennyson, Browning, Carlyle, and Swinburne, a Demidoff, an Emile Augier, a Revue des Deux Mondes, and a late number of an English magazine. She valued these things at once for their own sakes, but still more because she felt instinctively that Niaz had taken the trouble to get them there for her beforehand in this remote and uncivilized corner. She turned to the piano: a light piece by Sullivan lay open before her, and a number of airs from Chopin, Schubert, and Mendelssohn were scattered loosely on the top one above the other. Her heart was too full to utter a word, but she went straight up to her husband, threw her arms tenderly around his neck, and kissed him with the utmost fervour. Niaz smoothed her wavy fair hair gently with his hand, and his eyes sparkled with conscious pleasure as he returned her caress and kissed her forehead.

After a while, they went into the next room to dinner, a small hall, somewhat barbaric in type, but not ill-furnished; and Olga noticed that the two or three servants were very fierce and savage-looking Buriats of the most pronounced Tartar type. The dinner was a plain one, plainly served, of rough country hospitality; but the appointments were all European, and, though simple, good and sufficient. Niaz had said so much to her of the discomforts of his mountain stronghold that Olga was quite delighted to find things on the whole so comparatively civilized, clean, and European.

A few days' sojourn in the fort, it was rather that than a castle or a village, showed Olga pretty clearly what sort of life she was henceforth to expect. Her husband's subjects numbered about a hundred and fifty (with as many more women and children); they rendered him the most implicit obedience, and they evidently looked upon him entirely as a superior being. They were trained to a military discipline, and regularly drilled every morning by Niaz in the queer old semi-Chinese courtyard of the mouldering castle. Olga was so accustomed to a Russian military régime that this circumstance never struck her as being anything extraordinary; she regarded it only as part of the Baron's ancestral habits as a practically independent Tartar chieftain.

Week after week rolled away at the fort, and though Olga had absolutely no one to whom she could speak except her own husband (for the Buriats knew no Russian save the word of command), she didn't find time hang heavily on her hands in the quaint, old-fashioned village. The walks and rides about were really delightful; the scenery was grand and beautiful to the last degree; the Chinese-looking houses and Tartar dress were odd and picturesque, like a scene in a theatre. It was all so absurdly romantic. After all, Olga said to herself with a smile more than once, it isn't half bad being married to a Tartar chieftain up in the border mountains, when you actually come to try it. Only, she confessed in her own heart that she would probably always be very glad when the winter came again, and she got back from these mountain solitudes to the congenial gaiety of Tobolsk or Petersburg.

And Niaz, well, Niaz loved her distractedly. No husband on earth could possibly love a woman better.

Still, Olga could never understand why he sometimes had to leave her for three or four days together, and why during his absence, when she was left all alone at night in the solitary fort with those dreadful Buriats, they kept watch and ward so carefully all the time, and seemed so relieved when Niaz came back again. But whenever she asked him about it, Niaz only looked grave and anxious, and replied with a would-be careless wave of the hand that part of his duty was to guard the frontier, and that the Czar had not conferred a title and an order upon him for nothing. Olga felt frightened and disquieted on all such occasions, but somehow felt, from Niaz's manner, that she must not question him further upon the matter.

One day, after one of these occasional excursions, Niaz came back in high spirits, and kissed her more tenderly and affectionately than ever. After dinner, he read to her out of a book of French poems a grand piece of Victor Hugo's, and then made her sit down to the piano and play him his favourite air from Der Freischütz twice over. When she had finished, he leant back in his chair and murmured quietly in French (which they always spoke together), "And this is in the mountains of Tartary! One would say a soirée of St. Petersburg or of Paris."

Olga turned and looked at him softly. "What is the time, dearest Niaz?" she said with a smile. "Shall I be able to play you still that dance of Pinsuti's?"

Niaz pulled out his watch and answered quickly, "Only ten o'clock, darling. You have plenty of time still."

Something in the look of the watch he held in his hand struck Olga as queer and unfamiliar. She glanced at it sideways, and noticed hurriedly that Niaz was trying to replace it unobserved in his waistcoat pocket. "I haven't seen that watch before," she said suddenly; "let me look at it, dear, will you?"

Niaz drew it out and handed it to her with affected nonchalance; but in the undercurrent of his expression Olga caught a glimpse of a hang-dog look she had never before observed in it. She turned over the watch and looked on the back. To her immense surprise, it bore the initials "F. de K." engraved upon the cover.

"These letters don't belong to you, Niaz," she said, scanning it curiously.

Niaz moved uneasily in his chair. "No," he answered, "not to me, Olga. It's, it's an old family relic, an heirloom, in fact. It belonged to my mother's mother. She was—a Mademoiselle de Kérouac, I believe, from Morbihan, in Brittany."

Olga's eyes looked him through and through with a strange new-born suspicion. What could it all mean? She knew he was telling her a falsehood. Had the watch belonged—to some other lady? What was the meaning of his continued absences? Could he, but no. It was a man's watch, not a lady's. And if so, why, if so, then Niaz had clearly told her a falsehood in that too, and must be trying to conceal something about it.

That night, for the first time, Olga Davidoff began to distrust her Buriat husband.

Next morning, getting up a little early and walking on the parapet of the queer old fortress, she saw Niaz in the court below, jumping and stamping in a furious temper upon something on the ground. To her horror, she saw that his face was all hideously distorted by anger, and that as he raged and stamped the Tartar cast in his features, never before visible, came out quite clearly and distinctly. Olga looked on, and trembled violently, but dared not speak to him.

A few minutes later Niaz came in to breakfast, gay as usual, with a fresh flower stuck prettily in the button-hole of his undress coat and a smile playing unconcernedly around the clear-cut corners of his handsome thin-lipped mouth.

"Niaz," his wife said to him anxiously, "where is the watch you showed me last night?"

His face never altered for a moment as he replied, with the same bland and innocent smile as ever, "My darling, I have broken it all to little pieces. I saw it annoyed you in some way when I showed it to you yesterday, and this morning I took it out accidentally in the lower courtyard. The sight of it put me in a violent temper. 'Cursed thing,' I said, 'you shall never again step in so cruelly between me and my darling. There, take that, and that, and that, rascal!' and I stamped it to pieces underfoot in the courtyard."

Olga turned pale, and looked at him horrified. He smiled again, and took her wee hand tenderly in his. "Little one," he said, "you needn't be afraid; it's only our quick Buriat fashion. We lose our tempers sometimes, but it is soon over. It is nothing. A little whirlwind, and, pouf, it passes."

"But, Niaz, you said it was a family heirloom!"

"Well, darling, and for your sake I ground it to powder. Voilà, tout! Come, no more about it; it isn't worth the trouble. Let us go to breakfast."

Some days later Niaz went on an expedition again, "on the Czar's service for the protection of the frontier," and took more than half his able-bodied Tartars on the journey with him. Olga had never felt so lonely before, surrounded now by doubt and mystery in that awful solitary stronghold. The broken watch weighed gloomily upon her frightened spirits.

Niaz was gone for three days, as often happened, and on the fourth night, after she had retired to her lonely bedroom, she felt sure she heard his voice speaking low somewhere in the courtyard.

At the sound she sprang from her bed and went to the window. Yes, there, down in the far corner of the yard, without lights or noise, and treading cautiously, she saw Niaz and his men filing quietly in through the dim gloom, and bringing with them a number of boxes.

Her heart beat fast. Could it be some kind of smuggling? They lay so near the passes into Turkestan and China, and she knew that the merchant track from Yarkand to Semi-palatinsk crossed the frontier not far from Niaz's village.

Huddling on her dress hastily, she issued out alone and terrified, into the dark courtyard, and sought over the whole place in the black night for sight of Niaz. She could find him nowhere.

At last she mounted the staircase to the mouldering rampart. Generally the Tartar guards kept watch there constantly, but to-night the whole place seemed somehow utterly deserted. She groped her way along till she reached the far corner by a patch of ground which Niaz had told her was the Tartar burial-place.

There she came suddenly upon a great crowd of men below on the plain, running about and shouting wildly, with links and torches. Niaz stood in the midst, erect and military, with his Russian uniform gleaming fitfully in the flickering torchlight. In front of him six Turcoman merchants, with their hands bound behind their backs, knelt upon the ground, and beside him two Tartars held by either arm a man in European dress, whom Olga recognized at once as the English traveller from India by way of the Himalayas. Her heart stood still within her with terror, and she hung there, mute and unseen, upon the rampart above, wondering what in Heaven's name this extraordinary scene was going to end in. What could it mean? What could Niaz be doing in it? Great God, it was too horrible!

A Tartar came forward quietly from the crowd with a curved sword. At a word from Niaz he raised the sword aloft in the air. One second it glanced bright in the torchlight; the next second a Turcoman's head lay rolling in the dust, and a little torrent of blood spurted suddenly from the still kneeling corpse. Olga opened her mouth to scream at the horrid sight, but happily her voice at once forsook her as in a dream, and she stood fixed to the spot in a perfect fascination of awe and terror.

Then the Tartar moved on, obedient to a word and a nod from Niaz, and raised his sword again above the second Turcoman. In a moment, the second head too rolled down quietly beside the other. Without a minute's delay, as though it formed part of his everyday business, the practised headsman went on quietly to the next in order, and did not stop till all six heads lay grim and ghastly scattered about unheeded in the dust together. Olga shut her eyes, sickening, but still could not scream for very horror.

Next, Niaz turned to the English traveller, and said something to him in his politest manner. Olga couldn't catch the words themselves because of the distance, but she saw from his gestures that he was apologizing to the Englishman for his rough treatment. The Englishman in reply drew out and handed to Niaz a small canvas bag, a purse, and a watch. Niaz took them, bowing politely. "Hands off," he cried to the Tartars in Russian, and they loosed their prisoner. Then he made a sign, and the Englishman knelt. In a minute more his head lay rolling in the dust below, and Niaz, with a placid smile upon his handsome face, turned to give orders to the surrounding Tartars.

Olga could stand it no more. She dared not scream or let herself be seen; but she turned round, sick at heart, and groped her way, half paralyzed by fear, along the mouldering rampart, and then turned in at last to her own bedroom, where she flung herself upon the bed in her clothes, and lay, tearless but terrified, the whole night through in blinding misery.

She did not need to have it all explained to her. Niaz was nothing more, after all, than a savage Buriat robber chieftain.

IV

What a terribly long hypocrisy and suspense those six weeks of dreary waiting, before an answer to her letter could come from Tobolsk, and the Governor could send a detachment of the military to rescue her from this nest of murderous banditti!

How Olga hated herself for still pretending to keep on terms with Niaz! How she loathed and detested the man with whom she must yet live as wife for that endless time till the day of her delivery!

And Niaz couldn't help seeing that her manner was changed towards him, though he flattered himself that she had as yet only a bare suspicion, and no real knowledge of the horrible truth. What a sad thing that she should ever even have suspected it! What a pity if he could not keep her here to soothe and lighten his winter solitude!—for he loved her: yes, he really loved her, and he needed sympathy and companionship in all the best and highest instincts of his inner nature. These Buriats, what were they? a miserable set of brutal savages: mere hard-working robbers and murderers, good enough for the practical rough work of everyday life (such as knocking Turcoman merchants on the head), but utterly incapable of appreciating or sympathizing with the better tastes of civilized humanity. It was a hard calling, that of chieftain to these Tartar wretches, especially for a man of musical culture brought up in Paris; and he had hoped that Olga might have helped him through with it by her friendly companionship. Not, of course, that he ever expected to be able to tell her the whole truth: women will be women; and coming to a rough country, they can't understand the necessities laid upon one for rough dealing. No, he could never have expected her to relish the full details of a borderer's profession, but he was vexed that she should already begin to suspect its nature on so very short an acquaintance. He had told her he was like a Highland chieftain of the old times: did she suppose that the Rob Roys and Roderick Dhus of real life used to treat their Lowland captives with rose-water and chivalry? After all, women have really no idea of how things must be managed in the stern realities of actual existence.

So the six weeks passed slowly away, and Olga waited and watched, with smiles on her lips, in mute terror.

At last, one day, in broad daylight, without a moment's warning, or a single premonitory symptom, Olga saw the courtyard suddenly filled with men in Russian uniforms, and a friend of hers, a major of infantry at Tobolsk, rushing in at the head of his soldiers upon the Tartar barrack.

In one second, as if by magic, the courtyard had changed into a roaring battlefield, the Cossacks were firing at the Tartars, and the Tartars were firing at the Cossacks. There was a din of guns and a smoke of gunpowder; and high above all, in the Buriat language, she heard the voice of Niaz, frantically encouraging his men to action, and shouting to them with wild energy in incomprehensible gutturals.

The surprise had been so complete that almost before Olga realized the situation the firing began to die away. The fort was carried, and Niaz and his men stood, disarmed and sullen, with bleeding faces, in the midst of a hastily formed square of stout Cossacks, among the dead and dying strewn upon the ground.

Handsome as ever, but how she hated him!

His arm was wounded; and the Russian surgeon led him aside to bind it up. To Olga's amazement, while the surgeon was actually engaged in binding it, Niaz turned upon him like a savage dog, and bit his arm till the teeth met fiercely in the very middle. She shut her eyes, and half fainted with disgust and horror.

The surgeon shook him off, with an oath; and two Cossacks, coming up hastily, bound his hands behind his back, and tied his legs, quite regardless of his wounded condition.

Meanwhile, the Russian major had sought out Olga, "Madame la Baronne," he said respectfully, "I congratulate you upon your safety and your recovered freedom. Your father is with us; he will soon be here. Your letter reached him safely, in spite of its roundabout direction; and the Governor of Tobolsk despatched us at once upon this errand of release. Baron Niaz had long been suspected: your letter removed all doubts upon the subject."

A minute or two later, the Cossacks marched their prisoners out of the courtyard, two and two, into the great hall of the stronghold.

"I wish to bid farewell to my wife," Niaz cried to the major, in a loud voice. "I shall be sent to the mines, I suppose, and I shall never see her again in this world most probably."

The major allowed him to come near within speaking distance, under guard of two Cossacks.

"Madame la Baronne," he hissed out between his clenched teeth, "this is your hand. It was your hand that you gave me in marriage; it was your hand that wrote to betray me. Believe me, madame, come what may, your hand shall pay the penalty."

So much he said, passionately indeed, but with the offended dignity of a civilized being. Then the Tartar in him broke through the thin veneer of European culture, and he lolled his tongue out at her in savage derision, with a hideous menacing leer like an untamed barbarian. Till that moment, in spite of the horrible massacre she had seen with her own eyes, Olga had never suspected what profound depths of vulgar savagery lay unperceived beneath Alexander Niaz's handsome and aristocratic European features.

One more word he uttered coarsely: a word of foul reproach unfit to be repeated, which made Olga's cheek turn crimson with wrath and indignation even in that supreme moment of conflicting passions. She buried her face between her two hands wildly, and burst into a sudden flood of uncontrollable tears.

"March him away," cried the major in a stern voice. And they marched him away, still mocking, with the other prisoners.

That was the last Olga Davidoff then saw of her Buriat husband.

V

After Niaz had been tried and condemned for robbery and murder, and sent with the usual Russian clemency to the mines of Oukboul, Olga Davidoff could not bear any longer to live at Tobolsk. It was partly terror, partly shame, partly pride; but Tobolsk or even St. Petersburg she felt to be henceforth utterly impossible for her.

So she determined to go back to her kinsfolk in that dear old quiet England, where there are no Nihilists, and no Tartars, and no exiles, and where everybody lived so placidly and demurely. She looked back now upon The Laurels, Clapham, as the ideal home of repose and happiness.

It was not at Clapham, however, that Madame Niaz (as she still called herself) settled down, but in a quiet little Kentish village, where the London branch of the Davids family had retired to spend their Russian money.

Frank Davids, the son of the house, was Olga's second cousin; and when Olga had taken the pretty little rose-covered cottage at the end of the village, Frank Davids found few things more pleasant in life than to drop in of an afternoon and have a chat with his Russian kinswoman. Olga lived there alone with her companion, and in spite of the terrible scenes she had so lately gone through, she was still a girl, very young, very attractive, and very pretty.

What a wonderfully different life, the lawn-tennis with Frank and the curate and the Davids girls up at the big house, from the terror and isolation of the Buriat stronghold! Under the soothing influence of that placid existence, Olga Davidoff began at last almost to outlive the lasting effects of that one great horror. Stamped as it was into the very fabric of her being, she felt it now less poignantly than of old, and sometimes for an hour or two she even ventured to be careless and happy.

Yet all the time the awful spectre of that robber and murderer Niaz, who was nevertheless still her wedded husband, rose up before her, day and night, to prevent her happiness from being ever more than momentary.

And Frank, too, was such a nice, good fellow! Frank had heard from Madame Davidoff all her story (for madame had come over to see Olga fairly settled), and he pitied her for her sad romance in such a kind, brotherly fashion.

Once, and once only, Frank said a word to her that was not exactly brotherly. They were walking together down the footpath by the mill, and Olga had been talking to him about that great terror, when Frank asked her, in a quiet voice, "Olga, why don't you try to get a divorce from that horrible Niaz?"

Olga looked at him in blank astonishment, and asked in return, "Why, Frank, what would be the use of that? It would never blot out the memory of the past, or make that wretch any the less my wedded husband."

"But, Olga, you need a protector sorely. You need somebody to soothe and remove your lasting terror. And I think I know someone, Olga, I know someone who would give his whole life to save you, dearest, from a single day's fear or unhappiness."

Olga looked up at him like a startled child. "Frank," she cried, "dear, dear Frank, you good cousin, never say again another word like that, or you will make me afraid to walk with you or talk with you any longer. You are the one friend I have whom I can trust and confide in: don't drive me away by talking to me of what is so impossible. I hate the man: I loathe and abhor him with all my heart; but I can never forget that he is still my husband. I have made my choice, and I must abide by it. Frank, Frank, promise me, promise me, that you will never again speak upon the subject."

Frank's face grew saddened in a moment with a terrible sadness; but he said in a firm voice, "I promise," and he never broke his word from that day onward.

VI

Three years passed away quietly in the Kentish village, and every day Olga's unreasoning terror of Niaz grew gradually fainter and fainter. If she had known that Niaz had escaped from the mines, after eight months' imprisonment, and made his way by means of his Tartar friends across the passes to Tibet and Calcutta, she would not have allowed the sense of security to grow so strong upon her.

Meanwhile Frank, often in London, had picked up the acquaintance of a certain M. de Vouillemont, a French gentleman much about at the clubs, of whose delightful manners and wide acquaintance with the world and men he was never tired of talking to Olga. "A most charming man, indeed, De Vouillemont, and very anxious to come down here and see Hazelhurst. Besides, Olga, he has been even in Russia, and he knows how to talk admirably about everybody and everything. I've asked him down for Friday evening. Now, do, like a good girl, break your rule for once, and come and dine with us, although there's to be a stranger. It's only one, you know, and the girls would be so delighted if you'd help entertain him, for he speaks hardly any English, and their French, poor things, is horribly insular and boarding-schooly."

At last, with much reluctance, Olga consented, and on the Friday she went up to the big house at eight punctually.

Mrs. Davids and the girls were not yet in the drawing-room when she arrived; but M. de Vouillemont had dressed early, and was standing with his back to the room, looking intently at some pictures on the wall, as Olga entered.

As she came in, and the servant shut the door behind her, the stranger turned slowly. In a moment she recognized him. His complexion was disguised, so as to make him look darker than before; his black moustache was shaved off; his hair was differently cut and dressed; but still, as he looked her in the face, she knew him at once. It was Alexander Niaz!

Petrified with fear, she could neither fly nor scream. She stood still in the middle of the drawing-room, and stared at him fixedly in an agony of terror.

Niaz had evidently tracked her down, and come prepared for his horrid revenge. Without a moment's delay, his face underwent a hideous change, and from the cultivated European gentleman in evening clothes that he looked when she entered, he was transformed as if by magic into a grinning, gibbering Tartar savage, with his tongue lolling out once more, as of old in Siberia, in hateful derision of her speechless terror.

Seizing her roughly by the arm, he dragged her after him, not so much unresisting as rigid with horror, to the open fireplace. A marble fender ran around the tiled hearth. Laying her down upon the rug as if she were dead, he placed her small right hand with savage glee upon that ready-made block, and then proceeded deliberately to take out a small steel hatchet from inside his evening coat. Olga was too terrified even to withdraw her hand. He raised the axe on high, it flashed a second in the air, a smart throb of pain, a dreadful crunching of bone and sinew, and Olga's hand fell white and lifeless upon the tiled hearthplace. Without stopping to look at her for a second, he took it up brutally in his own, and flung it with a horrible oath into the blazing fire.

At that moment, the door opened, and Frank entered.

Olga, lying faint and bleeding on the hearth rug, was just able to look up at him imploringly and utter in a sharp cry of alarm the one word "Niaz."

Frank sprang upon him like an angry lion.

"I told her her hand should pay the penalty," the Tartar cried, with a horrible joy bursting wildly from his livid features; "and now it burns in the fire over yonder, as she herself shall burn next minute forever and ever in fire and brimstone."

As he spoke he drew a pistol from his pocket, and pointed it at her with his finger on the trigger.

Next moment, before he could fire, Frank had seized his hand, flung the pistol to the farther end of the drawing-room, and forced the Tartar down upon the floor in a terrible life-and-death struggle.

Niaz's face, already livid, grew purpler and purpler as they wrestled with one another on the carpet in that deadly effort. His wrath and vindictiveness gave a mad energy to his limbs and muscles. Should he be baulked of his fair revenge at last? Should the woman who had betrayed him escape scot-free with just the loss of a hand, and he himself merely exchange a Siberian for an English prison? No, no, never! by St. Nicholas, never! Ha, madame! I will murder you both! The pistol! the pistol! A thousand devils! let me go! I will kill you yet! I will kill you! I will kill you! Then he gasped, and grew blacker and purpler, blacker and purpler, blacker, blacker, blacker, ever blacker. Presently he gasped again. Frank's hand was now upon his mumbling throat. They rolled over and over in their frantic struggles. Then a long, slow inspiration. After that, his muscles relaxed. Frank loosed him a little, but knelt upon his breast heavily still, lest he should rise again in another paroxysm. But no: he lay quite motionless, quite motionless, and never stirred a single finger.

Frank felt his heart, no movement; his pulse, quite quiet; his lips, not a breath perceptible! Then he rose, faint and staggering, and rang for the servants.

When the doctor came hurriedly from the village to bandage up the Russian lady's arm, he immediately pronounced that M. de Vouillemont was dead, stone dead, not a doubt about it. Probably apoplexy under stress of violent emotion.

The inquest was a good deal hushed up, owing to the exceedingly painful circumstances of the case; and to this day very few people about Torquay (where she now lives) know how Mrs. Frank Davids, the quiet lady who dresses herself always in black, and has such a beautiful softened half-frightened expression, came to lose her right hand. But everybody knows that Mr. Davids is tenderness itself to her, and that she loves him in return with the most absolute and childlike devotion.

It was worth cutting off her right hand, after all, to be rid of that awful spectre of Niaz, and to have gained the peaceful love of Frank Davids.

JOHN CANN'S TREASURE

Cecil Mitford sat at a desk in the Record Office with a stained and tattered sheet of dark dirty-brown antique paper spread before him in triumph, and with an eager air of anxious inquiry speaking forth from every line in his white face and every convulsive twitch at the irrepressible corners of his firm pallid mouth. Yes, there was no doubt at all about it; the piece of torn and greasy paper which he had at last discovered was nothing more or less than John Cann's missing letter. For two years Cecil Mitford had given up all his spare time, day and night, to the search for that lost fragment of crabbed seventeenth-century handwriting; and now at length, after so many disappointments and so much fruitless anxious hunting, the clue to the secret of John Cann's treasure was lying there positively before him. The young man's hand trembled violently as he held the paper fast unopened in his feverish grasp, and read upon its back the autograph endorsement of Charles the Second's Secretary of State—"Letter in cypher from Io. Cann, the noted Buccaneer, to his brother Will'm, intercepted at Port Royal by his Ma'ties command, and despatched by General Ed. D'Oyley, his Ma'ties Captain-Gen'l and Governor-in-Chief of the Island of Jamaica, to me, H. NICHOLAS." That was it, beyond the shadow of a doubt; and though Cecil Mitford had still to apply to the cypher John Cann's own written key, and to find out the precise import of the directions it contained, he felt at that moment that the secret was now at last virtually discovered, and that John Cann's untold thousands of buried wealth were potentially his very own already.

He was only a clerk in the Colonial Office, was Cecil Mitford, on a beggarly income of a hundred and eighty a year, how small it seemed now, when John Cann's money was actually floating before his mind's eye; but he had brains and industry and enterprise after a fitful adventurous fashion of his own; and he had made up his mind years before that he would find out the secret of John Cann's buried treasure, if he had to spend half a lifetime on the almost hopeless quest. As a boy, Cecil Mitford had been brought up at his father's rectory on the slopes of Dartmoor, and there he had played from his babyhood upward among the rugged granite boulders of John Cann's rocks, and had heard from the farm labourers and the other children around the romantic but perfectly historical legend of John Cann's treasure. Unknown and incredible sums in Mexican doubloons and Spanish dollars lay guarded by a strong oaken chest in a cavern on the hilltop, long since filled up with flints and mould from the neighbouring summits. To that secure hiding-place the great buccaneer had committed the hoard gathered in his numberless piratical expeditions, burying all together under the shadow of a petty porphyritic tor that overhangs the green valley of Bovey Tracy. Beside the bare rocks that mark the site, a perfectly distinct pathway is worn by footsteps into the granite platform underfoot; and that path, little Cecil Mitford had heard with childish awe and wonder, was cut out by the pacing up and down of old John Cann himself, mounting guard in the darkness and solitude over the countless treasure that he had hidden away in the recesses of the pixies' hole beneath.

As young Mitford grew up to man's estate, this story of John Cann's treasure haunted his quick imagination for many years with wonderful vividness. When he first came up to London, after his father's death, and took his paltry clerkship in the Colonial Office, how he hated the place, with its monotonous drudgery, while John Cann's wealth was only waiting for him to take it and floating visibly before his prophetic eyes!—the story began for a while to fade out under the disillusioning realities of respectable poverty and a petty Government post. But before he had been many months in the West India department (he had a small room on the third floor, overlooking Downing Street) a casual discovery made in overhauling the archives of the office suddenly revived the boyish dream with all the added realism and cool intensity of maturer years. He came across a letter from John Cann himself to the Protector Oliver, detailing the particulars of a fierce irregular engagement with a Spanish privateer, in which the Spaniard had been captured with much booty, and his vessel duly sold to the highest bidder in Port Royal harbour. This curious coincidence gave a great shock of surprise to young Mitford. John Cann, then, was no mythical prehistoric hero, no fairy-king or pixy or barrow-haunter of the popular fancy, but an actual genuine historical figure, who corresponded about his daring exploits with no less a personage than Oliver himself! From that moment forth, Cecil Mitford gave himself up almost entirely to tracing out the forgotten history of the old buccaneer. He allowed no peace to the learned person who took care of the State Papers of the Commonwealth at the Record Office, and he established private relations, by letter, with two or three clerks in the Colonial Secretary's Office at Kingston, Jamaica, whom he induced to help him in reconstructing the lost story of John Cann's life.

Bit by bit Cecil Mitford had slowly pieced together a wonderful mass of information, buried under piles of ragged manuscript and weary reams of dusty documents, about the days and doings of that ancient terror of the Spanish Main. John Cann was a Devonshire lad, of the rollicking, roving seventeenth century, born and bred at Bovey Tracy, on the flanks of Dartmoor, the last survivor of those sea-dogs of Devon who had sallied forth to conquer and explore a new Continent under the guidance of Drake, and Raleigh, and Frobisher, and Hawkins. As a boy, he had sailed with his father in a ship that bore the Queen's letters of marque and reprisal against the Spanish galleons; in his middle life, he had lived a strange roaming existence, half pirate and half privateer, intent upon securing the Protestant religion and punishing the King's enemies by robbing wealthy Spanish skippers and cutting off the recusant noses of vile Papistical Cuban slave traders; in his latter days, the fierce, half-savage old mariner had relapsed into sheer robbery, and had been hunted down as a public enemy by the Lord Protector's servants, or later still by the Captains-General and Governors-in-Chief of his Most Sacred Majesty's Dominions in the West Indies. For what was legitimate warfare in the spacious days of great Elizabeth, had come to be regarded in the degenerate reign of Charles II. as rank piracy.

One other thing Cecil Mitford had discovered, with absolute certainty; and that was that in the summer of 1660, "the year of his Ma'tie's most happy restoration," as John Cann himself phrased it, the persecuted and much misunderstood old buccaneer had paid a secret visit to England, and had brought with him the whole hoard which he had accumulated during sixty years of lawful or unlawful piracy in the West Indies and the Spanish Main. Concerning this hoard, which he had concealed somewhere in Devonshire, he kept up a brisk vernacular correspondence in cypher with his brother William, at Tavistock; and the key to that cypher, marked outside "A clew to my Bro. John's secret writing," Cecil Mitford had been fortunate enough to unearth among the undigested masses of the Record Office. But one letter, the last and most important of the whole series, containing as he believed the actual statement of the hiding-place, had long evaded all his research: and that was the letter which, now at last, after months and months of patient inquiry, lay unfolded before his dazzled eyes on the little desk in his accustomed corner. It had somehow been folded up by mistake in the papers relating to the charge against Cyriack Skinner, of complicity in the Rye House Plot. How it got there nobody knows, and probably nobody but Cecil Mitford himself could ever have succeeded in solving the mystery.

As he gazed, trembling, at the precious piece of dusty much-creased paper, scribbled over in the unlettered schoolboy hand of the wild old sea-dog, Cecil Mitford could hardly restrain himself for a moment from uttering a cry. Untold wealth swam before his eyes: he could marry Ethel now, and let her drive in her own carriage! Ah, what he would give if he might only shout in his triumph. He couldn't even read the words, he was so excited. But after a minute or two, he recovered his composure sufficiently to begin deciphering the crabbed writing, which constant practice and familiarity with the system enabled him to do immediately, without even referring to the key. And this was what, with a few minutes' inspection, Cecil Mitford slowly spelled out of the dirty manuscript:—

"From Jamaica. This 23rd day of Jan'y,   "in the Yeare of our Lord 1663.

"My deare Bro., I did not think to have written you againe, after the scurvie Trick you have played me in disclosing my Affairs to that meddlesome Knight that calls himself the King's Secretary: but in truth your last Letter hath so moved me by your Vileness that I must needs reply thereto with all Expedicion. These are to assure you, then, that let you pray how you may, or gloze over your base treatment with fine cozening Words and fair Promises, you shall have neither lot nor scot in my Threasure, which is indeed as you surmise hidden away in England, but the Secret whereof I shall impart neither to you nor to no man. I have give commands, therefore that the Paper whereunto I have committed the place of its hiding shall be buried with my own Body (when God please) in the grave-yarde at Port Royal in this Island: so that you shall never be bettered one Penny by your most Damnable Treachery and Double-facedness. For I know you, my deare Bro., in very truth for a prating Coxcomb, a scurvie cowardlie Knave, and a lying Thief of other Men's Reputations. Therefore, no more herewith from your very humble Ser'vt., and Loving Bro.,

"IOHN CANN, Capt'n"

Cecil Mitford laid the paper down as he finished reading it with a face even whiter and paler than before, and with the muscles of his mouth trembling violently with suppressed emotion. At the exact second when he felt sure he had discovered the momentous secret, it had slipped mysteriously through his very fingers, and seemed now to float away into the remote distance, almost as far from his eager grasp as ever. Even there, in the musty Record Office, before all the clerks and scholars who were sitting about working carelessly at their desks at mere dilettante historical problems, the stupid prigs, how he hated them!—he could hardly restrain the expression of his pent-up feelings at that bitter disappointment in the very hour of his fancied triumph. Jamaica! How absolutely distant and unapproachable it sounded! How hopeless the attempt to follow up the clue! How utterly his day-dream had been dashed to the ground in those three minutes of silent deciphering! He felt as if the solid earth was reeling beneath him, and he would have given the whole world if he could have put his face between his two hands on the desk and cried like a woman before the whole Record Office.

For half an hour by the clock he sat there dazed and motionless, gazing in a blank disappointed fashion at the sheet of coffee-coloured paper in front of him. It was late, and workers were dropping away one after another from the scantily peopled desks. But Cecil Mitford took no notice of them: he merely sat with his arms folded, and gazed abstractedly at that disappointing, disheartening, irretrievable piece of crabbed writing. At last an assistant came up and gently touched his arm. "We're going to close now, sir," he said in his unfeeling official tone, just as if it were a mere bit of historical inquiry he was after—"and I shall be obliged if you'll put back the manuscripts you've been consulting into F. 27." Cecil Mitford rose mechanically and sorted out the Cyriack Skinner papers into their proper places. Then he laid them quietly on the shelf, and walked out into the streets of London, for the moment a broken-hearted man.

But as he walked home alone that clear warm summer evening, and felt the cool breeze blowing against his forehead, he began to reflect to himself that, after all, all was not lost; that in fact things really stood better with him now than they had stood that very morning, before he lighted upon John Cann's last letter. He had not discovered the actual hiding-place of the hoard, to be sure, but he now knew on John Cann's own indisputable authority, first, that there really was a hidden treasure; second, that the hiding-place was really in England; and third, that full particulars as to the spot where it was buried might be found in John Cann's own coffin at Port Royal, Jamaica. It was a risky and difficult thing to open a coffin, no doubt; but it was not impossible. No, not impossible. On the whole, putting one thing with another, in spite of his terrible galling disappointment, he was really nearer to the recovery of the treasure now than he had ever been in his life before. Till to-day, the final clue was missing; to-day, it had been found. It was a difficult and dangerous clue to follow, but still it had been found.

And yet, setting aside the question of desecrating a grave, how all but impossible it was for him to get to Jamaica! His small funds had long ago been exhausted in prosecuting the research, and he had nothing on earth to live upon now but his wretched salary. Even if he could get three or six months' leave from the Colonial Office, which was highly improbable, how could he ever raise the necessary money for his passage out and home, as well as for the delicate and doubtful operation of searching for documents in John Cann's coffin? It was tantalising, it was horrible, it was unendurable; but here, with the secret actually luring him on to discover it, he was to be foiled and baffled at the last moment by a mere paltry, petty, foolish consideration of two hundred pounds! Two hundred pounds! How utterly ludicrous! Why, John Cann's treasure would make him a man of fabulous wealth for a whole lifetime, and he was to be prevented from realizing it by a wretched matter of two hundred pounds! He would do anything to get it, for a loan, a mere loan; to be repaid with cent. per cent. interest; but where in the world, where in the world, was he ever to get it from?

And then, quick as lightning, the true solution of the whole difficulty flashed at once across his excited brain. He could borrow all the money if he chose from Ethel! Poor little Ethel; she hadn't much of her own; but she had just enough to live very quietly upon with her Aunt Emily; and, thank Heaven, it wasn't tied up with any of those bothering, meddling three-per-cent.-loving trustees! She had her little all at her own disposal, and he could surely get two or three hundred pounds from her to secure for them both the boundless buried wealth of John Cann's treasure.

Should he make her a confidante outright, and tell her what it was that he wanted the money for? No, that would be impossible, for though she had heard all about John Cann over and over again, she had not faith enough in the treasure, women are so unpractical, to hazard her little scrap of money on it; of that he felt certain. She would go and ask old Mr. Cartwright's opinion; and old Mr. Cartwright was one of those penny-wise, purblind, unimaginative old gentlemen who will never believe in anything until they've seen it. Yet here was John Cann's money going a-begging, so to speak, and only waiting for him and Ethel to come and enjoy it. Cecil had no patience with those stupid, stick-in-the-mud, timid people who can see no further than their own noses. For Ethel's own sake he would borrow two or three hundred pounds from her, one way or another, and she would easily forgive him the harmless little deception when he paid her back a hundredfold out of John Cann's boundless treasure.

II

That very evening, without a minute's delay, Cecil determined to go round and have a talk with Ethel Sunderland. "Strike while the iron's hot," he said to himself. "There isn't a minute to be lost; for who knows but somebody else may find John Cann's treasure before I do?"

Ethel opened the door to him herself; theirs was an old engagement of long standing, after the usual Government clerk's fashion; and Aunt Emily didn't stand out so stiffly as many old maids do for the regular proprieties. Very pretty Ethel looked with her pale face and the red ribbon in her hair; very pretty, but Cecil feared, as he looked into her dark hazel eyes, a little wearied and worn-out, for it was her music-lesson day, as he well remembered. Her music-lesson day! Ethel Sutherland to give music-lessons to some wretched squealing children at the West-end, when all John Cann's wealth was lying there, uncounted, only waiting for him and her to take it and enjoy it! The bare thought was a perfect purgatory to him. He must get that two hundred pounds to-night, or give up the enterprise altogether.

"Well, Ethel darling," he said tenderly, taking her pretty little hand in his; "you look tired, dearest. Those horrid children have been bothering you again. How I wish we were married, and you were well out of it!"

Ethel smiled a quiet smile of resignation. "They are rather trying, Cecil," she said gently, "especially on days when one has got a headache; but, after all, I'm very glad to have the work to do; it helps such a lot to eke out our little income. We have so very little, you know, even for two lonely women to live upon in simple little lodgings like these, that I'm thankful I can do something to help dear Aunt Emily, who's really goodness itself. You see, after all, I get very well paid indeed for the lessons."

"Ethel," Cecil Mitford said suddenly, thinking it better to dash at once into the midst of business; "I've come round this evening to talk with you about a means by which you can add a great deal with perfect safety to your little income. Not by lessons, Ethel darling; not by lessons. I can't bear to see you working away the pretty tips off those dear little fingers of yours with strumming scales on the piano for a lot of stupid, gawky school-girls; it's by a much simpler way than that; I know of a perfectly safe investment for that three hundred that you've got in New Zealand Four per Cents. Can you not have heard that New Zealand securities are in a very shaky way just at present?"

"Very shaky, Cecil?" Ethel answered in surprise. "Why, Mr. Cartwright told me only a week ago they were as safe as the Bank of England!"

"Mr. Cartwright's an ignorant old martinet," Cecil replied vigorously. "He thinks because the stock's inscribed and the dividends are payable in Threadneedle Street that the colony of New Zealand's perfectly solvent. Now, I'm in the Colonial Office, and I know a great deal better than that. New Zealand has over-borrowed, I assure you; quite over-borrowed; and a serious fall is certain to come sooner or later. Mark my words, Ethel darling; if you don't sell out those New Zealand Fours, you'll find your three hundred has sunk to a hundred and fifty in rather less than half no time!"

Ethel hesitated, and looked at him in astonishment. "That's very queer," she said, "for Mr. Cartwright wants me to sell out my little bit of Midland and put it all into the same New Zealands. He says they're so safe and pay so well."

"Mr. Cartwright indeed!" Cecil cried contemptuously. "What means on earth has he of knowing? Didn't he advise you to buy nothing but three per cents., and then let you get some Portuguese Threes at fifty, which are really sixes, and exceedingly doubtful securities? What's the use of trusting a man like that, I should like to know? No, Ethel, if you'll be guided by me, and I have special opportunities of knowing about these things at the Colonial Office, you'll sell out your New Zealands, and put them into a much better investment that I can tell you about. And if I were you, I'd say nothing about it to Mr. Cartwright."

"But, Cecil, I never did anything in business before without consulting him! I should be afraid of going quite wrong."

Cecil took her hand in his with real tenderness. Though he was trying to deceive her, for her own good, he loved her dearly in his heart of hearts, and hated himself for the deception he was remorsefully practising upon her. Yet, for her sake, he would go through with it. "You must get accustomed to trusting me instead of him, darling," he said softly. "When you are mine for ever, as I hope you will be soon, you will take my advice, of course, in all such matters, won't you? And you may as well begin by taking it now. I have great hopes, Ethel, that before very long my circumstances will be so much improved that I shall be able to marry you, I hardly know how quickly; perhaps even before next Christmas. But meanwhile, darling, I have something to break to you that I dare say will grieve you a little for the moment, though it's for your ultimate good, birdie, for your ultimate good. The Colonial Office people have selected me to go to Jamaica on some confidential Government business, which may keep me there for three months or so. It's a dreadful thing to be away from you so long, Ethel; but if I manage the business successfully, and I shall, I know, I shall get promoted when I come back, well promoted, perhaps to the chief clerkship in the Department; and then we could marry comfortably almost at once."

"To Jamaica! Oh, Cecil! How awfully far! And suppose you were to get yellow fever or something."

"But I won't, Ethel; I promise you I won't, and I'll guarantee it with a kiss, birdie; so now, that's settled. And then, consider the promotion! Only three months, probably, and when I come back, we can be actually married. It's a wonderful stroke of luck, and I only heard of it this morning. I couldn't rest till I came and told you."

Ethel wiped a tear away silently, and only answered, "If you're glad, Cecil dearest, I'm glad too."

"Well now, Ethel," Cecil Mitford went on as gaily as he could, "that brings me up to the second point. I want you to sell out these wretched New Zealands, so as to take the money with me to invest on good mortgages in Jamaica. My experience in West Indian matters, after three years in the Department, will enable me to lay it out for you at nine per cent.—nine per cent., observe, Ethel, on absolute security of landed property. Planters want money to improve their estates, and can't get it at less than that rate. Your three hundred would bring you in twenty-seven pounds, Ethel; twenty-seven pounds is a lot of money!"

What could poor Ethel do? In his plausible, affectionate manner, and all for her own good, too, Cecil talked her over quickly between love and business experience, coaxing kisses and nine per cent. interest, endearing names and knowledge of West Indian affairs, till helpless little Ethel willingly promised to give up her poor little three hundred, and even arranged to meet Cecil secretly on Thursday at the Bank of England, about Colonial Office dinner-hour, to effect the transfer on her own account, without saying a single word about it to Aunt Emily or Mr. Cartwright. Cecil's conscience, for he had a conscience, though he did his best to stifle it, gave him a bitter twinge every now and then, as one question after another drove him time after time into a fresh bit of deceit; but he tried to smile and smile and be a villain as unconcernedly and lightly as possible. Once only towards the end of the evening, when everything was settled, and Cecil had talked about his passage, and the important business with which he was entrusted, at full length, a gleam of suspicion seemed to flash for a single second across poor Ethel's deluded little brains. Jamaica, promotion, three hundred pounds, it was all so sudden and so connected; could Cecil himself be trying to deceive her, and using her money for his wild treasure hunt? The doubt was horrible, degrading, unworthy of her or him; and yet somehow for a single moment she could not help half-unconsciously entertaining it.

"Cecil," she said, hesitating, and looking into the very depths of his truthful blue eyes; "you're not concealing anything from me, are you? It's not some journey connected with John Cann?"

Cecil coughed and cleared his throat uneasily, but by a great effort he kept his truthful blue eyes still fixed steadily on hers. (He would have given the world if he might have turned them away, but that would have been to throw up the game incontinently.) "My darling Ethel," he said evasively, "how on earth could the Colonial Office have anything to do with John Cann?"

"Answer me 'yes' or 'no,' Cecil. Do please answer me 'yes' or 'no.'"

Cecil kept his eyes still fixed immovably on hers, and without a moment's hesitation answered quickly "no." It was an awful wrench, and his lips could hardly frame the horrid falsehood, but for Ethel's sake he answered "no."

"Then I know I can trust you, Cecil," she said, laying her head for forgiveness on his shoulder. "Oh, how wrong it was of me to doubt you for a second!"

Cecil sighed uneasily, and kissed her white forehead without a single word.

"After all," he thought to himself, as he walked back to his lonely lodgings late that evening, "I need never tell her anything about it. I can pretend, when I've actually got John Cann's treasure, that I came across the clue accidently while I was in Jamaica; and I can lay out three hundred of it there in mortgages; and she need never know a single word about my innocent little deception. But indeed in the pride and delight of so much money, all our own, she'll probably never think at all of her poor little paltry three hundred."

III

It was an awfully long time, that eighteen days at sea, on the Royal Mail Steamship Don, bound for Kingston, Jamaica, with John Cann's secret for ever on one's mind, and nothing to do all day, by way of outlet for one's burning energy, but to look, hour after hour, at the monotonous face of the seething water. But at last the journey was over; and before Cecil Mitford had been twenty-four hours at Date Tree Hall, the chief hotel in Kingston, he had already hired a boat and sailed across the baking hot harbour to Port Royal, to look in the dreary, sandy cemetery for any sign or token of John Cann's grave.

An old grey-haired negro, digging at a fresh grave, had charge of the cemetery, and to him Cecil Mitford at once addressed himself, to find out whether any tombstone about the place bore the name of John Cann. The old man turned the name over carefully in his stolid brains, and then shook his heavy grey head with a decided negative. "Massa John Cann, sah," he said dubiously, "Massa John Cann; it don't nobody buried here by de name ob Massa John Cann. I sartin, sah, becase I's sexton in dis here cemetry dese fifty year, an' I know de grabe ob ebbery buckra gentleman dat ebber buried here since I fuss came."

Cecil Mitford tossed his head angrily. "Since you first came, my good man," he said with deep contempt. "Since you first came! Why, John Cann was buried here ages and ages before you yourself were ever born or thought of."

The old negro looked up at him inquiringly. There is nothing a negro hates like contempt; and he answered back with a disdainful tone, "Den I can find out if him ebber was buried here at all, as well as you, sah. We has register here, we don't ignorant heathen. I has register in de church ob every pusson dat ebber buried in dis cemetery from de berry beginnin, from de year ob de great earthquake itself. What year dis Massa John Cann him die, now? What year him die?"

Cecil pricked up his ears at the mention of the register, and answered eagerly, "In the year 1669."

The old negro sat down quietly on a flat tomb, and answered with a smile of malicious triumph, "Den you is ignorant know-nuffin pusson for a buckra gentleman, for true, sah, if you tink you will find him grabe in dis here cemetery. Don't you nebber read your history book, dat all Port Royal drowned in de great earthquake ob de year 1692? We has register here for ebbery year, from de year 1692 downward; but de grabes, and de cemetery, and de register, from de year 1692 upward, him all swallowed up entirely in de great earthquake, bress de Lord!"

Cecil Mitford felt the earth shivering beneath him at that moment, as verily as the Port Royal folk had felt it shiver in 1692. He clutched at the headstone to keep him from falling, and sat down hazily on the flat tomb, beside the grey-headed old negro, like one unmanned and utterly disheartened. It was all only too true. With his intimate knowledge of John Cann's life, and of West Indian affairs generally, how on earth could he ever have overlooked it? John Cann's grave lay buried five fathoms deep, no doubt, under the blue waters of the Caribbean. And it was for this that he had madly thrown up his Colonial Office appointment, for this that he had wasted Ethel's money, for this that he had burdened his conscience with a world of lies; all to find in the end that John Cann's secret was hidden under five fathoms of tropical lagoon, among the scattered and waterlogged ruins of Old Port Royal. His fortitude forsook him for a single moment, and burying his face in his two hands, there, under the sweltering midday heat of that deadly sandbank, he broke down utterly, and sobbed like a child before the very eyes of the now softened old negro sexton.

IV

It was not for long, however. Cecil Mitford had at least one strong quality, indomitable energy and perseverance. All was not yet lost: if need were, he would hunt for John Cann's tomb in the very submerged ruins of Old Port Royal. He looked up once more at the puzzled negro, and tried to bear this bitter downfall of all his hopes with manful resignation.

At that very moment, a tall and commanding-looking man, of about sixty, with white hair but erect figure, walked slowly from the cocoa-nut grove on the sand-spit into the dense and tangled precincts of the cemetery. He was a brown man, a mulatto apparently, but his look and bearing showed him at once to be a person of education and distinction in his own fashion. The old sexton rose up respectfully as the stranger approached, and said to him in a very different tone from that in which he had addressed Cecil Mitford, "Marnin, sah; marnin, Mr. Barclay. Dis here buckra gentleman from Englan', him come 'quiring in de cemetery after de grabe of pusson dat dead before de great earthquake. What for him come here like-a-dat on fool's errand, eh, sah? What for him not larn before him come dat Port Royal all gone drowned in de year 1692?"

The new-comer raised his hat slightly to Cecil Mitford, and spoke at once in the grave gentle voice of an educated and cultivated mulatto. "You wanted some antiquarian information about the island, sir; some facts about some one who died before the Port Royal earthquake? You have luckily stumbled across the right man to help you; for I think if anything can be recovered about anybody in Jamaica, I can aid you in recovering it. Whose grave did you want to see?"

Cecil hardly waited to thank the polite stranger, but blurted out at once, "The grave of John Cann, who died in 1669."

The stranger smiled quietly. "What! John Cann, the famous buccaneer?" he said, with evident delight. "Are you interested in John Cann?"

"I am," Cecil answered hastily. "Do you know anything about him?"

"I know all about him," the tall mulatto replied. "All about him in every way. He was not buried at Port Royal at all. He intended to be, and gave orders to that effect; but his servants had him buried quietly elsewhere, on account of some dispute with the Governor of the time being, about some paper which he desired to have placed in his coffin."

"Where, where?" Cecil Mitford gasped out eagerly, clutching at this fresh straw with all the anxiety of a drowning man.

"At Spanish Town," the stranger answered calmly. "I know his grave there well to the present day. If you are interested in Jamaican antiquities, and would like to come over and see it, I shall be happy to show you the tomb. That is my name." And he handed Cecil Mitford his card, with all the courteous dignity of a born gentleman.

Cecil took the card and read the name on it: "The Hon. Charles Barclay, Leigh Caymanas, Spanish Town." How his heart bounded again that minute! Proof was accumulating on proof, and luck on luck! After all, he had tracked down John Cann's grave; and the paper was really there, buried in his coffin. He took the handkerchief from his pocket and wiped his damp brow with a feeling of unspeakable relief. Ethel was saved, and they might still enjoy John Cann's treasure.

Mr. Barclay sat down beside him on the stone slab, and began talking over all he knew about John Cann's life and actions. Cecil affected to be interested in all he said, though really he could think of one thing only: the treasure, the treasure, the treasure. But he managed also to let Mr. Barclay see how much he too knew about the old buccaneer: and Mr. Barclay, who was a simple-minded learned enthusiast for all that concerned the antiquities of his native island, was so won over by this display of local knowledge on the part of a stranger and an Englishman, that he ended by inviting Cecil over to his house at Spanish Town, to stop as long as he was able. Cecil gladly accepted the invitation, and that very afternoon, with a beating heart, he took his place in the lumbering train that carried him over to the final goal of his Jamaican expedition.

V

In a corner of the Cathedral graveyard at Spanish Town, overhung by a big spreading mango tree, and thickly covered by prickly scrub of agave and cactus, the white-haired old mulatto gentleman led Cecil Mitford up to a water-worn and weathered stone, on which a few crumbling letters alone were still visible. Cecil kneeled down on the bare ground, regardless of the sharp cactus spines that stung and tore his flesh, and began clearing the moss and lichen away from the neglected monument. Yes, his host was right! right, right, right, indubitably. The first two letters were IO, then a blank where others were obliterated, and then came ANN. That stood clearly for IOHN CANN. And below he could slowly make out the words, "Born at ... vey Tra ... Devon...." with an illegible date, "Died at P ...

Royal, May 12, 1669." Oh, great heavens, yes. John Cann's grave! John Cann's grave! John Cann's grave! Beyond any shadow or suspicion of mistake, John Cann and his precious secret lay buried below that mouldering tombstone.

That very evening Cecil Mitford sought out and found the Spanish Town gravedigger. He was a solemn-looking middle-aged black man, with a keen smart face, not the wrong sort of man, Cecil Mitford felt sure, for such a job as the one he contemplated. Cecil didn't beat about the bush or temporise with him in any way. He went straight to the point, and asked the man outright whether he would undertake to open John Cann's grave, and find a paper that was hidden in the coffin. The gravedigger stared at him, and answered slowly, "I don't like de job, sah; I don't like de job. Perhaps Massa John Cann's ghost, him come and trouble me for dat: I don't going to do it. What you gib me, sah; how much you gib me?"

Cecil opened his purse and took out of it ten gold sovereigns. "I will give you that," he said, "if you can get me the paper out of John Cann's coffin."

The negro's eyes glistened, but he answered carelessly, "I don't tink I can do it. I don't want to open grabe by night, and if I open him by day, de magistrates dem will hab me up for desecration ob interment. But I can do dis for you, sah. If you like to wait till some buckra gentleman die, John Cann grabe among de white man side in de grabeyard, I will dig grabe alongside ob John Cann one day, so let you come yourself in de night and take what you like out ob him coffin. I don't go meddle with coffin myself, to make de John Cann duppy trouble me, and magistrate send me off about me business."

It was a risky thing to do, certainly, but Cecil Mitford closed with it, and promised the man ten pounds if ever he could recover John Cann's paper. And then he settled down quietly at Leigh Caymanas with his friendly host, waiting with eager, anxious expectation, till some white person should die at Spanish Town.

What an endless aimless time it seemed to wait before anybody could be comfortably buried! Black people died by the score, of course: there was a small-pox epidemic on, and they went to wakes over one another's dead bodies in wretched hovels among the back alleys, and caught the infection and sickened and died as fast as the wildest imagination could wish them: but then, they were buried apart by themselves in the pauper part of the Cathedral cemetery. Still, no white man caught the small-pox, and few mulattoes: they had all been vaccinated, and nobody got ill except the poorest negroes. Cecil Mitford waited with almost fiendish eagerness to hear that some prominent white man was dead or dying.

A month, six weeks, two months, went slowly past, and still nobody of consequence in all Spanish Town fell ill or sickened. Talk about tropical diseases! why, the place was abominably, atrociously, outrageously healthy. Cecil Mitford fretted and fumed and worried by himself, wondering whether he would be kept there forever and ever, waiting till some useless nobody chose to die. The worst of it all was, he could tell nobody his troubles: he had to pretend to look unconcerned and interested, and listen to all old Mr. Barclay's stories about Maroons and buccaneers as if he really enjoyed them.

At last, after Cecil had been two full months at Spanish Town, he heard one morning with grim satisfaction that yellow fever had broken out at Port Antonio. Now, yellow fever, as he knew full well, attacks only white men, or men of white blood: and Cecil felt sure that before long there would be somebody white dead in Spanish Town. Not that he was really wicked or malevolent or even unfeeling at heart; but his wild desire to discover John Cann's treasure had now overridden every better instinct of his nature, and had enslaved him, body and soul, till he could think of nothing in any light save that of its bearing on his one mad imagination. So he waited a little longer, still more eagerly than before, till yellow fever should come to Spanish Town.

Sure enough the fever did come in good time, and the very first person who sickened with it was Cecil Mitford. That was a contingency he had never dreamt of, and for the time being it drove John Cann's treasure almost out of his fevered memory. Yet not entirely, even so, for in his delirium he raved of John Cann and his doubloons till good old Mr. Barclay, nursing at his bedside like a woman, as a tender-hearted mulatto always will nurse any casual young white man, shook his head to himself and muttered gloomily that poor Mr. Mitford had overworked his brain sadly in his minute historical investigations.

For ten days Cecil Mitford hovered fitfully between life and death, and for ten days good old Mr. Barclay waited on him, morning, noon, and night, as devotedly as any mother could wait upon her first-born. At the end of that time he began to mend slowly; and as soon as the crisis was over he forgot forthwith all about his illness, and thought once more of nothing on earth save only John Cann's treasure. Was anybody else ill of the fever in Spanish Town? Yes, two, but not dangerously. Cecil's face fell at that saving clause, and in his heart he almost ventured to wish it had been otherwise. He was no murderer, even in thought; but John Cann's treasure! John Cann's treasure! John Cann's treasure! What would not a man venture to do or pray, in order that he might become the possessor of John Cann's treasure!

As Cecil began to mend, a curious thing happened at Leigh Caymanas, contrary to almost all the previous medical experience of the whole Island. Mr. Barclay, though a full mulatto of half black blood, suddenly sickened with the yellow fever. He had worn himself out with nursing Cecil, and the virus seemed to have got into his blood in a way that it would never have done under other circumstances. And when the doctor came to see him, he declared at once that the symptoms were very serious. Cecil hated and loathed himself for the thought; and yet, in a horrid, indefinite way he gloated over the possibility of his kind and hospitable friend's dying. Mr. Barclay had tended him so carefully that he almost loved him; and yet, with John Cann's treasure before his very eyes, in a dim, uncertain, awful fashion, he almost looked forward to his dying. But where would he be buried? that was the question. Not, surely, among the poor black people in the pauper corner. A man of his host's distinction and position would certainly deserve a place among the most exalted white graves, near the body of Governor Modyford, and not far from the tomb of John Cann himself.

Day after day Mr. Barclay sank slowly but surely, and Cecil, weak and hardly convalescent himself, sat watching by his bedside, and nursing him as tenderly as the good brown man had nursed Cecil himself in his turn a week earlier. The young clerk was no hard-hearted wretch who could see a kind entertainer die without a single passing pang; he felt for the grey old mulatto as deeply as he could have felt for his own brother, if he had had one. Every time there was a sign of suffering or feebleness, it went to Cecil's heart like a knife, the very knowledge that on one side of his nature he wished the man to die made him all the more anxious and careful on the other side to do everything he could to save him, if possible, or at least to alleviate his sufferings. Poor old man! it was horrible to see him lying there, parched with fever and dying by inches; but then—John Cann's treasure! John Cann's treasure! John Cann's treasure! every shade that passed over the good mulatto's face brought Cecil Mitford a single step nearer to the final enjoyment of John Cann's treasure.

VI

On the evening when the Hon. Charles Barclay died, Cecil Mitford went out, for the first time after his terrible illness, to speak a few words in private with the negro sexton. He found the man lounging in the soft dust outside his hut, and ready enough to find a place for the corpse (which would be buried next morning, with the ordinary tropical haste), close beside the spot actually occupied by John Cann's coffin. All the rest, the sexton said with a horrid grin, he would leave to Cecil.

At twelve o'clock of a dark moonless night, Cecil Mitford, still weak and ill, but trembling only from the remains of his fever, set out stealthily from the dead man's low bungalow in the outskirts of Spanish Town, and walked on alone through the unlighted, unpaved streets of the sleeping city to the Cathedral precinct. Not a soul met or passed him on the way through the lonely alleys; not a solitary candle burned anywhere in a single window. He carried only a little dark lantern in his hand, and a very small pick that he had borrowed that same afternoon from the negro sexton. Stumbling along through the unfamiliar lanes, he saw at last the great black mass of the gaunt ungainly Cathedral, standing out dimly against the hardly less black abyss of night that formed the solemn background. But Cecil Mitford was not awed by place or season; he could think only of one subject, John Cann's treasure. He groped his way easily through scrub and monuments to the far corner of the churchyard; and there, close by a fresh and open grave he saw the well-remembered, half-effaced letters that marked the mouldering upright slab as John Cann's gravestone. Without a moment's delay, without a touch of hesitation, without a single tinge of womanish weakness, he jumped down boldly into the open grave and turned the light side of his little lantern in the direction of John Cann's undesecrated coffin.

A few strokes of the pick soon loosened the intervening earth sufficiently to let him get at a wooden plank on the nearer side of the coffin. It had mouldered away with damp and age till it was all quite soft and pliable; and he broke through it with his hand alone, and saw lying within a heap of huddled bones, which he knew at once for John Cann's skeleton. Under any other circumstances, such a sight, seen in the dead of night, with all the awesome accessories of time and place, would have chilled and appalled Cecil Mitford's nervous blood; but he thought nothing of it all now; his whole soul was entirely concentrated on a single idea, the search for the missing paper. Leaning over toward the breach he had made into John Cann's grave, he began groping about with his right hand on the floor of the coffin. After a moment's search his fingers came across a small rusty metal object, clasped, apparently, in the bony hand of the skeleton. He drew it eagerly out; it was a steel snuff-box. Prising open the corroded hinge with his pocket-knife, he found inside a small scrap of dry paper. His fingers trembled as he held it to the dark lantern; oh heavens, success! success! it was, it was—the missing document!

He knew it in a moment by the handwriting and the cypher! He couldn't wait to read it till he went home to the dead man's house; so he curled himself up cautiously in Charles Barclay's open grave, and proceeded to decipher the crabbed manuscript as well as he was able by the lurid light of the lantern. Yes, yes, it was all right: it told him with minute and unmistakable detail the exact spot in the valley of the Bovey where John Cann's treasure lay securely hidden. Not at John Cann's rocks on the hilltop, as the local legend untruly affirmed, John Cann had not been such an unguarded fool as to whisper to the idle gossips of Bovey the spot where he had really buried his precious doubloons, but down in the valley by a bend of the river, at a point that Cecil Mitford had known well from his childhood upward. Hurrah! hurrah! the secret was unearthed at last, and he had nothing more to do than to go home to England and proceed to dig up John Cann's treasure!

So he cautiously replaced the loose earth on the side of the grave, and walked back, this time bold and erect, with his dark lantern openly displayed (for it mattered little now who watched or followed him), to dead Charles Barclay's lonely bungalow. The black servants were crooning and wailing over their master's body, and nobody took much notice of the white visitor. If they had, Cecil Mitford would have cared but little, so long as he carried John Cann's last dying directions safely folded in his leather pocket-book.

Next day, Cecil Mitford stood once more as a chief mourner beside the grave he had sat in that night so strangely by himself: and before the week was over, he had taken his passage for England in the Royal Mail Steamer Tagus, and was leaving the cocoa-nut groves of Port Royal well behind him on the port side. Before him lay the open sea, and beyond it, England, Ethel, and John Cann's treasure.

VII

It had been a long job after all to arrange fully the needful preliminaries for the actual search after John Cann's buried doubloons. First of all, there was Ethel's interest to pay, and a horrid story for Cecil to concoct, all false, of course, worse luck to it, about how he had managed to invest her poor three hundred to the best advantage. Then there was another story to make good about three months' extra leave from the Colonial Office. Next came the question of buying the land where John Cann's treasure lay hidden, and this was really a matter of very exceptional and peculiar difficulty. The owner—pig-headed fellow!—didn't want to sell, no matter how much he was offered, because the corner contained a clump of trees that made a specially pretty element in the view from his dining-room windows. His dining-room windows, forsooth! What on earth could it matter, when John Cann's treasure was at stake, whether anything at all was visible or otherwise from his miserable dining-room windows? Cecil was positively appalled at the obstinacy and narrow-mindedness of the poor squireen, who could think of nothing at all in the whole world but his own ridiculous antiquated windows. However, in the end, by making his bid high enough, he was able to induce this obstructive old curmudgeon to part with his triangular little corner of land in the bend of the river. Even so, there was the question of payment: absurd as it seemed, with all John Cann's money almost in his hands, Cecil was obliged to worry and bother and lie and intrigue for weeks together in order to get that paltry little sum in hard cash for the matter of payment. Still, he raised it in the end: raised it by inducing Ethel to sell out the remainder of her poor small fortune, and cajoling Aunt Emily into putting her name to a bill of sale for her few worthless bits of old-fashioned furniture. At last, after many delays and vexatious troubles, Cecil found himself the actual possessor of the corner of land wherein lay buried John Cann's treasure.

The very first day that Cecil Mitford could call that coveted piece of ground his own, he could not restrain his eagerness (though he knew it was imprudent in a land where the unjust law of treasure-trove prevails), but he must then and there begin covertly digging under the shadow of the three big willow trees, in the bend of the river. He had eyed and measured the bearings so carefully already that he knew the very spot to a nail's breadth where John Cann's treasure was actually hidden. He set to work digging with a little pick as confidently as if he had already seen the doubloons lying there in the strong box that he knew enclosed them. Four feet deep he dug, as John Cann's instructions told him; and then, true to the inch, his pick struck against a solid oaken box, well secured with clamps of iron. Cecil cleared all the dirt away from the top, carefully, not hurriedly, and tried with all his might to lift the box out, but all in vain. It was far too heavy, of course, for one man's arms to raise: all that weight of gold and silver must be ever so much more than a single pair of hands could possibly manage. He must try to open the lid alone, so as to take the gold out, a bit at a time, and carry it away with him now and again, as he was able, covering the place up carefully in between, for fear of the Treasury and the Lord of the Manor. How abominably unjust it seemed to him at that moment, the legal claim of those two indolent hostile powers! to think that after he, Cecil Mitford, had borne the brunt of the labour in adventurously hunting up the whole trail of John Cann's secret, two idle irresponsible participators should come in at the end, if they could, to profit entirely by his ingenuity and his exertions!

At last, by a great effort, he forced the rusty lock open, and looked eagerly into the strong oak chest. How his heart beat with slow, deep throbs at that supreme moment, not with suspense, for he knew he should find the money, but with the final realization of a great hope long deferred! Yes, there it lay, in very truth, all before him, great shining coins of old Spanish gold, gold, gold, gold, arranged in long rows, one coin after another, over the whole surface of the broad oak box. He had found it, he had found it, he had really found it! After so much toilsome hunting, after so much vain endeavour, after so many heart-breaking disappointments, John Cann's treasure in very truth lay open there actually before him!

For a few minutes, eager and frightened as he was, Cecil Mitford did not dare even to touch the precious pieces. In the greatness of his joy, in the fierce rush of his overpowering emotions, he had no time to think of mere base everyday gold and silver. It was the future and the ideal that he beheld, not the piled-up heaps of filthy lucre. Ethel was his, wealth was his, honour was his! He would be a rich man and a great man now and henceforth forever! Oh, how he hugged himself in his heart on the wise successful fraud by which he had induced Ethel to advance him the few wretched hundreds he needed for his ever-memorable Jamaican journey! How he praised to himself his own courage, and ingenuity, and determination, and inexhaustible patience! How he laughed down that foolish conscience of his that would fain have dissuaded him from his master-stroke of genius. He deserved it all, he deserved it all! Other men would have flinched before the risk and expense of the voyage to Jamaica, would have given up the scent for a fool's errand in the cemetery at Port Royal, would have shrunk from ransacking John Cann's grave at dead of night in the Cathedral precincts at Spanish Town, would have feared to buy the high-priced corner of land at Bovey Tracy on a pure imaginative speculation. But he, Cecil Mitford, had had the boldness and the cleverness to do it every bit, and now, wisdom was justified of all her children. He sat for five minutes in profound meditation on the edge of the little pit he had dug, gloating dreamily over the broad gold pieces, and inwardly admiring his own bravery and foresight and indomitable resolution. What a magnificent man he really was, a worthy successor of those great freebooting, buccaneering, filibustering Devonians of the grand Elizabethan era! To think that the worky-day modern world should ever have tried to doom him, Cecil Mitford, with his splendid enterprise and glorious potentialities, to a hundred and eighty a year and a routine clerkship at the Colonial Office!

After a while, however, mere numerical cupidity began to get the better of this heroic mood, and Cecil Mitford turned somewhat languidly to the vulgar task of counting the rows of doubloons. He counted up the foremost row carefully, and then for the first time perceived, to his intense surprise, that the row behind was not gold, but mere silver Mexican pistoles. He rubbed his eyes and looked again, but the fact was unmistakable; there was only one row of yellow gold in the top layer, and all the rest was merely bright and glittering silver. Strange that John Cann should have put coins of such small value near the top of his box: the rest of the gold must certainly be in successive layers down further. He lifted up the big gold doubloons in the first row, and then, to his blank horror and amazement, came to, not more gold, not more silver, but—but—but—ay, incredible as it seemed, appalling, horrifying, a wooden bottom!

Had John Cann, in his care and anxiety, put a layer of solid oak between each layer of gold and silver? Hardly that, the oak was too thick. In a moment Cecil Mitford had taken out all the coins of the first tier, and laid bare the oaken bottom. A few blows of the pick loosened the earth around, and then, oh horror, oh ghastly disappointment, oh unspeakable heart-sickening revelation, the whole box came out entire. It was only two inches deep altogether, including the cover, it was, in fact, a mere shallow tray or saucer, something like the sort of thin wooden boxes in which sets of dessert-knives or fish-knives are usually sold for wedding presents!

For the space of three seconds Cecil Mitford could not believe his eyes, and then, with a sudden flash of awful vividness, the whole terrible truth flashed at once across his staggering brain. He had found John Cann's treasure indeed, the John Cann's treasure of base actual reality; but the John Cann's treasure of his fervid imagination, the John Cann's treasure he had dreamt of from his boyhood upward, the John Cann's treasure he had risked all to find and to win, did not exist, could not exist, and never had existed at all anywhere! It was all a horrible, incredible, unthinkable delusion! The hideous fictions he had told would everyone be now discovered; Ethel would be ruined; Aunt Emily would be ruined; and they would both know him, not only for a fool, a dreamer, and a visionary, but also for a gambler, a thief, and a liar.

In his black despair he jumped down into the shallow hole once more, and began a second time to count slowly over the accursed dollars. The whole miserable sum, the untold wealth of John Cann's treasure, would amount altogether to about two hundred and twenty pounds of modern sterling English money. Cecil Mitford tore his hair as he counted it in impotent self punishment; two hundred and twenty pounds, and he had expected at least as many thousands! He saw it all in a moment. His wild fancy had mistaken the poor outcast hunted-down pirate for a sort of ideal criminal millionaire; he had erected the ignorant, persecuted John Cann of real life, who fled from the king's justice to a nest of chartered outlaws in Jamaica, into a great successful naval commander, like the Drake or Hawkins of actual history. The whole truth about the wretched solitary old robber burst in upon him now with startling vividness; he saw him hugging his paltry two hundred pounds to his miserly old bosom, crossing the sea with it stealthily from Jamaica, burying it secretly in a hole in the ground at Bovey, quarrelling about it with his peasant relations in England, as the poor will often quarrel about mere trifles of money, and dying at last with the secret of that wretched sum hidden in the snuff-box that he clutched with fierce energy even in his lifeless skeleton fingers. It was all clear, horribly, irretrievably, unmistakably clear to him now; and the John Cann that he had once followed through so many chances and changes had faded away at once into absolute nothingness, now and for ever!

If Cecil Mitford had known a little less about John Cann's life and exploits he might still perhaps have buoyed himself up with the vain hope that all the treasure was not yet unearthed, that there were more boxes still buried in the ground, more doubloons still hidden further down in the unexplored bosom of the little three-cornered field. But the words of John Cann's own dying directions were too explicit and clear to admit of any such gloss or false interpretation. "In a strong oaken chest, bound round with iron, and buried at four feet of depth in the south-western angle of the Home Croft, at Bovey," said the document, plainly; there was no possibility of making two out of it in any way. Indeed, in that single minute, Cecil Mitford's mind had undergone a total revolution, and he saw the John Cann myth for the first time in his life now in its true colours. The bubble had burst, the halo had vanished, the phantom had faded away, and the miserable squalid miserly reality stood before him with all its vulgar nakedness in their place. The whole panorama of John Cann's life, as he knew it intimately in all its details, passed before his mind's eye like a vivid picture, no longer in the brilliant hues of boyish romance, but in the dingy sordid tones of sober fact. He had given up all that was worth having in this world for the sake of a poor gipsy pirate's penny-saving hoard.

A weaker man would have swallowed the disappointment or kept the delusion still to his dying day. Cecil Mitford was made of stronger mould. The ideal John Cann's treasure had taken possession of him, body and soul; and now that John Cann's treasure had faded into utter nonentity, a paltry two hundred pounds, the whole solid earth had failed beneath his feet, and nothing was left before him but a mighty blank. A mighty blank. Blank, blank, blank. Cecil Mitford sat there on the edge of the pit, with his legs dangling over into the hollow where John Cann's treasure had never been, gazing blankly out into a blank sky, with staring blank eyeballs that looked straight ahead into infinite space and saw utterly nothing.

How long he sat there no one knows; but late at night, when the people at the Red Lion began to miss their guest, and turned out in a body to hunt for him in the corner field, they found him sitting still on the edge of the pit he had dug for the grave of his own hopes, and gazing still with listless eyes into blank vacancy. A box of loose coin lay idly scattered on the ground beside him. The poor gentleman had been struck crazy, they whispered to one another; and so indeed he had: not raving mad with acute insanity, but blankly, hopelessly, and helplessly imbecile. With the loss of John Cann's treasure the whole universe had faded out for him into abject nihilism. They carried him home to the inn between them on their arms, and put him to bed carefully in the old bedroom, as one might put a new-born baby.

The Lord of the Manor, when he came to hear the whole pitiful story, would have nothing to do with the wretched doubloons; the curse of blood was upon them, he said, and worse than that; so the Treasury, which has no sentiments and no conscience, came in at the end for what little there was of John Cann's unholy treasure.

VIII

In the County Pauper Lunatic Asylum for Devon there was one quiet impassive patient, who was always pointed out to horror-loving visitors, because he had once been a gentleman, and had a strange romance hanging to him still, even in that dreary refuge of the destitute insane. The lady whom he had loved and robbed, all for her own good, had followed him down from London to Devonshire; and she and her aunt kept a small school, after some struggling fashion, in the town close by, where many kind-hearted squires of the neighbourhood sent their little girls, while they were still very little, for the sake of charity, and for pity of the sad, sad story. One day a week there was a whole holiday, Wednesday it was, for that was visiting day at the County Asylum; and then Ethel Sutherland, dressed in deep mourning, walked round with her aunt to the gloomy gateway at ten o'clock, and sat as long as she was allowed with the faded image of Cecil Mitford, holding his listless hand clasped hard in her pale white fingers, and looking with sad eager anxious eyes for any gleam of passing recognition in his. Alas, the gleam never came (perhaps it was better so), Cecil Mitford looked always straight before him at the blank whitewashed walls, and saw nothing, heard nothing, thought of nothing, from week's end to week's end.

Ethel had forgiven him all; what will not a loving woman forgive? Nay, more, had found excuses and palliations for him, which quite glossed over his crime and his folly. He must have been losing his reason long before he ever went to Jamaica, she said; for in his right mind he would never have tried to deceive her or himself in the way he had done. Did he not fancy he was sent out by the Colonial Office, when he had really gone without leave or mission? And did he not persuade her to give up her money to him for investment, and after all never invest it? What greater proofs of insanity could you have than those? And then that dreadful fever at Spanish Town, and the shock of losing his kind entertainer, worn out with nursing him, had quite completed the downfall of his reason. So Ethel Sutherland, in her pure beautiful woman's soul, went on believing, as steadfastly as ever, in the faith and the goodness of that Cecil Mitford that had never been. His ideal had faded out before the first touch of disillusioning fact; hers persisted still, in spite of all the rudest assaults that the plainest facts could make upon it. Thank heaven for that wonderful idealising power of a good woman, which enables her to walk unsullied through this sordid world, unknowing and unseeing.

At last one night, one terrible windy night in December, Ethel Sutherland was wakened from her sleep in the quiet little school-house by a fearful glare falling fiercely upon her bedroom window. She jumped up hastily and rushed to the little casement to look out towards the place whence the glare came. One thought alone rose instinctively in her white little mind—Could it be at Cecil's

Asylum? Oh, horror, yes; the whole building was in flames, and if Cecil were taken, even poor mad imbecile Cecil, what, what on earth would then be left her?

Huddling on a few things hastily, anyhow, Ethel rushed out wildly into the street, and ran with incredible speed where all the crowd of the town was running together, towards the blazing Asylum. The mob knew her at once, and recognized her sad claim; they made a little lane down the surging mass for her to pass through, till she stood beside the very firemen at the base of the gateway. It was an awful sight, poor mad wretches raving and imploring at the windows, while the firemen plied their hose and brought their escapes to bear as best they were able on one menaced tier after another. But Ethel saw or heard nothing, save in one third floor window of the right wing, where Cecil Mitford stood, no longer speechless and imbecile, but calling loudly for help, and flinging his eager arms wildly about him. The shock had brought him back his reason, for the moment at least: oh, thank God, thank God, he saw her, he saw her!

With a sudden wild cry Ethel burst from the firemen who tried to hold her back, leaped into the burning building and tore up the blazing stairs, blinded and scorched, but by some miracle not quite suffocated, till she reached the stone landing on the third story. Turning along the well-known corridor, now filled with black wreaths of stifling smoke, she reached at last Cecil's ward, and flung herself madly, wildly into his circling arms. For a moment they both forgot the awful death that girt them round on every side, and Cecil, rising one second superior to himself, cried only "Ethel, Ethel, Ethel, I love you; forgive me!" Ethel pressed his hand in hers gently, and answered in an agony of joy, "There is nothing to forgive, Cecil; I can die happy now, now that I have once more heard you say you love me, you love me."

Hand in hand they turned back towards the blazing staircase, and reached the window at the end where the firemen were now bringing their escape-ladder to bear on the third story. The men below beckoned them to come near and climb out on to the ladder, but just at that moment something behind seemed incomprehensibly to fascinate and delay Cecil, so that he would not move a step nearer, though Ethel led him on with all her might. She looked back to see what could be the reason, and beheld the floor behind them rent by the flames, and a great gap spreading downward to the treasurer's room. On the tiled floor a few dozen pence and shillings and other coins lay, white with heat, among the glowing rubbish; and the whole mass, glittering like gold in the fierce glare, seemed some fiery cave filled to the brim with fabulous wealth. Cecil's eye was riveted upon the yawning gap, and the corners of his mouth twitched horribly as he gazed with intense interest upon the red cinders and white hot coin beneath him. Instinctively Ethel felt at once that all was lost, and that the old mania was once more upon him. Clasping her arm tight round his waist, while the firemen below shouted to her to leave him and come down as she valued her life, she made one desperate effort to drag him by main force to the head of the ladder. But Cecil, strong man that he was, threw her weak little arm impetuously away, as he might have thrown a two-year-old baby's, and cried to her in a voice trembling with excitement, "See, see, Ethel, at last, at last; there it is, there it is in good earnest. JOHN CANN'S TREASURE!"

Ethel seized his arm imploringly once more. "This way, darling," she cried, in a voice choked by sobs and half stifled with the smoke. "This way to the ladder."

But Cecil broke from her fiercely, with a wild light in his big blue eyes, and shouting aloud, "The treasure, the treasure!" leaped with awful energy into the very centre of the seething fiery abyss. Ethel fell, fainting with terror and choked by the flames, on to the burning floor of the third story. The firemen, watching from below, declared next day that that crazy madman must have died stifled before he touched the heap of white hot ruins in the central shell, and the poor lady was insensible or dead with asphyxia full ten minutes before the flames swept past the spot where her lifeless body was lying immovable.

ISALINE AND I

I

"Well, Mademoiselle Isaline," I said, strolling out into the garden, "and who is the young cavalier with the black moustache?"

"What, monsieur," answered Isaline; "you have seen him? You have been watching from your window? We did not know you had returned from the Aiguille."

"Oh, yes, I've been back for more than an hour," I replied; "the snow was so deep on the Col that I gave it up at last, and made up my mind not to try it without a guide."

"I am so glad," Isaline said demurely. "I had such fears for monsieur. The Aiguille is dangerous, though it isn't very high, and I had been very distractedly anxious till monsieur returned."

"Thanks, mademoiselle," I answered, with a little bow. "Your solicitude for my safety flatters me immensely. But you haven't told me yet who is the gentleman with the black moustache."

Isaline smiled. "His name is M. Claude," she said; "M. Claude Tirard, you know; but we don't use surnames much among ourselves in the Pays de Vaud. He is the schoolmaster of the commune."

"M. Claude is a very happy man, then," I put in. "I envy his good fortune."

Isaline blushed a pretty blush. "On the contrary," she answered, "he has just been declaring himself the most miserable of all mankind. He says his life is not worth having."

"They always say that under those peculiar circumstances," I said. "Believe me, mademoiselle, there are a great many men who would be glad to exchange their own indifferently tolerable lot for M. Claude's unendurable misery."

Isaline said nothing, but she looked at me with a peculiar inquiring look, as if she would very much like to know exactly what I meant by it, and how much I meant it.

And what did I mean by it? Not very much after all, I imagine; for when it comes to retrospect, which one of us is any good at analyzing his own motives? The fact is, Isaline was a very pretty little girl, and I had nothing else to do, and I might just as well make myself agreeable to her as gain the reputation of being a bear of an Englishman. Besides, if there was the safeguard of M. Claude, a real indigenous suitor, in the background, there wasn't much danger of my polite attentions being misunderstood.

However, I haven't yet told you how I came to find myself on the farm at Les Pentes at all. This, then, is how it all came about. I was sick of the Temple; I had spent four or five briefless years in lounging about Brick Court and dropping in casually at important cases, just to let the world see I was the proud possessor of a well-curled wig; but even a wig (which suits my complexion admirably) palls after five years, and I said to myself that I would really cut London altogether, and live upon my means somewhere on the Continent. Very small means, to be sure, but still enough to pull through upon in Switzerland or the Black Forest. So, just by way of experiment as to how I liked it, I packed up my fishing-rod and my portmanteau (the first the most important), took the 7.18 express from the Gare de Lyon for Geneva, and found myself next afternoon comfortably seated on the verandah of my favourite hotel at Vevay. The lake is delightful, that we all know; but I wanted to get somewhere where there was a little fishing; so I struck back at once into the mountain country round Château d'Oex and Les Avants, and came soon upon the exact thing I wanted at Les Pentes.

Picture to yourself a great amphitheatre of open alp or mountain pasture in the foreground, with peaks covered by vivid green pines in the middle distance, and a background of pretty aiguilles, naked at their base, but clad near the summit with frozen masses of sparkling ice. Put into the midst of the amphitheatre a clear green-and-white torrent, with a church surrounded by a few wooden farmhouses on its slope, and there you have the commune of Les Pentes. But what was most delightful of all was this, that there was no hotel, no pension, not even a regular lodging-house. I was the first stranger to discover the capabilities of the village, and I was free to exploit them for my own private advantage. By a stroke of luck, it so happened that M. Clairon, the richest farmer of the place, with a pretty old-fashioned Vaudois farmhouse, and a pretty, dainty little Vaudoise daughter, was actually willing to take me in for a mere song per week. I jumped at the chance; and the same day saw me duly installed in a pretty little room, under the eaves of the pretty little farmhouse, and with the pretty little daughter politely attending to all my wants.

Do you know those old-fashioned Vaudois houses, with their big gable-ends, their deep-thatched roofs, their cobs of maize, and smoked hams, and other rural wealth, hanging out ostentatiously under the protecting ledges? If you don't, you can't imagine what a delightful time I had of it at Les Pentes. The farm was a large one for the Pays de Vaud, and M. Clairon actually kept two servants; but madame would have been scandalized at the idea of letting "that Sara" or "that Lisette" wait upon the English voyager; and the consequence was that Mademoiselle Isaline herself always came to answer my little tinkling hand-bell. It was a trifle awkward, for Mademoiselle Isaline was too much of a young lady not to be treated with deferential politeness; and yet there is a certain difficulty in being deferentially polite to the person who lays your table for dinner. However, I made the best of it, and I'm bound to say I managed to get along very comfortably.

Isaline was one of those pretty, plump, laughing-eyed, dimple-cheeked, dark little girls that you hardly ever see anywhere outside the Pays de Vaud. It was almost impossible to look at her without smiling; I'm sure it was quite impossible for her to look at any one else and not smile at them. She wore the prettiest little Vaudois caps you ever saw in your life; and she looked so coquettish in them that you must have been very hard-hearted indeed if you did not straightway fall head over ears in love with her at first sight. Besides, she had been to school at Lausanne, and spoke such pretty, delicate, musical French. Now, my good mother thought badly of my French accent; and when I told her I meant to spend a summer month or two in western Switzerland, she said to me, "I do hope, Charlie dear, you will miss no opportunity of conversing with the people, and improving yourself in colloquial French a little." I am certainly the most dutiful of sons, and I solemnly assure you that whenever I was not fishing or climbing I missed no opportunity whatsoever of conversing with pretty little Isaline.

"Mademoiselle Isaline," I said on this particular afternoon, "I should much like a cup of tea; can Sara bring me one out here in the garden?"

"Perfectly, monsieur; I will bring you out the little table on to the grass plot," said Isaline. "That will arrange things for you much more pleasantly."

"Not for worlds," I said, running in to get it myself; but Isaline had darted into the house before me, and brought it out with her own white little hands on to the tiny lawn. Then she went in again, and soon reappeared with a Japanese tray, bought at Montreux specially in my honour, and a set of the funniest little old China tea-things ever beheld in a London bric-à-brac cabinet.

"Won't you sit and take a cup with me, mademoiselle?" I asked.

"Ma foi, monsieur," answered Isaline, blushing again, "I have never tasted any except as pthisane. But you other English drink it so, don't you? I will try it, for the rest: one learns always."

I poured her out a cup, and creamed it with some of that delicious Vaudois cream (no cream in the world so good as what you get in the Pays de Vaud, you see I am an enthusiast for my adopted country, but that is anticipating matters), and handed it over to her for her approval. She tasted it with a little moue. English-women don't make the moue, so, though I like sticking to my mother tongue, I confess my inability to translate the word. "Brrrr," she said. "Do you English like that stuff! Well, one must accommodate one's self to it, I suppose;" and to do her justice, she proceeded to accommodate herself to it with such distinguished success that she asked me soon for another cup, and drank it off without even a murmur.

"And this M. Claude, then," I asked; "he is a friend of yours? Eh?"

"Passably," she answered, colouring slightly. "You see, we have not much society at Les Pontes. He comes from the Normal School at Geneva. He is instructed, a man of education. We see few such here. What would you have?" She said it apologetically, as though she thought she was bound to excuse herself for having made M. Claude's acquaintance.

"But you like him very much?"

"Like him? Well, yes; I liked him always well enough. Bat he is too haughty. He gives himself airs. To-day he is angry with me. He has no right to be angry with me."

"Mademoiselle," I said, "have you ever read our Shakespeare?"

"Oh, yes, in English I have read him. I can read English well enough, though I speak but a little."

"And have you read the 'Tempest'?"

"How? Ariel, Ferdinand, Miranda, Caliban? Oh, yes. It is beautiful."

"Well, mademoiselle," I said, "do you remember how Miranda first saw Ferdinand?"

She smiled and blushed again, she was such a little blusher. "I know what you would say," she said. "You English are blunt. You talk to young ladies so strangely."

"Well, Mademoiselle Isaline, it seems to me that you at Les Pentes are like Miranda on the island. You see nobody, and there is nobody here to see you. You must not go and fall in love, like Miranda, with the very first man you happen to meet with, because he comes from the Normal School at Geneva. There are plenty of men in the world, believe me, beside M. Claude."

"Ah, but Miranda and Ferdinand both loved one another," said Isaline archly; "and they were married, and both lived happily ever afterward." I saw at once she was trying to pique me.

"How do you know that?" I asked. "It doesn't say so in the play. For all I know, Ferdinand lost the crown of Naples through a revolution, and went and settled down at a country school in Savoy or somewhere, and took to drinking, and became brutally unsociable, and made Miranda's life a toil and a burden to her. At any rate, I'm sure of one thing; he wasn't worthy of her."

What made me go on in this stupid way? I'm sure I don't know. I certainly didn't mean to marry Isaline myself: ... at least, not definitely: and yet when you are sitting down at tea on a rustic garden seat, with a pretty girl in a charming white crimped cap beside you, and you get a chance of insinuating that other fellows don't think quite as much of her as you do, it isn't human nature to let slip the opportunity of insinuating it.

"But you don't know M. Claude," said Isaline practically, "and so you can't tell whether he is worthy of me or not."

"I'm perfectly certain," I answered, "that he can't be, even though he were a very paragon of virtue, learning, and manly beauty."

"If monsieur talks in that way," said Isaline, "I shall have to go back at once to mamma."

"Wait a moment," I said, "and I will talk however you wish me. You know, you agree to give me instruction in conversational French. That naturally includes lessons in conversation with ladies of exceptional personal attractions. I must practise for every possible circumstance of life.... So you have read Shakespeare, then. And any other English books?"

"Oh, many. Scott, and Dickens, and all, except Byron. My papa says a young lady must not read Byron. But I have read what he has said of our lake, in a book of extracts. It is a great pleasure to me to look down among the vines and chestnuts, there, and to think that our lake, which gleams so blue and beautiful below, is the most famous in poetry of all lakes. You know, Jean Jacques says, 'Mon lac est le premier,' and so it is."

"Then you have read Jean Jacques too?"

"Oh, mon Dieu, no. My papa says a young lady must especially not read Jean Jacques. But I know something about him, so much as is convenable. Hold here! do you see that clump of trees down there by the lake, just above Clarens? That is Julie's grove, 'le bosquet de Julie' we call it. There isn't a spot along the lake that is not thus famous, that has not its memories and its associations. It is for that that I could not choose ever to leave the dear old Pays de Vaud."

"You would not like to live in England, then?" I asked. (What a fool I was, to be sure.)

"Oh, ma foi, no. That would make one too much shiver, with your chills, and your fogs, and your winters. I could not stand it. It is cold here, but at any rate it is sunny.... Well, at least, it would not be pleasant.... But, after all, that depends.... You have the sun, too, sometimes, don't you?"

"Isaline!" cried madame from the window. "I want you to come and help me pick over the gooseberries!" And, to say the truth, I thought it quite time she should go.

A week later, I met M. Claude again. He was a very nice young fellow, there was not a doubt of that. He was intelligent, well educated, manly, with all the honest, sturdy, independent Swiss nature clearly visible in his frank, bright, open face. I have seldom met a man whom I liked better at first sight than M. Claude, and after he had gone away I felt more than a little ashamed of myself to think I had been half trying to steal away Isaline's heart from this good fellow, without really having any deliberate design upon it myself. It began to strike me that I had been doing a very dirty, shabby thing.

"Charlie, my boy," I said to myself, as I sat fishing with bottom bait and dangling my legs over the edge of a pool, "you've been flirting with this pretty little Swiss girl; and what's worse, you've been flirting in a very bad sort of way. She's got a lover of her own; and you've been trying to make her feel dissatisfied with him, for no earthly reason. You've taken advantage of your position and your fancied London airs and graces to run down by implication a good fellow who really loves her and would probably make her an excellent husband. Don't let this occur again, sir." And having thus virtuously resolved, of course I went away and flirted with Isaline next morning as vigorously as ever.

During the following fortnight, M. Claude came often, and I could not disguise from myself the fact that M. Claude did not quite like me. This was odd, for I liked him very much. I suppose he took me for a potential rival: men are so jealous when they are in love. Besides, I observed that Isaline tried not to be thrown too much with him alone; tried to include me in the party wherever she went with him. Also, I will freely confess that I felt myself every day more fond of Isaline's society, and I half fancied I caught myself trepidating a little inwardly now and then when she happened to come up to me. Absurd to be so susceptible; but such is man.

One lovely day about this time I set out once more to try my hand (or rather my feet) alone upon the Aiguille. Isaline put me up a nice little light lunch in my knapsack, and insisted upon seeing that my alpenstock was firmly shod, and my pedestrian boots in due climbing order. In fact, she loudly lamented my perversity in attempting to make the ascent without a guide; and she must even needs walk with me as far as the little bridge over the torrent beside the snow line, to point me out the road the guides generally took to the platform at the summit. For myself, I was a practised mountaineer, and felt no fear for the result. As I left her for the ice, she stood a long time looking and waving me the right road with her little pocket-handkerchief; while as long as I could hear her voice she kept on exhorting me to be very careful. "Ah, if monsieur would only have taken a guide! You don't know how dangerous that little Aiguille really is."

The sun was shining brightly on the snow; the view across the valley of the Rhone towards the snowy Alps beyond was exquisite; and the giants of the Bernese Oberland stood out in gloriously brilliant outline on the other side against the clear blue summer sky. I went on alone, enjoying myself hugely in my own quiet fashion, and watching Isaline as she made her way slowly along the green path, looking round often and again, till she disappeared in the shadow of the pinewood that girt round the tiny village. On, farther still, up and up and up, over soft snow for the most part; with very little ice, till at last, after three hours' hard climbing, I stood on the very summit of the pretty Aiguille. It was not very high, but it commanded a magnificent view over either side, the Alps on one hand, the counterchain of the Oberland on the other, and the blue lake gleaming and glowing through all its length in its green valley between them. There I sat down on the pure snow in the glittering sunlight, and ate the lunch that Isaline had provided for me, with much gusto. Unfortunately, I also drank the pint of white wine from the head of the lake—Yvorne, we call it, and I grow it now in my own vineyard at Pic de la Baume—but that is anticipating again: as good a light wine as you will get anywhere in Europe in these depressing days of blight and phylloxera. Now, a pint of vin du pays is not too much under ordinary circumstances for a strong young man in vigorous health, doing a hard day's muscular work with legs, arms, and sinews: but mountain air is thin and exhilarating in itself, and it lends a point to a half-bottle of Yvorne which the wine's own body does not by any means usually possess. I don't mean to say so much light wine does one any positive harm; but it makes one more careless and easy-going; gives one a false sense of security, and entices one into paying less heed to one's footsteps or to suspicious-looking bits of doubtful ice.

Well, after lunch I took a good look at the view with my field-glass; and when I turned it towards Les Pentes I could make out our farmhouse distinctly, and even saw Isaline standing on the balcony looking towards the Aiguille. My heart jumped a little when I thought that she was probably looking for me. Then I wound my way down again, not by retracing my steps, but by trying a new path, which seemed to me a more practicable one. It was not the one Isaline had pointed out, but it appeared to go more directly, and to avoid one or two of the very worst rough-and-tumble pieces.

I was making my way back, merrily enough, when suddenly I happened to step on a little bit of loose ice, which slid beneath my feet in a very uncomfortable manner. Before I knew where I was, I felt myself sliding rapidly on, with the ice clinging to my heel; and while I was vainly trying to dig my alpenstock into a firm snowbank, I became conscious for a moment of a sort of dim indefinite blank. It was followed by a sensation of empty space; and then I knew I was falling over the edge of something.

Whrrr, whrrr, whrrr, went the air at my ear for a moment; and the next thing I knew was a jar of pain, and a consciousness of being enveloped in something very soft. The jar took away all other feeling for a few seconds; I only knew I was stunned and badly hurt. After a time, I began to be capable of trying to realize the position; and when I opened my eyes and looked around me, I recognized that I was lying on my back, and that there was a pervading sensation of whiteness everywhere about. In point of fact, I was buried in snow. I tried to move, and to get on my legs again, but two things very effectually prevented me. In the first place, I could not stir my legs without giving myself the most intense pain in my spine; and in the second place, when I did stir them I brought them into contact on the one hand with a solid wall of rock, and on the other hand with vacant space, or at least with very soft snow unsupported by a rocky bottom. Gradually, by feeling about with my arms, I began exactly to realize the gravity of the position. I had fallen over a precipice, and had lighted on a snow-covered ledge half-way down. My back was very badly hurt, and I dared not struggle up on to my legs for fear of falling off the ledge again on the other side. Besides, I was half smothered in the snow, and even if anybody ever came to look for me (which they would not probably do till to-morrow) they would not be able to see me, because of the deep-covering drifts. If I was not extricated that night, I should probably freeze to death before morning, especially after my pint of wine. "Confound that Yvorne!" I said to myself savagely. "If ever I get out of this scrape I'll never touch a drop of the stuff again as long as I live." I regret to say that I have since broken that solemn promise twice daily for the past three years.

My one hope was that Isaline might possibly be surprised at my delay in returning, and might send out one of the guides to find me.

So there I lay a long time, unable even to get out of the snow, and with every movement causing me a horrid pain in my injured back. Still, I kept on moving my legs every now and then to make the pain shoot, and so prevent myself from feeling drowsy. The snow half suffocated me, and I could only breathe with difficulty. At last, slowly, I began to lose consciousness, and presently I suppose I fell asleep. To fall asleep in the snow is the first stage of freezing to death.

III

Noises above me, I think, on the edge of the precipice. Something coming down, oh, how slowly. Something comes, and fumbles about a yard or so away. Then I cry out feebly, and the something approaches. M. Claude's hearty voice calls out cheerily, "Enfin, le voilà!" and I am saved.

They let down ropes and pulled me up to the top of the little crag, clumsily, so as to cause me great pain: and then three men carried me home to the farmhouse on a stretcher. M. Claude was one of the three, the others were labourers from the village.

"How did you know I was lost, M. Claude?" I asked feebly, as they carried me along on the level.

He did not answer for a moment; then he said, rather gloomily, in German, "The Fräulein was watching you with a telescope from Les Pentes." He did not say Fräulein Isaline, and I knew why at once: he did not wish the other carriers to know what he was talking about.

"And she told you?" I said, in German too.

"She sent me. I did not come of my own accord. I came under orders." He spoke sternly, hissing out his gutturals in an angry voice.

"M. Claude," I said, "I have done very wrong, and I ask your forgiveness. You have saved my life, and I owe you a debt of gratitude for it. I will leave Les Pentes and the Fräulein to-morrow, or at least as soon as I can safely be moved."

He shook his head bitterly. "It is no use now," he answered, with a sigh; "the Fräulein does not wish for me. I have asked her, and she has refused me. And she has been watching you up and down the Aiguille the whole day with a telescope. When she saw you had fallen, she rushed out like one distracted, and came to tell me at the school in the village. It is no use, you have beaten me."

"M. Claude," I said, "I will plead for you. I have done you wrong, and I ask your forgiveness."

"I owe you no ill-will," he replied, in his honest, straightforward, Swiss manner. "It is not your fault if you too have fallen in love with her. How could any man help it? Living in the same house with her, too! Allons," he went on in French, resuming his alternative tongue (for he spoke both equally), "we must get on quick and send for the doctor from Glion to see you."

By the time we reached the farmhouse, I had satisfied myself that there was nothing very serious the matter with me after all. The soft snow had broken the force of the concussion. I had strained my spine a good deal, and hurt the tendons of the thighs and back, but had not broken any bones, nor injured any vital organ. So when they laid me on the old-fashioned sofa in my little sitting-room, lighted a fire in the wide hearth, and covered me over with a few rugs, I felt comparatively happy and comfortable under the circumstances. The doctor was sent for in hot haste; but on his arrival, he confirmed my own view of the case, and declared I only needed rest and quiet and a little arnica.

I was rather distressed, however, when madame came up to see me an hour later, and assured me that she and monsieur thought I ought to be moved down as soon as possible into more comfortable apartments at Lausanne, where I could secure better attendance. I saw in a moment what that meant: they wanted to get me away from Isaline. "There are no more comfortable quarters in all Switzerland, I am sure, madame," I said: but madame was inflexible. There was an English doctor at Lausanne, and to Lausanne accordingly I must go. Evidently, it had just begun to strike those two good simple people that Isaline and I could just conceivably manage to fall in love with one another.

Might I ask for Mademoiselle Isaline to bring me up a cup of tea? Yes, Isaline would bring it in a minute. And when she came in, those usually laughing black eyes obviously red with crying, I felt my heart sink within me when I thought of my promise to M. Claude; while I began to be vaguely conscious that I was really and truly very much in love with pretty little Isaline on my own account.

She laid the tray on the small table by the sofa, and was going to leave the room immediately. "Mademoiselle Isaline," I said, trying to raise myself, and falling back again in pain, "won't you sit with me a little while? I want to talk with you."

"My mamma said I must come away at once," Isaline replied demurely. "She is without doubt busy and wants my aid." And she turned to go towards the door.

"Oh, do come back, mademoiselle," I cried, raising myself again, and giving myself, oh, such a wrench in the spine: "don't you see how much it hurts me to sit up?"

She turned back, indecisively, and sat down in the big chair just beyond the table, handing me the cup, and helping me to cream and sugar. I plunged at once in medias res.

"You have been crying, mademoiselle," I said, "and I think I can guess the reason. M. Claude has told me something about it. He has asked you for your hand, and you have refused him. Is it not so?" This was a little bit of hypocrisy on my part, I confess, for I knew what she had been crying about perfectly: but I wished to be loyal to M. Claude.

Isaline blushed and laughed. "I do not cry for M. Claude," she said. "I may have other matters of my own to cry about. But M. Claude is very free with his confidences, if he tells such things to a stranger."

"Listen to me, Mademoiselle Isaline," I said. "Your father and mother have asked me to leave here to-morrow and go down to Lausanne. I shall probably never see you again. But before I go, I want to plead with you for M. Claude. He has saved my life, and I owe him much gratitude. He loves you; he is a brave man, a good man, a true and earnest man; why will you not marry him? I feel sure he is a noble fellow, and he will make you a tender husband. Will you not think better of your decision? I cannot bear to leave Les Pentes till I know that you have made him happy."

"Truly?"

"Truly."

"And you go away to-morrow?"

"Yes, to-morrow."

"Oh, monsieur!"

There isn't much in those two words; but they may be pronounced with a good deal of difference in the intonation; and Isaline's intonation did not leave one in much doubt as to how she used them. Her eyes filled again with tears, and she half started up to go. Ingrate and wretch that I was, forgetful of my promise to M. Claude, my eyes filled responsively, and I jumped to catch her and keep her from going, of course at the expense of another dreadful wrench to my poor back. "Isaline," I cried, unconsciously dropping the mademoiselle, and letting her see my brimming eyelids far too obviously, "Isaline, do wait awhile, I implore you, I beseech you! I have something to say to you."

She seated herself once more in the big chair. "Well, mon pauvre monsieur," she cried, "what is it?"

"Isaline," I began, trying it over again; "why won't you marry M. Claude?"

"Oh, that again. Well," answered Isaline boldly, "because I do not love him, and I love somebody else. You should not ask a young lady about these matters. In Switzerland, we do not think it comme il faut."

"But," I went on, "why do you not love M. Claude? He has every good quality, and—"

"Every good quality, and—he bores me," answered Isaline. "Monsieur," she went on archly, "you were asking me the other day what books I had read in English. Well, I have read Longfellow. Do you remember Miles Standish?"

I saw what she was driving at, and laughed in spite of myself. "Yes," I said, "I know what you mean. When John Alden is pleading with Priscilla on behalf of Miles Standish, Priscilla cuts him short by saying—"

Isaline finished the quotation herself in her own pretty clipped English, "Why don't you speak for yourself, John?"

I laughed. She laughed. We both looked at one another; and the next thing I remember was that I had drawn down Isaline's plump little face close to mine, and was kissing it vigorously, in spite of an acute darting pain at each kiss all along my spine and into my marrow-bones. Poor M. Claude was utterly forgotten.

In twenty minutes I had explained my whole position to Isaline: and in twenty minutes more, I had monsieur and madame up to explain it all to them in their turn. Monsieur listened carefully while I told him that I was an English advocate in no practice to speak of; that I had a few hundreds a year of my own, partly dependent upon my mother; that I had thoughts of settling down permanently in Switzerland; and that Isaline was willing, with her parents' consent, to share my modest competence. Monsieur replied with true Swiss caution that he would inquire into my statements, and that if they proved to be as represented, and if I obtained in turn my mother's consent, he would be happy to hand me over Isaline. "Toutefois," he added quietly, "it will be perhaps better to rescind your journey to Lausanne. The Glion doctor is, after all, a sufficiently skilful one." So I waited on in peace at Les Pontes.

Madame had insisted upon telegraphing the news of my accident to my mother, lest it should reach her first in the papers ("Je suis mère moi-même, monsieur," she said, in justification of her conduct). And next morning we got a telegram in reply from my mother, who evidently imagined she must hurry over at once if she wished to see her son alive, or at least must nurse him through a long and dangerous illness. Considering the injuries were a matter of about three days' sofa, in all probability, this haste was a little overdone. However, she would arrive by the very first rapide from Paris; and on the whole I was not sorry, for I was half afraid she might set her face against my marrying "a foreigner," but I felt quite sure anyone who once saw Isaline could never resist her.

That afternoon, when school was over, M. Claude dropped in to see how I was getting on. I felt more like a thief at that moment than I ever felt in my whole life before or since. I knew I must tell him the simple truth; but I didn't know how to face it. However, as soon as I began, he saved me the trouble by saying, "You need not mind explaining. Mademoiselle Isaline has told me all. Yon did your best for me, I feel sure; but she loves you, and she does not love me. We cannot help these things; they come and go without our being able to govern them. I am sorry, more than sorry; but I thank you for your kind offices. Mademoiselle Isaline tells me you said all you could on my behalf, and nothing on your own. Accept my congratulations on having secured the love of the sweetest girl in all Switzerland." And he shook my hand with an honest heartiness that cost me several more twinges both in the spine and the half-guilty conscience. Yet, after all, it was not my fault.

"Monsieur Claude," I said, "you are an honest fellow, and a noble fellow, and I trust you will still let me be your friend."

"Naturally," answered M. Claude, in his frank way. "I have only done my duty. You have been the lucky one, but I must not bear you a grudge for that; though it has cost my heart a hard struggle;" and, as he spoke, the tears came for a moment in his honest blue eyes, though he tried to brush them away unseen.

"Monsieur Claude," I said, "you are too generous to me. I can never forgive myself for this."

Before many days my mother came to hand duly; and though her social prejudices were just a trifle shocked, at first, by the farmhouse, with its hams and maize, which I had found so picturesque, I judged rightly that Isaline would soon make an easy conquest of her. My mother readily admitted that my accent had improved audibly to the naked ear; that Isaline's manners were simply perfect; that she was a dear, pretty, captivating little thing; and that on the whole she saw no objections, save one possible one, to my marriage. "Of course, Charlie," she said, "the Clairons are Protestants; because, otherwise, I could never think of giving my consent."

This was a poser in its way; for though I knew the village lay just on the borderland, and some of the people were Catholics while others were Reformed, I had not the remotest notion to which of the two churches Isaline belonged. "Upon my soul, mother dear," I said, "it has never struck me to inquire into Isaline's private abstract opinion on the subject of the Pope's infallibility or the Geneva Confession. You see, after all, it could hardly be regarded as an important or authoritative one. However, I'll go at once and find out."

Happily, as it turned out, the Clairons were Reformed, and so my mother's one objection fell to the ground immediately. M. Clairon's inquiries were also satisfactory; and the final result was that Isaline and I were to be quietly married before the end of the summer. The good father had a nice little vineyard estate at Pic de la Baume, which he proposed I should undertake to cultivate; and my mother waited to see us installed in one of the prettiest little toy châlets to be seen anywhere at the Villeneuve end of the lovely lake. A happier or sweeter bride than Isaline I defy the whole world, now or ever, to produce.

From the day of our wedding, almost, Isaline made it the business of her life to discover a fitting wife for good M. Claude; and in the end she succeeded in discovering, I will freely admit (since Isaline is not jealous), the second prettiest and second nicest girl in the whole Pays de Vaud. And what is more, she succeeded also in getting M. Claude to fall head over ears in love with her at first sight; to propose to her at the end of a week; and to be accepted with effusion by Annette herself, and with coldness by her papa, who thought the question of means a trifle unsatisfactory. But Isaline and I arranged that Claude should come into partnership in our vineyard business on easy terms, and give up schoolmastering for ever; and the consequence is that he and his wife have now got the companion châlet to ours, and between our two local connections, in Switzerland and England, we are doing one of the best trades in the new export wine traffic of any firm along the lake. Of course we have given up growing Yvorne, except for our own use, confining ourselves entirely to a high-priced vintage-wine, with very careful culture, for our English business: and I take this opportunity of recommending our famous phylloxera-proof white Pic de la Baume, London Agents—. But Isaline says that looks too much like an advertisement, so I leave off. Still, I can't help saying that a dearer little wife than Isaline, or a better partner than Claude, never yet fell to any man's lot. They certainly are an excellent people, these Vaudois, and I think you would say so too if only you knew them as well as I do.

PROFESSOR MILLITER'S DILEMMA

The Gospel Evangelists were naturally very proud of Professor Milliter. A small and despised sect, with not many great, not many rich, not many noble among them, they could comfort themselves at least with the reflection that they numbered in their fold one of the most learned and justly famous of modern English scientific thinkers. It is true, their place of meeting at Mortiscombe was but an upper chamber in a small cottage; their local congregation consisted of hardly more than three score members; and their nickname among their orthodox churchy neighbours was the very opprobrious and very ridiculous one of "the Shivering Ranters." Still, the Gospel Evangelists felt it was a great privilege to be permitted the ministrations of so learned and eloquent a preacher as Professor Milliter. The rector of the parish was an Oxford M.A., of the usual decorously stereotyped conventional pattern; but in point even of earthly knowledge and earthly consideration, said the congregation at Patmos Chapel, "he is not worthy to unloose the latchet of our pastor's shoe." For Professor Milliter was universally allowed to be the greatest living authority in England on comparative anatomy, the rising successor of Cuvier, and Owen, and Milne-Edwards, and Carpenter, in the general knowledge of animal structure.

Mortiscombe, as everybody knows, is the favourite little suburban watering-place, close by the busy streets and noisy wharves of a great English manufacturing centre. It is at Mortiscombe that the Western Counties College of Science is situated, away from the smoke and bustle of the whirring city: and it was in the Western Counties College of Science that Cyril Milliter ably filled the newly founded chair of Comparative Anatomy. When he was first appointed, indeed, people grumbled a little at the idea of a Professor at the College undertaking every Sunday to preach in a common conventicle to a low assembly of vulgar fanatics, as in their charitable Christian fashion they loved to call the Gospel Evangelists. But Cyril Milliter was a man of character and determination: he had fully made up his own mind upon theological questions; and having once cast in his lot with the obscure sect of Gospel Evangelists, to which his parents had belonged before him, he was not to be turned aside from his purpose by the coarse gibes of the ordinary public or the cynical incredulity of more cultivated but scarcely more tolerant polite society. "Not a Gospel Evangelist really and truly: you must surely be joking, Mr. Milliter," young ladies said to him at evening parties with undisguised astonishment; "why, they're just a lot of ignorant mill-hands, you know, who meet together in an upper room somewhere down in Ford's Passage to hear sermons from some ignorant lay preacher."

"Quite so," Cyril Milliter would answer quietly; "and I am the ignorant lay preacher who has been appointed to deliver those sermons to them. I was brought up among the Gospel Evangelists as a child, and now that I am a man my mature judgment has made me still continue among them."

Mortiscombe is well known to be a very advanced and liberal-minded place; so, after a time, people ceased to talk about the curious singularity of Cyril Milliter's Sunday occupation. All through the week the young professor lectured to his class on dry bones and the other cheerful stock-in-trade of his own department; and on Sundays he walked down erect, Bible in hand, to his little meeting-room, and there fervently expounded the Word, as it approved itself to his soul and conscience, before the handful of earnest artisans who composed his faithful but scanty congregation. A fiery and enthusiastic preacher was Cyril Milliter, devoured with zeal for what seemed to him the right doctrine. "There is only one thing worth living for in this fallen world," he used to say to his little group of attentive hearers, "and that is Truth. Truth, as it reveals itself in the book of nature, must be our quest during the working week: Truth, as it reveals itself in the written Word, must be our quest on these happy blessed seventh-day Sabbaths." There was a high eager light in his eye as he spoke, mingled with a clear intellectual honesty in his sharply cut features, which gave at once the stamp of reality to that plain profession of his simple, manly, earnest creed.

One other subject, however, beside the pursuit of truth, just at that moment deeply interested Cyril Milliter; and that subject assumed bodily form in the pretty little person of Netta Leaworthy. Right in front of Cyril, as he expounded the Word every Sunday morning, sat a modest, demure, dimpled English girl, with a complexion like a blushing apple-blossom, and a mouth like the sunny side of a white-heart cherry. She was only the daughter of an intelligent mill-hand, a foreman at one of the great factories in the neighbouring city, was dainty, whitefingered, sweet-voiced little Netta; but there was a Puritan freshness and demureness and simplicity about her that fairly won the heart of the enthusiastic young professor. Society at Mortiscombe had made itself most agreeable to Cyril Milliter, in spite of his heterodoxy, as Society always does to eligible young bachelors of good education; and it had thrown its daughters decorously in his way, by asking him to all its dinners, dances, and at-homes, with most profuse and urgent hospitality. But in spite of all the wiles of the most experienced among Society's mothers, Cyril Milliter had positively had the bad taste to fix his choice at last upon nobody better than simple, unaffected, charming little Netta.

For one sunny Sunday morning, after worship, Cyril had turned out into the fields behind the Common, for a quiet stroll among the birds and flowers: when, close by the stile in the upper meadow, he came unexpectedly upon Netta Leaworthy, alone upon the grass with her own fancies. She was pulling an ox-eye daisy carelessly to pieces as he passed, and he stopped a minute unperceived beside the hedge, to watch her deft fingers taking out one ray after another quickly from the blossom to the words of a foolish childish charm. Netta blushed crimson when she saw she was observed at that silly pastime, and Cyril thought to himself he had never seen anything in his life more lovely than the blushing girl at that moment. Learned and educated as he was, he had sprung himself from among the ranks of the many, and his heart was with them still rather than with the rich, the noble, and the mighty. "I will never marry among the daughters of Heth," he said to himself gently, as he paused beside her: "I will take to myself rather a wife and a helpmate from among the Lord's own chosen people."

"Ah, Miss Leaworthy," he went on aloud, smiling sympathetically at her embarrassment, "you are following up the last relics of a dying superstition, are you? 'One for money, two for health, Three for love, and four for wealth.' Is that how the old saw goes? I thought so. And which of the four blessings now has your daisy promised you I wonder?"

The tone he spoke in was so very different from that which he had just been using in the chapel at worship that Netta felt instinctively what it foreboded; and her heart fluttered tremulously as she answered in the quietest voice she could command, "I haven't finished it yet, Mr. Milliter; I have made five rounds already, and have a lot of rays left still in the middle of the daisy."

Cyril took it from her, laughingly, and went on with the rhyme, his conscience upbraiding him in an undertone of feeling meanwhile for such an unworthy paltering with old-world superstition, till he had gone twice round the spell, and finished abruptly with "Three for love!" "Love it is!" he cried gaily. "A good omen! Miss Leaworthy, we none of us love superstition: but perhaps after all it is something more than that; there may be a Hand guiding us from above, even in these everyday trifles! We must never forget, you know, that every hair of our heads is numbered."

Netta's heart fluttered still more violently within her as he looked at her so closely. Could it be that really, in spite of everything, the great, learned, good, clever young professor was going to ask her to be his wife? Netta had listened to him with joy Sunday after Sunday from his simple platform pulpit, and had felt in her heart that no man never expounded the gospel of love as beautifully as he did. She had fancied sometimes, girls cannot help fancying, be they as modest and retiring as they may, that he really did like her just a little. And she—she had admired and wondered at him from a distance. But she could hardly believe even now that that little vague day-dream which had sometimes floated faintly before her eyes was going to be actually realized in good earnest. She could answer nothing, her heart beat so; but she looked down to the ground with a flushed and frightened look which was more eloquent in its pretty simplicity than all the resources of the most copious language.

Cyril Milliter's mind, however, was pretty well made up already on this important matter, and he had been waiting long for just such an opportunity of asking Netta whether she could love him. And now, even without asking her, he could feel at once by some subtle inner sense that his eager question was answered beforehand, and that modest, maidenly little Netta Leaworthy was quite prepared to love him dearly.

For a moment he stood there looking at her intently, and neither of them spoke. Then Netta raised her eyes from the ground for a second's flash; and Cyril's glance caught hers one instant before she bent them down again in haste to play nervously with the mangled daisy. "Netta," he said, the name thrilling through his very marrow as he uttered it, "Netta, I love you."

She stood irresolute for a while, listening to the beating of her own heart, and then her eye caught his once more, timidly, but she spoke never a syllable.

Cyril took her wee white hand in his—a lady's hand, if ever you saw one, and raised it with chivalrous tenderness to his lips. Netta allowed him to raise it and kiss it without resistance. "Then you will let me love you?" he asked quickly. Netta still did not answer, but throwing herself back on the bank by the hedgerow began to cry like a frightened child.

Cyril sat down, all tremulous beside her, took the white hand unresisted in his, and said to her gently, "Oh, Netta, what is this for?"

Then Netta answered with an effort, through her tears, "Mr. Milliter, Mr. Milliter, how can you ever tell me of this?"

"Why not, Netta? Why not, my darling? May I not ask you to be my wife? Will you have me, Netta?"

Netta looked at him timidly, with another blush, and said slowly, "No, Mr. Milliter; I cannot. I must not."

"Why not, Netta? Oh, why not? Tell me a reason."

"Because it wouldn't be right. Because it wouldn't be fair to you. Because it wouldn't be true of me. You ought to marry a lady, someone in your own rank of life, you know. It would be wrong to tie your future down to a poor nameless nobody like me, when you might marry—marry—almost any lady you chose in all Mortiscombe."

"Netta, you pain me. You are wronging me. You know I care nothing for such gewgaws as birth or wealth or rank or station. I would not marry one of those ladies even if she asked me. And, as to my own position in life, why, Netta, my position is yours. My parents were poor God-fearing people, like your parents; and if you will not love me, then, Netta, Netta, I say it solemnly, I will never, never marry anybody."

Netta answered never a word; but, as any other good girl would do in her place, once more burst into a flood of tears, and looked at him earnestly from her swimming eyes in speechless doubt and trepidation.

Perhaps it was wrong of Cyril Milliter, on a Sunday, and in the public pathway too, but he simply put his strong arm gently round her waist, and kissed her a dozen times over fervidly without let or hindrance.

Then Netta put him away from her, not too hastily, but with a lingering hesitation, and said once more, "But, Mr. Milliter, I can never marry you. You will repent of this yourself by-and-by at your leisure. Just think, how could I ever marry you, when I should always be too frightened of you to call you anything but 'Mr. Milliter!'"

"Why, Netta," cried the young professor, with a merry laugh, "if that's all, you'll soon learn to call me, 'Cyril.'"

"To call you 'Cyril,' Mr. Milliter! Oh dear, no, never. Why, I've looked at you so often in meeting, and felt so afraid of you, because you were so learned, and wise, and terrible: and I'm sure I should never learn to call you by your Christian name, whatever happened."

"And as you can't do that, you won't marry me! I'm delighted to hear it, Netta, delighted to hear it; for if that's the best reason you can conjure up against the match, I don't think, little one, I shall find it very hard to talk you over."

"But, Mr. Milliter, are you quite sure you won't regret it yourself hereafter? Are you quite sure you won't repent, when you find Society doesn't treat you as it did, for my sake? Are you quite sure nothing will rise up hereafter between us, no spectre of class difference, or class prejudice, to divide our lives and make us unhappy?"

"Never!" Cyril Milliter answered, seizing both her hands in his eagerly, and looking up with an instinctive glance to the open heaven above them as witness. "Never, Netta, as long as I live and you live, shall any shadow of such thought step in for one moment to put us asunder."

And Netta, too proud and pleased to plead against her own heart any longer, let him kiss her once again a lover's kiss, and pressed his hand in answer timidly, and walked back with him blushing towards Mortiscombe, his affianced bride before the face of high heaven.

When Society at Mortiscombe first learnt that that clever young Professor Milliter was really going to marry the daughter of some factory foreman, Society commented frankly upon the matter according to the various idiosyncrasies and temperaments of its component members. Some of it was incredulous; some of it was shocked; some of it was cynical; some of it was satirical; and some of it, shame to say, was spitefully free with suggested explanations for such very strange and unbecoming conduct. But Cyril Milliter himself was such a transparently honest and straightforward man, that, whenever the subject was alluded to in his presence, he shamed the cynicism and the spitefulness of Society by answering simply, "Yes, I'm going to marry a Miss Leaworthy, a very good and sweet girl, the daughter of the foreman at the Tube Works, who is a great friend of mine and a member of my little Sunday congregation." And, somehow, when once Cyril Milliter had said that in his quiet natural way to anybody, however cynical, the somebody never cared to talk any more gossip thenceforward for ever on the subject of the professor's forthcoming marriage.

Indeed, so fully did the young professor manage to carry public sentiment with him in the end, that when the wedding-day actually arrived, almost every carriage in all Mortiscombe was drawn up at the doors of the small chapel where the ceremony was performed; and young Mrs. Milliter had more callers during the first fortnight after her honeymoon than she knew well how to accommodate in their tiny drawing-room. In these matters, Society never takes any middle course. Either it disapproves of a "mixed marriage" altogether, in which case it crushes the unfortunate offender sternly under its iron heel; or else it rapturously adopts the bride into its own magic circle, in which case she immediately becomes a distinct somebody, in virtue of the very difference of original rank, and is invited everywhere with empressement as a perfect acquisition to the local community. This last was what happened with poor simple blushing little Netta, who found herself after a while so completely championed by all Mortiscombe that she soon fell into her natural place in the college circle as if to the manner born. All nice girls, of whatever class, are potentially ladies (which is more than one can honestly say for all women of the upper ranks), and after a very short time Netta became one of the most popular young married women in all Mortiscombe. When once Society had got over its first disappointment because Cyril Milliter had not rather married one of its own number, it took to Netta with the greatest cordiality. After all, there is something so very romantic, you know, in a gentleman marrying a foreman's daughter; and something so very nice and liberal, too, in one's own determination to treat her accordingly in every way like a perfect equal.

And yet, happy as she was, Netta could never be absolutely free from a pressing fear, a doubt that Cyril might not repent his choice, and feel sorry in the end for not having married a real lady. That fear pursued her through all her little triumph, and almost succeeded in making her half jealous of Cyril whenever she saw him talking at all earnestly (and he was very apt to be earnest) with other women. "They know so much more than I do," she thought to herself often; "he must feel so much more at home with them, naturally, and be able to talk to them about so many things that he can never possibly talk about with poor little me." Poor girl, it never even occurred to her that from the higher standpoint of a really learned man like Cyril Milliter the petty smattering of French and strumming of the piano, wherein alone these grand girls actually differed from her, were mere useless surface accomplishments, in no way affecting the inner intelligence or culture, which were the only things that Cyril regarded in any serious light as worthy of respect or admiration. As a matter of fact, Netta had learnt infinitely more from her Bible, her English books, her own heart, and surrounding nature, than any of these well-educated girls had learnt from their parrot-trained governesses; and she was infinitely better fitted than any of them to be a life companion for such a man as Cyril Milliter.

For the first seven or eight months of Netta's married life all went smoothly enough with the young professor and his pretty wife. But at the end of that time an event came about which gave Netta a great deal of unhappiness, and caused her for the very first time since she had ever known him to have serious doubts about Cyril's affection. And this was just how it all happened.

One Sunday morning, in the upper chamber at Patmos, Cyril had announced himself to preach a discourse in opposition to sundry wicked scientific theories which were then just beginning seriously to convulse the little world of religious Mortiscombe. Those were the days when Darwin's doctrine of evolution had lately managed to filter down little by little to the level of unintelligent society; and the inquiring working-men who made up Cyril Milliter's little congregation in the upper chamber were all eagerly reading the "Origin of Species" and the "Descent of Man." As for Cyril himself, in his austere fashion, he doubted whether any good could come even of considering such heterodox opinions. They were plainly opposed to the Truth, he held, both to the Truth as expressed in the written Word, and to the Truth as he himself clearly read it in the great open book of nature. This evolution they talked about so glibly was a dream, a romance, a mere baseless figment of the poor fallible human imagination; all the plain facts of science and of revelation were utterly irreconcilable with it, and in five years' time it would be comfortably dead and buried for ever, side by side with a great load of such other vague and hypothetical rubbish. He could hardly understand, for his part, how sensible men could bother their heads about such nonsense for a single moment. Still, as many of his little flock had gone to hear a brilliant young lecturer who came down from London last week to expound the new doctrine at the Literary and Philosophical Institute, and as they had been much shaken in their faith by the lecturer's sophistical arguments and obvious misrepresentations of scientific principles, he would just lay before them plainly what science had to say in opposition to these fantastic and immature theorists. So on Sunday morning next, with Bible in one hand and roll of carefully executed diagrams in the other (for Cyril Milliter was no conventional formalist, afraid of shocking the sense of propriety in his congregation), he went down in militant guise to the upper chamber and delivered a fervent discourse, intended to smite the Darwinians hip and thigh with the arms of the Truth, both Scriptural and scientific, to slay the sophists outright with the sword of the Lord and of Gideon.

Cyril took for his text a single clause from the twenty-first verse of the first chapter of Genesis— "Every winged fowl after his kind." That, he said impressively, was the eternal and immutable Truth upon the matter. He would confine his attention that morning entirely to this one aspect of the case, the creation of the class of birds. "In the beginning," the Word told us, every species of bird had been created as we now see it, perfect and fully organized after its own kind. There was no room here for their boasted "development," or their hypothetical "evolution." The Darwinians would fain force upon them some old wife's tale about a monstrous lizard which gradually acquired wings and feathers, till at last, by some quaint Ovidian metamorphosis (into such childish heathenism had we finally relapsed), it grew slowly into the outward semblance of a crow or an ostrich. But that was not what the Truth told them. On the fourth day of creation, simultaneously with the fish and every living creature that moveth in the ocean, the waters brought forth "fowl that might fly above the earth in the open firmament of heaven." Such on this subject was the plain and incontrovertible statement of the inspired writer in the holy Scripture.

And now, how did science confirm this statement, and scatter at once to the winds the foolish, brain-spun cobwebs of our windy, vaporous, modern evolutionists? These diagrams which he held before him would sufficiently answer that important question. He would show them that there was no real community of structure in any way between the two classes of birds and reptiles. Let them observe the tail, the wings, the feathers, the breast-bone, the entire anatomy, and they would see at once that Darwin's ridiculous, ill-digested theory was wholly opposed to all the plain and demonstrable facts of nature. It was a very learned discourse, certainly; very crushing, very overwhelming, very convincing (when you heard one side only), and not Netta alone, but the whole congregation of intelligent, inquiring artisans as well, was utterly carried away by its logic, its clearness, and its eloquent rhetoric. Last of all, Cyril Milliter raised his two white hands solemnly before him, and uttered thus his final peroration.

"In conclusion, what proof can they offer us of their astounding assertions?" he asked, almost contemptuously. "Have they a single fact, a single jot or tittle of evidence to put in on this matter, as against the universal voice of authoritative science, from the days of Aristotle, of Linnæus, or of

Cuvier, to the days of Owen, of Lyell, and of Carpenter? Not one! Whenever they can show me, living or fossil, an organism which unites in itself in any degree whatsoever the characteristics of birds and reptiles, an organism which has at once teeth and feathers; or which has a long lizard-like tail and true wings; or which combines the anatomical peculiarities I have here assigned to the one class with the anatomical peculiarities I have here assigned to the other: then, and then only, will I willingly accede to their absurd hypothesis. But they have not done it. They cannot do it. They will never do it. A great gulf eternally separates the two classes. A vast gap intervenes impassably between them. That gulf will never be lessened, that gap will never be bridged over, until Truth is finally confounded with falsehood, and the plain facts of nature and the Word are utterly forgotten in favour of the miserable, inconsistent figments of the poor fallible human imagination."

As they walked home from worship that morning, Netta felt she had never before so greatly admired and wondered at her husband. How utterly he had crushed the feeble theory of these fanciful system-mongers, how clearly he had shown the absolute folly of their presumptuous and arrogant nonsense! Netta could not avoid telling him so, with a flush of honest pride in her beautiful face: and Cyril flushed back immediately with conscious pleasure at her wifely trust and confidence. But he was tired with the effort, he said, and must go for a little walk alone in the afternoon: a walk among the fields and the Downs, where he could commune by himself with the sights and sounds of truth-telling nature. Netta was half-piqued, indeed, that he should wish even so to go without her; but she said nothing: and so after their early dinner, Cyril started away abstractedly by himself, and took the lane behind the village that led up by steep inclines on to the heavy moorland with its fresh bracken and its purple heather.

As he walked along hastily, his mind all fiery-full of bones and fossils, he came at last to the oolite quarry on the broken hillside. Feeling tired, he turned in to rest awhile in the shade on one of the great blocks of building stone hewn out by the workmen; and by way of occupation he began to grub away with his knife, half-unconsciously as he sat, at a long flat slab of slaty shale that projected a little from the sheer face of the fresh cutting. As he did so, he saw marks of something very like a bird's feather on its upper surface. The sight certainly surprised him a little. "Birds in the oolite," he said to himself quickly; "it's quite impossible! Birds in the oolite! this is quite a new departure. Besides, such a soft thing as a feather could never conceivably be preserved in the form of a fossil."

Still, the queer object interested him languidly, by its odd and timely connection with the subject of his morning sermon; and he looked at it again a little more closely. By Jove, yes, it was a feather, not a doubt in the world of that now; he could see distinctly the central shaft of a tail-quill, and the little barbed branches given off regularly on either side of it. The shale on which it was impressed was a soft, light-brown mudstone; in fact, a fragment of lithographic slate, exactly like that employed by lithographers for making pictures. He could easily see how the thing had happened; the bird had fallen into the soft mud, long ages since, before the shale had hardened, and the form of its feathers had been distinctly nature-printed, while it was still moist, upon its plastic surface. But a bird in the oolite! that was a real discovery; and, as the Gospel Evangelists were no Sabbatarians, Cyril did not scruple in the pursuit of Truth to dig away at the thin slab with his knife, till he egged it out of the rock by dexterous side pressure, and laid it triumphantly down at last for further examination on the big stone that stood before him.

Gazing in the first delight of discovery at his unexpected treasure, he saw in a moment that it was a very complete and exquisitely printed fossil. So perfect a pictorial representation of an extinct animal he had never seen before in his whole lifetime; and for the first moment or two he had no time to do anything else but admire silently the exquisite delicacy and extraordinary detail of this natural etching. But after a minute, the professional interest again asserted itself, and he began to look more carefully into the general nature of its curious and unfamiliar anatomical structure.

As he looked, Cyril Milliter felt a horrible misgiving arise suddenly within him. The creature at which he was gazing so intently was not a bird, it was a lizard. And yet—no—it was not a lizard, it was a bird. "Why, these are surely feathers, yes, tail feathers, quite unmistakable.... But they are not arranged in a regular fan; the quills stand in pairs, one on each side of each joint in a long tail, for all the world exactly like a lizard's.... Still, it must be a bird; for, see, these are wings ... and that is certainly a bird's claw.... But here's the head; great heavens! what's this?... A jaw, with teeth in it...." Cyril Milliter leaned back, distractedly, and held his beating forehead between his two pale hands. To most scientific men it would have been merely the discovery of an interesting intermediate organism, something sure to make the reputation of a comparative anatomist; to him, it was an awful and sudden blow dealt unexpectedly from the most deadly quarter at all his deepest and most sacred principles. Religion, honour, Truth, the very fundamental basis of the universe itself, all that makes life worth living for, all that makes the world endurable, was bound up implicitly that moment for Cyril Milliter in the simple question whether the shadowy creature, printed in faint grey outline on the slab of shaly oolite before him, was or was not half bird and half lizard.

It may have been foolish of him: it may have been wrong: it may have been madness almost; but at that instant he felt dazzled and stunned by the crushing weight of the blow thus unexpectedly dealt at his whole preconceived theory of things, and at his entire mental scheme of science and theology. The universe seemed to swim aimlessly before him: he felt the solid ground knocked at once from beneath his feet, and found himself in one moment suspended alone above an awful abyss, a seething and tossing abyss of murky chaos. He had pinned all his tottering faith absolutely on that single frail support; and now the support had given way irretrievably beneath him, and blank atheism, nihilism, utter nothingness, stared him desperately in the face. In one minute, while he held his head tight between his two palms to keep it from bursting, and looked with a dull, glazed, vacant eye at the ghastly thing before him, only a few indistinct fossil bones, but to him the horridest sight he had ever beheld, a whole world of ideas crowded itself on the instant into his teeming, swimming brain. If we could compress an infinity of thought into a single second, said Shelley once, that second would be eternity; and on the brink of such a compressed eternity Cyril Milliter was then idly sitting. It seemed to him, as he clasped his forehead tighter and tighter, that the Truth which he had been seeking, and for which he had been working and fighting so long, revealed itself to him now and there, at last, in concrete form, as a visible and tangible Lie. It was no mere petrified lizard that he saw beneath his eyes, but a whole ruined and shattered system of philosophic theology. His cosmogony was gone; his cosmos itself was dispersed and disjointed; creation, nay, the Creator Himself, seemed to fade away slowly into nonentity before him. He beheld dimly an awful vision of a great nebulous mist, drifting idly before the angry storm-cyclones of the masterless universe, drifting without a God or a ruler to guide it; bringing forth shapeless monstrosities one after another on its wrinkled surface; pregnant with ravine, and rapine, and cruelty; vast, powerful, illimitable, awful; but without one ray of light, one gleam of love, one hope of mercy, one hint of divine purpose anywhere to redeem it. It was the pessimistic nightmare of a Lucretian system, translated hastily into terms of Cyril Milliter's own tottering and fading theosophy.

He took the thing up again into his trembling hands, and examined it a second time more closely. No, there could be no shadow of a doubt about it: his professional skill and knowledge told him that much in a single moment. Nor could he temporize and palter with the discovery, as some of his elder brethren would have been tempted to do; his brain was too young, and fresh, and vigorous, and logical not to permit of ready modification before the evidence of new facts. Come what might, he must be loyal to the Truth. This thing, this horrid thing that he held visibly before him, was a fact, a positive fact: a set of real bones, representing a real animal, that had once lived and breathed and flown about veritably upon this planet of ours, and that was yet neither a true bird nor a true lizard, but a half-way house and intermediate link between those two now widely divergent classes. Cyril

Milliter's mind was at once too honest and too intelligent to leave room for any doubts, or evasions, or prevarications with itself upon that fundamental subject. He saw quite clearly and instantly that it was the very thing the possibility of whose existence he had so stoutly denied that self-same morning. And he could not go back upon his own words, "Whenever they show me an organism which unites in itself the characteristics of birds and reptiles, then, and then only, will I accede to their absurd hypothesis." The organism he had asked for lay now before him, and he knew himself in fact a converted evolutionist, encumbered with all the other hideous corollaries which his own peculiar logic had been accustomed to tack on mentally to that hated creed. He almost felt as if he ought in pure consistency to go off at once and murder somebody, as the practical outcome of his own theories. For had he not often boldly asserted that evolutionism was inconsistent with Theism, and that without Theism, any real morality or any true right-doing of any kind was absolutely impossible?

At last, after long sitting and anxious pondering, Cyril Milliter rose to go home, carrying a heavy heart along with him. And then the question began to press itself practically upon him, What could he ever do with this horrible discovery? His first impulse was to dash the thing to pieces against the rock, and go away stealthily, saying naught about the matter to any man. But his inborn reverence for the Truth made him shrink back in horror, a moment later, from this suggestion of Satan, as he thought it, this wicked notion of suppressing a most important and conclusive piece of scientific evidence. His next idea was simply to leave it where it was, thus shuffling off the responsibility of publishing it or destroying it upon the next comer who chanced by accident to enter the quarry. After all, he said to himself, hypocritically, he wasn't absolutely bound to tell anybody else a word about it; he could leave it there, and it would be in much the same position, as far as science was concerned, as it would have been if he hadn't happened to catch sight of it accidentally as it lay that morning in the mother stone. But again his conscience told him next moment that such casuistry was dishonest and unworthy; he had found the thing, and, come what might, he ought to abide by the awful consequences. If he left it lying there in the quarry, one of the workmen would probably smash it up carelessly with a blow of his pick to-morrow morning, this unique survivor of a forgotten world, and to abandon it to such a fate as that would be at least as wicked as to break it to pieces himself of set purpose, besides being a great deal more sneakish and cowardly. No, whatever else he did, it was at any rate his plain duty to preserve the specimen, and to prevent it from being carelessly or wilfully destroyed.

On the other hand, he couldn't bear, either, to display it openly, and thereby become, as the matter envisaged itself to his mind, a direct preacher of evolutionism, that is to say, of irreligion and immorality. With what face could he ever rise and exhibit at a scientific meeting this evident proof that the whole universe was a black chaos, a gross materialistic blunder, a festering mass of blank corruption, without purpose, soul, or informing righteousness? His entire moral being rose up within him in bitter revolt at the bare notion of such cold-blooded treachery. To give a long-winded Latin classificatory name, forsooth, to a thing that would destroy the faith of ages! At last, after long pondering, he determined to carry the slab carefully home inside his coat, and hide it away sedulously for the present in the cupboard of his little physiological laboratory. He would think the matter over, he would take time to consider, he would ask humbly for light and guidance. But of whom? Well, well, at any rate, there was no necessity for precipitate action. To Cyril Milliter's excited fancy, the whole future of human thought and belief seemed bound up inextricably at that moment in the little slab of lithographic slate that lay before him; and he felt that he need be in no hurry to let loose the demon of scepticism and sin (as it appeared to him) into the peaceful midst of a still happily trusting and unsuspecting humanity.

He put his hand into his pocket, casually, to pull out his handkerchief for a covering to the thing, and, as he did so, his fingers happened to touch the familiar clasp of his little pocket Bible. The touch thrilled him strangely, and inspired him at once with a fresh courage. After all, he had the Truth there also, and he couldn't surely be doing wrong in consulting its best and most lasting interests. It was for the sake of the Truth that he meant for the present to conceal his compromising fossil. So he wrapped up the slab as far as he was able in his handkerchief, and hid it away, rather clumsily, under the left side of his coat. It bulged a little, no doubt; but by keeping his arm flat to his side he was able to cover it over decently somehow. Thus he walked back quickly to Mortiscombe, feeling more like a thief with a stolen purse in his pocket than he had ever before felt in the whole course of his earthly existence.

When he reached his own house, he would not ring, lest Netta should run to open the door for him, and throw her arms round him, and feel the horrid thing (how could he show it even to Netta after this morning's sermon?), but he went round to the back door, opened it softly, and glided as quietly as he could into the laboratory. Not show it to Netta, that was bad: he had always hitherto shown her and told her absolutely everything. How about the Truth? He was doing this, he believed, for the Truth's sake; and yet, the very first thing that it imposed upon him was the necessity for an ugly bit of unwonted concealment. Not without many misgivings, but convinced on the whole that he was acting for the best, he locked the slab of oolite up, hurriedly and furtively, in the corner cupboard.

He had hardly got it safely locked up out of sight, and seated himself as carelessly as he could in his easy chair, when Netta knocked softly at the door. She always knocked before entering, by force of habit, for when Cyril was performing delicate experiments it often disturbed him, or spoilt the result, to have the door opened suddenly. Netta had seen him coming, and wondered why he had slunk round by the back door: now she wondered still more why he did not "report himself," as he used to call it, by running to kiss her and announce his return.

"Come in," he said gravely, in answer to the knock; and Netta entered.

Cyril jumped up and kissed her tenderly, but her quick woman's eye saw at once that there was something serious the matter. "You didn't ring, Cyril darling," she said, half reproachfully, "and you didn't come to kiss your wifie."

"No," Cyril answered, trying to look quite at his ease (a thing at which the most innocent man in the world is always the worst possible performer), "I was in a hurry to get back here, as there was something in the way of my work I wanted particularly to see about."

"Why, Cyril," Netta answered in surprise; "your work! It's Sunday."

Cyril blushed crimson. "So it is," he answered hastily; "upon my word, I'd quite forgotten it. Goodness gracious, Netta, shall I have to go down to meeting and preach again to those people this evening?"

"Preach again? Of course you will, Cyril. You always do, dear, don't you?"

Cyril started back with a sigh. "I can't go to-night, Netta darling," he said wearily. "I can't preach to-night. I'm too tired and out of sorts, I'm not at all in the humour for preaching. We must send down somehow or other, and put off the brethren."

Netta looked at him in blank dismay. She felt in her heart there was something wrong, but she wouldn't for worlds ask Cyril what it was, unless he chose to tell her of his own accord. Still, she couldn't help reading in his eyes that there was something the matter: and the more she looked into them, the more poor Cyril winced and blinked and looked the other way in the vain attempt to seem unconcerned at her searching scrutiny. "I'll send Mary down with a little written notice," she said at last, "to fix on the door: 'Mr. Milliter regrets he will be unable, through indisposition, to attend worship at Patmos this evening.' Will that do, Cyril?"

"Yes," he answered uneasily. "That'll do, darling. I don't feel quite well, I'm afraid, somehow, after my unusual exertions this morning."

Netta looked at him hard, but said nothing.

They went into the drawing-room and for a while they both pretended to be reading. Then the maid brought up the little tea-tray, and Cyril was obliged to lay down the book he had been using as a screen for his crimson face, and to look once more straight across the room at Netta.

"Cyril," the little wife began again, as she took over his cup of tea to his easy chair by the bow window, and set it down quietly on the tiny round table beside him, "where did you go this afternoon?"

"On the Downs, darling."

"And whom did you meet there?"

"Nobody, Netta."

"Nobody, Cyril?"

"No, nobody."

Netta knew she could trust his word implicitly, and asked him no further. Still, a dreadful cloud was slowly rising up before her. She felt too much confidence in Cyril to be really jealous of him in any serious way; but her fears, womanlike, took that personal shape in which she fancied somebody or something must be weaning away her husband's love gradually from her. Had he seen some girl at a distance on the Downs, some one of the Mortiscombe ladies, with whom perhaps he had had some little flirtation in the days gone by, some lady whom he thought now would have made him a more suitable, companionable wife than poor little Netta? Had he wandered about alone, saying to himself that he had thrown himself away, and sacrificed his future prospects for a pure, romantic boyish fancy? Had he got tired of her little, simple, homely ways? Had he come back to the house, heartsick and disappointed, and gone by himself into the working laboratory on purpose to avoid her? Why was he so silent? Why did he seem so preoccupied? Why would he not look her straight in the face? Cyril could have done nothing to be ashamed of, that Netta felt quite sure about, but why did he behave as if he was ashamed of himself, as if there was something or other in his mind he couldn't tell her?

Meanwhile, poor Cyril was not less unhappy, though in a very different and more masculine fashion. He wasn't thinking so much of Netta (except when she looked at him so hard and curiously), but of the broken gods of his poor little scientific and theological pantheon. He was passing through a tempest of doubt and hesitation, compelled to conceal it under the calm demeanour of everyday life. That horrid, wicked, system-destroying fossil was never for a moment out of his mind. At times he hated and loathed the godless thing with all the concentrated force of his ardent nature. Ought he to harbour it under the shelter of his hospitable roof? Ought he to give it the deadly chance of bearing its terrible witness before the eyes of an innocent world? Ought he not to get up rather in the dead of night, and burn it to ashes or grind it to powder, a cruel, wicked, deceiving, anti-scriptural fossil that it was? Then again at other times the love of Truth came uppermost once more to chill his fiery indignation. Could the eternal hills lie to him? Could the evidence of his own senses deceive him? Was not the creature there palpably and visibly present, a veritable record of real existence; and ought he not loyally and reverently to accept its evidence, at whatever violence to his own most cherished and sacred convictions? If the universe was in reality quite other than what he had always hitherto thought it; if the doctrines he had first learned and then taught as certain and holy were proved by plain facts to be mere ancient and fading delusions, was it not his bounden duty manfully to resign his life-long day-dream, and to accept the Truth as it now presented itself to him by the infallible evidence of mute nature, that cannot possibly or conceivably lie to us?

The evening wore away slowly, and Cyril and Netta said little to one another, each absorbed in their own thoughts and doubts and perplexities. At last bedtime came, but not much sleep for either. Cyril lay awake, looking out into the darkness which seemed now to involve the whole physical and spiritual world; seeing in fancy a vast chaotic clashing universe, battling and colliding for ever against itself, without one ray of hope, or light, or gladness left in it anywhere. Netta lay awake, too, wondering what could have come over Cyril; and seeing nothing but a darkened world, in which Cyril's love was taken away from her, and all was cold, and dull, and cheerless. Each in imagination had lost the keystone of their own particular special universe.

Throughout the next week, Cyril went on mechanically with his daily work, but struggling all the time against the dreadful doubt that was rising now irresistibly within him. Whenever he came home from college, he went straight to his laboratory, locked the door, and took the skeleton out of the cupboard. It was only a very small skeleton indeed, and a fossil one at that; but if it had been a murdered man, and he the murderer, it could hardly have weighed more terribly than it actually did upon Cyril Milliter's mind and conscience. Yet it somehow fascinated him; and in all his spare time he was working away at the comparative anatomy of his singular specimen. He had no doubts at all about it now: he knew it perfectly for what it was, an intermediate form between birds and reptiles. Meanwhile, he could not dare to talk about it even to Netta; and Netta, though the feeling that there was something wrong somewhere deepened upon her daily, would not say a word upon the subject to Cyril. But she had discovered one thing, that the secret, whatever it was, lay closed up in the laboratory cupboard; and as her fears exaggerated her doubts, she grew afraid at last almost to enter the room which held that terrible, unspeakable mystery.

Thus more than a fortnight passed away, and Cyril and Netta grew daily less and less at home with one another. At last, one evening, when Cyril seemed gloomier and more silent than ever, Netta could bear the suspense no longer. Rising up hastily from her seat, without one word of warning, she went over to her husband with a half-despairing gesture of alarm, and, flinging her arms around him with desperate force, she cried passionately through her blinding tears, "Cyril, Cyril, Cyril, you must tell me all about it."

"About what, darling?" Cyril asked, trembling with half-conscious hypocrisy, for he knew in his heart at once what she meant as well as she did.

"Cyril," she cried again, looking him straight in the face steadily, "you have a secret that you will not tell me."

"Darling," he answered, smoothing her hair tenderly with his hand, "it is no secret. It is nothing. You would think nothing of it if you knew. It's the merest trifle possible. But I can't tell you. I can not tell you."

"But you must, Cyril," Netta cried bitterly. "You had never any secret from me, I know, till that dreadful Sunday, when you went out alone, and wouldn't even let me go with you. Then you came back stealthily by the back door, and never told me. And you brought something with you: of that I'm certain. And you've got the something locked up carefully in the laboratory cupboard. I don't know how I found it all out exactly, but I have found it out, and I can't bear the suspense any longer, and so you must tell me all about it. Oh, Cyril, dear Cyril, do, do tell me all about it!"

Cyril faltered, faltered visibly; but even so, he dare not tell her. His own faith was going too terribly fast already; could he let hers go too, in one dreadful collapse and confusion? It never occurred to him that the fossil would mean little or nothing to poor Netta; he couldn't help thinking of it as though every human being on earth would regard it with the same serious solemnity and awe as he himself did. "I cannot tell you, Netta," he said, very gently but very firmly. "No, I dare not tell you. Some day, perhaps, but not now. I must not tell you."

The answer roused all Netta's worst fears more terribly than ever. For a moment she almost began to doubt Cyril. In her terror and perplexity she was still too proud to ask him further; and she went back from her husband, feeling stung and repulsed by his cruel answer, and made as though she did not care at all for his strange refusal. She took up a scientific paper from the heap on the table, and pretended to begin reading it. Cyril rose and tried to kiss her, but she pushed him away with an impatient gesture. "Never," she said haughtily. "Never, Cyril, until you choose to tell me your private secret."

Cyril sank back gloomily into his chair, folded his hands into one another in a despondent fashion, and looked hard at the vacant ceiling without uttering a single word.

As Netta held the paper aimlessly before her that minute, by the merest chance her eye happened to fall upon her husband's name printed in the article that lay open casually at the middle page. Even at that supreme moment of chagrin and torturing doubt, she could not pass by Cyril's name in print without stopping to read what was said about him. As she did so, she saw that the article began by hostile criticism of the position he had taken up on the distinction between birds and reptiles in a recent paper contributed to the Transactions of the Linnæan Society. She rose from her place silently, put the paper into his hands and pointed to the paragraph with her white forefinger, but never uttered a single syllable. Cyril took it from her mechanically, and read on, not half thinking what he was reading, till he came to a passage which attracted his attention perforce, because it ran somewhat after this fashion—

"Professor Milliter would have written a little less confidently had he been aware that almost while his words were passing through the press a very singular discovery bearing upon this exact subject was being laid before the Academy of Sciences at Berlin. Dr. Hermann von Meyer has just exhibited to that body a slab of lithographic slate from the famous oolitic quarry at Solenhofen, containing the impression of a most remarkable organism, which he has named Archæopteryx lithographica. This extraordinary creature has the feathers of a bird with the tail of a lizard; it is entirely destitute of an os coccygis; it has apparently two conical teeth in the upper jaw; and its foot is that of a characteristic percher." And so forth for more than a column, full of those minute anatomical points which Cyril had himself carefully noticed in the anatomy of his own English specimen.

As he read and re-read that awful paragraph, Netta looking on at him half angrily all the time, he grew more and more certain every moment that the German professor had simultaneously made the very same discovery as himself. He drew a long sigh of relief. The worst was over; the murder was out, then; it was not to be he who should bear the responsibility of publishing to the world the existence and peculiarities of that wicked and hateful fossil. A cold-blooded German geologist had done so already, with no more trace of remorse and punctiliousness in the business than if it had been the merest old oyster-shell or spider or commonplace cockroach! He could hardly keep in his excited feelings; the strain of personal responsibility at least was lightened; and though the universe remained as black as ever, he could at any rate wash his own hands of the horrid creature. Unmanly as it may seem, he burst suddenly into tears, and stepped across the room to throw his arms round Netta's neck. To his surprise, for he scarcely remembered that she could not yet realize the situation, Netta repelled him with both hands stretched angrily before her, palm outwards.

"Netta," he said, imploringly, recognizing immediately what it was she meant, "come with me now into the laboratory, and see what it is that I have got in the cupboard."

Netta, all trembling and wondering, followed him in a perfect flutter of doubt and anxiety. Cyril slowly unlocked the cupboard, then unfastened a small drawer, and last of all took out a long flat object, wrapped up mysteriously in a clean handkerchief. He laid it down reluctantly upon the table, and Netta, amazed and puzzled, beheld a small smooth slab of soft clay-stone, scored with what seemed like the fossil marks of a few insignificant bones and feathers. The little woman drew a long breath.

"Well, Cyril?" she said interrogatively, looking at it in a dubious mood.

"Why, Netta," cried her husband, half angry at her incomprehensible calmness, "don't you see what it is? It's terrible, terrible!"

"A fossil, Cyril, isn't it? A bird, I should say."

"No, not a bird, Netta; nor yet a lizard; but that half-way thing, that intermediate link you read about just now over yonder in the paper."

"But why do you hide it, Cyril? You haven't taken it anywhere from a museum."

"Oh, Netta! Don't you understand? Don't you see the implications? It's a creature, half bird and half reptile, and it proves, absolutely proves, Netta, beyond the faintest possibility of a doubt, that the evolutionists are quite right—quite scientific. And if it once comes to be generally recognized, I don't know, I'm sure, what is ever to become of religion and of science. We shall every one of us have to go and turn evolutionists!"

It is very sad to relate, but poor Netta, her pent-up feelings all let loose by the smallness of the evil, as it seemed to her, actually began to smile, and then to laugh merrily, in the very face of this awful revelation. "Then you haven't really got tired of me, Cyril?" she cried eagerly. "You're not in love with somebody else? You don't regret ever having married me?"

Cyril stared at her in mute surprise. What possible connection could these questions have with the momentous principles bound up implicitly in the nature-printed skeleton of Archæopteryx lithographica? It was a moment or so before he could grasp the association of ideas in her womanly little brain, and understand the real origin of her natural wife-like fears and hesitations.

"Oh, Cyril," she said again, after a minute's pause, looking at the tell-tale fossil with another bright girlish smile, "is it only that? Only that wretched little creature? Oh, darling, I am so happy!" And she threw her arms around his neck of her own accord, and kissed him fervently twice or thrice over.

Cyril was pleased indeed that she had recovered her trust in him so readily, but amazed beyond measure that she could look at that horrible anti-scriptural fossil absolutely without the slightest symptom of flinching. "What a blessed thing it must be," he thought to himself, "to be born a woman! Here's the whole universe going to rack and ruin, physically and spiritually, before her very eyes, and she doesn't care a fig as soon as she's quite satisfied in her own mind that her own particular husband hasn't incomprehensibly fallen in love with one or other of the Mortiscombe ladies!" It was gratifying to his personal feelings, doubtless; but it wasn't at all complimentary, one must admit, to the general constitution of the universe.

"What ought I to do with it, Netta?" he asked her simply, pointing to the fossil; glad to have any companionship, even if so unsympathetic, in his hitherto unspoken doubts and difficulties.

"Do with it? Why, show it to the Geological Society, of course, Cyril. It's the Truth, you know, dearest, and why on earth should you wish to conceal it? The Truth shall make you perfect."

Cyril looked at her with mingled astonishment and admiration. "Oh, Netta," he answered, sighing profoundly, "if only I could take it as quietly as you do! If only I had faith as a grain of mustard-seed! But I have been reduced almost to abject despair by this crushing piece of deadly evidence. It seems to me to proclaim aloud that the evolutionists are all completely right at bottom, and that everything we have ever loved and cherished and hoped for, turns out an utter and absolute delusion."

"Then I should say you were still bound, for all that, to accept the evidence," said Netta quietly. "However, for my part, I may be very stupid and silly, and all that sort of thing, you know, but it doesn't seem to me as if it really mattered twopence either way."

Cyril looked at her again with fresh admiration. That was a point of view that had not yet even occurred to him as within the bounds of possibility. He had gone on repeating over and over again to his congregation and to himself that if evolution were true, religion and morality were mere phantoms, until at last he had ceased to think any other proposition on the subject could be even thinkable. That a man might instantly accept the evidence of his strange fossil, and yet be after all an indifferent honest citizen in spite of it, was an idea that had really never yet presented itself to him. And he blushed now to think that, in spite of all his frequent professions of utter fidelity, Netta had proved herself at last more loyal to the Truth in both aspects than he himself had done. Her simple little womanly faith had never faltered for a moment in either direction.

That night was a very happy one for Netta: it was a somewhat happier one than of late, even for Cyril. He had got rid of the cloud between himself and his wife: he had made at least one person a confidante of his horrid secret: and, above all, he had learnt that some bold and ruthless German geologist had taken off his own shoulders the responsibility of announcing the dreadful discovery.

Still, it was some time before Cyril quite recovered from the gloomy view of things generally into which his chance unearthing of the strange fossil had temporarily thrown him. Two things mainly contributed to this result.

The first was that a few Sundays later he made up his mind he ought in common honesty to exhibit his compromising fossil to the congregation in the upper chamber, and make a public recantation of his recent confident but untenable statements. He did so with much misgiving, impelled by a growing belief that after all he must trust everything implicitly to the Truth. It cost him a pang, too, to go back upon his own deliberate words, so lately spoken; but he faced it out, for the Truth's sake, like an honest man, as he had always tried to be, save for those few days when the wicked little slab of slate lay carefully hidden away in the inmost recesses of the laboratory cupboard. To his immense surprise, once more, the brethren seemed to think little more of it than Netta herself had done. Perhaps they were not so logical or thorough-going as the young professor: perhaps they had more of unquestioning faith: perhaps they had less of solid dogmatic leaven; but in any case they seemed singularly little troubled by the new and startling geological discovery. However, they were all much struck by the professor's honesty of purpose in making a straightforward recantation of his admitted blunder; he had acted honest and honourable, they said, like a man, and they liked him better for it in the end, than if he'd preached, and hedged, and shilly-shallied to them about it for a whole year of Sundays together. Now, the mere fact that his good congregation didn't mind the fossil much reacted healthily on Cyril Milliter, who began to suspect that perhaps after all he had been exaggerating the religious importance of speculative opinions on the precise nature of the cosmogony.

The second thing was that, shortly after the great discovery, he happened to make the acquaintance of the brilliant young evolutionist from London, and found to his surprise that on the whole most of their opinions agreed with remarkable unanimity. True, the young evolutionist was not a Gospel Evangelist, and did not feel any profound interest in the literal or mystical interpretation of the first chapter of Genesis. But in all essentials he was as deeply spiritual as Cyril Milliter himself; and the more Cyril saw of him and talked with him, the more did he begin to suspect that the truth may in reality have many facets, and that all men may not happen to see it in exactly the self-same aspect. It dawned upon him slowly that all the illumination in the world might not be entirely confined to the narrow circle of the Gospel Evangelists. Even those terrible evolutionists themselves, it seemed, were not necessarily wholly given over to cutting throats or robbing churches. They might have their desires and aspirations, their faith and their hope and their charity, exactly like other people, only perhaps in a slightly different and more definite direction. In the end, Cyril and his former bugbear became bosom friends, and both worked together amicably side by side in the self-same laboratory at the College of Science.

To this day, Professor Milliter still continues to preach weekly to the Gospel Evangelists, though both he and they have broadened a good deal, in a gradual and almost imperceptible fashion, with the general broadening of ideas and opinions that has been taking place by slow degrees around us during the last two decades. His views are no doubt a good deal less dogmatic and a good deal more wide and liberal now than formerly. Netta and he live happily and usefully together; and over the mantelpiece of his neat little study, in the cottage at Mortiscombe, stands a slab of polished slate containing a very interesting oolitic fossil, of which the professor has learnt at last to be extremely proud, the first discovered and most perfect existing specimen of Archæopteryx lithographica. He can hardly resist a quiet smile himself, nowadays, when he remembers how he once kept that harmless piece of pictured stone wrapt up carefully in a folded handkerchief in his laboratory cupboard for some weeks together, as though it had been a highly dangerous and very explosive lump of moral dynamite, calculated to effect at one fell swoop the complete religious and ethical disintegration of the entire divine universe.

IN STRICT CONFIDENCE

I

Harry Pallant was never more desperately in love with his wife Louie than on the night of that delightful dance at the Vernon Ogilvies'. She wore her pale blue satin, with the low bodice, and her pretty necklet of rough amber in natural lumps, which her husband had given her for a birthday present just three days earlier. Harry wasn't rich, and he wasn't able to do everything that he could have wished for Louie, a young barrister, with no briefs to speak of, even if he ekes out his petty professional income with literary work, can't afford to spend very much in the way of personal adornment upon the ladies of his family, but he loved his pretty little wife dearly, and nothing pleased him better than to see Louie admired as she ought to be by other people. And that evening, to be sure, she was looking her very sweetest and prettiest. Flushed a little with unwonted excitement, in the glow of an innocent girlish flirtation, as she stood there talking to Hugh Ogilvie in the dim recess by the door of the conservatory, Harry, watching her unobserved from a nook of the refreshment-room, thought he had never in his life seen her look more beautiful or more becomingly animated. Animation suited Louie Pallant, and Hugh Ogilvie thought so too, as he half whispered his meaningless compliments in her dainty little ear, and noted the blush that rose quickly to her soft cheek, and the sudden droop of her long eyelashes above her great open hazel-grey eyes.

"Hugh's saying something pretty to Louie, I'm sure," Harry thought to himself with a smile of pleasure, as he looked across at the sweet little graceful girlish figure. "I can see it at once in her face, and in her hands, playing so nervously with the edge of her fan. Dear child, how she lets one read in her eyes and cheeks her every tiny passing feeling! Her pretty wee mouth is like an open book! Hugh's telling her confidentially now that she's the belle of the evening. And so she is; there's not a doubt about it. Not a girl in the place fit to hold a candle to my Louie; especially when she blushes, she's sweet when she blushes. Now she's colouring up again. By Jove, yes, he must be positively making love to her. There's nothing I enjoy so much as seeing Louie enjoying herself, and being made much of. Too many girls, bright young girls, when they marry early, as Louie has done, settle down at once into household drudges, and never seem to get any happiness worth mentioning out of their lives in any way. I won't let it be so with Louie. Dear little soul, she shall flit about as much as she likes, and enjoy herself as the fancy seizes her, like a little butterfly, just like a butterfly. I love to see it!" And he hugged one clasped hand upon the other silently.

Whence the astute reader will readily infer that Harry Pallant was still more or less in love with his wife Louie, although they had been married for five years and upwards.

Presently Louie and Hugh went back into the ballroom, and for the first time Harry noticed that the music had struck up some minutes since for the next waltz, for which he was engaged to Hugh's sister, Mrs. Wetherby Ferrand. He started hastily at the accusing sound, for in watching his wife he had forgotten his partner. Returning at once in search of Mrs. Ferrand, he found her sitting disconsolate in a corner waiting for him, and looking (as was natural) not altogether pleased at his ungallant treatment.

"So you've come at last, Harry!" Mrs. Ferrand said, with evident pique. They had been friends from childhood, and knew one another well enough to use both their Christian names and the critical freedom of old intimacy.

"Yes, Dora, I've come at last," Harry answered, with an apologetic bow, as he offered her his arm, "and I'm so sorry I've kept you waiting; but the fact is I was watching Louie. She's been dancing with Hugh, and she looks perfectly charming, I think, this evening."

Mrs. Ferrand bit her lip. "She does," she answered coldly, with half a pout. "And you were so busy watching her, it seems, you forgot all about me, Harry."

Harry laughed. "It was pardonable under the circumstances, you know, Dora," he said lightly. "If it had been the other way, now, Louie might have had some excuse for being jealous."

"Who said I was jealous?" Mrs. Ferrand cried, colouring up. "Jealous of you, indeed! What right have I got to be jealous of you, Harry? She may dance with Hugh all night long, for all I care for it. She's danced with him now three times already, and I dare say she'll dance with him as often again. You men are too conceited. You always think every woman on earth is just madly in love with you."

"My dear child," Harry answered, with a faint curl of his lip, "you quite misunderstand me. Heaven knows I at least am not conceited. What on earth have I got to be conceited of? I never thought any woman was in love with me in all my life except Louie; and what in the name of goodness even she can find to fall in love with in me, a fellow like me, positively passes my humble comprehension."

"She's going to dance the next waltz but one with Hugh, he tells me," Mrs. Ferrand replied drily, as if changing the conversation.

"Is she? Hugh's an excellent fellow," Harry answered carelessly, resting for a moment a little aside from the throng, and singling out Louie at once with his eye among the whirling dancers. "Ah, there she is, over yonder. Do you see?—there, with that Captain Vandeleur. How sweetly she dances, Dora! And how splendidly she carries herself! I declare, she's the very gracefullest girl in all the room here."

Mrs. Ferrand dropped half a mock curtsey. "A polite partner would have said 'bar one,' Harry," she murmured petulantly. "How awfully in love with her you are, my dear boy. It must be nice to have a man so perfectly devoted to one.... And I don't believe either she half appreciates you. Some women would give their very eyes, do you know, to be as much loved by any man as she's loved by you, Harry." And she looked at him significantly.

"Well, but Ferrand—"

"Ah, poor Wetherby! Yes, yes; of course, of course, I quite agree with you. You're always right, Harry. Poor Wetherby is the worthiest of men, and in his own way does his very best, no doubt, to make me happy. But there is devotion and devotion, Harry. Il y a fagots et fagots. Poor dear Wetherby is no more capable—"

"Dora, Dora, for Heaven's sake, I beg of you, no confidences. As a legal man, I must deprecate all confidences, otherwise than strictly in the way of business. What got us first into this absurd groove, I wonder? Oh yes, I remember, Louie's dancing. Shall we go on again? You must have got your breath by this time. Why, what's the matter, Dora? You look quite pale and flurried."

"Nothing, Harry. Nothing, nothing, I assure you. Not quite so tight, please; go quietly, I'm rather tired.... Yes, that'll do, thank you. The room's so very hot and close this evening. I can hardly breathe, I feel so stifled. Tight-lacing, I suppose poor dear Wetherby would say. I declare, Louie isn't dancing any longer. How very odd! She's gone back again now to sit by Hugh there. What on earth can be the reason, I wonder!"

"Captain Vandeleur's such an awfully bad waltzer, you know," Harry answered unconcernedly. "I dare say she was glad enough to make some excuse or other to get away from him. The room's so very hot and stifling."

"Oh, you think so," and Dora Ferrand gave a quiet little smile, as one who sees clearly below the surface. "I dare say. And she's not sorry either to find some good reason for another ten minutes' chat with Hugh, I fancy."

But Harry, in his innocence, never noticed her plain insinuation. "He's as blind as a bat," Dora Ferrand thought to herself, half contemptuously. "Just like poor dear Wetherby! Poor dear Wetherby never suspects anything! And that girl Louie doesn't half appreciate Harry either. Just like me, I suppose, with that poor dear stupid old stockbroker. Stockbroker, indeed! What in the name of all that's sensible could ever have induced me to go and marry a blind old stick of a wealthy stockbroker? If Harry and I had only our lives to live again, but there, what's the use of bothering one's head about it? We've only got one life apiece, and that we generally begin by making a mull of."

II

Three days later Harry Pallant went down as usual to his rooms in the Temple, and set to work upon his daily labour. The first envelope he opened of the batch upon his table was from the editor of the Young People's Monitor. It contained the week's correspondence. Harry Pallant glanced over the contents hastily, and singled out a few enclosures from the big budget with languid curiosity.

Of course everybody knows the Young People's Monitor. It is one of the most successful among the penny weeklies, and in addition to its sensational stories and moral essays, it gives advice gratis to all and sundry in its correspondence columns upon every conceivable subject that our common peccant or ignorant humanity can possibly inquire about. Now, Harry Pallant happened to be the particular person employed by the editor of this omniscient journal to supply the answers to the weekly shoals of anxious interrogators de omni scibili. His legal learning came in handy for the purpose, and being a practised London journalist as well, his knowledge of life stood him in good stead at this strange piece of literary craftsmanship. But the whole affair was "in strict confidence," as the Monitor announced. It was a point of honour between himself and the editor that the secret of the correspondence column should be jealously guarded from all and several; so Harry Pallant, accustomed, lawyer-like, to keeping secrets, had never mentioned his connection with the Monitor in this matter even to Louie. It came as part of his week's work at his chambers in the Temple, and it was duly finished and sent off to press, without note or comment, on the same day, in true business-like barrister fashion.

The first letter that Harry opened and listlessly glanced through with his experienced eye was one of the staple Monitor kind, Stella or Euphemia had quarrelled, in a moment of pique, with her lover, and was now dying of anxiety to regain his affections. Harry scribbled a few words of kindly chaff and sound advice in reply upon a blank sheet of virgin foolscap, and tossed the torn fragments of letter number one into the capacious mouth of his waste-paper basket.

The second letter requested the editor's candid opinion upon a short set of amateur verses therewith enclosed. Harry's candid opinion, muttered to himself beneath his moustache, was too unparliamentary for insertion in full; but he toned its verbal expression down a little in his written copy, and passed on hastily to the others in order.

"Camilla" would like to know, in strict confidence (thrice underlined), what is the editor's opinion of her style of handwriting. "A Draper's Assistant" is desirous to learn how the words "heterogeneous" and "Beethoven" are usually pronounced in the best society. "Senex," having had a slight difference as to the buttered toast with his present landlady (in whose house he has lodged for forty years), would be glad of any advice as to how, at his age, he is to do without her. "H. J. K." has just read with much surprise a worthless pamphlet, proving that the inhabitants of the northern divisions of Staffordshire and Warwickshire are the lost Ten Tribes of Israel, and cannot imagine how this reckless assertion can be scripturally reconciled with the plain statements of the prophet Habakkuk, which show that the descendants of Manasseh are really to be looked for in the county of Sligo. And so forth, though every variety of male feebleness and feminine futility, in answer to all which Harry turned off his hasty rejoinder with the dexterous ease acquired of long practice and familiar experience.

At last he came in due course to a small white envelope, of better paper and style than the others, marked "17" in red pencil on the back in the formal hand of the systematic editor. He turned it over with mechanical carelessness. To his immense amusement and no little surprise, he saw at once, by the writing of the address, that the note came from his own Louie!

What could Louie have to ask of advice or information from the anonymous editor of the Young People's Monitor?

He stood for a moment, with a quiet smile playing about his lips, thinking to himself that he had often wondered whether he should ever get a letter thus incognito from any person among his private acquaintances. And now he had got one from Louie herself. How very funny! How truly ridiculous! And how odd too that she shouldn't even have told him beforehand she was going to write for counsel or assistance to the Young People's Monitor!

And then a strange doubt flashed idly for a moment across his mind, a doubt that he felt immediately ashamed of. What possible subject could there be on which Louie could want advice and aid from an editor, a stranger, an unknown and anonymous impersonal entity, rather than from him, Harry, her own husband, her natural guide, assistant, and counsellor? It was odd, very odd, nay, even disquieting. Harry hardly knew what to make of the unexpected episode.

But next moment he had dismissed his doubts, though he stood still toying with the unopened envelope. He was half afraid to look inside it. Louie had only written, he felt sure, about some feminine trifle or other, some foolish point of petty etiquette, how to fold napkins mitre-fashion, or whether "P.P.O." cards should be turned down at the upper right or the lower left-hand corner, some absurd detail about which she would have laughed outright at his personal opinion, but would defer at once to the dignity of print, and the expressed verdict of the Young People's Monitor. So great is the power of printer's ink, that if you say a thing face to face, your own wife even will take no notice of it; but if you set it up in type anonymously, she, and the world at large to boot, will treat it like an inspired oracle in stone fallen down direct from the seventh heaven.

And yet somehow Harry Pallant couldn't make up his mind at once to break open the tiny envelope of that mysterious, incomprehensible letter.

At last he broke it, and read it hurriedly. As he did so a terrible, ominous pang came across his heart, and the writing, familiar as it was, swam illegibly in dancing lines before his strained and aching vision.

"Dear Mr. Editor," the letter began, somewhat shakily, "you give your advice and assistance to many people. Will you give it to me? Will you help me? Will you save me?

"This is my position. I was married young to a man I did not love, but liked and respected. I thought love would come afterwards. It never came. On the contrary, the longer I have lived with him the less I care for him. Not that he is unkind to me, he is good enough and generous enough in all conscience; but he inspires me with no affection and no enthusiasm. Till lately this was all I felt. I did not love him, but I jogged along comfortably somehow.

"Now, however, I find to my dismay that I am in love, not with him, but with another man a hundred times more congenial to my tastes and feelings in every way. I have done no wrong, but I think of him and live in him all my time. I cannot for a moment dismiss him from my thoughts. Oh, what am I to do? Tell me, help me!

"I can never love my husband, of that I am certain. I can never leave off loving the other, of that I am still more confident. Can you advise me? Can you relieve me? This torture is too terrible. It is killing me, killing me.

"Yours ever, in strict confidence, "EGERIA."

Harry Pallant gazed at that awful accusing letter in blank horror and speechless bewilderment. He could not even cry or groan. He could not utter a word or shed a tear. The shock was so sudden, so crushing, so unexpected, so irretrievable!

He had never till that moment in the faintest degree doubted that Louie loved him as he loved her, devotedly, distractedly.

Why, that very morning, before he came away on his journey to the Temple, Louie had kissed him so tenderly and affectionately, and called him "darling," and wished he hadn't always to go to that horrid City. How the memory stung him!

Yes; that was the hardest thought of all. If Louie wrote it, Louie was a hypocrite. Not only did she not now love him, not only had she never loved him, but, lowest depth of misery and shame, she had pretended to love him when in her heart of hearts she hated and despised him. He couldn't believe it. He wouldn't believe it. In her own words, it was too terrible!

If Louie wrote it? He turned the letter over once more. Ah, yes, there was no denying it. It was Louie's handwriting, Louie's, Louie's. His brain reeled, but he could not doubt it or palter over it for a moment. Not even disguised, her very own handwriting. It was the seal of doom for him, yet he could not even pretend to disbelieve it.

He sat there long, incapable of realizing the full horror of that crushing, destroying, annihilating disclosure. It was useless trying to realize it, thank God for that! It so dazed and stunned and staggered and bewildered him that he fell for a time into a sort of hopeless lethargy, and felt and saw and thought of nothing.

At last he roused himself. He must go out. He rose from the table by the dingy window, took up his hat dreamily in his hand, and walked down the stairs, out of the gateway, and into the full tide of life and bustle in busy Fleet Street.

The cooler air upon his forehead and the sight of so many hurrying, active figures sobered and steadied him. He walked with rapid strides as far as Charing Cross Station, and then back again. After that, he came into his chambers once more, sat down resolutely at his table by himself, and began to write in a trembling shaky hand his answer to "Egeria."

How often he had written a different answer to just the same type of tragic little letter, an answer of the commonplace conventional morality, a small set sermon on the duties of wives and the rights of husbands, as though there was nothing more in that fearful disclosure than the merest fancy; and now, when at last it touched himself, how profoundly awful in their mockery of the truth those baldly respectable answers seemed to him!

"EGERIA.—Your letter shall be treated, as you wish, in strict confidence. No one but ourselves shall ever know of it. You need not fear that H. P. will any longer prove a trouble to you. By the time you read this you will have learnt, or will shortly learn, that he is not in a position to cause you further discomfort. This is the only intimation you will receive of his intention. You will understand what it all means soon after you read this communication."

He rang the hand-bell on the table for his boy, put the answers into a long blue envelope, and said mechanically in a dry voice, "To the Young People's Monitor. For press immediately." The boy nodded a mute assent, and took them off to the office in silent obedience.

As soon as he was gone Harry Pallant locked the door, flung himself upon the table with his head buried madly in his arms, and sobbed aloud in terrible despondency. He had found at least the relief of tears.

There was only one comfort. He was fully insured, and Hugh Ogilvie was a rich man. Louie at least would be well provided for. He cared for nothing except for Louie. If Louie was happier, happier without him, what further need had he got for living?

He had never thought before of Hugh, but now, now, Dora's words came back to him at once, and he saw it all, he saw it all plainly.

Heaven be praised, they had no children! If they had had children, well, well, as things now stood, he could do what was best for Louie's happiness.

III

For the next two days Louie could not imagine what sudden change had come so inexplicably over Harry Pallant. He was quite as tender and as gentle as ever, but so silent, sad, and incomprehensible. Louie coaxed him and petted him in vain; the more she made of him the more Harry seemed to retreat within himself, and the less could she understand what on earth he was thinking of.

On the Thursday night, when Harry came back from his work in the City, he said to Louie in an off-hand tone, "Louie, I think of running down to-morrow to dear old Bilborough."

"What for, darling?"

"Well, you know, I've been fearfully out of sorts lately, worried or something, and I think three or four days at the seaside would be all the better for me, and for you too, darling. Let's go to the Red Lion, Louie. I've telegraphed down to-night for rooms, and I dare say, I shall get rid there of whatever's troubling me."

The Red Lion at Bilborough was the hotel at which they had passed their honeymoon, and where they had often gone at various times since for their summer holiday. Louie was delighted at the proposed trip, and smoothed her husband's hair softly with her hand.

"My darling," she said, "I'm so glad you're going there. I've noticed for the last few days you looked fagged and worried. But Bilborough's just the right place. Bilborough always sets you up again."

Harry smiled a faint, unhappy smile. "I've no doubt," he answered evasively, "I shall leave all my trouble behind at Bilborough."

They started by the early train next day, Louie hastily packing their little portmanteau overnight, and got down to Bilborough before noon. As soon as they were fairly settled in at the Lion, Harry kissed his wife tenderly, and, with a quiet persistence in his voice said, on a sudden, "Louie, I think I shall go and have a swim before lunch-time."

"A swim, Harry! So soon?—already?"

"Yes," Harry answered, with a twitching mouth, and looking at her nervously. "There's nothing like a swim you know, Louie, to wash away the cobwebs of London."

"Well, don't be long, darling," Louie said, with some undisguised anxiety. "I've ordered lunch, remember, for one."

"For one, Louie?" Harry cried with a start. "Why for one, dearest? I don't understand you.... Oh, I see. How very stupid of me! Yes, yes, I'll be back by one o'clock.... That is to say, if I'm not back, don't you wait lunch for me."

He moved uneasily to the door, and then he turned back again with a timid glance, and drew a newspaper slowly from his pocket. "I've brought down this morning's Young People's Monitor with me, Louie," he said, in a tremulous voice, after a short pause. "I know you sometimes like to see it."

He watched her narrowly to observe the effect, but Louie took it from him without a visible tremor. "Oh, I'm so glad, Harry," she said in her natural tone, without betraying the least excitement. "How awfully kind of you to get it for me! There's something in it I wanted to see about."

Something in it she wanted to see about! Harry's heart stood still for a second within him! What duplicity! What temerity! What a terrible mixture of seeming goodness and perfect composure! And yet it was Louie, and he couldn't help loving her! He kissed her once more, a long, hard kiss, upon the forehead, and went out, leaving her there with the paper clasped tightly in her small white fingers. Though she said nothing he could see that her fingers trembled as she held it. Yes yes, there could be no doubt about it; she was eagerly expecting the answer, the fatal answer, the answer to "Egeria" in the correspondence column.

IV

Louie stood long at the window, with the paper still clutched eagerly in her hand, afraid to open it and read the answer, and yet longing to know what the Young People's Monitor had to say in reply to "Egeria." So she watched Harry go down to the bathing machines and enter one, it was still early in the season, and he had no need to wait; and then she watched them turning the windlass and letting it run down upon the shelving beach; and then she watched Harry swimming out and stemming the waves in his bold, manly fashion, he was a splendid swimmer; and after that, unable any longer to restrain her curiosity, she tore the paper open with her finger, and glanced down the correspondence column till she reached the expected answer to "Egeria."

She read it over wondering and trembling, with a sudden awful sense of the editor's omniscience as she saw the letters "H. P."—her husband's initials—Harry Pallant. "H. P.!" what could he mean by it?

And then a vague dread came across her soul. What could "Egeria" and the editor of the Young People's Monitor have to do with Harry Pallant?

She read it over again and again. How terrifying! how mysterious! how dimly incomprehensible! Who on earth could have told the editor, that impersonal entity, that "Egeria's" letter had any connection with her own husband, Harry Pallant? And yet he must have known it, evidently known it. And she herself had never suspected the allusion. Yes, yes, it was clear to her now; the man about whom "Egeria" had written was Harry—Harry—Harry—Harry. Could it have been that that had so troubled him of late? She couldn't bear to distrust Harry; but it must have been that, and nothing else. Harry was in love with Dora Ferrand; or, if not, Dora Ferrand was in love with Harry, and Harry knew it, and was afraid he might yield to her, and had ran away from her accordingly. He had come to Bilborough on purpose to escape her, to drag himself away from her, to try to forget her. Oh, Harry, Harry!—and she loved him so truly. To think he should deceive her, to think he should keep anything from her! It was too terrible, too terrible! She couldn't bear to think it, and yet the evidence forced it upon her.

But how did the editor ever come to know about it? And what was this mysterious, awful message that he gave Dora about Harry Pallant?

"You need not fear that H. P. will any longer prove a trouble to you." Why? Did Harry mean to leave London altogether? Was he afraid to trust himself there with Dora Ferrand? Did he fear that she would steal his heart in spite of him? Oh, Dora, Dora! the shameless creature! When Louie came to think it all over, her effrontery and her wickedness were absolutely appalling.

She sat there long, turning the paper over helplessly in her hand, reading its words every way but the right way, pondering over what Harry had said to her that morning, putting her own interpretation upon everything, and forgetting even to unpack her things and make herself ready for lunch in the coffee-room.

Presently, a crowd upon the beach below languidly attracted her passing attention. The coastguard from the look-out was gesticulating frantically, and a group of sailors were seizing in haste upon a boat on the foreshore. They launched it hurriedly and pulled with all their might outward, the people on the beach gathering thicker meanwhile, and all looking eagerly towards some invisible object far out to sea, in the direction of the Race with the dangerous current. Louie's heart sank ominously within her. At that very moment the chambermaid of the hotel rushed in with a pale face, and cried out in merciless haste, "Oh, ma'am, Mrs. Pallant! quick! quick!—he's drowning! he's drowning! Mr. Pallant's swum too far out, and's got into the Race, and they've put the boat off to try and save him!"

In a second, half the truth flashed terribly upon Louie Pallant's distracted intelligence. She saw that it was Harry himself who wrote the correspondence for the Young People's Monitor, and that he had swum out to sea of his own accord to the end of his tether, on purpose to drown himself as if by accident. But she didn't yet perceive, obvious as it seemed, that Harry thought she herself had written "Egeria's" letter in her own person. She thought still he was in love with Dora, and had drowned himself because he couldn't tear himself away from her for ever.

V

They brought Harry Pallant ashore, cold and lifeless, and carried him up in haste to the hotel. There the village doctor saw him at once, and detected a faint tremor of the heart. At the end of an hour the lungs began to act faintly of themselves, and the heart beat a little in some feeble fashion.

With care Harry Pallant came round, but it took a week or two before he was himself again, and Louie nursed him meanwhile in fear and trembling, with breathless agony. She had one consolation—Harry loved her. In the long nights the whole truth dawned upon her, clear and certain. She saw how Harry had opened the letter, had jumped at once to the natural conclusion, and had tried to drown himself in order to release her. Oh, why had he not trusted her? Why had he not asked her? A woman naturally thinks like that; a man knows in his own soul that a man could never possibly do so.

She dared not tell him yet, for fear of a relapse. She could only wait and watch, and nurse him tenderly. And all the time she knew he distrusted her, knew he thought her a hypocrite and a traitor. For Harry's sake she had to bear it.

At last, one day, when he was getting very much stronger, and could sit up in a chair and look bitterly out at the sea, she said to him in a gentle voice, very tentatively, "Harry, Dora Ferrand and her husband have gone to spend the summer in Norway."

Harry groaned. "How do you know?" he asked. "Has Hugh written to you? What is it to us? Who told you about it?"

Louie bit her lip hard to keep back the tears. "Dora telegraphed to me herself," she answered softly. "She telegraphed to me as soon as ever"—she hesitated a moment—"as soon as ever she saw your answer to her in the Monitor."

Harry's face grew white with horror. "My answer to her!" he cried in a ghastly voice, not caring to ask at the moment how Louie came to know it was he who wrote the answers in the Young People's Monitor. "My answer to you, you mean, Louie. It was your letter—yours, not Dora's. You can't deceive me. I read it myself. My poor child, I saw your handwriting."

It was an awful thing that, in spite of all, he must have it out with her against his will; but he would not flinch from it, he would settle it then and there, once and for ever. She had introduced it herself; she had brought it down upon her own head. He would not flinch from it. It was his duty to tell her.

Louie laid her hand upon his arm. He did not try to cast it off. "Harry," she said, imploringly, persuasively, "there is a terrible mistake here, a terrible misunderstanding. It was unavoidable; you could not possibly have thought otherwise. But oh, Harry, if you knew the suffering you have brought upon me, you would not speak so, darling, you would not speak so."

Harry turned towards her passionately and eagerly. "Then you didn't want me to die, Louie?" he cried in a hoarse voice. "You didn't really want to get rid of me?"

Louie withdrew her hand hastily as if she had been stung. "Harry," she gasped, as well as she was able, "you misunderstood that letter altogether. It was not mine, it was Dora Ferrand's. Dora wrote it, and I only copied it. If you will listen a minute I will tell you all, all about it."

Harry flung himself back half incredulously on his chair, but with a new-born hope lighting up in part the gloom of his recovered existence.

"I went over to Dora Ferrand's the day after the Ogilvies' dance," Louie began tremulously, "and I found Dora sitting in her boudoir writing a letter. I walked up without being announced, and when Dora saw me she screamed a little, and then she grew as red as fire, and burst out crying, and tried to hide the letter she was writing. So I went up to her and began to soothe her, and asked her what it was, and wanted to read it. And Dora cried for a long time, and wouldn't tell me, and was dreadfully penitent, and said she was very, very miserable. So I said, 'Dora, is there anything wrong between you and Mr. Ferrand?' And she said, 'Nothing, Louie; I give you my word of honour, nothing. Poor Wetherby's as kind to me as anybody could be. But—' And then she began crying again as if her heart would burst, worse than ever. And I took her head on my shoulder, and said to her, 'Dora, is it that you feel you don't love him?' And Dora was in a dreadfully penitent fit, and she flung herself away from me, and said to me, 'Oh, Louie, don't touch me! Don't kiss me! Don't come near me! I'm not fit to associate with a girl like you, dear.... Oh, Louie, I don't love him; and, what's worse, I love somebody else, darling.' Well, then, of course, I was horribly shocked, and I said, 'Dora, Dora, this is awfully wicked of you!' And Dora cried worse than before, and sobbed away, and wouldn't be comforted. And there was a copy of the Monitor lying on the table, and I saw it open at the correspondence, and I said, 'Were you writing for advice to the Monitor, Dora?' And she looked up and nodded 'Yes.' So I coaxed her and begged her to show me the letter, and at last she showed it to me; but she wouldn't tell me who she was in love with, Harry; and, oh, Harry, my darling, my darling, I never so much as dreamt of its being you, dear, the thought never even crossed my mind. I ran over everybody I could imagine she'd taken a fancy to, but I never for a moment thought of you, darling. I suppose, Harry, I loved you too dearly even to suspect it. And then, I dare say, Dora saw I didn't suspect it; but, anyhow, she went on and finished the letter, it was nearly done when I came in to her, and after that she said she couldn't bear to send it in her own handwriting, for fear anybody should know her and recognize it. So I said if she liked I'd copy it out for her, for by that time I was crying just as hard as she was, and so sorry for her and for poor Mr. Ferrand; and it never struck me that anybody could ever possibly think that I wrote it about myself. And—and—and that's all, Harry."

Harry listened, conscience-smitten, to the artless recital, which bore its own truth on the very surface of it, as it fell from Louie's trembling lips, and then he held her off at arm's length when she tried to fall upon his neck and kiss him, whispering in a loud undertone, "Oh, Louie, Louie, don't, don't! I don't deserve it! I have been too wicked—too mistrustful!"

Louie drew forth a letter from her pocket and handed it to him silently. It was in Dora's handwriting. He read it through in breathless anxiety.

"Louie, I dare not call you anything else now. You know it all by this time. We have heard about Harry's accident from your sister. Nobody but ourselves knows it was not an accident. And I have seen the answer in the Monitor. Of course Harry wrote it. I see it all now. You can never forgive me. It is I who have brought all this misery upon you. I am a wretched woman. Do not reproach me, I reproach myself more bitterly than anything you could say would ever reproach me. But don't forgive me and pity me either. If you forgive me I shall have to kill myself. It's all over now. I will do the only thing that remains for me, keep out of your way and his forever. Poor Wetherby is going to take me for the summer to Norway, as I telegraphed to you. We are just starting. When we return we shall winter in Italy. I will leave London in future altogether. Nobody but our three selves need ever know or suspect the reason. Harry will recover, and you two will be happy yet. But I, I shall be as miserable for ever, as I truly deserve to be.

"Your wretched friend,   "D. F."

Harry crumpled up the letter bitterly in his hand. "Poor soul," he said. "Louie, I forgive her. Can I myself ever hope for forgiveness?"

Louie flung herself fiercely upon him. "My darling," she cried, "we will always trust one another in future. You couldn't help it, Harry. It was impossible for you to have judged otherwise. But oh, my darling, what I have suffered! Let us forgive her. Harry, and let us love one another better now."

THE SEARCH PARTY'S FIND

I can stand it no longer. I must put down my confession on paper, since there is no living creature left to whom I can confess it.

The snow is drifting fiercer than ever to-day against the cabin; the last biscuit is almost finished; my fingers are so pinched with cold I can hardly grasp the pen to write with. But I will write, I must write, and I am writing. I cannot die with the dreadful story unconfessed upon my conscience.

It was only an accident, most of you who read this confession perhaps will say; but in my own heart I know better than that, I know it was a murder, a wicked murder.

Still, though my hands are very numb, and my head swimming wildly with delirium, I will try to be coherent, and to tell my story clearly and collectedly.

I was appointed surgeon of the Cotopaxi in June, 1880. I had reasons of my own, sad reasons, for wishing to join an Arctic expedition. I didn't join it, as most of the other men did, from pure love of danger and adventure. I am not a man to care for that sort of thing on its own account. I joined it because of a terrible disappointment.

For two years I had been engaged to Dora, I needn't call her anything but Dora; my brother, to whom I wish this paper sent, but whom I daren't address as "Dear Arthur"—how could I, a murderer?—will know well enough who I mean; and as to other people, it isn't needful they should know anything about it. But whoever you are, whoever finds this paper, I beg of you, I implore you, I adjure you, do not tell a word of it to Dora. I cannot die unconfessed, but I cannot let the confession reach her; if it does, I know the double shock will kill her. Keep it from her. Tell her only he is dead, dead at his post, like a brave man, on the Cotopaxi exploring expedition. For mercy's sake don't tell her that he was murdered, and that I murdered him.

I had been engaged, I said, two years to Dora. She lived in Arthur's parish, and I loved her, yes, in those days I loved her purely, devotedly, innocently. I was innocent then myself, and I really believe good and well-meaning. I should have been genuinely horrified and indignant if anybody had ventured to say that I should end by committing a murder.

It was a great grief to me when I had to leave Arthur's parish, and my father's parish before him, to go up to London and take a post as surgeon to a small hospital. I couldn't bear being so far away from Dora. And at first Dora wrote to me almost every day with the greatest affection. (Heaven forgive me, if I still venture to call her Dora! her, so good and pure and beautiful, and I, a murderer.) But, after a while, I noticed slowly that Dora's tone seemed to grow colder and colder, and her letters less and less frequent. Why she should have begun to cease loving me, I cannot imagine; perhaps she had a premonition of what possibility of wickedness was really in me. At any rate, her coldness grew at last so marked that I wrote and asked Arthur whether he could explain it. Arthur answered me, a little regretfully, and with brotherly affection (he is a good fellow, Arthur), that he thought he could. He feared, it was painful to say so, but he feared Dora was beginning to love a newer lover. A young man had lately come to the village of whom she had seen a great deal, and who was very handsome and brave and fascinating. Arthur was afraid he could not conceal from me his impression that Dora and the stranger were very much taken with one another.

At last, one morning, a letter came to me from Dora. I can put it in here, because I carried it away with me when I went to Hammerfest to join the Cotopaxi, and ever since I have kept it sadly in my private pocket-book.

"Dear Ernest" (she had always called me Ernest since we had been children together, and she couldn't leave it off even now when she was writing to let me know she no longer loved me), "Can you forgive me for what I am going to tell you? I thought I loved you till lately; but then I had never discovered what love really meant. I have discovered it now, and I find that, after all, I only liked you very sincerely. You will have guessed before this that I love somebody else, who loves me in return with all the strength of his whole nature. I have made a grievous mistake, which I know will render you terribly unhappy. But it is better so than to marry a man whom I do not really love with all my heart and soul and affection; better in the end, I am sure, for both of us. I am too much ashamed of myself to write more to you. Can you forgive me?

"Yours, "DORA."

I could not forgive her then, though I loved her too much to be angry; I was only broken-hearted, thoroughly stunned and broken-hearted. I can forgive her now, but she can never forgive me, Heaven help me!

I only wanted to get away, anywhere, anywhere, and forget all about it in a life of danger. So I asked for the post of surgeon to Sir Paxton Bateman's Cotopaxi expedition a few weeks afterwards. They wanted a man who knew something about natural history and deep-sea dredging, and they took me on at once, on the recommendation of a well-known man of science!

The very day I joined the ship at Hammerfest, in August, I noticed immediately there was one man on board whose mere face and bearing and manner were at first sight excessively objectionable to me. He was a handsome young fellow enough, one Harry Lemarchant, who had been a planter in Queensland, and who, after being burned up with three years of tropical sunshine was anxious to cool himself apparently by a long winter of Arctic gloom. Handsome as he was, with his black moustache and big dark eyes rolling restlessly, I took an instantaneous dislike to his cruel thin lip and cold proud mouth the moment I looked upon him. If I had been wise, I would have drawn back from the expedition at once. It is a foolish thing to bind one's self down to a voyage of that sort unless you are perfectly sure beforehand that you have at least no instinctive hatred of any one among your messmates in that long forced companionship. But I wasn't wise, and I went on with him.

From the first moment, even before I had spoken to him, I disliked Lemarchant; very soon I grew to hate him. He seemed to me the most recklessly cruel and devilish creature (God forgive me that I should say it!) I had ever met with in my whole lifetime. On an Arctic expedition, a man's true nature soon comes out, mine did certainly, and he lets his companions know more about his inner self in six weeks than they could possibly learn about him in years of intercourse under other circumstances. And the second night I was on board the Cotopaxi I learnt enough to make my blood run cold about Harry Lemarchant's ideas and feelings.

We were all sitting on deck together, those of us who were not on duty, and listening to yarns from one another, as idle men will, when the conversation happened accidentally to turn on Queensland, and Lemarchant began to enlighten us about his own doings when he was in the colony. He boasted a great deal about his prowess as a disperser of the black fellows, which he seemed to consider a very noble sort of occupation. There was nobody in the colony, he said, who had ever dispersed so many blacks as he had; and he'd like to be back there, dispersing again, for, in the matter of sport, it beat kangaroo-hunting, or any other kind of shooting he had ever yet tried his hand at, all to pieces.

The second-lieutenant, Hepworth Paterson, a nice kind-hearted young Scotchman, looked up at him a little curiously, and said, "Why, what do you mean by dispersing, Lemarchant? Driving them off into the bush, I suppose: isn't that it? Not much fun in that, that I can see, scattering a lot of poor helpless black naked savages."

Lemarchant curled his lip contemptuously (he didn't think much of Paterson, because his father was said to be a Glasgow grocer), and answered in his rapid, dare-devil fashion: "No fun! Isn't there, just! that's all you know about it, my good fellow. Now I'll give you one example. One day, the inspector came in and told us there were a lot of blacks camping out on our estate down by the Warramidgee river. So we jumped on our horses like a shot, went down there immediately, and began dispersing them. We didn't fire at them, because the grass and ferns and things were very high, and we might have wasted our ammunition; but we went at them with native spears, just for all the world like pig-sticking. You should have seen those black fellows run for their lives through the long grass, men, women, and little ones together. We rode after them, full pelt; and as we came up with them, one by one, we just rolled them over, helter-skelter, as if they'd been antelopes or bears or something. By-and-by, after a good long charge or two, we'd cleared the place of the big blacks altogether; but the gins and the children, some of them, lay lurking in among the grass, you know, and wouldn't come out and give us fair sport, as they ought to have done, out in the open: children will pack, you see, whenever they're hard driven, exactly like grouse, after a month or two's steady shooting. Well, to make them start and show game, of course we just put a match to the grass; and in a minute the whole thing was in a blaze, right down the corner to the two rivers. So we turned our horses into the stream, and rode alongside, half a dozen of us on each river; and every now and then, one of the young ones would break cover, and slide out quietly into the stream, and try to swim across without being perceived, and get clean away into the back country. Then we just made a dash at them with the pig-spears; and sometimes they'd dive, and precious good divers they are, too, those Queenslanders, I can tell you; but we waited around till they came up again, and then we stuck them as sure as houses. That's what we call dispersing the natives over in Queensland: extending the blessings of civilization to the unsettled parts of the back country."

He laughed a pleasant laugh to himself quietly as he finished this atrocious, devilish story, and showed his white teeth all in a row, as if he thought the whole reminiscence exceedingly amusing.

Of course, we were all simply speechless with horror and astonishment. Such deliberate brutal murderousness, gracious heavens! what am I saying? I had half forgotten for the moment that I, too, am a murderer.

"But what had the black fellows done to you?" Paterson asked with a tone of natural loathing, after we had all sat silent and horror-stricken in a circle for a moment. "I suppose they'd been behaving awfully badly to some white people somewhere, massacring women or something, to get your blood up to such a horrid piece of butchery."

Lemarchant laughed again, a quiet chuckle of conscious superiority, and only answered: "Behaving badly! Massacring white women! Lord bless your heart, I'd like to see them! Why, the wretched creatures wouldn't ever dare to do it. Oh, no, nothing of that sort, I can tell you. And our blood wasn't up either. We went in for it just by way of something to do, and to keep our hands in. Of course you can't allow a lot of lazy hulking blacks to go knocking around in the neighbourhood of an estate, stealing your fowls and fruit and so forth, without let or hindrance. It's the custom in Queensland to disperse the black fellows. I've often been out riding with a friend, and I've seen a nigger skulking about somewhere down in a hollow among the tree-ferns; and I've just drawn my six-shooter, and said to my friend, 'You see me disperse that confounded nigger!' and I've dispersed him right off, into little pieces, too, you may take your oath upon it."

"But do you mean to tell me, Mr. Lemarchant," Paterson said, looking a deal more puzzled and shocked, "that these poor creatures had been doing absolutely nothing?"

"Well, now, that's the way of all you home-sticking sentimentalists," Lemarchant went on, with an ugly simper. "You want to push on the outskirts of civilization and to see the world colonized, but you're too squeamish to listen to anything about the only practicable civilizing and colonizing agencies. It's the struggle for existence, don't you see: the plain outcome of all the best modern scientific theories. The black man has got to go to the wall; the white man, with his superior moral and intellectual nature, has got to push him there. At bottom, it's nothing more than civilization. Shoot 'em off at once, I say, and get rid of 'em forthwith and for ever."

"Why," I said, looking at him, with my disgust speaking in my face (Heaven forgive me!), "I call it nothing less than murder."

Lemarchant laughed, and lit his cigar; but after that, somehow, the other men didn't much care to talk to him in an ordinary way more than was necessary for the carrying out of the ship's business.

And yet he was a very gentlemanly fellow, I must admit, and well read and decently educated. Only there seemed to be a certain natural brutality about him, under a thin veneer of culture and good breeding, that repelled us all dreadfully from the moment we saw him. I dare say we shouldn't have noticed it so much if we hadn't been thrown together so closely as men are on an Arctic voyage, but then and there it was positively unendurable. We none of us held any communications with him whenever we could help it; and he soon saw that we all of us thoroughly disliked and distrusted him.

That only made him reckless and defiant. He knew he was bound to go the journey through with us now, and he set to work deliberately to shock and horrify us. Whether all the stories he told us by the ward-room fire in the evenings were true or not, I can't tell you, I don't believe they all were; but at any rate he made them seem as brutal and disgusting as the most loathsome details could possibly make them. He was always apologizing, nay, glorying, in bloodshed and slaughter, which he used to defend with a show of cultivated reasoning that made the naked brutality of his stories seem all the more awful and unpardonable at bottom. And yet one couldn't deny, all the time, that there was a grace of manner and a show of polite feeling about him which gave him a certain external pleasantness, in spite of everything. He was always boasting that women liked him; and I could easily understand how a great many women who saw him only with his company manners might even think him brave and handsome and very chivalrous.

I won't go into the details of the expedition. They will be found fully and officially narrated in the log, which I have hidden in the captain's box in the hut beside the captain's body. I need only mention here the circumstances immediately connected with the main matter of this confession.

One day, a little while before we got jammed into the ice off the Liakov Islands, Lemarchant was up on deck with me, helping me to remove from the net the creatures that we had dredged up in our shallow soundings. As he stooped to pick out a Leptocardium boreale, I happened to observe that a gold locket had fallen out of the front of his waistcoat, and showed a lock of hair on its exposed surface. Lemarchant noticed it too, and with an awkward laugh put it back hurriedly. "My little girl's keepsake!" he said in a tone that seemed to me disagreeably flippant about such a subject. "She gave it to me just before I set off on my way to Hammerfest."

I started in some astonishment. He had a little girl then, a sweetheart he meant, obviously. If so, Heaven help her! poor soul, Heaven help her! For any woman to be tied for life to such a creature as that was really quite too horrible. I didn't even like to think upon it.

I don't know what devil prompted me, for I seldom spoke to him, even when we were told off on duty together; but I said at last, after a moment's pause, "If you are engaged to be married, as I suppose you are from what you say, I wonder you could bear to come away on such a long business as this, when you couldn't get a word or a letter from the lady you're engaged to for a whole winter."

He went on picking out the shells and weeds as he answered in a careless, jaunty tone, "Why, to tell you the truth, Doctor, that was just about the very meaning of it. We're going to be married next summer, you see, and for reasons of her papa's, the deuce knows what!—my little girl couldn't possibly be allowed to marry one week sooner. There I'd been, knocking about and spooning with her violently for three months nearly; and the more I spooned, and the more tired I got of it, the more she expected me to go on spooning. Well, I'm not the sort of man to stand billing and cooing for a whole year together. At last the thing grew monotonous. I wanted to get an excuse to go off somewhere, where there was some sort of fun going on, till summer came, and we could get spliced properly (for she's got some tin, too, and I didn't want to throw her over); but I felt that if I'd got to keep on spooning and spooning for a whole winter, without intermission, the thing would really be one too many for me, and I should have to give it up from sheer weariness. So I heard of this precious expedition, which is just the sort of adventure I like; I wrote and volunteered for it; and then I managed to make my little girl and her dear papa believe that as I was an officer in the naval reserve I was compelled to go when asked, willy-nilly. 'It's only for half a year, you know, darling,' and all that sort of thing, you understand the line of country; and meanwhile I'm saved the bother of ever writing to her, or getting any letters from her either, which is almost in its way an equal nuisance."

"I see," said I shortly. "Not to put too fine a point upon it, you simply lied to her."

"Upon my soul," he answered, showing his teeth again, but this time by no means pleasantly, "you fellows on the Cotopaxi are really the sternest set of moralists I ever met with outside a book of sermons or a Surrey melodrama. You ought all to have been parsons, every man Jack of you; that's just about what you're fit for."

On the fourteenth of September we got jammed in the ice, and the Cotopaxi went to pieces. You will find in the captain's log how part of us walked across the pack to the Liakov Islands, and settled ourselves here on Point Sibiriakoff in winter quarters. As to what became of the other party, which went southwards to the mouth of the Lena, I know nothing.

It was a hard winter, but by the aid of our stores and an occasional walrus shot by one of the blue-jackets, we managed to get along till March without serious illness. Then, one day, after a spell of terrible frost and snow, the Captain came to me, and said, "Doctor, I wish you'd come and see Lemarchant, in the other hut here. I'm afraid he's got a bad fever."

I went to see him. So he had. A raging fever.

Fumbling about among his clothes to lay him down comfortably on the bearskin (for of course we had saved no bedding from the wreck), I happened to knock out once more the same locket that I had seen when he was emptying the drag-net. There was a photograph in it of a young lady. The seal-oil lamp didn't give very much light in the dark hut (it was still the long winter night on the Liakov Islands), but even so I couldn't help seeing and recognizing the young lady's features. Great Heaven support me! uphold me! I reeled with horror and amazement. It was Dora.

Yes; his little girl, that he spoke of so carelessly, that he lied to so easily, that he meant to marry so cruelly, was my Dora.

I had pitied the woman who was to be Harry Lemarchant's wife even when I didn't know who she was in any way; I pitied her terribly, with all my heart, when I knew that she was Dora, my own Dora. If I have become a murderer, after all, it was to save Dora, to save Dora from that unutterable, abominable ruffian.

I clutched the photograph in the locket eagerly, and held it up to the man's eyes. He opened them dreamily. "Is that the lady you are going to marry?" I asked him, with all the boiling indignation of that terrible discovery seething and burning in my very face.

He smiled, and took it all in in half a minute. "It is," he answered, in spite of the fever, with all his old dare-devil carelessness. "And now I recollect they told me the fellow she was engaged to was a doctor in London, and a brother of the parson. By Jove, I never thought of it before that your name, too, was actually Robinson. That's the worst of having such a deuced common name as yours; no one ever dreams of recognizing your relations. Hang it all, if you're the man, I suppose now, out of revenge, you'll be wanting next to go and poison me."

"You judge others by yourself, I'm afraid," I answered sternly. Oh, how the words seem to rise up in judgment against me at last, now the dreadful thing is all over!

I doctored him as well as I was able, hoping all the time in my inmost soul (for I will confess all now) that he would never recover. Already in wish I had become a murderer. It was too horrible to think that such a man as that should marry Dora. I had loved her once and I loved her still; I love her now; I shall always love her. Murderer as I am, I say it nevertheless, I shall always love her.

But at last, to my grief and disappointment, the man began to mend and get better. My doctoring had done him good; and the sailors, though even they did not love him, had shot him once or twice a small bird, of which we made fresh soup that seemed to revive him. Yes, yes, he was coming round; and my cursed medicines had done it all. He was getting well, and he would still go back to marry Dora.

The very idea put me into such a fever of terror and excitement that at last I began to exhibit the same symptoms as Lemarchant himself had done. The Captain saw I was sickening, and feared the fever might prove an epidemic. It wasn't: I knew that. Mine was brain, Lemarchant's was intermittent; but the Captain insisted upon disbelieving me. So he put me and Lemarchant into the same hut, and made all the others clear out, so as to turn it into a sort of temporary hospital.

Every night I put out from the medicine-chest two quinine powders apiece, for myself and Lemarchant.

One night, it was the 7th of April (I can't forget it), I woke feebly from my feverish sleep, and noticed in a faint sort of fashion that Lemarchant was moving about restlessly in the cabin.

"Lemarchant," I cried authoritatively (for as surgeon I was, of course, responsible for the health of the expedition), "go back and lie down upon your bearskin this minute! You're a great deal too weak to go getting anything for yourself as yet. Go back this minute, sir, and if you want anything, I'll pull the string, and Paterson'll come and see what you're after." For we had fixed up a string between the two huts, tied to a box at the end, as a rough means of communication.

"All right, old fellow," he answered, more cordially than I had ever yet heard him speak to me. "It's all square, I assure you. I was only seeing whether you were quite warm and comfortable on your rug there."

"Perhaps," I thought, "the care I've taken of him has made him really feel a little grateful to me." So I dozed off and thought nothing more at the moment about it.

Presently, I heard a noise again, and woke up quietly, without starting, but just opened my eyes and peered about as well as the dim light of the little oil-lamp would allow me.

To my great surprise, I could make out somehow that Lemarchant was meddling with the bottles in the medicine-chest.

"Perhaps," thought I again, "he wants another dose of quinine. Anyhow, I'm too tired and sleepy to ask him anything just now about it."

I knew he hated me, and I knew he was unscrupulous, but it didn't occur to me to think he would poison the man who had just helped him through a dangerous fever.

At four I woke, as I always did, and proceeded to take one of my powders. Curiously enough, before I tasted it, the grain appeared to me to be rather coarser and more granular than the quinine I had originally put there. I took a pinch between my finger and thumb, and placed it on my tongue by way of testing it. Instead of being bitter, the powder, I found, was insipid and almost tasteless.

Could I possibly in my fever and delirium (though I had not consciously been delirious) have put some other powder instead of the quinine into the two papers? The bare idea made me tremble with horror. If so, I might have poisoned Lemarchant, who had taken one of his powders already, and was now sleeping quietly upon his bearskin. At least, I thought so.

Glancing accidentally to his place that moment, I was vaguely conscious that he was not really sleeping, but lying with his eyes held half open, gazing at me cautiously and furtively through his closed eyelids.

Then the horrid truth flashed suddenly across me. Lemarchant was trying to poison me.

Yes, he had always hated me; and now that he knew I was Dora's discarded lover, he hated me worse than ever. He had got up and taken a bottle from the medicine-chest, I felt certain, and put something else instead of my quinine inside my paper.

I knew his eyes were fixed upon me then, and for the moment I dissembled. I turned round and pretended to swallow the contents of the packet, and then lay down upon my rug as if nothing unusual had happened. The fever was burning me fiercely, but I lay awake, kept up by the excitement, till I saw that he was really asleep, and then I once more undid the paper.

Looking at it closely by the light of the lamp, I saw a finer powder sticking closely to the folded edges. I wetted my finger, put it down and tasted it. Yes, that was quite bitter. That was quinine, not a doubt about it.

I saw at once what Lemarchant had done. He had emptied out the quinine and replaced it by some other white powder, probably arsenic. But a little of the quinine still adhered to the folds in the paper, because he had been obliged to substitute it hurriedly; and that at once proved that it was no mistake of my own, but that Lemarchant had really made the deliberate attempt to poison me.

This is a confession, and a confession only, so I shall make no effort in any way to exculpate myself for the horrid crime I committed the next moment. True, I was wild with fever and delirium; I was maddened with the thought that this wretched man would marry Dora; I was horrified at the idea of sleeping in the same room with him any longer. But still, I acknowledge it now, face to face with a lonely death upon this frozen island, it was murder, wilful murder. I meant to poison him, and I did it.

"He has set this powder for me, the villain," I said to myself, "and now I shall make him take it without knowing it. How do I know that it's arsenic or anything else to do him any harm? His blood be upon his own head, for aught I know about it. What I put there was simply quinine. If anybody has changed it, he has changed it himself. The pit that he dug for another, he himself shall fall therein."

I wouldn't even test it, for fear I should find it was arsenic, and be unable to give it to him innocently and harmlessly.

I rose up and went over to Lemarchant's side. Horror of horrors, he was sleeping soundly! Yes, the man had tried to poison me; and when he thought he had seen me swallow his poisonous powder, so callous and hardened was his nature that he didn't even lie awake to watch the effect of it. He had dropped off soundly, as if nothing had happened, and was sleeping now, to all appearance, the sleep of innocence. Being convalescent, in fact, and therefore in need of rest, he slept with unusual soundness.

I laid the altered powder quietly by his pillow, took away his that I had laid out in readiness for him, and crept back to my own place noiselessly. There I lay awake, hot and feverish, wondering to myself hour after hour when he would ever wake and take it.

At last he woke, and looked over towards me with unusual interest. "Hullo, Doctor," he said quite genially, "how are you this morning, eh? getting on well, I hope." It was the first time during all my illness that he had ever inquired after me.

I lied to him deliberately to keep the delusion up. "I have a terrible grinding pain in my chest," I said, pretending to writhe. I had sunk to his level, it seems. I was a liar and a murderer.

He looked quite gay over it, and laughed. "It's nothing," he said, grinning horribly. "It's a good symptom. I felt just like that myself, my dear fellow, when I was beginning to recover."

Then I knew he had tried to poison me, and I felt no remorse for my terrible action. It was a good deed to prevent such a man as that from ever carrying away Dora, my Dora, into a horrid slavery. Sooner than that he should marry Dora, I would poison him, I would poison him a thousand times over.

He sat up, took the spoon full of treacle, and poured the powder as usual into the very middle of it. I watched him take it off at a single gulp without perceiving the difference, and then I sank back exhausted upon my roll of sealskins.

All that day I was very ill; and Lemarchant, lying tossing beside me, groaned and moaned in a fearful fashion. At last the truth seemed to dawn upon him gradually, and he cried aloud to me: "Doctor, Doctor, quick, for Heaven's sake! you must get me out an antidote. The powders must have got mixed up somehow, and you've given me arsenic instead of quinine, I'm certain."

"Not a bit of it, Lemarchant," I said, with some devilish malice; "I've given you one of my own packets, that was lying here beside my pillow."

He turned as white as a sheet the moment he heard that, and gasped out horribly, "That—that—why, that was arsenic!" But he never explained in a single word how he knew it, or where it came from. I knew. I needed no explanation, and I wanted no lies, so I didn't question him.

I treated him as well as I could for arsenic poisoning, without saying a word to the captain and the other men about it; for if he died, I said, it would be by his own act, and if my skill could still avail, he should have the benefit of it; but the poison had had full time to work before I gave him the antidote, and he died by seven o'clock that night in fearful agonies.

Then I knew that I was really a murderer.

My fingers are beginning to get horribly numb, and I'm afraid I shan't be able to write much longer. I must be quick about it, if I want to finish this confession.

After that came my retribution. I have been punished for it, and punished terribly.

As soon as they all heard Lemarchant was dead, a severe relapse, I called it, they set to work to carry him out and lay him somewhere. Then for the first time the idea flashed across my mind that they couldn't possibly bury him. The ice was too deep everywhere, and underneath it lay the solid rock of the bare granite islands. There was no snow even, for the wind swept it away as it fell, and we couldn't so much as decently cover him. There was nothing for it but to lay him out upon the icy surface.

So we carried the stark frozen body, with its hideous staring eyes wide open, out by the jutting point of rock behind the hut, and there we placed it, dressed and upright. We stood it up against the point exactly as if it were alive, and by-and-by the snow came and froze it to the rock; and there it stands to this moment, glaring for ever fiercely upon me.

Whenever I went in or out of the hut, for three long months, that hideous thing stood there staring me in the face with mute indignation. At night, when I tried to sleep, the murdered man stood there still in the darkness beside me. O God! I dared not say a word to anybody: but I trembled every time I passed it, and I knew what it was to be a murderer.

In May, the sun came back again, but still no open water for our one boat. In June, we had the long day, but no open water. The captain began to get impatient and despondent, as you will read in the log: he was afraid now we might never get a chance of making the mouth of the Lena.

By-and-by, the scurvy came (I have no time now for details, my hands are so cramped with cold), and then we began to run short of provisions. Soon I had them all down upon my hands, and presently we had to place Paterson's corpse beside Lemarchant's on the little headland. Then they sank, one after another, sank of cold and hunger, as you will read in the log, till I alone, who wanted least to live, was the last left living.

I was left alone with those nine corpses propped up awfully against the naked rock, and one of the nine the man I had murdered.

May Heaven forgive me for that terrible crime; and for pity's sake, whoever you may be, keep it from Dora—keep it from Dora!

My brother's address is in my pocket-book.

The fever and remorse alone have given me strength to hold the pen. My hands are quite numbed now. I can write no longer.

There the manuscript ended. Heaven knows what effect it may have upon all of you, who read it quietly at home in your own easy-chairs in England; but we of the search party, who took those almost illegible sheets of shaky writing from the cold fingers of the one solitary corpse within the frozen cabin on the Liakov Islands, we read them through with such a mingled thrill of awe and horror and sympathy and pity as no one can fully understand who has not been upon an Arctic expedition. And when we gathered our sad burdens up to take them off for burial at home, the corpse to which we gave the most reverent attention was certainly that of the self-accused murderer.

HARRY'S INHERITANCE

I

Colonel Sir Thomas Woolrych, K.C.B. (retired list), was a soldier of the old school, much attached to pipe-clay and purchase, and with a low opinion of competitive examinations, the first six books of Euclid, the local military centres, the territorial titles of regiments, the latest regulation pattern in half-dress buttons, and most other confounded new-fangled radical fal-lal and trumpery in general. Sir Thomas believed as firmly in the wisdom of our ancestors as he distrusted the wisdom of our nearest descendants, now just attaining to years of maturity and indiscretion. Especially had he a marked dislike for this nasty modern shopkeeping habit of leaving all your loose money lying idly at your banker's, and paying everybody with a dirty little bit of crumpled paper, instead of pulling out a handful of gold, magnificently, from your trousers pocket, and flinging the sovereigns boldly down before you upon the counter like an officer and a gentleman. Why should you let one of those bloated, overfed, lazy banker-fellows grow rich out of borrowing your money from you for nothing, without so much as a thank-you, and lending it out again to some other poor devil of a tradesman (probably in difficulties) at seven per cent. on short discount? No, no; that was not the way Sir

Thomas Woolrych had been accustomed to live when he was an ensign (sub-lieutenant they positively call it nowadays) at Ahmednuggur, in the North-West Provinces. In those days, my dear sir, a man drew his monthly screw by pay-warrant, took the rupees in solid cash, locked them up carefully in the desk in his bungalow, helped himself liberally to them while they lasted, and gave IOU's for any little trifle of cards or horses he might happen to have let himself in for meanwhile with his brother-officers. IOU's are of course a gentlemanly and recognized form of monetary engagement, but for bankers' cheques Sir Thomas positively felt little less than contempt and loathing.

Nevertheless, in his comfortable villa in the park at Cheltenham (called Futteypoor Lodge, after that famous engagement during the Mutiny which gave the Colonel his regiment and his K.C.B.-ship) he stood one evening looking curiously at his big devonport, and muttered to himself with more than one most military oath, "Hanged if I don't think I shall positively be compelled to patronize these banker-fellows after all. Somebody must have been helping himself again to some of my sovereigns."

Sir Thomas was not by nature a suspicious man, he was too frank and open-hearted himself to think ill easily of others, but he couldn't avoid feeling certain that somebody had been tampering unjustifiably with the contents of his devonport. He counted the rows of sovereigns over once more, very carefully; then he checked the number taken out by the entry in his pocket-book; and then he leaned back in his chair with a puzzled look, took a meditative puff or two at the stump of his cigar, and blew out the smoke, in a long curl that left a sort of pout upon his heavily moustached lip as soon as he had finished. Not a doubt in the world about it, somebody must have helped himself again to a dozen sovereigns.

It was a hateful thing to put a watch upon your servants and dependents, but Sir Thomas felt he must really do it. He reckoned up the long rows a third time with military precision, entered the particulars once more most accurately in his pocket-book, sighed a deep sigh of regret at the distasteful occupation, and locked up the devonport at last with the air of a man who resigns himself unwillingly to a most unpleasant duty. Then he threw away the fag-end of the smoked-out cigar, and went up slowly to dress for dinner.

Sir Thomas's household consisted entirely of himself and his nephew Harry, for he had never been married, and he regarded all womankind alike from afar off, with a quaint, respectful, old-world chivalry; but he made a point of dressing scrupulously every day for dinner, even when alone, as a decorous formality due to himself, his servants, society, the military profession, and the convenances in general. If he and his nephew dined together they dressed for one another; if they dined separately they dressed all the same, for the sake of the institution. When a man once consents to eat his evening meal in a blue tie and a morning cutaway, there's no drawing a line until you finally find him an advanced republican and an accomplice of those dreadful War Office people who are bent upon allowing the service to go to the devil. If Colonel Sir Thomas Woolrych, K.C.B., had for a single night been guilty of such abominable laxity, the whole fabric of society would have tottered to its base, and gods and footmen would have felt instinctively that it was all up with the British constitution.

"Harry," Sir Thomas said, as soon they sat down to dinner together, "are you going out anywhere this evening, my boy?"

Harry looked up a little surlily, and answered after a moment's hesitation, "Why, yes, uncle, I thought—I thought of going round and having a game of billiards with Tom Whitmarsh."

Sir Thomas cleared his throat, and hemmed dubiously. "In that case," he said at last, after a short pause, "I think I'll go down to the club myself and have a rubber. Wilkins, the carriage at half-past nine. I'm sorry, Harry, you're going out this evening."

"Why so, uncle? It's only just round to the Whitmarshes', you know."

Sir Thomas shut one eye and glanced with the other at the light through his glass of sherry, held up between finger and thumb critically and suspiciously. "A man may disapprove in toto of the present system of competitive examinations for the army," he said slowly; "for my part, I certainly do, and I make no secret of it; admitting a lot of butchers and bakers and candlestick makers plump into the highest ranks of the service: no tone, no character, no position, no gentlemanly feeling; a great mistake—a great mistake; I told them so at the time. I said to them, 'Gentlemen, you are simply ruining the service.' But they took no notice of me; and what's the consequence? Competitive examination has been the ruin of the service, exactly as I told them. Began with that; then abolition of purchase; then local centres; then that abominable strap with the slip buckle, there, there, Harry, upon my soul, my boy, I can't bear to think of it. But a man may be opposed, as I said, to the whole present system of competitive examination, and yet, while that system still unfortunately continues to exist (that is to say, until a European War convinces all sensible people of the confounded folly of it), he may feel that his own young men, who are reading up for a direct commission, ought to be trying their hardest to get as much of this nonsensical humbug into their heads as possible during the time just before their own examinations. Now, Harry, I'm afraid you're not reading quite as hard as you ought to be doing. The crammer's all very well in his way, of course, but depend upon it, the crammer by himself won't get you through it. What's needed is private study."

Harry turned his handsome dark eyes upon his uncle, a very dark, almost gipsy-looking face altogether, Harry's, and answered deprecatingly, "Well, sir, and don't I go in for private study? Didn't I read up Samson Agonistes all by myself right through yesterday?"

"I don't know what Samson Something-or-other is," the old gentleman replied testily. "What the dickens has Samson Something-or-other got to do with the preparation of a military man, I should like to know, sir?"

"It's the English Literature book for the exam., you know," Harry answered, with a quiet smile. "We've got to get it up, you see, with all the allusions and what-you-may-call-its, for direct commission. It's a sort of a play, I think I should call it, by John Milton."

"Oh, it's the English Literature, is it?" the old Colonel went on, somewhat mollified. "In my time, Harry, we weren't expected to know anything about English literature. The Articles of War, and the Officer's Companion, By Authority, that was the kind of literature we used to be examined in. But nowadays they expect a soldier to be read up in Samson Something-or-other, do they really? Well, well, let them have their fad, let them have their fad, poor creatures. Still, Harry, I'm very much afraid you're wasting your time, and your money also. If I thought you only went to the Whitmarshes' to see Miss Milly, now, I shouldn't mind so much about it. Miss Milly is a very charming, sweet young creature, certainly, extremely pretty, too, extremely pretty, I don't deny it. You're young yet to go making yourself agreeable, my boy, to a pretty girl like that; you ought to wait for that sort of thing till you've got your majority, or at least, your company, a young man reading for direct commission has no business to go stuffing his head cram full with love and nonsense. No, no; he should leave it all free for fortification, and the general instructions, and Samson Something-or-other, if soldiers can't be made nowadays without English literature. But still, I don't so much object to that, I say, a sweet girl, certainly, Miss Milly, what I do object to is your knocking about so much at billiard-rooms, and so forth, with that young fellow Whitmarsh. Not a very nice young fellow, or a good companion for you either, Harry. I'm afraid, I'm afraid, my boy, he makes you spend a great deal too much money."

"I've never yet had to ask you to increase my allowance, sir," the young man answered haughtily, with a curious glance sideways at his uncle.

"Wilkins," Sir Thomas put in, with a nod to the butler, "go down and bring up a bottle of the old Madeira. Harry, my boy, don't let us discuss questions of this sort before the servants. My boy, I've never kept you short of money in any way, I hope; and if I ever do, I trust you'll tell me of it, tell me of it immediately."

Harry's dark cheeks burned bright for a moment, but he answered never a single word, and went on eating his dinner silently, with a very hang-dog look indeed upon his handsome features.

II

At half-past nine Sir Thomas drove down to the club, and, when he reached the door, dismissed the coachman. "I shall walk back, Morton," he said. "I shan't want you again this evening. Don't let them sit up for me. I mayn't be home till two in the morning."

But as soon as the coachman had had full time to get back again in perfect safety, Sir Thomas walked straight down the club steps once more, and up the Promenade, and all the way to Futteypoor Lodge. When he got there, he opened the door silently with his latch-key, shut it again without the slightest noise, and walked on tip-toe into the library. It was an awkward sort of thing to do, certainly, but Sir Thomas was convinced in his own mind that he ought to do it. He wheeled an easy chair into the recess by the window, in front of which the curtains were drawn, arranged the folds so that he could see easily into the room by the slit between them, and sat down patiently to explore this mystery to the very bottom.

Sir Thomas was extremely loth in his own mind to suspect anybody; and yet it was quite clear that someone or other must have taken the missing sovereigns. Twice over money had been extracted. It couldn't have been cook, of that he felt certain; nor Wilkins either. Very respectable woman, cook, very respectable butler, Wilkins. Not Morton; oh dear no, quite impossible, certainly not Morton. Not the housemaid, or the boy: obviously neither; well-conducted young people, every one of them. But who the dickens could it be then? for certainly somebody had taken the money. The good old Colonel felt in his heart that for the sake of everybody's peace of mind it was his bounden duty to discover the real culprit before saying a single word to anybody about it.

There was something very ridiculous, of course, not to say undignified and absurd, in the idea of an elderly field officer, late in Her Majesty's service, sitting thus for hour after hour stealthily behind his own curtains, in the dark, as if he were a thief or a burglar, waiting to see whether anybody came to open his devonport. Sir Thomas grew decidedly wearied as he watched and waited, and but for his strong sense of the duty imposed upon him of tracking the guilty person, he would once or twice in the course of the evening have given up the quest from sheer disgust and annoyance at the absurdity of the position. But no; he must find out who had done it: so there he sat, as motionless as a cat watching a mouse-hole, with his eye turned always in the direction of the devonport, through the slight slit between the folded curtains.

Ten o'clock struck upon the clock on the mantelpiece, half-past ten—eleven. Sir Thomas stretched his legs, yawned, and muttered audibly, "Confounded slow, really." Half-past eleven. Sir Thomas went over noiselessly to the side table, where the decanters were standing, and helped himself to a brandy and seltzer, squeezing down the cork of the bottle carefully with his thumb, to prevent its popping, till all the gas had escaped piecemeal. Then he crept back, still noiselessly, feeling more like a convicted thief himself than a Knight Commander of the Most Honourable Order of the Bath, and wondering when the deuce this pilfering lock-breaker was going to begin his nightly depredations. Not till after Harry came back most likely. The thief, whoever he or she was, would probably be afraid to venture into the library while there was still a chance of Harry returning unexpectedly and disturbing the whole procedure. But when once Harry had gone to bed, they would all have heard from Morton that Sir Thomas was going to be out late, and the thief would then doubtless seize so good an opportunity of helping himself unperceived to the counted sovereigns.

About half past eleven, there was a sound of steps upon the garden-walk, and Harry's voice could be heard audibly through the half-open window. The colonel caught the very words against his will. Harry was talking with Tom Whitmarsh, who had walked round to see him home; his voice was a little thick, as if with wine, and he seemed terribly excited (to judge by his accent) about something or other that had just happened.

"Good night, Tom," the young man was saying, with an outward show of carelessness barely concealing a great deal of underlying irritation. "I'll pay you up what I lost to-morrow or the next day. You shall have your money, don't be afraid about it."

"Oh, it's all right," Tom Whitmarsh's voice answered in an off-hand fashion. "Pay me whenever you like, you know, Woolrych. It doesn't matter to me when you pay me, this year or next year, so long as I get it sooner or later."

Sir Thomas listened with a sinking heart. "Play," he thought to himself. "Play, play, play, already! It was his father's curse, poor fellow, and I hope it won't be Harry's. It's some comfort to think, anyhow, that it's only billiards."

"Well, good night, Tom," Harry went on, ringing the bell as he spoke.

"Good night, Harry. I hope next time the cards won't go so persistently against you."

The cards! Phew! That was bad indeed. Sir Thomas started. He didn't object to a quiet after-dinner rubber on his own account, naturally: but this wasn't whist; oh, no; nothing of the sort. This was evidently serious playing. He drew a long breath, and felt he must talk very decidedly about the matter to Harry to-morrow morning.

"Is my uncle home yet, Wilkins?"

"No, sir; he said he wouldn't be back probably till two o'clock, and we wasn't to sit up for him."

"All right then. Give me a light for a minute in the library. I'll take a seltzer before I go upstairs, just to steady me."

Sir Thomas almost laughed outright. This was really too ridiculous. Suppose, after all the waiting, Harry was to come over and discover him sitting there in the darkness by the window, what a pretty figure he would cut before him. And besides, the whole thing would have to come out then, and after all the thief would never be discovered and punished. The Colonel grew hot and red in the face, and began to wish to goodness he hadn't in the first place let himself in, in any way, for this ridiculous amateur detective business.

But Harry drank his seltzer standing by the side table, with no brandy, either; that was a good thing, no brandy. If he'd taken brandy, too, in his present excited condition, when he'd already certainly had quite as much as was at all good for him, Sir Thomas would have been justly and seriously angry. But, after all, Harry was a good boy at bottom, and knew how to avoid such ugly habits. He took his seltzer and his bedroom candle. Wilkins turned out the light in the room, and Harry went upstairs by himself immediately.

Then Wilkins turned the key in the library door, and the old gentleman began to reflect that this was really a most uncomfortable position for him to be left in. Suppose they locked him in there till to-morrow morning! Ah! happy thought; if the worst came to the worst he could get out of the library window and let himself in at the front door by means of his latch-key.

The servants all filed upstairs, one by one, in an irregular procession; their feet died away gradually upon the upper landings, and a solemn silence came at last over the whole household. Sir Thomas's heart began to beat faster: the excitement of plot interest was growing stronger upon him. This was the time the thief would surely choose to open the devonport. He should know now within twenty minutes which it was of all his people, whom he trusted so implicitly, that was really robbing him.

And he treated them all so kindly, too. Ha, the rascal! he should catch it well, that he should, whoever he was, as soon as ever Sir Thomas discovered him.

Not if it were Wilkins, though; not if it were Wilkins. Sir Thomas hoped it wasn't really that excellent fellow Wilkins. A good old tried and trusty servant. If any unexpected financial difficulties—

Hush, hush! Quietly now. A step upon the landing.

Coming down noiselessly, noiselessly, noiselessly. Not Wilkins; not heavy enough for him, surely; no, no, a woman's step, so very light, so light and noiseless. Sir Thomas really hoped in his heart it wasn't that pretty delicate-looking girl, the new housemaid. If it was, by Jove, yes, he'd give her a good lecture then and there, that very minute, about it, offer to pay her passage quietly out to Canada, and—recommend her to get married decently, to some good young fellow, on the earliest possible opportunity.

The key turned once more in the lock, and then the door opened stealthily. Somebody glided like a ghost into the middle of the room. Sir Thomas, gazing intently through the slit in the curtains, murmured to himself that now at last he should fairly discover the confounded rascal.

Ha! How absurd! He could hardly help laughing once more at the ridiculous collapse to his high-wrought expectations. And yet he restrained himself. It was only Harry! Harry come down, candle in hand, no doubt to get another glass of seltzer. The Colonel hoped not with brandy. No; not with brandy. He put the glass up to his dry lips, Sir Thomas could see they were dry and feverish even from that distance; horrid thing, this gambling!—and he drained it off at a gulp, like a thirsty man who has tasted no liquor since early morning.

Then he took up his candle again, and turned, not to the door. Oh, no. The old gentleman watched him now with singular curiosity, for he was walking not to the door, but over in the direction of the suspected devonport. Sir Thomas could hardly even then guess at the truth. It wasn't, no it wasn't, it couldn't be Harry! not Harry that ... that borrowed the money!

The young man took a piece of stout wire from his pocket with a terrible look of despair and agony. Sir Thomas's heart melted within him as he beheld it. He twisted the wire about in the lock with a dexterous pressure, and it opened easily. Sir Thomas looked on, and the tears rose into his eyes slowly by instinct; but he said never a word, and watched intently. Harry held the lid of the devonport open for a moment with one hand, and looked at the rows of counted gold within. The fingers of the other hand rose slowly and remorsefully up to the edge of the desk, and there hovered in an undecided fashion. Sir Thomas watched still, with his heart breaking. Then for a second Harry paused. He held back his hand and appeared to deliberate. Something within seemed to have affected him deeply. Sir Thomas, though a plain old soldier, could read his face well enough to know what it was; he was thinking of the kind words his uncle had said to him that very evening as they sat together down there at dinner.

For half a minute the suspense was terrible. Then, with a sudden impulse, Harry shut the lid of the devonport down hastily; flung the wire with a gesture of horror and remorse into the fireplace; took up his candle wildly in his hand; and rushed from the room and up the stairs, leaving the door open behind him.

Then Sir Thomas rose slowly from his seat in the window corner; lighted the gas in the centre burner; unlocked the devonport, with tears still trickling slowly down his face; counted all the money over carefully to make quite certain; found it absolutely untouched; and flung himself down upon his knees wildly, between shame, and fear, and relief, and misery. What he said or what he thought in that terrible moment of conflicting passions is best not here described or written; but when he rose again his eyes were glistening, more with forgiveness than with horror (anger there never had been); and being an old-fashioned old gentleman, he took down his big Bible from the shelf, just to reassure himself about a text which he thought he remembered somewhere in Luke: "Joy shall be in heaven over one sinner that repenteth, more than over ninety and nine just persons, which need no repentance." "Ah, yes," he said to himself; "he repented; he repented. He didn't take it. He felt he couldn't after what I said to him." And then, with the tears still rolling silently down his bronzed cheeks, he went up stairs to bed, but not to sleep; for he lay restless on his pillow all night through with that one terrible discovery weighing like lead upon his tender old bosom.

III

Next morning, after breakfast, Sir Thomas said in a quiet tone of command to Harry, "My boy, I want to speak to you for a few minutes in the library."

Harry's cheek grew deadly pale and he caught his breath with difficulty, but he followed his uncle into the library without a word, and took his seat at the table opposite him.

"Harry," the old soldier began, as quietly as he was able, after an awkward pause, "I want to tell you a little, a little about your father and mother."

Harry's face suddenly changed from white to crimson, for he felt sure now that what Sir Thomas was going to talk about was not the loss of the money from the devonport a week earlier; and on the other hand, though he knew absolutely nothing about his own birth and parentage, he knew at least that there must have been some sort of mystery in the matter, or else his uncle would surely long since have spoken to him quite freely of his father and mother.

"My dear boy," the Colonel went on again, in a tremulous voice, "I think the time has now come when I ought to tell you that you and I are no relations by blood; you are, you are my nephew by adoption only."

Harry gave a sudden start of surprise, but said nothing.

"The way it all came about," Sir Thomas went on, playing nervously with his watch-chain, "was just this. I was in India during the Mutiny, as you know, and while I was stationed at Boolundshahr, in the North-West Provinces, just before those confounded niggers, I mean to say, before the sepoys revolted, your father was adjutant of my regiment at the same station. He and your mother, well, Harry, your mother lived in a small bungalow near the cantonments, and there you were born; why, exactly eight months before the affair at Meerut, you know, the beginning of the Mutiny. Your father, I'm sorry to say, was a man very much given to high play, in short, if you'll excuse my putting it so, my boy, a regular gambler. He owed money to almost every man in the regiment, and amongst others, if I must tell you the whole truth, to me. In those days I sometimes played rather high myself, Harry; not so high as your poor father, my boy, for I was always prudent, but a great deal higher than a young man in a marching regiment has any right to do, a great deal higher. I left off playing immediately after what I'm just going to tell you; and from that day to this, Harry, I've never touched a card, except for whist or cribbage, and never will do, my boy, if I live to be as old as Methuselah."

The old man paused and wiped his brow for a second with his capacious handkerchief, while Harry's eyes, cast down upon the ground, began to fill rapidly with something or other that he couldn't for the life of him manage to keep out of them.

"On the night before the news from Meerut arrived," the old soldier went on once more, with his eye turned half away from the trembling lad, "we played together in the major's rooms, your father and I, with a few others; and before the end of the evening your father had lost a large sum to one of his brother-officers. When we'd finished playing, he came to me to my quarters, and he said 'Woolrych, this is a bad job. I haven't got anything to pay McGregor with.'

"'All right, Walpole,' I answered him, your father's name was Captain Walpole, Harry—'I'll lend you whatever's necessary.'

"'No, no, my dear fellow,' he said, 'I won't borrow and only get myself into worse trouble. I'll take a shorter and easier way out of it all, you may depend upon it.'

"At the moment I hadn't the slightest idea what he meant, and so I said no more to him just then about it. But three minutes after he left my quarters I heard a loud cry, and saw your father in the moonlight out in the compound. He had a pistol in his hand. Next moment, the report of a shot sounded loudly down below in the compound, and I rushed out at once to see what on earth could be matter.

"Your father was lying in a pool of blood, just underneath a big mango-tree beside the door, with his left jaw shattered to pieces, and his brain pierced through and through from one side to the other by a bullet from the pistol.

"He was dead, stone dead. There was no good doctoring him. We took him up and carried him into the surgeon's room, and none of us had the courage all that night to tell your mother.

"Next day, news came of the rising at Meerut.

"That same night, while we were all keeping watch and mounting guard, expecting our men would follow the example of their companions at head-quarters, there was a sudden din and tumult in the lines, about nine in the evening, when the word was given to turn in, and McGregor, coming past me, shouted at the top of his voice, 'It's all up, Woolrych. These black devils have broken loose at last, and they're going to fire the officers' quarters.'

"Well, Harry, my boy, I needn't tell you all about it at full length to-day; but in the end, as you know, we fought the men for our own lives, and held our ground until the detachment came from Etawah to relieve us. However, before we could get to the Bibi's bungalow, the sepoys used to call your mother the Bibi, Harry, those black devils had broken in there, and when next morning early I burst into the ruined place, with three men of the 47th and a faithful havildar, we found your poor mother, well, there, Harry, I can't bear to think of it, even now, my boy: but she was dead, too, quite dead, with a hundred sabre-cuts all over her poor blood-stained, hacked-about body. And in the corner, under the cradle, the eight-month-old baby was lying and crying, crying bitterly; that was you, Harry."

The young man listened intently, with a face now once more ashy white, but still he answered absolutely nothing.

"I took you in my arms, my boy," the old Colonel continued in a softer tone; "and as you were left all alone in the bungalow there, with no living soul to love or care for you, I carried you away in my arms myself, to my own quarters. All through the rest of that terrible campaign I kept you with me, and while I was fighting at Futteypoor, a native ayah was in charge of you for me. Your poor father had owed me a trifling debt, and I took you as payment in full, and have kept you with me as my nephew ever since. That is all your history, Harry."

The young man drew a deep breath, and looked across curiously to the bronzed face of the simple old officer. Then he asked, a little huskily, "And why didn't my father's or mother's relations reclaim me, sir? Do they know that I am still living?"

Sir Thomas coughed, and twirled his watch-chain more nervously and uneasily than ever. "Well, you see, my boy," he answered at last, after a long pause, "your mother, I must tell you the whole truth now, Harry, your mother was a Eurasian, a half-caste lady, very light, almost white, but still a half-caste, you know, and—and—well, your father's family—didn't exactly acknowledge the relationship, Harry."

Harry's face burnt crimson once more, and the hot blood rushed madly to his cheeks, for he felt in a moment the full force of the meaning that the Colonel wrapped up so awkwardly in that one short embarrassed sentence.

There was another long pause, during which Harry kept his burning eyes fixed fast upon Sir Thomas, and Sir Thomas looked down uncomfortably at his boots and said nothing. Then the young man found voice again feebly to ask, almost in a whisper, one final question.

"Had you ... had you any particular reason for telling me this story about my birth and my parents at this exact time ... just now, uncle?"

"I had, Harry. I—I have rather suspected of late ... that ... that you are falling somehow into ... into your poor father's unhappy vice of gambling. My boy, my boy, if you inherit his failings in that direction, I hope his end will be some warning to you to desist immediately."

"And had you ... any reason to suspect me of ... of any other fault ... of ... of any graver fault ... of anything really very serious, uncle?"

The Colonel held his head between his hands, and answered very slowly, as if the words were wrung from him by torture: "If you hadn't yourself asked me the question point-blank, Harry, I would never have told you anything about it. Yes, my boy, my dear boy, my poor boy; I know it all ... all ... all ... absolutely."

Harry lifted up his voice in one loud cry and wail of horror, and darted out of the room without another syllable.

"I know that cry," the Colonel said in his own heart, trembling. "I have heard it before! It's the very cry poor Walpole gave that night at Boolundshahr, just before he went out and shot himself!"

IV

Harry had rushed out into the garden; of that, Sir Thomas felt certain. He followed him hastily, and saw him by the seat under the lime-trees in the far corner; he had something heavy in his right hand. Sir Thomas came closer and saw to his alarm and horror that it was indeed the small revolver from the old pistol-stand on the wall of the vestibule.

Even as the poor old soldier gazed, half petrified, the lad pushed a cartridge home feverishly into one of the chambers, and raised the weapon, with a stern resolution, up to his temple. Sir Thomas recognized in that very moment of awe and terror that it was the exact attitude and action of Harry's dead father. The entire character and tragedy seemed to have handed itself down directly from father to son without a single change of detail or circumstance.

The old man darted forward with surprising haste, and caught Harry's hand just as the finger rested upon the trigger.

"My boy! my boy!" he cried, wrenching the revolver easily from his trembling grasp, and flinging it, with a great curve, to the other end of the garden. "Not that way! Not that way! I haven't reproached you with one word, Harry; but this is a bad return, indeed, for a life devoted to you. Oh, Harry! Harry! not by shuffling off your responsibilities and running away from them like a coward, not by that can you ever mend matters in the state you have got them into, but by living on, and fighting against your evil impulses and conquering them like a man, that's the way, the right way, to get the better of them. Promise me, Harry, promise me, my boy, that whatever comes you won't make away with yourself, as your father did; for my sake, live on and do better. I'm an old man, an old man, Harry, and I have but you in the world to care for or think about. Don't let me be shamed in my old age by seeing the boy I have brought up and loved as a son dying in disgrace, a poltroon and a coward. Stand by your guns, my boy; stand by your guns, and fight it out to the last minute."

Harry's arm fell powerless to his side, and he broke down utterly, in his shame and self-abasement flinging himself wildly upon the seat beneath the lime-trees and covering his face with his hands to hide the hot tears that were bursting forth in a feverish torrent.

"I will go," he said at last, in a choking voice, "I will go, uncle, and talk to Milly."

"Do," the Colonel said, soothing his arm tenderly. "Do, my boy. She's a good girl, and she'll advise you rightly. Go and speak to her; but before you go, promise me, promise me."

Harry rose, and tried to shake off Sir Thomas's heavy hand, laid with a fatherly pressure upon his struggling shoulder. But he couldn't; the old soldier was still too strong for him. "Promise me," he said once more caressingly, "promise me; promise me!"

Harry hesitated for a second, in his troubled mind; then, with an effort, he answered slowly, "I promise, uncle."

Sir Thomas released him, and he rushed wildly away. "Remember," the Colonel cried aloud, as he went in at the open folding windows, "remember, Harry, you are on your honour. If you break parole I shall think very badly, very badly indeed, of you."

But as the old man turned back sadly into his lonely library, he thought to himself, "I wonder whether I oughtn't to have dealt more harshly with him! I wonder whether I was right in letting him off so easily for two such extremely, such extremely grave breaches of military discipline!"

V

"Then you think, Milly, that's what I ought to do? You think I'd better go and never come back again till I feel quite sure of myself?"

"I think so, Harry, I think so.... I think so.... And yet ... it's very hard not to see you for so long, Harry."

"But I shall write to you every day, Milly, however long it may be; and if I conquer myself, why, then, Milly, I shall feel I can come back fit to marry you. I'm not fit now, and unless I feel that I've put myself straight with you and my uncle, I'll never come back again, never, never, never!"

Milly's lip trembled, but she only answered bravely, "That's well, Harry; for then you'll make all the more effort, and for my sake I'm sure you'll conquer. But, Harry, I wish before you go you'd tell me plainly what else it is that you've been doing besides playing and losing your uncle's money."

"Oh, Milly, Milly, I can't, I mustn't. If I were to tell you that you could never again respect me, you could never love me."

Milly was a wise girl, and pressed him no further. After all, there are some things it is better for none of us to know about one another, and this thing was just one of them.

So Harry Walpole went away from Cheltenham, nobody knew whither, except Milly; not daring to confide the secret of his whereabouts even to his uncle, nor seeing that sole friend once more before he went, but going away that very night, on his own resources, to seek his own fortune as best he might in the great world of London. "Tell my uncle why I have gone," he said to Milly; "that it is in order to conquer myself; and tell him that I'll write to you constantly, and that you will let him know from time to time whether I am well and making progress."

It was a hard time for poor old Sir Thomas, no doubt, those four years that Harry was away from him, he knew not where, and he was left alone by himself in his dreary home; but he felt it was best so; he knew Harry was trying to conquer himself. How Harry lived or what he was doing he never heard; but once or twice Milly hinted to him that Harry seemed sorely in want of money, and Sir Thomas gave her some to send him, and every time it was at once returned, with a very firm but gentle message from Harry to say that he was able, happily, to do without it, and would not further trouble his uncle. It was only from Milly that Sir Thomas could learn anything about his dear boy, and he saw her and asked her about him so often that he learned at last to love her like a daughter.

Four years rolled slowly away, and at the end of them Sir Thomas was one day sitting in his little library, somewhat disconsolate, and reflecting to himself that he ought to have somebody living with him at his time of life, when suddenly there came a ring and a knock that made him start with surprise and pleasure, for he recognized them at once as being Harry's. Next moment, the servant brought him a card, on which was engraved in small letters, "Dr. H. Walpole," and down in the left-hand corner, "Surrey Hospital."

Sir Thomas turned the card over and over with a momentary feeling of disappointment, for he had somehow fancied to himself that Harry had gone off covering himself with glory among Zulus or Afghans, and he couldn't help feeling that beside that romantic dream of soldierly rehabilitation a plain doctor's life was absurdly prosaic. Next moment, Harry himself was grasping his hand warmly, and prose and poetry were alike forgotten in that one vivid all-absorbing delight of his boy recovered.

As soon as the first flush of excitement was fairly over, and Harry had cried regretfully, "Why, uncle, how much older you're looking!" and Sir Thomas had exclaimed in his fatherly joy, "Why, Harry, my boy, what a fine fellow you've turned out, God bless me!" Harry took a little bank bag of sovereigns from his coat pocket and laid it down, very red, upon the corner of the table. "These are yours, uncle," he said simply.

Sir Thomas's first impulse was to say, "No, no, my boy; keep them, keep them, and let us forget all about it," but he checked himself just in time, for he saw that the best thing all round was to take them quietly and trouble poor Harry no more with the recollection. "Thank you, my boy," the old soldier answered, taking them up and pocketing them as though it were merely the repayment of an ordinary debt. ("The School for the Orphan Children of Officers in the Army will be all the richer for it," he thought to himself) "And now tell me, Harry, how have you been living, and what have you been doing ever since I last saw you?"

"Uncle," Harry cried, he hadn't unlearnt to think of him and call him by that fond old name, then, "uncle, I've been conquering myself. From the day I left you I've never touched a card once, not once, uncle."

"Except, I suppose, for a quiet rubber?" the old Colonel put in softly.

"Not even for a rubber, uncle," Harry answered, half smiling; "nor a cue nor a dice-box either, nor anything like them. I've determined to steer clear of all the dangers that surround me by inheritance, and I'm not going to begin again as long as I live, uncle."

"That's well, Harry, that's well. And you didn't go in for a direct commission, then? I was in hopes, my boy, that you would still, in spite of everything, go into the Queen's service."

Harry's face fell a little. "Uncle," he said, "I'm sorry to have disappointed you; sorry to have been compelled to run counter to any little ambitions you might have had for me in that respect; but I felt, after all you told me that day, that the army would be a very dangerous profession for me; and though I didn't want to be a coward and run away from danger, I didn't want to be foolhardy and heedlessly expose myself to it. So I thought on the whole it would be wiser for me to give up the direct commission business altogether, and go in at once for being a doctor. It was safer, and therefore better in the end both for me and for you, uncle."

Sir Thomas took the young man's hand once more, and pressed it gently with a fatherly pressure. "My boy," he said, "you are right, quite right, a great deal more right, indeed, than I was. But how on earth have you found money to keep yourself alive and pay for your education all these years, tell me Harry?"

Harry's face flushed up again, this time with honest pride, as he answered bravely, "I've earned enough by teaching and drawing to pay my way the whole time, till I got qualified. I've been qualified now for nine months, and got a post as house-surgeon at our hospital; but I've waited to come and tell you till I'd saved up that money, you know, out of my salary, and now I'm coming back to settle down in practice here, uncle."

Sir Thomas said nothing, but he rose from his chair and took both Harry's hands in his with tears. For a few minutes, he looked at him tenderly and admiringly, then he said in his simple way, "God bless you! God bless you! I couldn't have done it myself, my boy. I couldn't have done it myself, Harry."

There was a minute's pause, and then Sir Thomas began again, "What a secretive little girl that dear little Miss Milly must be, never to have told me a word of all this, Harry. She kept as quiet about all details as if she was sworn to the utmost secrecy."

Harry rose and opened the library door. "Milly!" he called out, and a light little figure glided in from the drawing-room opposite.

"We expect to be married in three weeks, uncle, as soon as the banns can be published," Harry went on, presenting his future wife as it were to the Colonel. "Milly's money will just be enough for us to live upon until I can scrape together a practice, and she has confidence enough in me to believe that in the end I shall manage to get one."

Sir Thomas drew her down to his chair and kissed her forehead. "Milly," he said, softly, "you have chosen well. Harry, you have done wisely. I shall have two children now instead of one. If you are to live near me I shall be very happy. But, Harry, you have proved yourself well. Now you must let me buy you a practice."

www.ingramcontent.com/pod-product-compliance
Lightning Source LLC
Chambersburg PA
CBHW061216170626
46809CB00003B/1379